Drop the Gloves

A.L. Heard

Drop the Gloves

Front Cover Art by Veronica

For information on commissions and to view more of her artwork, visit her on Instagram @sailorlun2

ISBN: 979-8-9911881-2-8 (ebook edition)

ISBN: 979-8-9911881-3-5 (Paperback edition)

1

"Oh, sweetie!" Evan's mom pulled him into a bone-crushing hug. He had to bend down so she could reach him, and even then she was on her tippy toes. "I'm going to miss you so stinkin' much!"

Evan held on a little longer before letting go. "I'll miss you too. But hey, we play Toronto in the pre-season and in November, so I'll be back soon."

His mom dabbed at her eyes. "I know, I know. I just miss my baby."

For as long as Evan could remember, it'd been him and his mom. He'd grown up in Peterborough, Ontario and been fortunate not to have to live too far away while he played in the OHL. That hadn't made the separation any easier for either of them, though. He'd always felt bad leaving her for hockey, especially when it became more permanent once the Pittsburgh Riveters drafted him a few years ago, but it helped that he knew he had her full support.

"Pittsburgh's not that far," he reminded her. "I'm only a 65-minute flight away."

Carol Abernathy had been thrilled that her son was drafted, obviously, but she'd been a little disappointed it hadn't been by a Canadian team. The only thing that had soothed her was that Pittsburgh was a helluva lot closer than British Columbia.

"It's 650 kilometers," she grumbled. They'd hashed this out several times, and he knew it was exactly 647.2 kilometers of decent roads from his condo to his childhood home, but he figured he could spot her the couple extra.

"It is a whole other country," he agreed. It was hard to suppress a smile. "Better watch out. A few more years and I'll sound like a Yinzer for sure."

She rolled her eyes at his teasing. "Evan, have you heard yourself? You sound like you walked straight out of a Tim Hortons commercial, your accent's so thick."

This startled a laugh from him. "It is not!"

His mom waved it off and grew serious again. "Text me when you land."

"I will."

"I'll be watching every game, sweetie."

"I know, Mom. You don't have to—"

"You guys are going to do great this year! I have a good feeling."

Evan gave her a look. She said that every year, without fail. It wasn't until December hit that she'd start being skeptical of the Riveters' odds, though he suspected that was more about being superstitious that she'd jinx them. Even when they'd been mathematically eliminated from the playoffs his first season, she'd refused to say anything negative.

"A good feeling, eh?" he teased.

"I do! This is going to be your best year yet." Then she pushed over his suitcase, telling him he needed to be the one to walk away because she never would. "Good luck!"

"Thanks, Mom." His chest was tight. He hated goodbyes, even if they were only temporary. He gave her one more hug and a quick peck on the top of her head, well below his shoulder level, before he took the hint and left. The one time he sneaked a look back, she was still standing there, waving and watching him. Ugh, he was going to miss being home.

He knew how much she'd sacrificed to make his NHL career possible. Hockey was expensive, and as a single mom, it hadn't always been easy for her to put together the money for team fees. He probably hadn't gotten new gear until he played Junior hockey, settling instead for his cousins' hand-me-downs or thrifted items on consignment at local shops.

He'd felt *really* good paying off his mom's mortgage once he'd signed his contract with the Riveters. His mom hadn't stopped grinning that entire summer as she bragged to everyone that her son was a big NHL star, an embarrassment he'd endured because if anyone deserved that right, it was Carol Abernathy.

It didn't mean he felt good about walking away.

———

The promised sixty-five minutes after it had taken off, the plane touched down and started gliding to the terminal. Most passengers were restless as they taxied, hands ready on their seatbelts for the go-ahead to start collecting their things. Evan barely stirred, even when the seatbelt light went off and everyone around him practically sprang to their feet.

It wasn't that he wasn't happy to be back. Pittsburgh was home. He'd fully embraced the city that had not only drafted him but given him a shot as a rookie. It wasn't as busy and crowded as Toronto, but still boasted all the city-life he wanted. More affordable, too. He'd snagged a nice condo near the practice facility, a new build that would've cost seven digits in Toronto's suburbs.

He'd held off getting attached until the end of last season when his entry-level contract ended and the team had signed him on for another three years. Even though the Riveters lost in the second round last season to the Blue Crabs, the coaches must've liked what they'd seen from Evan, since he'd been offered a pretty decent contract right after. Now that he had a guaranteed three more years in Pittsburgh, he could let himself love the city.

So it wasn't anxiety about the season that was keeping him in his seat or that made him the last person off the plane. It was the fans.

Both a blessing and a curse, Pittsburgh *really* loved their sports teams. They wholeheartedly supported their players, always kind to them face-to-face (even if they might blast them online or on the radio) and never booing their own team at home games no matter how dire it got. Unfortunately, they were also very good at recognizing players in public and felt a sort of camaraderie with them that more often than not had them approaching said players. Evan didn't know how many times he'd been spotted at Starbucks or Target or just out for a run, always resulting in someone coming up to talk to him about last night's game or how the team was doing or to compliment him on his stats.

While some of his teammates appreciated the recognition and celebrity status it offered them, Evan kind of hated it.

He was too shy to be intelligible when he was put on the spot, and he was terrified he'd say something about the team or coaches that would be taken out of context and come back to bite him in the ass. Any time he went out in public, he wore a Pirates hat pulled low and kept his head down. If he weren't 6'5, it might actually work more than it did.

Today he lucked out: he made it out of the airport without anyone noticing him, and he counted that as a win. Thank God for the off-season—it would be next to impossible to sneak around once hockey was back on TV.

The Uber driver who picked him up wasn't the chatty type, and Evan was left to mindlessly scroll on his phone as they traveled to and then through the city proper to get to his place north of Pittsburgh. There were new messages in the team chat as people updated their arrival status. Evan added his name to the list of Riveters in town, receiving a dozen happy emojis celebrating his return.

Lawson
Drinks tonight? My place @ 8
Should give us time to recover before practice
tomorrow

Doyle
Yinz are doing practice??
We still got 2 weeks of freedom and u r
voluntarily hanging out with coach? Lame.

Woodward
lmao coach is in the office all day
Mel's in charge

4

Besides some of us are captains and need to set an example for the rest of you scrubs

Doyle

u r an alternate captain. Don't let it go to your head woodsy

Kates

You had me at coach is in the office and lost me at Mel's in charge

Lawson

Why? Mel's great

Kates

Her drills are 10x harder than coach's

Lawson

Fair

Melissa Gamble was their defensive coach. One of the first female coaches in the NHL, she'd worked damn hard to get where she was and twice as hard to stay there. Her father owned the Nevada Scorpions, and even though she'd started her career there, she'd jumped ship as soon as she could: she wasn't going to be called a nepotism hire.

Evan might dread her drills like the rest of the team—they *were* brutal, and she required perfection before she let them off the hook—but he respected the hell out of her. He'd mostly played wing in the OHL, but the Riveters had shifted him to center his rookie year. It had definitely been an adjustment, since, like most young wingers, the idea of a backcheck was something of a foreign concept. Mel had worked with him a lot his first year to get him up to snuff, and he was eternally grateful for that.

Abernathy

I'm in for drinks tonight

Doyle

Aren't you like 15??

Just bc it's legal in Canada doesn't mean we can give beer to infants

Abernathy
I'm 21 1/2

Woodward
Lil sus you're bringing in the half there
No adult does that

Lawson
Don't worry about them abs
You grow a better beard than woodsy
ever has

Woodward
🍺

Antonov
He's right

Woodward
Nover you ain't even on this continent rn you
can stfu
Tell me again how to say 'fuck you' in Russian

Evan was smiling as he lumbered out of the Uber and headed up to his condo. Despite their teasing, he'd really missed the guys. Sure, they kept in touch over the summer, but with everyone spread out across the world, there'd been little more than memes and pictures sent in the group chat for nearly two months. He felt fortunate that he'd ended up on a team he clicked so well with.

The air in his condo was a little stagnant, and the only things even remotely edible were ramen and ketchup, but it was great to be back. His space, the one he'd earned and carved out for himself. His city and his team, ready for another go at the Stanley Cup. For once, he agreed with his mom's overly optimistic prediction: he had a good feeling about this season.

2

"Abs! Good to see you!" Lawson pulled him into a hug as soon as Evan entered the kitchen. Before he could say or do anything, there was a beer in his hand. Not only was Lawson a good captain, he was also a good host.

"Cheers," Lawson said and clinked their IC Lights together. "How was your summer, kid?"

"I'm not a kid," Evan said automatically. Pittsburgh had gotten shit from the media for having one of the oldest teams in the league a few years ago. That might've been why he and a few other younger players had gotten contracts this season as the team worked to add young blood to the lineup. But it still meant most of the Riveters were a decade older than him, and Evan definitely felt like a kid half the time. Hell, he'd had Lawson's trading card in middle school. But he was a real NHL player and could actually see over several people's heads: he wasn't a kid anymore, even in this crowd. "It was good. Hung out at home for a bit. Played golf."

Lawson made a face. He hated golf. "Cool. Hey, did you meet any of the new guys?"

Evan nodded. "I met a few of them last year at training camp. I know they're pumped to be playing this pre-season—"

7

"Huh? No, not the kids." He nodded toward the backyard, where a bunch of the guys were laughing by the pool. A backyard pool in Pittsburgh. What a waste. "I meant the trades."

Evan followed Lawson's gaze. They'd lost a few players during the off-season to trades and retirement, but while Evan was aware of the roster changes, it was too early for his brain to have really adjusted to the changes.

"Not yet," Evan said and then froze as he spotted him. Riley fucking Barczyk, in the flesh.

Barczyk was a pest throughout the league. Aside from his antics like slashing people's sticks out of their hands at the face-off circle and allegedly licking someone during a scrum in front of the net, he had legendary fighting status. He might only be 5'9 (and from this distance and without the benefit of skates, Evan thought that might be generous), but he'd beaten just about every heavyweight in the league. And the bastard, annoying as he was, wasn't some lowly enforcer: he could score. Maybe not top-line or anything, but he put up a solid 20 goals every season. Enough to make teams overlook his penalty minutes.

As of July 1st, he was a member of the Riveters. A solid pickup during free agency for sure. Reportedly very likable once you got to know him. The only problem was Evan did *not* want to know him or like him or have anything to do with him.

Riley Barczyk was a jerk.

"C'mon," Lawson said. He'd grabbed Evan's elbow and was leading him toward the back patio. "I'll introduce you to them. Barzy does this great impression of Coach—"

"I've gotta piss." Evan spun out of Lawson's grasp, nearly spilling both their drinks. "I'll catch up in a few, 'kay?"

Lawson frowned and watched Evan flee in the opposite direction of the bathrooms, though thankfully he let Evan go. Evan let his feet carry him to the quiet end of the house by the guest rooms—an area he knew well, since he'd lived in one of those rooms for six months after making the regular season roster but before he'd settled on a condo. He went inside his old room, just as impersonal as he remembered it, and sat on the edge of the bed to collect himself. Deep breath in through his nose, out through his mouth. In, out. In, out.

Fuck. He did *not* like Riley Barczyk.

Barczyk had been a thorn in the Riveters' side the past two years while he played for the Philadelphia Gliders. Pittsburgh and Philly never got along sports-wise. Or anything-wise, he supposed. When it came to hockey, it was particularly vicious. Just thinking about his last game in Philly gave Evan hives. The Philly crowd always roared, whether the Gliders were winning or losing. The only thing that changed was their tone. Evan felt more like a performer than a hockey player whenever they played there.

And Barczyk had been the king of the whole spectacle.

The fans went wild whenever he pulled his shenanigans, which he did often. It was impossible to concentrate when Barczyk was on the ice, and it only made Evan feel more like a rookie than he usually did. If he couldn't tune out one jerk, how could he be relied on during important games? If they were in the Stanley Cup Finals and someone gave him a hard time, he couldn't let that impact his performance. He thought he'd done a pretty good job during their three Philly games last season. He hadn't even flinched when Barczyk had charged at him by the boards.

If only Barczyk hadn't injured him during that play. If only he could think of anything else when he looked at Barczyk. If only they weren't on the same damn team and he'd be thinking about it constantly.

Trust Barczyk to be a liability even when he was on the same team as you. Go fucking figure.

The first step to getting over it was to get his ass back out there and stop moping in the guest room. Face his fears or whatever. Not that he was *scared* of Barczyk. It was—

Okay, you're stalling. Stop it. Just go out there. I guarantee you he doesn't remember that game. He hurts people all the time and never cares. You don't get that kind of reputation by caring.

Evan could actually learn a thing or two from that mentality. Evan was big, strong, and fast, even among other NHL players. In the couple of times Evan had dealt hard hits, he'd always felt so bad that when he saw those players again, he tended to go easier on them than he should, much to his coach's annoyance. He just didn't want to hurt anyone, but that opinion hadn't done him any favors.

One time, he'd checked a guy so hard, he'd fallen down and not gotten back up. Evan had abandoned the play to circle back and check on him, which had earned him a crosscheck from behind for his efforts. Apparently, it had looked like he was going back to finish the job.

Which actually sounded like something Barczyk might do.

Be more like Barczyk. What a joke.

Evan left his refuge and went out onto the back deck with the rest of the guys. Not everyone had returned to town yet—most notably the Europeans and Russians were unaccounted for—but there was a decent number of Riveters in attendance. Evan stood between Turner and Moreau, two of the other centers, and accepted a fistbump from Woodward while he tried to figure out what the hell everyone was talking about.

"Everett?" Moreau asked.

"Not a chance!" Barczyk said. "He's all bark, no bite, anyway."

"Gagnon!" Lawson said.

This time Barczyk frowned. "Didn't he retire over a decade ago? I ain't that old, sorry."

"Nilsson!" Kates said.

"Which one?" Barczyk shot back.

"The bigger one. He's got like two feet on you, Barzy."

They all laughed, though Barczyk looked unbothered by the jab. You'd need thick skin to be under six feet in this league.

"I've fought Anders," Barczyk said calmly. As he took a long swig from his beer, he ran a hand through his curls. Evan had never seen Barczyk up close without hockey gear on, and he hadn't realized his hair was a mess of brown curls on top with an undercut along the sides to give him a combination of mohawk and mullet. How...well, how Barczyk, to need even his hair to be a statement. "Can't reach his face but got him right in the gut before the refs rescued him."

More laughter. Barczyk smirked, clearly pleased to be the center of everyone's attention; if Evan had been in his place, he'd have stuttered so much the joke would've been incomprehensible.

"Best fight you ever had!" Doyle challenged.

Barczyk shrugged. "I dunno, man. I've had too many to remember them all. Maybe the best was the time Mattherson knocked out my tooth." He opened wide to show off his missing front tooth. Everyone leaned in, like they didn't know that was part of Barczyk's trademark look. "Otherwise they all kinda blend together."

They continued to fawn over Barczyk's fighting prowess. Evan was pretty sure some of them had been on the receiving end of Barczyk's fists—just another notch in his belt, apparently—and he definitely knew no one here had appreciated his antics last season. There'd been a lot of colorful language after he'd taken down Evan, but hey, guess it was easier to join in on the laughs than carry a grudge.

Unfortunately, Evan hadn't heard anything funny yet.

When the pizza arrived, everyone was too busy eating to continue the Barczyk party. Evan grabbed himself a slice—he wasn't that hungry, but he didn't want to make a whole thing of it—and a spot as far away from Barczyk as possible. That put him between their two biggest defensemen, Calhoun and Kates, who spent the next half hour arguing over whether Hawaiian pizza was "not that bad" (per Calhoun) or "an abomination and insult to tastebuds everywhere" (per Kates). It was a completely stupid conversation that made Evan wonder how many times the two men had been concussed over the years, but it was definitely less annoying than pretending he couldn't stand Riley Barczyk.

All Evan had to do was figure out how to survive the whole season like this, hiding from Barczyk and not making it obvious he hated the guy. Great.

3

EVAN PUSHED INTO THE TRAINING FACILITY, RELIEVED TO BE out of the summer heat. He'd never quite adjusted to the humidity in Pittsburgh, or to the heat. But rinks were familiar everywhere in the world. In a few days, he'd hit the ice again with his teammates, and he'd really feel like he was home.

But today was for off-ice training in the gym. It wasn't as if he'd spent all summer doing nothing. He'd gone on runs through Peterborough. He'd skated at the rink where he'd grown up and done drills with some of the same coaches who'd helped him get this far. Still, he didn't feel ready for the physical stress of another NHL season. He'd need to spend some serious time on a treadmill and at the weight rack to feel up to snuff again.

Today he'd focus on getting his lungs back. Despite his new contract and the security it afforded him, Evan didn't want to look out of shape when the pre-season started. In some ways, the pre-season was more competitive than the early regular season games because every rookie, prospect, and AHL-hopeful had something to prove.

Competitive might not be the best word, he considered. Aggressive. That was it. Too many players were hanging their egos on so few games.

Evan had been in the same position, so he understood why people went so hard.

That didn't mean he was going to let anyone show him up, though. He might have nothing on the line, but this was his chance to focus on his play and developing chemistry with his linemates. After only a handful of years in the league and just off his entry-level contract, he wasn't established enough to slack off.

"Abs!"

Evan detoured from the gym to the locker room. He was here to run and sweat, and was already in his workout clothes with a playlist ready to go, but he was curious who else had decided to do some optional training. He followed the voices to the locker room, and almost instantly regretted it.

"Abs!" Kates cheered when he saw Evan. "Thought I saw you sneaking in. Working out today?"

Kates was sitting on the benches with Woodward and Barczyk. No skates or gear in sight, so they must be here for the gym like Evan. He nodded to each of them and tried not to tense up when he noticed Barczyk's stall was only two down from his. Even the locker room wouldn't be safe.

"Yeah, just going for a run." Evan hated how awkward he felt. This was *his* space! Kates and Woodward were *his* teammates! His! Long before Barczyk had shown up in town. Ugh. Why couldn't he pretend he didn't care about him?

"Boring!" Kates said at the same time Woodward said, "Ew."

Barczyk said nothing, instead cocking his head to the side as he appraised Evan. Because that would totally help Evan feel less self-conscious.

"Well, I should..." Evan started to back out of the room and wished he hadn't come in here at all.

"Want some company?" Barczyk offered, earning him betrayed looks from Kates and Woodward.

"I'm good!" Evan said a little too quickly, his voice much higher than he'd have liked. He held up his earbuds in a belated attempt to not seem rude. "Got my tunes ready to go."

Tunes!? Oh my fucking God.

Barczyk's eyes lit up, as if he could hear Evan's thoughts. More likely, he had pest powers that sniffed out embarrassment and preyed upon weakness. "Whatcha listening to?" he asked, sounding far too amused for Evan's liking.

His cheeks flushed. He suddenly couldn't remember a single band he liked or even the name of a song. Was music even real? "I—"

"Why are my players dicking around in the locker room? Go chat in the parking lot. You're here, you're working. Capisce?" Coach Jack strode past Evan into the locker room and right out the far side that led to the coaches' offices. He barely glanced at them as he went through, his eyes glued to the clipboard in his hands. From his vantage point, Evan couldn't read much of it, but it looked like player stats and drills. He recognized one from last year's training camp and suspected it was prep for this year's camp. It was Evan's first year *not* attending, and he was relieved to be past that part of his career.

As soon as the office door closed behind him, Barczyk arched an eyebrow. "Coach Brooks always got a stick up his ass?"

"Jack," all three of them corrected in unison, before Kates offered, "And yes."

"Coach Jack?" Barczyk repeated cautiously, like he thought maybe they were pulling his leg.

"There was this, like, whole thing," Woodward explained. "When Coach Mel joined the team. Some of the older guys refused to call her Coach Gamble, so she owned being Coach Mel. Then Coach Jack showed solidarity and made us all call him by his first name too. Better get used to it, because every time you fuck it up, we're gonna have to do laps. And I am *not* doing laps. I will tape your fucking mouth shut if I have to."

"Aww," Barczyk said with a pout. "But my mouth is my most charming feature."

Evan took advantage of their laughter to disappear to the gym. Maybe if he ran hard enough, he could outrun Barczyk's knowing smile.

———

Riley Barczyk was drafted in 2016 by the New Jersey Kings. He played two seasons for them, putting up records in PIMs (Penalty Infraction Minutes) and hits. He was then traded to Vermont, where he played another two seasons before moving to the New York Rough Riders. Most recently, he played for the Philadelphia Gliders before being picked up by the Pittsburgh Riveters when his three-year contract ended. He currently has a two-year, $9 million contract with the Riveters.

Evan could understand why the team had acquired Barczyk. It was a good move on paper: he put up points and could act in a semi-enforcer/instigator role. The team needed that kind of grit, especially after getting manhandled so much last season in the playoffs. They'd lost to the Blue Crabs in the second round because players like Nilsson and Vlasic could knock them off the puck. It made sense from a management point of view, and it had been praised all over social media by sports journalists and fans.

It didn't mean Evan had to like it.

Evan closed the article, then for good measure, he tossed his phone onto the coffee table so he wouldn't be tempted to look up anything else. He hated that he was curious about stupid Riley Barczyk. Blackwell and Reese were also new to the team, but Evan hadn't bothered to look *them* up. But one night listening to Barczyk's stupid stories about fighting every heavyweight in the league, and now he couldn't get the guy out of his head.

He's not going to fight you, he reminded himself. Evan flexed his right shoulder unconsciously, caught himself, and instead gritted his teeth.

Sure, Barczyk wasn't *going* to fight him, but the jackass had already done his damage last season.

What Evan needed to do was get his mind off hockey. It was going to be a long year if he kept obsessing over one player.

A long two *years,* he corrected. This wasn't some temporary arrangement. Barczyk was here for a while, same as him.

All the more reason for Evan to get over his shit. This wasn't a middle school bully. This was a teammate who might kind of be a dick, but Evan had played with lots of guys who were dicks. Besides, there were plenty of other people on the team. Right now he was seeing more of Barczyk than usual because not everyone was in town yet. Once the season started for real, it wouldn't be an issue.

Probably.

Unless we get put on the same line, some masochistic part of him supplied. *Then we'll see each other all the time.*

Fuck.

He dove for his phone.

> **Abernathy**
> Hey have you heard anything about lines??

> **Lawson**
> Hi abs how's your evening going?
> Mine's fine thanks

> **Abernathy**
> sorry

> **Lawson**
> I'm just fucking with you
> You're still playing center if that's what you're wondering but I haven't heard much else
> Won't know until training camp finishes up but I'm guessing you're third line

That wasn't what Evan was getting at, but it was a relief to know he'd moved up to the third line. He'd mostly been on the fourth line the past couple of years, and he knew he wasn't ready for the top six, not when he knew the players he was competing with. Maybe on another team, he'd be able to hold down second-line duties, but not on the Riveters. He was dying to ask about potential linemates, but he didn't want to push his luck. Lawson had given him as much as he could right now—it was true; there were no guarantees until after training camp, and even then, things could change at any time.

> **Abernathy**
> Thx
> I'll do my best

Lawson
Of course you will kid
You earned it

Evan didn't bother correcting the 'kid' thing. He had the feeling that was going to stick with him for a few more years. At least until a few more of the younger rookies funneled onto the team and took over the mantle.

This time, he shut his phone off completely before he put it away. He didn't need the temptation to overthink. Instead, he grabbed the remote and put on a movie so he could fall asleep in peace.

4

EVAN DIDN'T GET AN ANSWER ABOUT LINES UNTIL THE PRE-season started a few weeks later.

After training camp, the rest of the team started official practices. Evan knew the lines in practice didn't necessarily mean anything—especially when there were ten players there competing for four spots—so he tried not to read too much into things. Yeah, he had to play on a line with Barczyk, but he also played on lines with younger guys like Dalton, Winchester, and Maxwell, as well as experienced players like Antonov, Woodward, and Vassiliev. Too much was up in the air, so he didn't worry about what it all 'meant.'

The worst part was the mini-games and scrimmages, where he had to go *against* Barczyk. He tried not to cringe whenever they were fighting for the puck or if Barczyk was barreling down towards him. He shouldn't have to worry; this was a practice. No one went *that* hard, and Barczyk was more than half a foot shorter than him. It was already a fluke he'd hurt Evan in the first place.

"Get over it," Evan muttered under his breath. He was standing on the goal line to the right of the net, with Barczyk on the left. Once Coach Jack blew the whistle, they'd be racing down the ice for a puck to bring in and shoot on their backup goalie, Reese. "Get over it. You skate fast enough, and it won't even matter."

He was right.

The whistle blew, and he was off. He'd learned a long time ago never to go 100% during practices—that was how players got injured or you burnt yourself out too early in the season—but he always liked to be able to. He liked to pull out that little bit of extra hustle or muscle as necessary, in case he needed to prove a point or impress the coaches.

He did that now, sprinting faster than he had outside a game since the last time scouts were looking at him. He got to the puck first, going so fast he nearly lost his balance on the sharp turn to head back to the net. He passed Barczyk, who hadn't even reached the pylon where he could turn around, and now focused on coming in on Reese.

Reese pushed out of the crease, blocker and glove up.

Evan hated one-on-ones with goalies. They were all so talented and could read him like an open book. It's why he usually just shot and got it over with, because they always made the save, anyway. But he had some time with Barczyk so far behind, so he faked left before pulling back to the right and trying for the back door. He just *barely* stuffed it in before Reese got back over.

"Nice hustle, Abernathy!" Coach Jack said, and there was some applause from the rest of the team. "Try that in a game, why don't you?" Then he blew the whistle for the next pair.

Evan preened at the praise as he got back in line. A few of the guys patted his shoulder and said things like, "Nice one, kid" or "Heckuva move there at the end, kid."

Kid. Always kid. He supposed as nicknames went, it wasn't terrible, but he *really* wanted to be seen as one of the guys. Not one of the 'young' guys they always felt the need to babysit when they went out as a team. Hopefully, being old enough to drink now would help him look like an actual adult this season.

He'd completely forgotten about Barczyk until he skated up behind Evan.

"You've got wheels on you," he said. He was looking straight up to meet Evan's eye, but he exuded so much confidence Evan felt like he was the shorter one. "Not everyone as big as you can move that fast."

Evan noted both the praise and the lack of 'kid.' He wasn't so sure he liked the way his heart fluttered in response. Didn't he hate this guy? He didn't *want* Barczyk to like him.

Though it was kind of satisfying.

It's about the respect, he decided. *That* counted.

"Thanks," he eventually said. Then, because he was too stupidly polite to stop there, he added, "You've been looking pretty good out there, too."

A roguish smile spread across Barczyk's face. It made him look young, like a teenager up to no good. "I *have* been looking pretty."

Evan flushed, his shoulders tensing up almost all the way to his ears in embarrassment. "I didn't—that's not—"

"I'm just fucking with you." Barczyk slapped his stick against Evan's shinguard. "I am pretty, but I wasn't fishing for compliments. How come I never noticed you before? I feel like a big guy who can move like that would've been someone I was forced to fight."

And instantly, the small gains Barczyk had made in Evan's good opinion were lost.

"I don't know," he said coldly. "I played you plenty of times when you were on the Gliders." Then he turned away before he could see Barczyk's reaction.

———

The Riveters' first pre-season game was less than a week away, and the coaches had finally seen enough that they were put out lines. When his phone pinged with the email—complete with preliminary roster, practice schedule, and travel info—Evan's eyes immediately went to the third and fourth lines. He dreaded it a little, mostly because he wondered which of his friends still had a shot of making the team this season and who would be sent down to the AHL.

There was a lot of young talent on the farm team, but not all of them were ready to make the leap to the NHL. Evan felt for them—he'd been in the same position only a few years ago, starting his first season in the AHL after getting some chances in the pre-season, and only moving up to the NHL after the trade deadline had made room for him—but he wasn't surprised when he saw the names. Walker, Stevens, and Maxwell were still in the mix for the forwards, and O'Brien, Leonard, and Pope for defense. There were other names, guys Evan didn't know as well, and he was so distracted trying to place them that he only glanced at the second line by chance.

Woodward - Abernathy - Barczyk.

Son of a bitch.

It made sense, unfortunately. The top line wouldn't see play for a while, which gave him and some other guys the opportunity to push up. Evan's old linemates had both retired, so of course he'd see some new faces. And there was one very competent fresh face that would work well in that right wing spot.

He didn't know what he'd been expecting, but still Evan felt like his hopes had been crushed. How was he going to concentrate on playing if he was so stressed out about his own winger? And what could he possibly say or do? Barczyk was a perfectly reasonable player. Evan had seen that during practice. He had great hands and good hockey sense. Yeah, he ran his mouth, but everyone chirped each other. There was no way Evan could complain about him without sounding like an asshole or exposing his own weakness.

Besides, everyone else liked the guy. Even Doyle, who had four career fights against Barczyk, laughed along with everyone else when Barczyk told stories and did impressions of other players.

...had Barczyk entertained the Gliders with an impression of Evan hitting the boards and hobbling to the bench?

Unable to keep any sort of chill about it, Evan switched from his message app to his phone and hit the first number listed under Favorites.

"Mom," Evan whined on the phone as soon as the call connected. "I don't like my linemate."

"Hello, Evan," his mom deadpanned. "Miss you too."

"Sorry. Miss you, love you, should've called sooner. Better?"

"Hmmm," she hummed. "A little. So what's this about your linemate?"

"Remember last season when I got hurt—?"

"You mean when that rat from the Gliders laid a dirty hit on you, and you missed the rest of the game and a few days of practice to make sure your shoulder was okay? That time?"

"Yeah, that time." He smiled fondly. He was pretty sure his mom would've been standing on the couch, screaming at her TV when it happened. He'd had a dozen texts from her by the time the trainers had finished looking him over, and the last few had been mostly expletives about Barczyk and the refs missing that obvious call.

"What about it?"

"Well, I'm sure you saw that the guy who hit me is on the team"— there was zero chance his mom hadn't taken down his name and number after the hit, and even less likely she wouldn't have noticed the Riveters had acquired him—"and he's going to be my linemate to start the pre-season."

Silence.

"Mom?" He looked at his phone to make sure the call was still going.

"Riley Barczyk will be on a line with you," she repeated slowly, like she was speaking some foreign language and wasn't quite sure the words she'd put together meant what she thought they did. "Oh, sweetie. Well, it's hockey. You don't have to like your teammates, just play with them."

"Liking helps," he grumbled. "I flinch every time I have the puck and he comes near me. If he's on a line with me, he's *supposed* to do that."

His mom sighed sympathetically. "Yeah, you'll have to work on that. I'm sorry, baby, but looks like you'll have to deal with Barczyk for the foreseeable future. I doubt Coach Jack would appreciate a call from your mom about it. Didn't work in Pee Wee, certainly won't work in the NHL."

"Ugh," he grumbled. It wasn't like he thought his mom could magically fix things, but he was a teensy bit disappointed she couldn't.

"How's practice going? I assume you've already had to work with him there? He can't be a total disaster if the team picked him up."

He knew his mom was dying for details. Usually, he talked hockey with her all the time, but he'd been so stressed he'd redirected all of their text exchanges to be about her work or their family. For the past few days, it'd been nothing but cat videos and memes.

"Practice is fine. I've been doing well, I think. Coach seems happy, anyway. And no, Barczyk isn't a *total* disaster," Evan admitted. It'd be so easy to brush off Barczyk as a pest if he weren't so damn *good*. He wasn't like those players who only got contracts to be obnoxious and draw penalties. Whatever else he might say about Barczyk, the guy was a decent player.

"So use him to your advantage. Get as many points as you can and let *him* do the dirty work. You can make this work, sweetie, I promise."

That was true. Despite his size, Evan was terrible at fighting. He also hated it. As a bottom-six player, it was expected for him to be in some scrums. But if *Barczyk* was out with him, maybe *he* could take care of the heavy lifting. The guy seemed to *enjoy* fighting. It was kind of perfect. Eventually, if Evan could make it to the second line, he wouldn't have those expectations on him. He could get away with stepping away from fights.

"Thanks, Mom," he said with genuine relief. He could *totally* make this work. Granted, he wasn't over wanting to stay the hell away from Barczyk on the ice. A game plan would help, though. "You're the best."

"I know," she teased. "Glad I could make you feel better. Lunch in a few weeks when you're in town?"

The Riveters played the Toronto Terrors in Toronto for their last pre-season game. He'd already sent tickets to his mom. One of his cousins was on the Terrors, even though his family lived out in Alberta. The three of them would grab lunch, then Evan would try not to injure his cousin during the game. Weird that the only time they saw each other was during hockey season, but that was pro-hockey life.

"Sure. I'll text you when I've got my flight info."

"Thanks, sweetie. Good luck. And not just in the games. Hope you survive having Barczyk on your line. He'll get you your goals, but he'll probably cost you a few with his shenanigans."

"Probably. Love you."

"Love you too, Evan."

Riley

RILEY WAS THE MASTER OF NEW TEAMS.

A lot of guys hated changing teams, and Riley got that. It was a huge pain to move, and it was easy for resentment or feelings of inadequacy to build up. Riley knew who he was and what he could do, so he didn't care. Hockey was a game, yeah, but the NHL was a business. He'd learned early on to make himself a brand. If people were talking about him and he was producing, then he'd be fine. If teams weren't going to be loyal to him, he didn't need to be loyal to them, and honestly, that'd been really freeing.

Some guys wouldn't be able to go from a three-year stint in Philly to Pittsburgh. They'd be thinking too much about the fans and the past, remembering all the times they'd been booed by the place they were moving to. Their memories were too long if they let it dictate their future. Pittsburgh was a damn good team on the rise, and Riley wasn't going to take less money on a worse team just because it might ruffle some feathers in Philly.

Anything he owed to Philadelphia ended the second his contract was up and they weren't interested in re-signing him. He expected no less from the team, and he hated the double standard that he should continue to care after they didn't. Somehow *he* was the asshole for moving on, when in reality he was forced to move on because the GM was done with him. Like, what the fuck?

Good thing Riley was comfortable being an asshole. It made things a lot easier most of the time.

He didn't always get a warm welcome when he joined a new team. Came with the territory of being a pest: there was usually someone he'd pissed off, fought, or hurt. He took it as a challenge to try to turn it around, to get the guys to realize he was only a jackass during games and for the media. Not to toot his own horn or anything, but Riley considered himself a nice, sociable guy. A couple of beers and jokes usually smoothed things over. Occasionally, one grump would continue to hold a grudge, and Riley learned not to push. If they wanted to be cranky, that was their business. Despite his efforts to have fun with his teammates, he wasn't there to make friends.

The Riveters weren't standoffish to start, which was nice. He didn't have to perform too much early on. They seemed to appreciate his talents (especially his intangibles), and his previous team affiliation was a mark in his favor.

"Philly's gonna hate us even more," Lawson said with a gleam in his eyes. "It's gonna be so much fun."

Riley appreciated that kind of chaotic captain energy, in all honesty. They needed more of that in the league, instead of all the guys being a little too prim and proper. It was boring, and never quite represented how those people acted on the ice or in the locker room. He saw it as dishonest, like they were playing a part.

Though Riley was playing a part too, he supposed.

———

It took all of two days for the Riveters to fully accept him as one of their own. One party at Lawson's place, then a team lunch, and he was golden. It made something in him unclench. As much as he pretended he didn't mind people hating him, it bothered him a teensy bit.

Just when I gotta see them every day, he decided. *It wears on you to have someone be a dick to your face day in and day out.*

The only guy he couldn't get a read of was Abernathy. The guy was huge (huge!), but one of those gentle giant types. Wouldn't hurt a fly even if that fly were holding his mother at gunpoint. Too nice for Riley's tastes.

Scratch that. That was exactly Riley's type. He liked big men, and he liked nice men, but being fucked by them off the ice was usually a lot better experience than getting fucked over by them on it. The last thing he needed was a nice guy linemate who wouldn't carry his weight.

Abernathy, Mr. Nice Guy, seemed a likely candidate for a linemate. Riley looked him up online, watched some highlights, read over the stats. He was a solid third-liner. A little green still, getting his feet under him in the NHL, but Riley figured they could get stuff done this season.

Except Abernathy seemed to give zero fucks about Riley. Again, he was nice, so he politely engaged in any conversation Riley started, didn't snub him during practice, and never even hinted at being unhappy that Riley was on the team. It was just...*too* polite. Like he was using it as a barrier to keep from actually getting to know Riley or having more than a superficial connection.

Which was fine. Riley wasn't looking for friends, and he knew not everyone was as loud as him. Some guys were shy, who cared?

Riley, apparently, cared.

He had no idea why it bugged him that Abernathy was a touch formal with him, but it did. Riley wasn't everyone's cup of tea for sure, but it didn't seem like he could do anything to get Abernathy to warm up to him. What did a guy have to do to get a real laugh when he told a joke? Or a real smile when they made eye contact? Or—

"Oh, fuck," he said abruptly one evening. He was watching YouTube on the couch with his cat Sophia draped over him, and she shot him an annoyed look at the outburst. "Sorry," he said and rubbed behind her ear until she purred. "Just realized I might have a crush on my teammate. Fuck, I hate it when this happens."

'When-this-happens' had occurred exactly twice before. Once in Mites, when he was too young to understand he was in love with his goalie, and then again in Pee Wee when he crushed hard on a guy who'd just moved to town specifically for their team. That one he'd been able to chalk up to him being mysterious and having a cute accent that didn't make him sound like he'd walked right out of a Red Sox game.

That cute accent? Midwest. God, Riley was still embarrassed about that one.

Evan Abernathy was admittedly very worthy of a crush. He was handsome with his sandy brown hair and had big brown puppy dog eyes that he probably didn't even know he was using whenever the coaches yelled at him. He was obviously in great shape, and he was tall. Maybe it was a jealousy thing, but Riley had always been into tall guys. Big hands, big thighs, big—

"Sophia," he whined to the Persian. "What am I gonna do?"

She blinked at him.

"Nothing? Ohhh, smart. Who's such a smart girl?" he cooed, and Sophia blinked again in agreement.

Flings with teammates were already ill-advised, and Abernathy didn't ping his gaydar. It was probably just him accidentally reading Abernathy's distance as him playing hard to get. What he *really* needed was to get Abernathy to loosen up like the rest of the Riveters, and then Riley would be able to prove to himself that was what was going on. It was a weird, unfortunate feeling of inadequacy, not actual romantic feelings.

Once they were friends, he wouldn't be interested in Abernathy anymore.

"Thanks, Sophia." He pulled the cat up and kissed the top of her head. She mewed in annoyance but allowed the manhandling. "I appreciate your helping me talk it out."

5

THE PRE-SEASON CAME AND WENT IN A WHIRLWIND. IT FELT
great to get back on the ice with his team, to hear the fans cheering them
on again. He wasn't as much in shape as he'd like, and he was thankful
for that because while he was struggling through the burn in his legs, he
couldn't focus on the fact that Riley Barczyk was his right wing.

When he did make the mistake of thinking about it, well, then he
made sloppy plays.

Like a bad pass to Barczyk against the Brooklyn Bootleggers that led
to a turnover and a goal the other way.

Or the flubbed shot after Barczyk set him up beautifully in front of
the net. Evan had looked up, recognized it was Barczyk curling out from
behind the net because he was chewing on his stupid mouthguard, and
messed up what should've been an easy backdoor goal.

Or the time he lost a face-off because all he could hear was Barczyk
to his right, chirping the winger on the Buffalo Bears about a stain on
his jersey.

Worst was the time he skated directly into Barczyk in the neutral
zone because he'd been too busy *thinking* that he forgot to just *play*.

"Jesus, Abs," Barczyk grumbled on the bench after the collision.
"You like 250 pounds? Like running into a brick wall."

"220 pounds," Evan said self-consciously, more embarrassed about his mistake than his weight.

"What are you, Barzy?" Woodward teased. "A buck thirty?"

Barczyk threw his head back and cackled. "Look at this guy," he said, jabbing Woodward with his elbow. "Fucking clown. I'll have you know I'm 175 pounds, thank you."

This got all the guys laughing. If true, that would put Barczyk a good ten pounds under their next smallest player, one of the rookies who was at least taller than Barczyk though not leaner.

"You're like a chihuahua," Pope said. "Small, mean, and loud as fuck."

Evan thought the comparison was pretty on the nose, but Barczyk scoffed. "I ain't mean. I'm a nice guy, honest. Just not to anyone wearing something other than green and yellow."

By the time they reached Toronto, Evan had locked in enough that he was playing actual hockey with only the occasional Barczyk-related hiccup. He still made poor plays that the coaches chewed him out for, but they were infrequent enough that they didn't connect them with Barczyk. It was a blessing and a curse that they hadn't. He secretly hoped they'd notice the bad line chemistry and make a change, but that would require there to actually be a problem: they had a decent number of goals for and few against. It might not be ideal for Evan, but he couldn't deny it was working.

Or at least...working well enough.

"You hesitate a lot," Barczyk said in the locker room after their game against the Toronto Terrors. They'd lost 3-2 in a shootout. Evan hadn't scored, but his cousin had in the shootout; he'd have to remember to text him about it. They'd made a bet at lunch earlier about who'd get the most points, and he now owed his cousin a pack of beer that he'd have to pay up on when the Terrors came to town in November.

Evan tensed. "What do you mean?" He knew exactly what Barczyk meant.

"On the ice." He still had his gear on from the waist down; from the waist up he was naked, a gold necklace of large interlocking chains dangling around his neck highlighting the smooth planes of his chest.

His hair, normally a wild mess of curls, was sweat-damp and clung to his forehead. "You hesitate."

Fuck. It was true, and while a lot of it currently was Barczyk-related, Evan couldn't blame all of it on him. He did hesitate whenever he got the chance to check. When he was in the zone, he played hard and didn't *try* to avoid big hits...but then he'd hit someone, and it would look like it hurt. Evan knew he was a big guy—his mom often said watching him play was like watching a tiger cub trying to play with house cats, unaware of his size and strength—and he didn't want to injure anyone, a sentiment that had crystalized even more after his injury last season. After those bigger hits, he would find himself slowing down before making contact, never quite following through and going too easy on opponents, especially if he'd already made contact with them that game.

It had on a couple of unfortunate occasions resulted in the other team scoring.

But that was a can of worms Evan didn't want to get into, period. He 100% didn't want to get into it with Barczyk, the last guy on the planet who'd understand. Barczyk didn't play easy on anyone ever, as evidenced by how rough he'd played this pre-season. It was the fucking pre-season, and they were both players with rostered spots (read: absolutely nothing to prove), and he'd gotten into three fights so far. Three! That was more than Evan had in his whole career!

(Easy enough, since Evan had exactly zero career fights.)

So instead, he pulled the one thread that would look the least bad and might seem the most relatable.

"My cousin's on the Terrors," he said apologetically.

Barczyk considered this. "So you were going easy on him?" he asked skeptically.

"Probably?" Evan admitted. "I don't want anyone to get hurt, but I *really* don't want to hurt him."

"You're so Canadian." Barczyk said it like an accusation. He bent over to untie his skates, exposing his back and a purple bruise on his ribs.

"Thank you?"

"If I had family in the league, I'd be more like the Nilssons. Those boys know you can't give family an inch or they'll take a mile. My sis plays hockey, but I always played with her. Always got pissy when I wouldn't pass to her, though. My other siblings play lacrosse, and my cousins all play rugby and soccer. If they played hockey, we'd fucking *murder* each other on the ice." Barczyk said this with a kind of manic delight that implied he in fact wished it were true because he'd like nothing more.

"Oh," Evan said, because he really didn't know how to respond to that. It was probably in the league's best interest that the rest of the Barczyk clan had gravitated to other sports.

"Who's your cousin?" Barczyk asked. "Auchter? He's big too. Canadian, I think. Played against him in Juniors. Helluva shot."

"Yeah." He was surprised Barczyk had guessed. It wasn't something that Evan hid or anything, but he didn't typically talk about his family within the league. There were four of them currently, all spread across North America. It was a little surreal that he was talking about this with Barczyk of all people when he hadn't discussed it with the guys on the team he considered friends. "He does have a good shot."

"And like I said, he's big. He can take you hitting him, promise. But it's not just tonight. You hesitate all the time. This a new thing or...?"

Evan's cheeks burned. "I—"

Barczyk leaned forward and smacked Evan's thigh. It kinda hurt. "Here's a secret for ya. It's hockey. You're gonna hit people, and they're gonna hit you back. If you walk away from a game without a few bruises, did you even really play?" He paused as if he expected Evan to answer, but then kept going. "If someone can't handle it when you knock 'em over or rough 'em up, then that's a them-problem. We're all adults. You gotta learn to shake that shit off."

Aaaand it was over, that brief moment of camaraderie between them. As friendly as Barczyk was with his teammates, he really didn't give a shit about anyone else. And apparently Evan's inability to let go of his injury was a poor reflection on *him* instead of a sign that Barczyk played a dangerous game and didn't care about collateral damage.

"Right," Evan said stiffly. "I'll keep that in mind."

He really would, though not for any of the reasons Barczyk might assume.

Barczyk nodded approvingly and stood up. He shimmied out of his hockey pants, and Evan took that as a cue the conversation was over; he looked away so he wouldn't get an eyeful of Barczyk's jock.

It wasn't over.

"I can do some checking drills with you, if you want," Barczyk offered. "When we get back home. Some easy ones just to get you to follow through with your hits. We can use some of those big pylon dummy-things if you don't wanna hit a person."

Evan's head snapped back. Barczyk's crotch was unfortunately eye level, and he had to quickly look up. He was so flustered he stuttered, "Uhm, I guess...maybe...it's not a big deal—"

"Cool," Barczyk said, thankfully not looking at Evan as he then pulled off his hockey shorts and tossed them into his bag. "I'll set it up when we're back home. See you on the bus." Then he grabbed a towel and walked his naked ass toward the showers. Evan was so stunned that he couldn't help it...he looked, realized he was staring at Riley Barczyk's ass, and quietly turned away.

What the fuck just happened?

6

EVAN ASSUMED BARCZYK WOULD FORGET ALL ABOUT HIS offer—if anyone in the league said shit just to say it, it was Riley Barczyk—but after practice a few days before the home opener, Evan was about to skate off the rink when he felt a tug on his jersey.

"Hey," Barczyk said. "Thought you wanted to practice checks. I got Coach Mel to help us out since that's more what her D-boys do, and I pulled in some of the rookies so it wouldn't look like anyone thought *you* were the problem or anything."

"Oh." That was actually kind of nice, and 'kind of nice' wasn't a descriptor he was used to attributing to Barczyk. Plus, having Coach Mel run things made it seem a lot more official, and he wouldn't have to deal with Barczyk one-on-one. "That's great, actually. Uhm. Thanks."

He turned back to the rink where Coach Mel was directing some of the assistants to put out large dummies and pylons while a few other players skated around one of the goals. It was mostly the bottom six forwards and the younger defensemen, making it look a lot more like an actual practice rather than something Barczyk had put together just because he noticed Evan couldn't get his shit together.

Coach Mel blew the whistle, and everyone gathered around. "Barczyk's brought it to my attention that some of us need a refresher on how to hit, and I agree. We play a clean game, but being physical is part of hockey. You guys are our grinders: you don't get the pretty minutes, and sometimes it's on you to rough up the other team and tire 'em out. I can't have my defense pulling their punches, and the only way lines three and four see more minutes is if you're doing more 'n just standing around while lines one and two catch their breaths."

While most of the players nodded along, an eager look in their eyes, Evan gulped. Coach Mel had pretty clearly laid out what was expected of him, and he wasn't living up to it. Sure, he scored, and his plus/minus wasn't terrible, but he was in no way 'roughing up' anyone. It had never really mattered before. There wasn't as much checking at lower levels, or at least he'd never needed to worry about it, because he was always bigger than everyone. People hit him, bounced off, and he went about his business. As long as he'd played hard, his coaches were satisfied with his physicality.

But this was the NHL, and that had definitely been something he'd noticed early on. There was a lot more hitting, because not only was it allowed, it was expected. Not only that: everyone was big. Granted, not everyone was 6'5, but there were plenty of guys about his size. Up until now, his coaches had definitely *said* they'd like him to be more physical, but he'd always considered it more like a footnote in their feedback. It sounded like it was no longer optional for him. If this was what he had to do to up his game—and, to some extent, it was definitely a mental roadblock for him to get over—then he'd do whatever Coach Mel asked.

Honestly, he appreciated the direct instruction. Throughout the drills, Coach Mel explained exactly what she wanted them to do, why she wanted it, and how much they could get away with before they'd be risking a penalty.

"Harder!" she yelled as Evan once again pulled up a little short on his check to a dummy. "Abernathy! C'mon, you're a big guy. If you ain't knocking these things over when you check them, I know you're not putting enough into it."

"Sorry, Coach," he said. He meant it too. He just didn't know what to do about it.

"Don't look like someone kicked your puppy. C'mere, kid."

He skated over, glad that the drills were still going so no one would pay attention to them. "Yes, Coach?" he asked, hanging his head.

"What's the problem here? You not taking this seriously?"

"I am! I swear, it's just—" He huffed, looked around the empty bleachers for any excuse that wouldn't be as bad as the truth but found none. "I don't want to hurt anyone. And yes, I know they're dummies. It's hard to get out of that mentality."

Coach Mel raised her eyebrows. "You don't want to hurt anyone?"

He nodded.

"In hockey?"

He winced but nodded again.

"Look, Abernathy, if you don't wanna hurt anyone, go find yourself a rec league or something. This is the big leagues. You can't play games in this league being scared of shit like that. Everyone knows the risks when they step onto the ice. I don't want to see anyone go down, but my priority is my players. If word gets out you won't check, you're gonna be a sitting duck out there. You've gotten away with it so far because you're big, but it only takes one to notice before they all will."

That was unfortunately true: no one but Barczyk had noticed, and thankfully he hadn't until he was on the Riveters. Evan was pretty sure he'd have told everyone on the Gliders if he'd figured it out last season, and then Evan would've gotten a lot more than an injured shoulder.

Coach Mel watched that compute for him before continuing. "I need you to see this kind of stuff"—she gestured to the surrounding ice, his teammates and the drills and the ever-continuing *thud* as dummies hit the boards or the ice—"as your top priority right now. This is gonna keep you from getting hurt, and it's gonna get you the puck a lot more."

"Yes, ma'am."

"We're gonna keep these practices going for you and a couple of the rookies who are on the opposite end of the spectrum and need to learn to play a clean fucking game for once in their goddamned lives. Now, I know you're not a defenseman, so you're not my problem in games, but I don't want liabilities. So, I'm giving you a little homework. We start the season at home against Boston. They've got a lot of big, tough guys in the lineup. I need you to make five hits this game."

"Five!?" He balked at the suggestion. "Couldn't we start with, like, *one?*"

She considered. "Every goal you score, we can decrease that by one. You scoring four goals?"

"Against Boston? Not likely—"

"Then five," she said dismissively. "Five good, clean hits. You take a penalty for one, that's on me, but at this rate, I'll count it as a step in the right direction. You got it?"

Like he had a choice. "Yes, ma'am."

"Atta boy. Get back in line. Gotta get those reps in."

As he skated to the back of the line, he caught a glimpse of Barczyk racing around the back of the net and then laying a huge shoulder slam into a dummy, wedging it against the boards before they both flopped to the ground. The dummy landed on top of Barczyk, earning laughter and stick taps from the boys.

"Barczyk!" Coach Mel called in exasperation. "That's boarding! Every time!"

"Just having some fun," he said with a huge grin. "Gotta get it outta my system before game night." He pushed the dummy off him, stood up, and then carefully put the thing back in place. He patted it on the back like it was a good friend before skating off.

A menace for sure...but Evan begrudgingly admired his no-fear approach. If Evan could get even a smidge of that confidence...too bad it came with a colossal ego and a blasé attitude Evan wanted nothing to do with.

"Nice hit," he deadpanned as Barczyk stopped behind him in line. "Really showed him who's boss."

Barczyk just laughed, unbothered. "I did, right? Teach him to think twice before he joins the equipment for a hockey team."

Evan looked away so Barczyk wouldn't see him smile.

7

THE ONE THING EVAN HAD LEARNED OVER THE YEARS: HOME openers were *loud*. He put on his best suit (navy with a yellow tie and pocket square), slicked back his hair as best he could, and resigned himself to The Experience.

The Riveters went all out for opening night. The Experience included the players arriving at a red carpet outside the main entrance to the arena. Fans crowded behind velvet ropes, taking pictures, begging for autographs, or cheering on the team. It wasn't quite as over-whelming as it'd been his first season, when he'd felt blinded by the lights and deafened by the sheer volume. Even so, his couple of years had only gained him the composure to sign anything handed to him and to remember to smile while he did. He even took a few selfies with people wearing ABERNATHY 21 jerseys. It still shocked him that people would pay money to wear his name.

With their roster, he was surprised anyone remembered he was on the team at all.

Evan had almost reached the entrance when he heard some mock boos behind him. He turned and saw Riley Barczyk getting out of a limo, his hair done up in an exaggerated mohawk of messy curls. He wore a black suit with a deep green vest and a golden tie that glittered as cameras flashed, the arms of his suit jacket a touch too tight, making his biceps bulge. He swaggered onto the red carpet looking more like a boxer coming to a match, though given his history, that wasn't too far off.

There were a few people holding out jerseys from his former teams for him to autograph, and there were a dozen homemade signs held up. Things like "BARCZYK #1 GOON!" and "BARCZYK PIM COUNTER: ∞" plus one notable poster that had a sketch of Barczyk holding a giant wrench and whacking members of the Boston Militia. Barczyk laughed and signed them all, fistbumping people and taking pictures where he pretended to punch people. Evan watched as a teenage girl absolutely swooned when he did this for her, tears in her eyes and her parents filming the whole thing.

Strange how quickly things had changed. They hadn't played a real game yet (he didn't know people besides his mom *watched* pre-season games anymore), but Barczyk had gone from Enemy Number One to Team Heartthrob. Which, fine, he was objectively attractive even if his mohawk/undercut combo was a bit much, and he needed to find a new tailor to make sure his clothes actually fit. Still, it irked Evan how easily everyone forgot Barczyk was a fucking menace on the ice.

Maybe not so much forgot but were willing to overlook it. He was on their side now, after all, and this seemed to be another thing Riley Barczyk was very good at: putting on a show for the crowd.

When Barczyk spotted him, Evan had to resist the urge to run away. He stood there at the entrance like a good linemate, even held the door open for Barczyk, and followed him into the arena.

"Love the energy out there," Barczyk said. "Youse really know how to hype up a team with this shit."

"Yinz," he corrected. When he saw Barczyk's confusion, he added, "They don't say *youse* or *y'all* around here. It's *yinz*." Then he started heading to the player area and away from the madness outside. Even through the doors, he could hear the fans shouting as someone new arrived.

"Oh." Barczyk rushed to catch up to Evan, falling into step beside him. "Well, *yinz* really know how to do opening night. Makes a guy feel special, y'know?" He smiled up at Evan, his missing tooth a mini-void in

38

his mouth. He'd apparently lost it in a fight his rookie year and refused to get it fixed until he retired. Practical, since his face did seem to get hit a lot; he'd just break the replacement.

"The fans do love us," Evan agreed. This time it was Barczyk who held the door for him as they arrived at the player zone, free from fans and reporters. Enough of the team had already arrived that Evan was able to weasel away from Barczyk without seeming rude, and he enjoyed a pre-game meal with Winchester, Dalton, and Pope. The three of them were the youngest on the team and tended to get stuck together whenever the other guys started talking about wives, girlfriends, and kids.

"You survived the gauntlet," Dalton teased when Evan sat down at their table. They'd been road roommates last year when Evan was still on his entry contract, so he knew how much opening night messed with Evan's nerves.

"Somehow," he agreed. "You guys ready to score some goals tonight?"

The team had a tradition of buying a new watch for whoever scored the first goal of the season, and every year Evan hoped it would be him. He was also terrified of it, because the last thing he needed was an expensive watch to break. That didn't make him want the honor any less, though.

"Always," Winchester said.

"I score two goals a season," Pope grumbled into his meal. He always ate the same thing before a game: a bowl of cereal. The type didn't matter, only that it was nearly overflowing and soggy. Evan assumed it was some superstition that'd lasted since childhood, but he never asked. No point in asking a hockey player about their routine: there either was no answer or a really stupid one.

"You're a defenseman," Evan pointed out. "You do just fine."

"Did you see him check Zelly during that practice with Coach Mel?" Winchester asked. "I think I dislocated my shoulder just watching him."

Pope shrugged like he didn't care, but he had an almost-smile. "Hitting people's fun."

Hitting people was not fun, in Evan's opinion. He'd almost forgotten about Coach Mel's homework assignment, and now his stomach twisted itself into fresh knots. Evan tried to visualize himself pushing people off the pucks, bodying people in the corners, and hitting people in open ice. If he pictured it enough, maybe he'd do it by accident during the game.

The trick worked. During the first period, someone on the Militia broke off from his defender. He was wheeling out of the left corner, completely open with all the time in the world to make a pass or take a shot. Evan was the closest to him, so he raced over. Without letting himself think about it, he skated through him, their chests colliding and the other guy spinning like a top before going down. The puck bounced harmlessly into the neutral zone.

"Nice work, kid!" Kates called. He'd been the defender who'd gotten burned, and his relief that nothing had happened was palpable. "Now go score or something!"

Evan's heart pounded, and his skin buzzed. He'd done it! Surely one good physical play early would be enough to call the experiment a success. But any hope he had of coach Mel forgetting about his homework assignment was short-lived.

While she stood at the far end of the bench during the game and never glanced towards him or the rest of the offense, she came by his stall after the first intermission. "Looking better out there," she said, arms crossed as she stopped in front of him. Like all the coaches, she wore a suit during games. Unlike the other coaches, hers was green to match the Riveters' home jerseys. "Only one hit so far and no goals. Looks like you owe me four more."

"Yes, Coach." He hoped no one heard, and he really hoped he wasn't blushing too badly.

"Way to cover for Kates," she continued. She smacked his head with her clipboard, then turned toward the corner where a few defensemen had their stalls. "Kates, you turned the puck over three times that period. Which team you playing for tonight?" she yelled as she walked away.

As soon as she was gone, Barczyk slid over. With their linemate Vassilev off for an interview, there was no buffer between them. "You owe the Coach hits?" he asked with a crooked smile that revealed a dimple. Evan's eye snagged on the dimple before he looked away in annoyance.

"Something like that," he grumbled. "Look, I—"

"You should focus on Number 52. He's the biggest guy they've got on defense. You two match up pretty well size-wise, but you're faster. You nudge him a little, get him worked up, and he'll give you all the space you need to score."

Evan blinked at him. "It's just that easy?"

"Yeah, kinda. I mean, he's a veteran player. You roughing him up won't get him pissy, but if you run your mouth a little it will. He *hates* it when young guys get the better of him. Call him old man or some shit like that. Just be ready to have a shoving match in front of the crease if you do."

"Oh." He wasn't sure he wanted any of the things Barczyk had said, but he was right about them being the same size. Maybe Evan could use that to meet his check quota. And if Barczyk was right, maybe it would give them some scoring opportunities. "I'll keep that in mind." Then begrudgingly, "Thanks."

Barczyk winked at him and slid back over to his own stall. "Any time, liney."

8

THE RIVETERS WON THE FIRST GAME OF THE SEASON, A narrow 2-1 win over Boston. The honor of the first goal of the season went to Lawson—no surprise there, he was captain for a reason—and the first game-winning goal was a breakaway from Antonov. Evan watched Lawson accept the fancy Rolex, and when he joked about adding it to his collection, Evan felt a pang of envy. Lawson was nearly a decade into his career and had the accolades to go with it; when Evan imagined himself in his 30s, he hoped to have achieved what Lawson had.

Instead, he was getting fake punched by Riley Barczyk after the game.

"Fuck yeah, Abs," Barczyk said, punctuating each word with a hit. Evan gritted his teeth and had to remind himself that Barczyk wasn't trying to be an asshole. Not currently, anyway. "You almost got as many checks in today as I did. Fun, right?"

"Uhm." It wasn't *fun*, not when he had to pay so much attention to it, but Evan could admit that it was a relief to have succeeded. Five checks exactly, and it hadn't negatively impacted his offense. Their line hadn't scored, but they'd gotten a decent number of shots and chances. Admittedly, a couple of those were generated *because* Evan was being more aggressive. If he were more skilled at picking the right opportunities instead of going after all of them, it really might help. "It was okay," he conceded.

Not the worst game ever, at least.

"Ha! You hated it. Too bad, you're good at it."

"Am not."

"Okay, you're not, but you could be. You gonna keep it up?"

Evan didn't know what expression his face made, but it made Barczyk laugh.

"Hey, it's just a tool," Barczyk said. "Something to break out when you need it. You don't have to go all Hulk or anything every game."

"Just a tool?" Evan grumbled. "It's the only one you use." And then he wanted to kick himself for saying it out loud.

But Barczyk only grinned wider, showing off his stupid missing tooth. "Hey, I'm a simple man. If you're good with a hammer, no point in learning how to use a wrench."

"That—" He wanted to say it didn't make any sense, but given that Barczyk had made his entire career out of 'using a hammer,' he was maybe onto something. "Okay. I'll keep it in mind. I'll maybe break out the hammer this season."

Barczyk's answering smile was mischievous with the missing tooth, with none of the menace he usually associated with Barczyk's presence.

———

Coach Mel didn't prescribe him any more hit quotas. She congratulated him and warned him about upcoming practices, and that was that. He was grateful that he wouldn't be under the microscope for his checking for a while, because it made him too damn self-conscious during games. There was already a lot of pressure to perform, and he didn't want another way he might not measure up to expectations.

That said, he would try to play a more physical game. He saw the way it worked for Barczyk, a guy half his size, and there was definite potential in trying to do the same.

Not as much as Barczyk, obviously, because Barczyk just went for it. All the time. The guy couldn't go a shift without hitting somebody or something. How his body wasn't just one giant bruise, Evan didn't know. The fans loved it, the other teams hated it, and more and more, Evan appreciated it. After a few games watching it front and center, he had to admire the consistency of Barczyk's game and its effectiveness.

Or maybe he was just glad not to be on the receiving end of it.

That final realization made him sick. It came during a game against Chicago after Barczyk delivered a late check to Aliaksei Sokolov. Sokolov went down awkwardly and came up clutching his ribs. Evan got to see the check up close, only a few feet behind Barczyk on the play, and he hated himself because his first thought was, *thank fuck he isn't checking me like that anymore.*

When the ref gave Barczyk a deserved penalty, instead of taking it and quietly going to the box, he mouthed off the whole time.

"Ref, c'mon. He's got eighty pounds on me at least. If he falls over for that, that's his fault. Tell him to learn how to skate."

"Being small doesn't give you a free pass, Barczyk," the ref said. He seemed more amused than upset, like this was a song and dance they'd done before. "Get in the box."

"Would it help if I said sorry?"

"Doubt it. You say it to Sokolov, it'd probably just make it worse."

"Nah, that guy loves me. Ain't that right, Socks?"

Sokolov glared at him and cursed under his breath in Russian. Barczyk looked disappointed, but he went to the box without complaint after that. While Barczyk was making himself comfortable in the penalty box, Evan reclaimed his spot on the bench, feeling guilty for his own relief. Sokolov could've gotten really hurt, and all he could think was *phew! not me this time!*

He also didn't like how callous Barczyk had been about the whole thing. He hadn't said sorry, not that Evan had expected him to (he knew firsthand Barczyk didn't apologize for hits). Still, it was the lack of remorse after. He hadn't even looked back to see if Sokolov had been okay, just kept playing and had the gall to look surprised by the penalty. It was no wonder Barczyk was one of the most hated players in the league.

It also became apparent after his penalty why he still got contracts. Not only did Barczyk score the next time their line was out, but he drew a penalty when Sokolov angrily crosschecked him well after the goal. Barczyk sat on the ice, chewing his stupid mouthguard like always, and grinning up at Sokolov while Evan and Vassy stepped in to keep the angry Russian from pounding Barczyk into the ice.

"Buh bye," Barczyk said with a wave as the refs dragged Sokolov away. "Make sure you watch the replay of my goal! It was a nice one! Sorry you dropped your coverage, big guy!"

"You are asshole," Vassy said as he offered Barczyk a hand and pulled him up. "Complete shithead."

"Don't I know it," Barczyk said, fistbumping him. "Thanks for having my back, guys." He looked to Evan as he said this, offering one of his wide smiles like he was telling a great joke and Evan was in on it.

Evan felt like he *was* the joke.

––––––

"He's just so...so..." Evan huffed into his phone later, completely at a loss how to describe Riley Barczyk to his mom.

"Heartless?" his mom offered. "Reckless? Cold-blooded?"

Evan growled, suddenly wanting to defend Barczyk. He wasn't heartless or cold-blooded—not the way he celebrated each and every player on the Riveters. If someone made a good play, delivered a clean check, scored, did anything even remotely positive during a game or practice, Barczyk was the first and loudest among those cheering. He was a great hype man, and it came from his genuine enthusiasm for his teammates' success.

But he couldn't defend everything about Barczyk. Despite his redeemable qualities, he was a rough guy to play against.

"Reckless," he decided. "He's really reckless, and I hate watching it up close, because the things he's doing to other players, he did to *me* last season. And it doesn't even faze him! It doesn't register with him that he's hurting people."

"Well, sweetie," his mom said. "Lots of players either have to or like to play rough. Barczyk's a bit of both. He's good, but he's small. He's not as fast as you, so I guess he learned early on that if he was physical, it would make up for it."

"Oh my *God*, Mom. Are *you* defending him? After calling him heartless?"

His mom laughed. "I'm just explaining. I didn't say I agree with it, but I've seen it before in hundreds of other players. You hear me telling you to play like that?"

"No."

"I know he's a pest, but I never minded it until he hit you," she said. "I have a list a mile long of players I've got a grudge against because they checked you or hooked you or tripped you, starting with that jerk in your first game. You remember that kid?"

"Mom, that was like...almost two decades ago."

"And I haven't forgotten the little shit who tripped my baby boy and sent him headfirst into the net. Obviously, he was also a small child, and I would've taken out my anger on his parents and not him, but still. Haven't forgotten it." A pause. "Where was I going with this?"

"Barczyk."

"Oh, right. So I didn't mind when he was doing it to other people around the league, because it honestly makes for some great highlights when he does it. The problem was he did it to you, and now he's on top of my list of players I hold a grudge against."

Evan laughed. "Thanks? I think?"

She laughed with him. "You feel better now that you've gotten that off your chest?"

"Yeah, actually. Sorry for ranting, but thanks for listening."

"Always, sweetie pie. But I should let you go. You're flying out early tomorrow, aren't you?"

"Not that early, but yeah." The Riveters had an 11 a.m. flight to Carolina. He wasn't looking forward to it, but it was one of the easier flights on their schedule. "Night, Mom. I'll call you after we play the Reapers."

"Good luck. I'll be cheering you on."

"I know you will. Night."

"Night, sweetie. Love you."

9

A WEEK AND A HALF LATER, THEY HOSTED THE FLORIDA Pythons, which sucked. The Pythons were a killer team, and the Riveters were coming off their first back-to-back of the season. They were all tired, exhausted from their loss yesterday (an overtime loss at that, even worse). As soon as the puck dropped at center ice, with Turner squaring off for the opening face-off against the Pythons' lead scorer, the Riveters were sloppy. A few minutes into the game, Evan got his first shift, and yep, he was no exception.

His line couldn't get any momentum, and he left the ice after his first few shifts feeling insanely frustrated. The real issue: he was getting manhandled left and right. Any time he got anywhere within five feet of the puck, he'd have at least one Python player on him, bodying him off track and clogging up all the passing lanes. He couldn't remember having so little space and time in a game, and it was driving him crazy.

When the second period rolled around, Evan didn't know what came over him. This one defender, Smith, kept pushing him around. He'd wait until the refs' backs were turned and then slashed or cross-checked Evan, and once tripped him by hooking his stick behind Evan's knee. Maybe it was all the talk about using his body, maybe it was

Barczyk's influence, but in the waning minutes of the second period, Evan had reached his limits.

"You wanna fucking go?" he found himself yelling as Smith pushed him again.

Smith looked startled for a moment—he actually did a double-take —and then grinned widely around his mouthguard. "You sure you wanna do that, 21?"

Normally, that would be when Evan would come to his senses and realize, no, he absolutely did not want to do that. He liked his teeth and not being in the penalty box, thank you very much. Except he knew that if he backed out now, it would only get worse. It was already fucking awful, enduring Smith's pestering, and if he didn't stick up for himself, it would be open season for the rest of the game.

So he did the mature thing; he dropped his gloves.

Smith's eyes lit up in delight. He threw aside his stick and gloves, and brought up his fists. Oh, right. The fighting part. Evan managed to block the first punch and took the other to his shoulder pad. Not bad. He had no idea what to do with his own hands, so he clenched them hard and started swinging wildly. He hit Smith, though he wasn't tracking where or how hard, but he figured any contact was good contact. But Smith had a hand on Evan's shoulder and was doing a good job manhandling him so Evan couldn't get in a decent punch. It also put him at the mercy of Smith's more skilled jabs. In his adrenaline rush, Evan didn't feel anything until the one that connected square with his nose.

All that worrying about his teeth getting knocked out, he'd forgotten about his nose.

When he inevitably fell to the ice seconds later with Smith on top of him trying to get a few more blows in before the refs pulled them apart, Evan felt dizzy.

When he finally got up, recollecting his helmet, gloves, and stick so the refs could escort him and Smith to their respective penalty boxes, it was to cheers from the crowd and stick taps from his teammates. He felt like a gladiator, putting on a show for the masses.

Too bad he'd lost. They killed gladiators who fought as bad as him, didn't they?

After he sat down in the penalty box, he ran a hand through his sweaty hair. An attendant offered him a towel, which he took as a hint and dabbed at his face. Yep, blood. Great. He held the towel in place over his nose, sighed, and tilted his head back so he could look at the jumbotron. Sure enough, they were replaying the fight. Evan thought he looked reasonably good when he dropped his gloves. Less so after that. After they showed the punch to his face that took him out, Evan winced. He'd fought like shit. Looked like a damn rookie.

Granted, it was his first career fight. He was lucky he got any hits in.

"21!"

Evan looked over to the other penalty box, where Smith was leering at him.

"You fight like shit, kid."

Kid. Always a stupid kid.

"You fight like an old man, fuckface," he yelled back and turned to watch the game. He didn't look back at him the rest of the penalty, or at the fans pounding on the glass behind him. He just wanted this game to be over so he could sulk in peace.

God, what if he had media tonight? He didn't want to answer questions about the worst fight in the history of hockey fights. He didn't have the training to be diplomatic about Smith provoking him or his own incompetence.

"Fuck me," he grumbled. He put his helmet back on and watched the clock tick by. Because it was a five-minute penalty, he'd have to wait for his time to expire and for a stoppage in play before he could head to the bench. He could kiss the rest of his shifts goodbye until the third period, and he wouldn't be surprised if he sat more than usual as punishment for taking such a dumb penalty in a game where the team was already struggling.

All in all? Not worth it.

Not to be outdone, Barczyk joined him in the box shortly after. He skated hard into the Python's zone, chasing an errant puck. The goalie covered it well before Barczyk got there, but Barczyk didn't slow down and instead did a hard stop right in front of the crease. Snow flew and covered the goalie, who glared up at Barczyk.

A grand total of three seconds later—Evan counted, holding his breath because he knew what was about to happen—Barczyk was cross-checked from behind. He stumbled, fell into the goalie, and then immediately threw off his right glove to deliver a blind right hook at the person who'd hit him. He got in a great hit to the jaw of the Python's defenseman. By the time he'd regained his balance, Barczyk had both fists up.

Unfortunately for him, the defenseman had no interest in fighting. He skated away, holding his jaw, while the goalie skated after him in solidarity. Barczyk stood in the crease with his arms out in a *what the fuck?* gesture, and even from the box, there was no mistaking his bewilderment.

When the refs gave Barczyk his own five-minute major, Evan kind of felt bad for him.

"I didn't even get to fight!" Barczyk complained as he stormed into the box. He threw his helmet into the corner, gave Smith the finger, and sat down with a thump a little too close to Evan. His chestnut curls were sweaty and almost straight, matted against the sides of his head. "The asshole hit me first! What kind of jackass doesn't fight back when punches are thrown?"

"You did snow his goalie," Evan pointed out.

"Et tu, Abs?" Barczyk grumbled. He leaned back against the glass, oblivious to the fans taking selfies behind them. At least they were in Pittsburgh and it was their own fans. Evan hated being in the box during away games, because the crowds could be rude if not downright vulgar as they heckled him.

"I'm just saying—"

"That because I'm an asshole, I deserved it?"

"I didn't—" Evan blushed. "I would never—"

"Call me an asshole to my face?" He'd been staring glumly at the rafters, but his gaze shifted briefly to Evan, an eyebrow raised in challenge.

Evan felt like a jerk, because it wasn't like Barczyk was wrong. He didn't think much of Barczyk's personality and definitely didn't approve of his style of play, but he wouldn't say that to a teammate. Honestly, he was surprised he'd called Smith a fuckface out loud, but

Smith was on another team and he'd never have to live with the consequences of that one.

"It's okay," Barczyk said. He knocked his knee into Evan's. While he'd been upset about the penalty, he looked completely unbothered to hear that his own linemate thought he was a dick. "I am an asshole. I'm an asshole who snows goalies and smashes into people and punches them. But right now, I'm *your* asshole and I punch them for *you*. So if guys like Smith are being jagoffs"—he said this last part loudly while glaring at the other penalty box, the Pittsburghism earning hoots from the nearby fans—"you let me handle it, 'kay?"

The admission shouldn't have meant anything, yet it tore through Evan like a bolt of lightning. He squirmed uncomfortably, suddenly too hot and his heart beating madly. Before he could figure out how to respond, though, Barczyk nudged him with his elbow.

"Think they'll kill my penalty for me?"

Evan blinked and turned his attention back to the ice. He'd forgotten they were in the middle of a game. "Uhm, yeah. Hope so."

They stayed quiet after that. He felt bad for what he'd said. Or almost said. After his one embarrassing attempt at a fight, Evan better understood what Barczyk went through every time he dropped his gloves. It took a lot to put yourself out there, in front of tens of thousands of people (hundreds of thousands if you included TV viewers), and he did it multiple times a season. Evan might not agree with some of the asinine reasons Barczyk fought, but he found he respected Barczyk's readiness to stick up for himself a bit more.

He and Smith got out of the box during a stoppage, and Smith scowled at Evan. Barczyk waved at him and blew a kiss, which seemed to scare him off. Thank God. Evan wasn't sure he wanted to continue trash talking without the safety of plexiglass between them.

"Hey," Evan said, turning back to Barczyk before he closed the penalty box door. With his stick, he tapped Barczyk's skate. "See you in a few? Try not to be too lonely without me."

Barczyk grinned at him, missing tooth on full display. "Aww, Abs, you softie. Gonna miss me for my last minute in the slammer?"

"Not really," he said, his own smile hard to control. He pushed the door shut and skated away, well aware that Barczyk was laughing behind him.

When he returned to the bench, his teammates were supportive and made a point of congratulating him on his first fight.

"Smith's a dick," Lawson said and patted Evan on the back. Evan preened a little whenever he got their captain's attention. "Way to stand up to him."

Lawson and the others diplomatically didn't comment on the outcome beyond a neutral, "We've all been there." He appreciated them overlooking how pathetic he'd looked.

Well...there was one player who wasn't good at diplomacy.

"That your first fight or something?" Barczyk asked as soon as he'd been freed from the penalty box. They sat together on the bench, bracketed by Vassiliev to their right and Dalton to their left, waiting their turn to go on the ice. He was chewing his stupid mouthguard, per usual. He did it so often, it didn't do much guarding of his mouth. Even to shut him up. "Sorry, I should've asked when we were in the box. I was kinda..."

"Distracted?"

"Something like that." He waited expectantly.

"Ugh, yes. That was my first career fight," Evan grumbled. "You surprised?"

"Not really. A guy who doesn't like checking people wouldn't like fighting them, either." Barczyk frowned as he looked Evan up and down. "It's just you're so...so *big*. You should win every fight. Hell, you breathe on me too hard, I'll probably go flying."

Evan wilted. "I don't think I've ever thrown a punch before today."

"Oh, don't worry, I believe you. No one would accuse you of knowing what you were doing."

A line change rescued Evan from Barczyk's chirping. They jumped over the boards and rushed onto the ice, and Evan was happy to go back to actual hockey. The Riveters were fired up after his fight, at least. It was like they'd decided if Evan Abernathy was willing to get into a fight, they could suck it up and play better. They'd scored twice in the five minutes Evan had been trapped in the box, and they'd been buzzing the whole third.

Smith and the Pythons, on the other hand, seemed to have lost steam. Like the whole thing was embarrassing or something. *Same*, Evan thought. *Hard same.*

But he ignored his own embarrassment because he had to.

With the ice tilted in their favor, the Riveters came out of the game with a 4-1 win.

"Wish we could've gotten you a Gordie Howe hat trick," Barczyk joked as they headed back down the tunnel after the game. "That would've been something. Could've redeemed ourselves if we'd pulled that off."

Evan highly doubted he'd ever get a Gordie Howe hat trick. He very rarely got a goal and an assist in the same game, and he certainly didn't plan on fighting again. Getting all three in a single game seemed impossible.

"Abernathy."

They both stopped in their tracks and turned around. Coach Jack was still by the bench where Doyle was waiting to go onto the ice with Calhoun.

"Yeah?" Evan asked nervously.

"Get over here. You're third star."

Evan stood there dumbly. "What?"

"You're the third star of the game," Coach repeated wryly. "You go on first. C'mon, kid. They're about to call it. Don't worry, they'll give you a puck. Just throw it to the fans and smile. You'll be fine."

"Oh." He'd never been one of the three stars of the game. And to think he got it for *that* fight. He trudged back, wondering what his mom and his friends back home would say about all this.

He waved to the fans, threw the puck to a couple of kids by the penalty box, and disappeared off the ice as soon as he was allowed.

When he stepped into the locker room, the team erupted in cheers.

"I didn't even score," Evan muttered when he sat down at his stall. Not that he didn't enjoy or want the praise—he really, *really* did—but he hadn't earned it. He hadn't done anything, except lose.

That didn't seem to matter, though: he was the hero of the hour. As the team got undressed, showered, and went through their various post-game routines, Evan kept getting pats on the back, noogies, and whoops of encouragement from everyone, the coaches included. It was weirdly gratifying, like instead of completing fucking things up, he'd done something right. Surreal, since as far as he was concerned, it had been the least hockey-thing he'd ever done.

Fighting's part of hockey, a voice that sounded suspiciously like Barczyk whispered. *Can't ignore it just because you don't like it.*

Evan mulled it over on his drive home, then dreamed of fighting a hundred Smiths while Barczyk coached him from the sidelines. Strangely, it wasn't a nightmare.

10

Despite getting the Third Star against the Pythons, the achievement was short-lived. Evan had a mediocre game against the Tennessee Outlaws and was falling behind in practice.

He needed to get out of his own head. This checking and fighting garbage, the Barczyk stuff, it was throwing his game off. It was small enough right now for him to fix it. He just needed to make the effort and stop it from getting out of hand.

Pretty much everyone on the team had their coping mechanisms. For Moreau and Doyle, it was recreational drinking (with whiskey being their preferred drink); Kates, Antonov, and Farrell had established a video game club where they played Mario Kart religiously on road trips; a lot of them used exercise; Lawson had taken up knitting when his daughter was born and routinely made whole scarfs on plane rides.

For Evan? He had a very specific way of detoxing from hockey.

"Hey, Dalty," Evan said after practice a couple days after the Outlaws game. "You feeling putt-y?"

Dalton's eyes lit up. "Hell yeah, bro." He offered a fistbump to Evan, which he gladly accepted. "Wanna grab dinner too? It's my cheat day, and I could really go for a milkshake."

"Sure." He frowned. "Your dinner isn't going to be just milkshakes, right?"

"No," Dalton scoffed. "...maybe."

Evan thought over their options. There was a new place he'd been meaning to check out, just to be thorough in his mini-golf of Pittsburgh knowledge, that was inside a bar/restaurant.

"You wanna go to that new fancy place in the Strip?" he asked. "They might have milkshakes."

"Milkshakes?"

Both turned to see Barczyk walking behind them to the parking lot. "What's this about milkshakes? And putty? Doesn't sound healthy, guys."

Dalton laughed, like a traitor. "Not putty, putty. Putt putt. Like, mini-golf." He hooked a thumb at Evan. "Abs here loves it. We go a couple of times a season. Wanna come?"

Actually, traitor was too nice of a word for Edward Dalton. Maybe his middle name was Judas.

"Mini-golf?" Barczyk gave Evan a look like he was reevaluating everything he knew about him. "I don't want to intrude."

Good, Evan thought, but he would never in a million years be rude enough to say it out loud.

"Nah, bro," Dalton said. "The more the merrier. And maybe if you come, I might not lose every round."

Barczyk didn't take his eyes off Evan. "Abs is that good, huh?"

"Real good. Understands the angles and how hard to hit and all that. I don't think he's ever done a course over par, even when he's never been there before."

Barczyk's expression lit up with delight. "Never?" he teased, and Evan felt like his cheeks were on fire. "I need to see this in action. Count me in."

———

They agreed to meet in an hour, giving them time to go home and change. It meant they drove separately, thank God, because Evan didn't know if he could handle more Barczyk. Mini-golf was his escape from this sort of thing, but here was Barczyk, tagging along like they were friends or something.

Barczyk probably thought they were friends, and that only made Evan's chest constrict with guilt. Barczyk had been nothing but friendly to Evan since joining the team. More than friendly, honestly. He'd talked to Evan more about his checking and fighting fears than literally anyone else on the team, and he'd spotted it back in the pre-season whereas some of these guys Evan had played with for three years and hadn't noticed at all. If last season hadn't happened, things would be great. Evan would've enthusiastically welcomed Barczyk to the team, and they'd be more in sync on the ice.

Okay, maybe not *enthusiastically* because he still didn't agree with Barczyk's reckless style of play. The point was he wouldn't be so on edge all the dang time.

Barczyk was already at the kiosk when Evan arrived, trying to figure out the machine and get their game started. Evan tried his best to picture Barczyk as just one of the guys on the team and not...well, Riley Barczyk.

Evan observed from a distance as he tried to reevaluate Barczyk through unbiased eyes.

Barczyk's mohawk of messy, poofy curls was ridiculous on a grown man...but Evan would've loved it when he was a kid. Evan could never pull it off, but he could a) appreciate someone trying and b) admit that Barczyk did pull it off. His look of perfectly fitted jeans (where the hell did he find jeans that fit hockey thighs?) and a green tee just tight enough to hint at how toned he was only made him look cooler than he had any right to be, though he lost points for his gold chain. His credit card was out as he paid for all three of them to play, which was pretty decent of him, and he was polite to the staff when they offered him help getting putters and balls.

That was when he noticed Evan, a smile lighting up his face as he waved him over, and Evan was forced to stop lurking in the entry.

"Wanna grab a drink while we wait for Dalty?" Barczyk offered as he tossed Evan a yellow ball. "He drives ten under the speed limit. It'll take him another twenty to show up."

Evan caught the ball and pocketed it in his joggers. He felt like a slob compared to Barczyk, since Evan looked like he was coming from the gym while Barczyk at least looked like he was out to have fun with friends.

"No thanks," he said. "It's a little early for a beer."

"Beer?" Barczyk laughed, that stupid dimple on his left cheek on display again and grabbing Evan's attention more than it should. "What about all that milkshake talk? We gotta get some to rub it in Dalty's face that he was late."

Evan didn't mean for it to happen, but he smiled. "Yeah," he said, realizing he'd been scowling before. Maybe this would be good for him. Hanging out with Barczyk without hockey might help him fix his brain to read Barczyk as friend and not guy-who-injured-me. "That seems fair. Let's get two of the biggest milkshakes they've got."

The milkshakes were massive, on par with a liter of beer by the look of it, and Barczyk's face brightened when the server dropped them off for them.

"Dalty's got the right idea. These ain't no joke." Barczyk dove right in, ignoring the straw and licking up whipped cream from the top. Some ended up on his nose, and he went cross-eyed as he tried to lick it off.

"Hold up." Evan took out his phone and pulled up the camera. He worried Barczyk would get the spot off before Evan could take a picture, but instead he grinned big and held up his massive milkshake. He managed to wink just as Evan snapped the picture. "Ugh," he grumbled as he sent it to Dalty. "You are unfairly photogenic."

Barczyk winked again. "Don't I know it."

Evan sipped his own milkshake—chocolate milk with chocolate brownie topped with whipped cream and a chocolate syrup drizzle, more sugar than he normally consumed in a week—and saw that Dalty was messaging him back. He waited patiently, expecting a middle finger emoji or a *bros nooooo*, but the longer he waited, the more confused he was. When the message finally came through, his shoulders sagged and he groaned.

"What's up?" Barczyk asked. He was almost done with his milkshake, like some bottomless pit.

"Dalty can't make it. His piece of shit truck that he bitches about all the time broke down. He didn't even make it out of the parking lot. He's in a tow truck right now."

"Oh." Then Barczyk shrugged. "Sucks. He need a ride home or anything?"

"No, it sounds like Lawson is going to pick him up and get him set up with a rental. But he's not making it for mini-golf." Evan turned over his phone in annoyance as he laid it between them. "Sorry, if you don't wanna—"

"Let's get on the course, then," Barczyk said before Evan could finish. He hopped off his bar stool, chugged the last of his milkshake, and slid it into the center of their high top. "We'll take turns shooting for Dalty. We're gonna get him such a bad score." There was an amused glint in his eyes, the same mischievous one he got on the ice when he was about to royally piss someone off. Except here at the putt shack bar, it seemed endearing instead of malicious.

Part of Evan didn't want to be stuck alone with Barczyk, but mostly he didn't want to give up on his afternoon of zen. Maybe it would be kind of fun if they were messing with Dalton in a harmless way.

See, Barczyk's a friend. Friends play pranks on each other. You've got this.

"Sure," Evan said. "Let's do it."

Barczyk, it turned out, wasn't very good at mini-golf. He was better than average, if only because he had decent aim, but he didn't seem to have the patience to inspect the course or line up his shots, and he wanted to muscle his way through everything. He even did a toe drag with his putter a few times to get it in position, and when he was waiting for Evan to take his turn, he'd bounce the ball on the end of his putter.

"Can you not stay still for even a minute?" Evan said slowly, breathing evenly as he steadied his hands and lined up the shot. There was a moving bridge to get across, and he had to time it perfectly or the whole hole was ruined.

"Nope." Evan could hear the bounce of the ball behind him. "You should see my bed in the morning. I'm tangled up in the sheets, and the pillows are on the floor. When I was a kid, my ma said they should put me in a straightjacket to sleep, otherwise, it looked like a tornado ran through my room. Very localized to the bed, but a couple of times I knocked over all the stuff on my nightstand. Broke a lamp once. Ma wasn't happy about that one."

Evan tuned him out, waited, then shot. The ball went across the bridge, teetering a little at the end, but landing within an inch of the hole. Evan clenched his fist and mouthed a pleased, "Yes!"

"Hey, nice! Way better than when I tried."

"You tried to saucer it over the bridge," Evan said as he walked around to the hole. He tapped the ball in and allowed himself a few seconds to be happy about his score so far.

"What do you do? Imagine you're going five-hole?"

"I don't visualize it like hockey," he said. "They're completely different."

Barczyk raised an eyebrow and looked between the putter in one hand, the ball in the other, then back at Evan. "I don't think they're as unalike as you think, bro. We can do Topgolf sometime. I'll show you what I mean." He dropped the orange ball—Dalton's ball—and squared up at the start. "Dalty's been having such a terrible game today. Think he'll make it in less than ten?"

"Doubtful." Evan grabbed his ball and stepped off the course.

He snickered and watched some truly terrible mini-golf, amusing only because of Barczyk's theatrics. Back-handed shots while facing away from the course. Squatting down so he could use the putter like a pool cue. Making everything a bounce shot instead of trying to take the most direct path. It was impressive how many ways he could find to play mini-golf wrong. Of course, Evan could argue that he'd found as many odd ways to exploit ice hockey too, so it shouldn't be that surprising he'd do it with any sport or game.

When they reached the end, there was a scoreboard that showed their final scores, and Barczyk insisted they take a selfie with it in the background to show Dalty.

Abs: 13
Barzy: 20
Dalty: 74

Evan smiled, then froze when Barczyk slung his arm around Evan's shoulder (no easy feat given their height difference) and pulled him down. Evan watched on the camera display as Barczyk made a duck face; Evan belatedly tried not to look constipated. Neither of them quite succeeded.

"Perfect," Barczyk said gleefully as he released Evan. He started messing around on his phone, and Evan took a step back to get some air. "Gonna put this on Insta. What's your username? I'm gonna tag both of you guys, even though this is obviously a Dalty callout post."

"Evanabernathy21," he mumbled. His shoulder had felt too warm with Barczyk's arm around it, and now it was too cold.

"How professional," Barczyk said, though he was too busy with his phone to put his usual teasing tone behind it.

Before Evan could ask what Barczyk used as his handle, his phone pinged with a notification.

@bardownbarzy has tagged you in an Instagram post.

It was certainly on brand; Evan had to give him that.

At the Puttshack with my boys @evanabernathy21 and @eddydalton78 - par for the course is 15 and Abs beat it!? 🏌️ Dalty don't quit your day job 😂😂😂

Evan hit the like button. He figured it was time to head back home. His head felt a lot clearer, even after having Barczyk for company.

"Let's grab dinner," Barczyk said, dragging Evan by the sleeve of his sweatshirt toward the bar. "I'm starving. Who knew you could work up an appetite with mini-golf?"

"I uhm...uh—"

They were seated at the bar with two more milkshakes in front of them and burgers on the way before Evan had properly formed a sentence. Well shit.

"You're good at mini-golf," Barczyk said. "I can see why you score so much. Even with a goalie, the net's a lot bigger than those holes."

"I don't score that much," Evan said. "I haven't scored yet this season."

Barczyk shrugged. "But you did good in the pre-season. You've got good hands and a wicked shot. Good game sense, too. I mean, the only thing really stopping you from being in the top six is..." He looked at Evan expectantly.

"That I'm not good enough?"

"What? No. Jesus, Abs, have you been listening to me at all? You've got all the skills. You just don't take advantage of your other assets."

"My other assets? I don't—"

"Fuck, if I had your size," Barczyk said wistfully, then shook his head. "Actually, it's better that I don't. I've got no restraint. You, though, you've got too much. You fix your checking and your fighting, and every team in the league'll want you."

"I don't know about that." Evan's cheeks were burning. This conversation wasn't happening. Riley Barczyk wasn't gushing with praise over him. Maybe the milkshakes were spiked or something.

"I promise it's true." Barczyk's face lit up. "Hey! I've got an idea!"

Evan grimaced. He had a feeling he wouldn't like Barczyk's idea. "What? I sign up for boxing lessons?"

"No. I mean, yes, you totally should, but who's got time for that? I can help. You did all that checking practice with Coach Mel, and it did wonders for you. Huge improvement—"

"I still don't check much."

"But you do it more, and that's what you needed. And don't interrupt. The only thing that's missing is your fighting game. That fight the other day with Smith was weak, bro. Like I know I've had some less than stellar fights and gotten my ass handed to me, so I get it, it's not easy, but that was kind of embarrassing. Good for you for doing it. We're all proud of you for sticking up for yourself. But yikes, man. Yikes."

Yep, Evan's cheeks were on fire. His ears and neck, too. This was the worst.

"And how would you help exactly? Be my enforcer?"

"I do that anyway," Barczyk said dismissively. "That's not what you need. If you're gonna throw your body, even if it's only now and then, you gotta be willing to drop the gloves too. And you need to not look like a kitten swatting at a ball of yarn when you do it, or people are gonna antagonize you more 'cuz they've got nothing to be afraid of."

"A kitten and a ball of yarn?" He sighed and pinched the bridge of his nose. What was he doing here, listening to this? All the stress he'd let go of during mini-golf was seeping back in with every word Barczyk said.

"See." Barczyk pointed at him and smirked. "You're pissed right now, but I ain't afraid because I know you're not gonna do anything about it. You're this giant, polite Canadian boy who'll offer to pay at the end of the meal and thank me for my advice, even though I can tell you fucking hate it."

Evan gritted his teeth. He wanted to deny it, but it was pretty spot on. He did hate it, he would thank Barczyk, and he would offer to pay.

"Well, you paid for the mini-golf—"

Barczyk burst out laughing. Mercifully, their burgers arrived, and Barczyk had a mouthful of fries for the next few minutes. Evan thought he'd escaped; he should've known better.

"So," Barczyk said as he chased down his entire side of fries with more milkshake. "I can help you learn to fight."

"Who says I want to learn how to fight?"

Barczyk snorted. "Yeah right. Every hockey player wants to know how to fight." Then, after a moment of appraisal, he straightened up. "Oh shit. Sorry. You're serious."

"Yes, I'm serious. I've gone this long without fighting. It's not part of my game."

"Okay, well, that's great, but it *is* part of the game of hockey, which you play."

"Plenty of leagues—"

"So when you join one of them, you're set. Right now we're talking about the NHL, and fighting is definitely still part of the game. If you can throw a few reasonable punches when necessary, it'll do you a world of good."

"And you'll just generously teach me how to do it? Out of the goodness of your heart?"

"Yes?" Barczyk's nose scrunched up in confusion. "That so hard to believe?"

"Kind of. I mean, what's in it for you?" Evan pressed. A guy with that many penalty minutes didn't seem like a team player, so why would he offer to help Evan? What was in it for him? At the very least, he seemed to love being the center of attention. If Evan started laying people out left, right, and center, wouldn't that detract from the Barczyk Show?

"I won't have to kick someone's ass for you when you bite off more than you can chew. Like you did with Smith."

"You gonna keep rubbing that in my face?" Evan grumbled. He wished he could eat in peace, but he found he wasn't all that hungry anymore.

"Have another fight where you don't suck, and I won't be able to." Barczyk said it reasonably, like it was the obvious solution to a problem that wouldn't exist if Barczyk would just drop it.

"And what does your so-called fighting lesson look like?"

"Uh..." Barczyk's eyes crossed as he thought about it. "I dunno. The curriculum's a work in progress. Probably like the checking drills. Just...practice. Lots of reps. Make sure you know the basics."

"I know the basics—"

"I mean, make sure you can *execute* the basics. I don't want you getting your hands stuck in your gloves when you try to drop them or something."

Evan rolled his eyes, though now his heart was racing because, oh no, was that a thing? Given his luck, it would be.

"Look, I appreciate the offer—"

Barczyk held up his hands to stop him. "You don't have to say anything right now. If you're not up for it, cool. If you change your mind later, also cool. It's a long season."

"I'll think about it," he said. It was true—he would think about the time Barczyk offered to teach him how to fight for a long time, probably longer than they'd be teammates—but he had no intention of taking him up on the offer. "Thanks."

Whether or not Barczyk believed him, he let it go. "Cool. Hey, you gonna eat all those fries or what?"

11

"Abernathy."

Evan froze. He'd been re-taping his stick for practice when Coach Jack's voice gave him a mini-heart attack. "Yes, Coach?" he asked. His stupid voice wavered. Fuck.

Coach Jack pretended he didn't notice. "My office for a minute?"

Oh shit. Something Coach didn't want to say in front of the rest of the team. This was worse than Evan had thought. "Sure."

Coach Jack's office had floor-to-ceiling bookshelves along two walls, completely stuffed with hockey and sports books. They weren't for show, either: Evan knew Coach Jack had read each and every one of them, front to back, several times. He often had one with him on road trips, a pen and highlighter and pad of paper in hand as he annotated them page by page. The wall behind his desk had two high windows, and the rest was covered with photos and memorabilia. Most coaches had bragging walls like this, though a fair share of Coach Jack's was covered with pictures of his daughter, who was making her way up through the local youth volleyball programs.

"I told her any sport she wanted," Coach Jack said when he saw Evan looking at the photos. "Any sport at all. She picked a sport I know nothing about. Youthful rebellion." He took a seat and gestured for Evan to do the same. "How's the season going for you so far?"

"Uh, pretty well?" Then he coughed and tried again. "I think I've been doing okay. My line, we get pretty good zone time. Not a lot of goals yet, but we're still working on the chemistry, I think. I was a little skeptical about working with Barczyk..." A few weeks ago, this would've been where he made his case to get on a different line, even if it meant dropping to the fourth. After mini-golf, though, they were kind of friends; he had to acknowledge that any on-ice issues were his fault. "But I think we're getting there."

"Glad to hear it. You guys had me worried there for a moment during pre-season, not going to lie, but I've liked what I've seen since then. The goals will come, and your line hasn't given up too many."

Evan preened at the praise...until he realized he wouldn't have been called into the head coach's office for a one-on-one if everything was fine. He knew the drill. Compliment sandwich: good comment, real comment about what he needed to improve, good comment, goodbye.

"But...?"

Coach Jack made a face. "So against the Pythons..."

Oof. He should've seen it coming. After that fiasco of a fight, it was a miracle Evan hadn't been pulled aside mid-game.

"I won't get in any more fights," he blurted. "I know it was a disaster and—"

"Whoa," Coach Jack said and put up his hands. "Let's slow that down. I'm not here to say you should or shouldn't fight."

"...you're not?"

"Well, you shouldn't fight too much if you can help it," he conceded. "Really, I wanted to check in with you and talk about your style of play. You're a big guy, and you're using all of your assets to their fullest. Coach Mel said she worked with you and several of the guys on checking, and honestly, I've noticed an improvement in your game since then. I was wondering if there was anything else I could do to help you come into your own and feel more comfortable with your physicality."

Evan didn't know what to say to that, so he joked, "I don't know. A membership to a boxing gym?" Coach Jack looked like he was considering it, so he quickly added, "I don't actually want that."

"Oh." He sounded disappointed. "Well, I've got the next best thing in mind. Barczyk."

The bottom dropped out of Evan's stomach. "What about him?"

"I think you could benefit a lot from working with him. He's half your size and wins just about every fight he's in. Playing with him, you could learn a few things. It's part of why I put you two on a line together. I figure your levelheadedness might rub off on him. A pest is only as good as his temper, and no one so far's been able to keep him in check."

Evan blushed. "I don't know if *I*—"

"Relax, Abernathy," Coach Jack said. "I'm not making Barczyk your responsibility. Like I said, you're a good influence. That's all I need from you. That and an actual win when you get in a scrap. Six foot five and you lose to a guy who has to reach up to punch you. All I'm asking is that you watch Barczyk and maybe, I don't know, try to incorporate some of what he does into your game."

When he tried to imagine himself acting more like Barczyk in games, he couldn't picture it. It was so foreign to him to say or do the things Barczyk did, it would be like wearing a costume, disingenuous at best and a complete train wreck at the worst.

"Not all of it," Coach Jack continued. "Like I said, I don't need you to fight, and I don't want unnecessary penalties. We're looking for a few tweaks here and there, not a total 180 in your game. You've got a great shot, and you skate harder than half my guys. I've always appreciated that about you. You've got spirit, kid. Lots of potential, and I can't wait to see what you do with it."

"Thanks," he said a little too earnestly. Coach Jack was trying to encourage him, trying to point out parts of his game that he could improve, and, honestly, it was fantastic to hear that the only thing lacking was being more physical. That meant everything else—i.e. basically 90% of hockey—was good.

He just needed to figure out if he cared enough about that final 10% to do something about it.

"But I'm serious. If you need anything from me, or Coach Mel, or any of the staff, we're all ears. I know I ask a lot from you guys during the season, but it's a two-way street. I'll get you what you need if I can."

"I appreciate that," Evan said, because he really did. There weren't many coaches who would let you know privately what they thought you could improve on. Throughout his youth hockey career, they'd very loudly and publicly said what they weren't happy about. The best way to show that appreciation would be to act on what Coach had said. "I'll do my best."

When he got back to the locker room, a lot of the team had already cleared out to hit the ice. There were only a few stragglers, and thankfully one of them was exactly who he needed.

"Hey, Abs," Barczyk said when Evan slid next to him on the bench. "What's—?"

"I'm in."

Barczyk looked at him, head tilted in confusion. "In what?"

"For your fighting lessons. I'm in."

"For real?" Barczyk's eyes went wide. He looked like a kid on their birthday. "Fuck yeah, Abs! When do we start?"

Coach Jack walked through the locker room on his way to the ice, sparing an approving nod at Evan and Barczyk. Evan gulped and turned back to Barczyk. "How about today?"

"Today?" Barczyk winced. "I gotta take my cat to the vet, and she gets real pissy after." But before Evan could get too down about it, he said, "Tomorrow after practice okay?"

Evan had absolutely no clue what his plans were tomorrow, but he'd make it work. "Perfect." He held out his hand. "Tomorrow after practice."

Instead of shaking his hand, Barczyk grabbed it and pulled him in for a hug that wasn't more than their chests bumping together, then clapped him hard on the back. "Fuck. Yeah. Let's fucking go!"

What had Evan gotten himself into?

12

Twenty-four hours was the perfect amount of time for Evan to reconsider whether he was making a huge mistake. It was a pendulum of doubt, swinging back and forth between 'this is a good idea' and 'what the fuck was I thinking,' and it had just landed back at 'what the fuck' when practice ended. He was wondering how to weasel out of it when Barczyk appeared at his side on the ice, blocking the exit.

"Ready, bro? Don't worry, I'll take it easy on you today."

"Uhm." His stupid brain couldn't come up with an excuse, and then his stupid mouth said, "Yeah, sure."

Nobody looked twice as Barczyk dragged him to one of the circles, well away from the boards and benches. By the time they were at the face-off dot, everyone else had disappeared back to the locker room. Thankfully, today was a closed practice, not open to the public; Evan was relieved there'd be no witnesses. As good as Barczyk was at fighting and as bad as Evan was, he didn't need anyone seeing him getting beaten up by a guy that seemed like half his size.

"Today is just about the basics," Barczyk said. "We won't get to any actual punches, I don't think."

"Today? How many lessons do you have planned?" Evan had *not* signed up for that.

"The Barczyk School of Hockey Fights is a work in progress," he said. "I've only got the first three lessons planned out, but we might need to improvise."

"Three!?" he squeaked.

"Minimum three. Abs, you suck at this. You're really good at hockey, so maybe you'll be a quick study, but it took me years to get good at this. I don't think it's unreasonable to think you'll need three lessons to get non-sucky."

"Years? I thought you were just naturally good at being annoying."

"Oh, I am," Barczyk said, shameless as always. "But perfection at anything takes time. So let's start with the gear."

"Gear?"

"Yeah, the gear. Lots of rookie mistakes with people who can't handle their gear." He nodded to Evan. "I'm coming in hot. We're about to fight. Drop your gloves."

"Oh." Evan shook off his left glove, switched his stick to his left hand, and did the same with his right glove. He looked up to see Barczyk's bewildered expression, like Evan had grown a second head.

"What the fuck was that? Why do you still have your stick? Like, holy fuck, Abs. I'd have knocked you out cold by now!"

Evan blushed. Right. In a fight, people wouldn't wait for you to take off your gloves and gingerly put down your stick. He reached down for his gloves. "Can I try that again?"

Barczyk crossed his arms across his chest. "Please."

The second time, Evan did better. He dropped his stick first, wincing slightly as it hit the ice, then shook off both gloves at the same time. One got stuck, but still, overall he did way better. He thought it was good enough to move on, but Barczyk looked as unimpressed as before.

"You are in greater need of my services than I thought. You've gotta be faster, and you've gotta get it out of the blast radius. Look where you left your stick. It's right in front of you! You're gonna trip over it or break it."

Evan looked down. Barczyk had a point. There was more to this fighting thing than he thought, and they hadn't done any actual fighting yet.

"Okay, let's try something different." He backed away from Evan. "Time me."

"Time you?"

"Yeah, time me. Do a ready, set, go. You don't need a stopwatch. One-Mississippi it."

"One-Mississippi—? Oh." As a kid, Evan had seen people on TV and in movies count seconds that way, but he'd never done it himself. "Okay, yeah." He waited for Barczyk to give him a nod of approval before starting: "Ready...set...go!"

As soon as he said go, Barczyk tossed aside his gloves and sticks and had his fists up. Evan hadn't even gotten through one full Mississippi. He gulped, both impressed and a little concerned. Maybe he was lucky Barczyk had checked him and not fought him. It seemed like that was the better option.

"Wow," Evan said as Barczyk went to retrieve his gear.

"That's how long you've got until a guy like me is going for your face, so you've gotta be that fast too."

They spent fifteen minutes just dropping and picking up their gear. Evan would never have thought to practice this, so it was a relief he could at least have one takeaway.

"All right," Barczyk said when he deemed Evan could drop everything at an acceptable speed. "You've got the hang of it. Hard to do it in the heat of the moment, but you shouldn't embarrass yourself."

"Wow," he deadpanned. "I'm glad you're proud." He was ready to call the lesson a success and go home, but Barczyk cut him off before he got the chance.

"Now time for the most complex part of hockey fights."

Evan froze, mouth dry. "I thought you said we weren't going punching today."

"We won't. God, you're not ready for that. We've gotta get you swinging on solid ground before we put you on ice."

If Barczyk had said that to him in August, Evan would've thought it was super condescending—Evan had been skating since he was four and was perfectly capable of staying on his feet, thank you very much. Only two months later, he wasn't even annoyed. He'd had all of one fight, made a fool of himself, and had to concede that it wasn't as easy as it looked. Barczyk was the expert here.

"So what are we doing instead? What's the most important part of fighting?"

"Jerseys," Barczyk said grimly, almost apologetic. "We've gotta work on your jersey-pulling game."

"Jerseys?" he asked, but it clicked as he said it. He knew players often grabbed each other's jerseys during a fight. You could use them to hold the other person in place while you punched them, or to keep them at arm's length to avoid getting punched yourself. Some more ambitious players tried to take off the other person's jersey, pulling it up over their head, effectively blinding and trapping them. "Oh. Right."

"Show me what you've got," Barczyk said. He still had his mouth-guard with him, chewing it as he made Evan drop his gloves and reach for his jersey. Once Evan had done it a few times, Barczyk nodded. "Good. You've got a lotta reach, so use that. Keep the people you don't want to fight away from you and then pull them in when you're ready to punch. You could also shake 'em a bit, try to throw them off balance."

"I can handle that," Evan said, mostly because he liked the idea of 'keeping away people you don't want to fight.'

Barczyk chuckled—a deep, throaty sound that Evan unexpectedly felt in his gut. "Yeah, only because I'm *letting* you manhandle me."

And again, the words hit Evan oddly, leaving him more unbalanced than if Barczyk had pushed him. He gulped. "So you gonna fight back?"

"I'm gonna try to grab your jersey, yeah. No punching." He held out a finger sternly, but his eyes lit up in amusement. "I don't need you giving me a shiner."

"No punching," Evan repeated. His heart was in his throat. He was suddenly hyperaware of how close he and Barczyk were. It hadn't mattered when Evan had been the only one grabbing, but this was more...what? Intense? Personal?

Intimate?

He shook off the thought and instead skated away to grab his gloves and get some space. Space that almost immediately evaporated, because as soon as he'd squared up with Barczyk, he winked at Evan and dropped his gloves with lightning speed. Evan threw his gloves at

Barczyk more than onto the ice, but he dodged Barczyk's first attempt to grab hold of his jersey. Not the second, though, and before he could return the favor, Barczyk had gently slapped his face.

"How the fuck"—Evan took a deep breath, heart racing—"do you do that so fast?"

"Lots and lots of practice. Let's go again."

They did it again and again and again, like they were practicing a dance, so quickly that Evan soon lost his self-consciousness about their proximity. He focused on the task at hand, trying to get faster at it. He got better at aiming his hand for Barczyk's chest, grabbing a fistful of coarse fabric. Sometimes their hands knocked into each other as they lunged, and after a few minutes, Evan was breathless and laughing. This was stupidly fun.

And maybe chasing that feeling made him bold and reckless. As they squared up again, Evan went for it. He was going to try to pull Barczyk's jersey over his head.

When Barczyk dove for him, Evan side-stepped him and instead of going for the front, he reached for the back of Barczyk's jersey. Barczyk squawked indignantly and flailed to stop Evan as he started pulling the jersey (and Evan appreciated that he didn't start punching out of instinct), but there wasn't much he could do once Evan got it over his face. The helmet made it impossible for him to take it off, and instead Barczyk was trapped in his practice jersey. Eventually his knees knocked against Evan's, and they both went down onto the ice in a heap: Barczyk fell backwards and Evan didn't let go quick enough, tumbling after and landing right on top of him.

"Jesus, Abs, you weigh a ton," Barczyk said through laughter as he wiggled and tried to get his jersey off his face. Evan, proud of himself, showed mercy and helped. When Barczyk's face reappeared, rosy-cheeked and grinning from ear to ear with his stupid missing tooth on display, Evan froze. His heart did a weird flip-flop he didn't understand, while his dick reacted in a way he definitely did.

"You might win a fight yet," Barczyk said. He leaned back on his elbows and looked up at Evan, and yeah, Evan's dick was feeling a certain way about having Barczyk pinned beneath him. "You gonna get off me or what?"

"Huh?" His brain hadn't put those words in the right order at first, and his cheeks burned before he realized what Barczyk had actually said. "Right. Sorry. Lemme just..." He untangled himself from Barczyk and backed away. How was the ice not melting, because fuck it was too hot in here?

"I think that's a successful first lesson," Barczyk said as he picked himself up, stopping to grab his mouthguard from the ice. He popped it back in his mouth, chewing on the end like that wasn't absolutely disgusting. "Probably can't get much done on the road trip next week. We'll figure something out when we're back in town?"

Evan didn't know if he could handle any more rounds with Barczyk, but he nodded. "Yeah, sure thing," he said, distracted.

He turned his back on Barczyk and headed off the ice. He changed as quickly as possible, avoiding eye contact with the few guys left chatting in the locker room, and disappeared into the showers (a refreshing *cold* shower). It was an enormous relief that Barczyk had disappeared by the time Evan finished, because Evan he absolutely zero clue how he would ever look Barczyk in the eye again after...whatever the heck had just happened on the ice.

13

Evan had learned how to compartmentalize a long time ago. It was an important skill when you had a high-pressure life, and he'd had to add it to his coping skills as a kid. Between school and money issues and hockey and travel, there'd always been something stressing him out. He'd gotten good at ignoring the things he couldn't control right now. Couldn't pay for new skates? That was a weekend problem. Grade dropping in French class? He'd worry about it after practice.

Accidentally got a boner while roughhousing with a teammate? He'd put a pin in that and circle back, hopefully never.

He hadn't had to do much compartmentalization since he'd graduated from high school, and even less since he'd made the Riveters' official roster and moved up from the AHL. Mini-golf and the occasional cheat day were enough to mellow him out, but that was before Riley Barczyk, so Evan carefully packed away the incident after practice and decided he would ignore it until absolutely necessary.

He figured it would be easy enough. At home, he could shift his focus to TV. At the gym, he could use his heart rate and breathing to ground himself. He figured at practices and games, there'd be plenty of distractions built in. That would give him time to figure out what the fuck had happened, and if it was a fluke or an actual problem. Ideally, he'd ignore the issue indefinitely.

The one wrinkle in his plan: they had a road trip to Vermont and New York. Normally, Evan sat with Dalton on the team bus and plane rides. Maybe he'd taken that for granted, because he grabbed himself a window seat and started fiddling with his phone while the rest of the team filed onto the plane. He'd just pulled up his travel playlist when someone sat next to him. He'd looked up, expecting to say hi to Dalton, and found it wasn't Dalton at all.

It was Barczyk.

"There's nothing more boring than plane rides," Barczyk whined. "Amirite?"

Evan blinked at him. "I think you picked the wrong career if you don't like flying."

Barczyk pouted. Pouted! "Sucks, right? At least I just think it's boring. Can you imagine traveling as much as we do and being scared to fly? Had a teammate like that back in Jersey. Basically had to hide in the bathroom or sleep the whole flight."

"Who was it?" Evan asked.

"Nah, bro, I'm not telling. He was embarrassed about it."

"Oh." That was rather decent of Barczyk. "You've played on a bunch of teams, right?"

Barczyk shrugged. "I've played on my fair share, yeah." It amazed Evan that he seemed unfazed by it. Unexpected or frequent trades caused a lot of anxiety and bitterness among players. If the Riveters ever traded Evan, he might cry.

"It doesn't bother you?" he asked. "To get traded so much?"

"It's not always trades. Sometimes it's just time to move on. But no, not really." He took in Evan's skeptical look and laughed, nudging Evan with his elbow. "For real, I don't mind. Sometimes, a change of scenery is a good thing. And it's cool to get to live in different cities."

"But aren't you worried you might get stuck somewhere you don't want to be?"

"What, like Manitoba?" he joked. "There's good and bad in every city and team, and even being ambitious, I don't think I'll make it to every NHL team before I retire. Having a team is all I need, and I'm not worried about finding new ones."

Evan weighed his words carefully. "With the way you play," he said slowly, "you're not worried about burning any bridges?"

Barczyk didn't even hesitate. "Not really. I put up good numbers. I'll always find a team. And if a team has their panties in a bunch about something I did on the ice, then they're not a good fit for me, anyway. I mean, if I can go from Philadelphia to Pittsburgh and have management not think it's an issue, I'm good."

"I guess." Then, because apparently joking around with Barczyk was a thing he did now, he added, "Good numbers? Like what, PIMs?" He hadn't checked recently, but he was pretty sure Barczyk was always top ten in penalty minutes.

"Abs, you givin' me shit right now?" He put a hand to his heart. "I'm hurt that you think my career is based solely on my penalties." He paused, then said, "It's also on how many fans love to hate me."

"That's not something to brag about!" Evan said, though Barczyk's amusement was infectious.

"Isn't it? Y'all hated me while I was in Philly. Don't even try to deny it. But how many Barczyk jerseys have you seen since I joined the team? I've been in Pittsburgh a couple of months, and I can't go anywhere around town without seeing someone wearing my number."

It was true. The same Pittsburghers who'd complained about him last season had fully embraced him and loved nothing more than to cheer him on after big hits.

So instead of arguing, Evan said, "You can't keep it up forever. You can't be getting into fights all the time when you're thirty."

"First of all, I ain't thirty yet. Second of all, why the fuck not?"

"Because you won't want to?"

It was Barczyk's turn to look at him skeptically. "Maybe," he conceded, though Evan could tell he was just humoring him. "So anyway, there aren't a lot of fighters on the Nor'easters right now, but I still recommend you hold off on dropping the gloves until we get in another practice sesh or two."

Evan swallowed around the sudden lump in his throat. He hadn't thought about their last practice until just now, and he knew he wouldn't be able to think of anything else for the rest of the flight. "Okay," he said, his voice hoarser than he'd like. He shifted uncomfortably in his seat.

"We're gonna be too busy on the road," Barczyk went on. Thankfully, he seemed unaware of Evan's squirming; if he noticed, maybe he'd attribute it to takeoff. "There's a gym at my apartment with a padded area. I don't know if they have boxing gloves or anything, but we could figure something out."

Practice. At Barczyk's apartment building. Would he expect Evan to go to his place too? The only thing that had saved Evan the last time was they'd been at the rink, so escape had been easy. How was he supposed to run away if he got hard while hanging out in Barczyk's living room?

Ugh. That was the worst sentence I've ever thought in my life.

"Yeah, maybe." Any hope he'd had of Barczyk giving up on this was long gone. As soon as Evan had taken him up on the offer, he should've known he was stuck.

That's not true. Barczyk might nag me about it, but if I said I wasn't interested anymore, he'd let me stop.

So the real question was, did he want to stop? While he had no idea how effective Barczyk's lessons were, they *felt* effective. It'd bolstered his confidence (though not his interest in getting into a fight; more like his confidence that he'd make it out without looking like an idiot), and Coach Jack had encouraged it. Even if he never fought again, it might help how the coaches saw him. And somehow Barczyk was not the worst person to hang out with.

Y'know. Except for Evan's dick going rogue.

Once, he reasoned. *Just once. It won't happen again.*

...right?

It won't. It's not like you find Barczyk attractive.

...well, you know *he's conventionally good-looking, but you're not attracted to him. There's a difference. One-hundred percent.*

"We'll figure something out when we're back in town," Evan added, because they should. Maybe not at Barczyk's apartment building. There had to be neutral ground somewhere.

"Cool." Barczyk offered Evan his fist (which he reluctantly bumped) then dug through his backpack. Pulling out ginormous headphones, he put them on his head, keeping one ear open. "I'm gonna take a nap. Lemme know if we're gonna crash or if someone does something stupid, 'kay?"

"You'd want to know if we're going to crash?"

"Hmm, good point. Only wake me up if someone does something stupid that I should make fun of." Then he slipped the headphone over his right ear. Within seconds, Evan could feel the slight vibration of a bass line, followed shortly by Barczyk's light snoring. Evan stared at him for a moment before shaking his head and turning back to his own phone. He did not get Barczyk at all...but he was turning out to be not nearly as bad as Evan had thought. That was something, at least.

Riley

WARM-UPS WERE BORING. COMPLETELY UNSTRUCTURED chaos. Not that Riley necessarily minded chaos. The chaos of a good play or a line brawl, that was fun. This was just...everyone going through the motions until the real thing started. Riley was one of the rare players who didn't have a pre-game routine. No regimen of stretches, no skating exercises, no must-do superstition that would bring disaster if performed wrong, nothing. Sixteen minutes of dicking around.

Today, Riley did some slow laps to get his feet moving and kill time.

The arena was slowly filling, with a fair number of green and yellow jerseys mixed with the Nor'easters' baby blue and black. Riley expected it to be a tough game, which was always a plus in his book. Though honestly, he was just glad they played in Vermont during October and not, say, February; when he'd played here, Riley had always liked the fanbase in Vermont, but he sure as fuck didn't miss the weather.

Riley spotted Abernathy standing alone by the boards. He was stickhandling with a furrowed brow, like something was on his mind. Which was a problem. Abernathy was a decent player, but the more his brain was spinning, the worse he did. Put him against his cousin, he tanked. Make him think about checking, he tanked. Have him get in his own head about fighting...shit, that one was on Riley if it happened tonight.

Without letting himself think it through too much, he skated over to Abernathy and swung his stick like a baseball bat so it smacked him on the ass.

"What the—?" Abernathy turned, spotted Riley, and glared. Well, he was *trying* to glare, but when his face soured like that, he looked more like a disgruntled kitten than anything else. "What are you doing?"

"For good luck," Riley said, because it was the first thing he could think of.

"How exactly is hitting my ass good luck?"

Riley shrugged. "I dunno, but if you score today, we'll know it worked."

Abernathy rolled his eyes and turned away. Still, he was smiling slightly and not glowering at the ice anymore. Mission accomplished.

He whacked Abernathy on the ass again. "If it works, I'll be more than happy to do it again next game," he called over his shoulder as he skated away. He didn't believe in luck, but sometimes shit like this helped guys get out of (or into) their own heads. If it worked, it worked. Riley wasn't about to question the process.

(And hey, he wasn't going to give up an excuse to give Abernathy's ass attention. Riley was almost out of crush territory, but he was only human. He deserved his fun.)

Sometimes he wished he *did* have some sort of good luck charm for himself. Not often, but there were days he could use a little nudge away from his thoughts. Especially when he played his growing list of former teams.

Riley didn't like looking back. The teams he'd played for, the guys he'd played with, it'd been good times, but it was over. Plus, going down memory lane would mean thinking about why he'd left and who exactly he was smashing into the boards. It was the number on their backs and their value to their team that he targeted, not the guy he'd won a Cup with or the guy whose kid's birthday party he'd gone to.

It was more fun that way. Less mental load or whatever. Because at the end of the day, Riley loved playing his style of hockey. All out, all the time, ready for anything. It was a style that had earned him minutes throughout his career, because he wasn't afraid of the hard matchups. Most of the guys were bigger than him, but as his youth coaches always told him, he had more grit. There was nothing more satisfying than upending a guy twice his size or making them lose their shit when he got under their skin.

Which he'd done in Vermont, again and again. Most of his former teammates had also moved on, retired, or jumped ship to warmer climates when their contracts allowed, but there were some franchise players who remembered him. Sometimes guys like that thought friendships off the ice mattered. Like Riley shouldn't be throwing his weight around against them.

Like they hadn't loved Riley for doing it when he was on their side.

"What the fuck, Riley!?" David Bates screamed at him after a questionable late hit. (Okay, *really* questionable, but it was a juicy opportunity.) "Why you always gotta be such a dick?"

"What's that about my dick?" Riley asked. "You miss it?"

Now, he'd never once done anything sexual with anyone on the Nor'easters. Not even hinted at it, because he knew it wouldn't go well. Which was too bad, since Vermont seemed like a decent place to be queer, but that didn't always carry over to sports-dominated spaces. Riley had read the locker room on day one and decided, nah, he wasn't going to push his luck. Despite popular opinion, Riley knew how to keep his head down and mouth shut.

But that was when he had to share space with the homophobes. Now that he only saw them maybe three times a season and promptly got on a plane after, he used it against them.

The sucker punch was a calculated risk. Given he wasn't even facing Bates when he punched Riley in the jaw, he knew he'd get the call from the refs. He was laughing as he tumbled to the ice, because it was just too fucking easy. Leaning back on his elbows, he made sure to spread his legs and waggle his eyebrows. Which was probably stupid. The whistle had blown, and the refs were coming, but that was no reason to tempt Bates to finish what he'd started.

Bates took a stride towards Riley, looking like he was about to tackle him. Riley tensed, because having a 215-pound defenseman land on him wasn't going to be pleasant, but it never happened. Abernathy had skated between Bates and Riley, a human shield that was way too gentle when he said, "How about we calm down here."

It was kind of sexy, actually.

"How about you get the fuck out of my way?" Bates said.

Abernathy had a hand on Bates' chest. A light touch, but a warning nonetheless.

Definitely sexy.

"Nope," Abernathy said. "Not happening. You're going to the box."

Bates looked about to escalate things (fuck, Abernathy was *not* ready for another fight, period. Could Riley get up in time?) but a ref came to the rescue. Abernathy kept his protective guard until Bates was far enough away, then he turned to Riley.

"I feel like you probably deserved some of that."

"Maaaybe." Riley batted his eyelashes. "You defending my honor, Abs?"

Abernathy blushed. He did that a lot around Riley, though Riley couldn't figure out why. At first, he'd assumed it was because Abernathy was starstruck or annoyed by Riley, then he learned the guy was a little shy and figured it was because he was a bit awkward when put on the spot. There were other options, of course, but Riley didn't think they were very likely. Good Canadian boys tended not to be interested in the loud-mouthed American. Not in Riley's experience, anyway.

"Not a chance," Abernathy said. "I can't take on the whole league for one guy." He took off a glove and leaned over to offer Riley his hand.

Riley let himself be pulled up. "What's the damage?" He worked his jaw and felt his lip for blood.

"You're as ugly as when you started," Abernathy said and patted Riley's helmet like he was a little kid. Granted, the height difference was comical sometimes. Riley let it go, because it didn't feel condescending like when Abernathy did it. It'd bugged the hell out of him when it'd been guys like Bates. "No harm done."

"Good." Riley rubbed at his jaw one last time—it would be sore for a few days, ugh—then grinned and poked his tongue through the hole where he'd lost a tooth years ago. "My ma would kill me if I lost another tooth."

Abernathy raised an eyebrow. "I'm shocked you've only lost the one."

"Samesies. Oh!" He looked around the ice, spotted his missing mouthguard, and swiped it before heading back to the bench.

"You're disgusting, you know that?" Abernathy said. He wrinkled his nose as Riley stuffed it back into his mouth.

"Builds the immune system," he said, words muffled by the mouthguard. Part of why he rarely wore it: it made it too hard for other people to understand when he chirped them. "It's why I never get sick."

"Still gross," Abernathy said, so quiet he probably didn't think Riley could hear him. It was cute.

...shit. As they sat down together on the bench to watch the Riveters' power play line get to work, Riley side-eyed Abernathy. Yep, Riley definitely still thought Abernathy was cute. He turned back to the ice and tried to get his head back in the game, all while wondering how long it would take to get over this stupid crush.

14

THEY RETURNED TO PITTSBURGH FIVE DAYS LATER. THEY got a win in Vermont, then lost in overtime to the Buffalo Bears. Instead of focusing on the team's small jump in the standings, all Evan could think about was stupid Riley Barczyk's invitation to his apartment gym.

When it had been Future Evan's problem, days away and not quite real, he'd been able to ignore it. Now he was stuck next to Barczyk on a plane (again), forced to pick a day that worked for him (was never an option?).

"I can't do Wednesday," Barczyk muttered as he scrolled through his phone. He was wearing a hoodie over his button-down shirt and chewing the end of one string. Could that man go a day without chewing on something? Maybe if Evan got him a pack of gum, half his anger problems would go away. "Sophia's got an appointment with the groomer. Lemme check the rest of the week…"

Knowing he had about a minute before Barczyk just picked a day and time for them, Evan needed to act. This was his chance to decline the offer once and for all, but what he said instead was: "Couldn't we just use the team gym after practice Tuesday?"

Barczyk didn't argue with the venue change, just flipped his calendar back a few days. "Yeah, that'll work. We can meet up with Dalty, S'more, and Vassy for drinks after at that new place. You're going to that, right?"

Shit. He'd forgotten about whatever new bar Dalton had found out about and insisted a bunch of them go to. The whole point of practicing at a neutral location was so there was no risk or expectation to hang out after. At least the bar wasn't going to be weirdly intimate like Barczyk's apartment. As a bonus, there'd be other people there to defuse the one-sided tension that was making Evan act like an idiot.

"Yeah." He gulped. "I'm going."

"Cool, that settles it. We can practice and then head over." Barczyk added a calendar event that read 'Abs 🥊 👊,' then looked up at Evan with a lopsided grin, that stupid sweatshirt string still in his mouth. "We'll have you in fighting form by Thanksgiving."

"It was Thanksgiving last week," he said automatically. He'd had a video chat with his mom, which had become their tradition years ago when he'd moved to live with his first billet team out in Ottawa. Nothing like a turkey breast sandwich, boxed stuffing, and canned cranberries while hundreds of miles away from family to hit home he needed to be thankful for all the times they could share holidays together.

Barczyk made a pinched face, squinting at Evan like he wasn't sure if he wanted to contradict Evan or let it slide. Apparently he couldn't be bothered, because he shrugged and said, "Right. So by the end of November, you should be ready to graduate from the Barczyk School of Kicking Ass and Taking Names."

"Is there a diploma that comes with that?" Evan asked.

"I can maybe hook you up with a certificate," Barczyk said. "But I can't sign it until after you win a fight."

"Sounds like you won't be signing it," he grumbled. He saw Barczyk about to argue, so he said, "You're teaching me as insurance in case I get in a fight again. I'm not trying to pick fights."

"Aww, you're no fun, Abs. You'd be a real contender if you wanted to be. I mean, if I can hold my own"—he pointed to his chest, but all Evan noticed was that even sitting, he had to look down farther than usual—"then the sky's the limit for a guy like you."

"A guy like me?"

"Yeah. A Canadian giant. What, you part sasquatch?"

Even with teammates, Barczyk couldn't shut up.

"Scottish," he said.

Barczyk squinted at him. "Hmmm." Then he stretched and wiggled deeper into his seat, eyes fluttering shut. Still with the string in his mouth. "My family's Polish. My grampa speaks it and everything. Rest up, Abs. We've got a lot of work to do."

————

It felt like he blinked and when he opened his eyes, he was at the far end of the team gym where the mats were laid away from the weight racks. He poked the mats with his foot, suddenly worried they weren't thick enough. It couldn't be worse than falling and hitting the ice, though, right?

He'd gotten there before Barczyk, and, not knowing how to prepare for fighting practice, he sat on the mat and stretched.

"You're pretty flexible for a big guy," Barczyk called, startling Evan so badly that he nearly pulled a muscle in his groin. "Is that useful in hockey if you're not a goalie?"

Evan took a measured breath in and out, then gently rose out of the stretch before turning to Barczyk. "Shouldn't you..." He trailed off as he saw Barczyk in a too-big Riveters tee with the sleeves cut off (why?) and bicycle shorts. Very tight spandex bicycle shorts. He also stood close enough to Evan that his dick was at eye level.

Evan immediately went back down to stretch again so he could regroup and try to forget the mental image of Barczyk's dick outlined in dark spandex.

You've seen him naked before, he reminded himself. *In the locker room and showers. Dozens of times. You don't care about his dick.*

His own dick disagreed. He bit the inside of his cheek and prayed he didn't get hard. Why was this happening? Thank fuck his own gym shorts were loose.

Barczyk poked him in the side with his bare foot. "Bro, stop. You're not going to pull anything. That's not how fighting works."

Thankfully, Barczyk's annoyingness worked as well as a cold shower. Evan pushed out of the fake stretch and stood up, crossed his arms over his chest, and scowled at Barczyk (mostly to remind himself he barely liked Riley Barczyk so he couldn't be attracted to him).

Or any guy, he told himself firmly, as if that put the period at the end of his worries.

"So how *does* fighting work?" Evan asked.

"Well, aside from the equipment stuff we already worked on, mostly just punching."

"That's it?"

"No, but the other stuff is too advanced for you. Took me years to master tripping someone while we're fighting, and it's hard to wrestle guys to the ice without practice. No offense, but I don't want you tackling or tripping me when a good right hook will do the trick."

There was a bag slung around Barczyk's shoulder—it was a testament to how out of it Evan was that he hadn't noticed it before—and he pulled out what looked like a pair of goalie blockers. He tossed aside the bag and started putting them on his hands. "I stole these from my apartment gym so we could work on stuff, so don't break them. Hopefully no one misses them and checks the security cameras."

"You don't need to worry about breaking them," Evan said. They looked deceptively soft, but he was more worried about bruising his knuckles than doing any damage to the pads. "I don't think I can punch hard enough."

"Let's see what you've got." Barczyk raised the mitts and squared his feet. "Put 'em up."

Evan rolled his shoulders before balling his hands into fists. He raised his fists, aimed for Barczyk's right blocker, and stepped into the punch—

Barczyk jumped to the side, swinging the blocker out of Evan's reach. Evan's momentum carried him a few steps forward, and he had to scramble to keep from faceplanting.

"What the fuck, Barczyk!?" he yelled, not sure if he was more surprised or angry. "If this is some stunt to piss me off so I'll punch harder, I swear—"

"Not a stunt." Barczyk used his mouth to undo one of the mitts and wiggled his hand out. "Trying to keep you from busting up your hand." He motioned Evan over. "C'mere."

Still peeved, he strode over.

"Gimme your hand."

He lifted his hand and watched goosebumps rise along his arm as Barczyk lightly grabbed his wrist.

"Make a fist."

He did, and Barczyk knocked him with the blocker on his other hand.

"Never do that again!"

"Ow!" Evan tried to jerk away from Barczyk, but he tightened his grip. "What was that for? I thought I was doing the hitting today."

"Not like that, you're not. Jesus, didn't your dad ever teach you how to punch?"

"I don't have a dad," Evan grumbled.

"Okay, then your mom. Hockey moms are scarier than the dads. She didn't teach you?"

"She told me not to fight because I might hurt someone."

"Well," Barczyk drawled. "She wasn't wrong, but you're just going to hurt yourself. Make another fist."

"You gonna hit me again?"

"If necessary, yes. Do it."

Evan did, though this time he dodged Barczyk's swing.

"Ehhh! Wrong! Look at your hand, dummy. What do you see?"

When he looked, all Evan saw was his hand and not the mortal error Barczyk seemed to think he was committing. "My fist?"

"Yeah. And where's your thumb?"

"In my fist?" This time he caught Barczyk's mitt. "Stop that," Evan said. He pulled the mitt off Barczyk's hand and threw it across the gym. "What are you—?"

"If you put your thumb in your fist and throw a punch, you could break your thumb. You're trying to hurt the other person, not yourself."

"Oh." He looked at his fist, then carefully opened and closed his hand so his thumb was now wrapped outside his fingers. "Like this?"

"Hallelujah, he gets it! Now open and close your fist a bajillion times so you get it right. Both hands. I gotta go find that other glove thing."

As much as it aggravated him, he did as he was told. He couldn't complain about Barczyk treating him like a complete beginner, because apparently he was a complete beginner. He couldn't even make a fist properly, for fuck's sake. It made him feel like a rookie again...except that Barczyk never treated him like a 'kid.' Sure, he gave Evan shit, but it was never about his age like most of the guys did.

They went through punches. Barczyk threw words at him like 'upper cut' and 'right hook' and 'haymaker.' Evan didn't bother trying to remember them, too focused on replicating the punches he demonstrated. Admittedly, it was satisfying to hit something and put his full weight behind it. He held back at first, not so much worried about hurting Barczyk but knocking him over. When he proved he could absorb the hits, Evan let loose.

After the hit last season and his brief flirtation with the Injury Reserve, Evan had worried part of him might try to return the favor. He couldn't deny that he'd daydreamed about Barczyk getting his just desserts, and maybe even toyed with the idea of doing it himself. Not that he would initiate anything, but the fantasy had satisfied him in a primal way.

Now that he had the opportunity to do something, all he worried about was his form.

By the end, he was sweating and panting. His body twitched as new muscle memories formed, and he was sure he'd dream about fighting tonight.

Squatting down to rest, Evan tried to catch his breath. His arms were exhausted, and sweat was pouring off him. "I'm gonna call it a day."

"Nope." He looked up and watched Barczyk take off the gloves and then offer them to him. "My turn. Call it payback, but I wanna get my reps in too."

"Oh." He took the sweaty gloves and stared at them. "What do I do exactly?"

Barczyk flexed his hands and bounced back and forth on his feet while he jabbed at the air. "Put 'em on and hold 'em up. It ain't rocket science."

Right. Evan put them on, trying not to think about how Barczyk's hands had just been in them. It felt intimate to share gear, even if it was borrowed/stolen. Evan wouldn't share hockey gloves or skates or hockey socks or literally anything except maybe a stick. Now Barczyk's clammy hands might as well be wrapped around his.

Evan ignored the desire for hand sanitizer. He'd have to shower after this anyway. Instead he held up his hands about eye level with Barczyk and waited.

Barczyk took one look at him and narrowed his eyes. "Seriously?"

"What?" he asked self-consciously. How had Evan managed to fuck up holding up a glove?

"What's the average height of players in the league?" Barczyk asked.

"Uhh..."

"It's 6'1. How tall am I?"

Not 6'1, that was for sure, but he didn't want to say that out loud. "I feel like this is a trap."

"Forget your delicate sensibilities, Abs. I'm 5'9. I can't practice punching people my height when everyone's got a couple of inches on me. I gotta practice hitting up, because there's no one my size to fight. Look at you. What if I wanted to fight a giant?"

"Maybe don't fight them?"

Barczyk ignored him. He nudged the gloves higher until he was satisfied with the height of his imaginary opponent, then got his fists up. There was a moment when it looked like a switch turned, and he went from kind-of-annoying teammate to locked-in fighter. It was like Evan wasn't even there as blow after blow came. It was a good thing Evan didn't hold any illusions that he was good at this, because thirty seconds of absorbing Barczyk's punches would've been enough to dispel that idea. His speed and power were one thing, but his intensity was something else.

Honestly, it was kind of sexy.

Wait, no! Anyone would be sexy showing off this kind of competence. It's not Barczyk that's sexy. It's his skill.

Evan didn't feel much better after the clarification, because his dick was getting hard again and the proximity to Barczyk made it difficult to argue he wasn't a factor. If he wasn't attracted to Barczyk, then his body wouldn't be reacting, right?

As his brain wobbled between 'this is a problem' and 'this is normal,' Barczyk went at it. When he abruptly stopped, Evan blinked back to awareness. Were they done? Already? Was he disappointed?

"Get rid of those." Barczyk waved a hand at the gloves as he ran a hand through his mess of damp curls. His hair was darker when it was wet, with none of the slight blond twinge to it. "Ready for a big-boy fight?"

"Wh-what?" Evan froze with the left glove halfway off. He gulped.

"Don't freak out on me." Barczyk walked over to his duffel bag and pulled out two pairs of boxing gloves. "You've got massive hands, so hopefully they fit."

"We're going to fight?"

Barczyk held up the gloves. "No? It's just practice. I mean, try not to let me slug you in the face, but I'm not going to whale on you or anything." He paused. "No kidney shots. Those suck."

As he traded one pair of padded gloves for another, Evan tried not to stare through the ridiculously enormous gap in Barczyk's sleeves, revealing glimpses of his bare chest and stomach. Evan's mouth went dry when he spotted a bead of sweat running down his side. Why the heck did Barczyk mutilate his shirt like that?

"Did you have brothers you fought with as a kid or something?" Evan asked, more to distract himself than anything else.

"Sure. I've got an older brother and two sisters, and, yeah, we fought all the time. Ma said it was like WrestleMania 24/7 until we moved out. Now she misses the chaos." He gave Evan a once-over. "Only child, right?"

"Is it that obvious?"

"Kind of." He knocked his fists together a few times. "This does kind of make it hard to practice dropping your gloves and pulling up the other person's jersey. I'll have to figure that out for next time."

"Next time—?" Evan barely got the words out before Barczyk was swinging at him. He knew Barczyk was pulling his punches, but it didn't make it any easier to stop him. Evan spent the next minute scrambling to block and dodge before he finally managed to throw a few punches. The first few went so wide, Barczyk didn't need to dodge them, but after he found his stride, they got better. Once again, he was reminded of dancing, moving back and forth to try to hit the other guy. An intense dance where Evan was still learning the steps and Barczyk could probably do this blindfolded with an arm tied behind his back.

...that was pretty much what it would be like to fight with your jersey pulled over your head, so Barczyk really could do that.

They went at it for a few minutes, then stopped for a water break. After Barczyk critiqued his form, they started all over. Rinse and repeat several times over.

"Last round," Barczyk eventually announced. "We've gotta hit the showers before we go to Dalty's mixer thingy."

"Think I'll actually hit you this time?"

"You've hit me a couple of times." When Evan shot him a skeptical look, Barczyk laughed and said, "Okay, you've *grazed* me a couple of times. Problem is you're getting too close. You've got the reach, so use it. You can start swinging earlier than I can. You should be making contact before I can throw my first punch."

Fair point, though it wouldn't help as much against people his own size. But as they squared up again, Evan decided if he could just land one decent shot on Barczyk, this whole thing would be worth it. They circled each other for a few steps before Evan thought, to hell with waiting around, and stepped just outside of Barczyk's reach. He jabbed and grazed Barczyk's chest before he jumped out of the way.

"You can't jump away on the ice," Evan said as he followed, trying to press his advantage.

"I can skate away. It's similar."

And that's when it happened. While Barczyk was running his mouth, Evan took him by surprise and got him square in the jaw. Both their eyes went wide. Evan worried Barczyk might be pissed or embarrassed, but instead his face stretched wide in a grin and he pounced. Evan squawked as he toppled backward onto the mat with Barczyk on top of him. At first he thought Barczyk was attacking him as he punched at Evan's ribs, but none of it hurt.

"Abs, you son of a gun!" Barczyk said, hitting him the whole time. "That would've been a KO on the ice. Fuck yeah, bro!"

Soon Evan was laughing along with him, enjoying the thrill of the moment. It was unfortunate that it took him a few seconds to properly process their compromising position, with Barczyk sitting right on his pelvis. His full weight was pushing down on Evan, his crotch pressed against Evan's lower abdomen so that he could continue his barrage of playful punches. Evan's body had already reacted before he'd noticed, and the effect was only amplified now that he felt his hardening cock straining towards Barczyk's ass.

"Hey, quit it," Evan said, voice thick and a little desperate. He tried to squirm away, out from under Barczyk and away to safety, but it only made things worse. He knew the exact second Barczyk noticed Evan's half-hard dick, because he stopped his joking assault.

"I, uhm..." Evan had no idea what to say. "Sorry, it's—"

His lame attempt at an apology was cut off by a sharp gasp as Barczyk sat back on his thighs, his ass pressing even more firmly against Evan's groin.

"Sorry?" Barczyk raised an eyebrow and then looked down his own torso. Evan followed his gaze and landed on Barczyk's slowly hardening cock, in no way hidden beneath his spandex shorts.

And fuck, Evan was bizarrely tempted to reach out and touch—

Panic choked him, and he lay there frozen and silent and terrified.

" 'S okay," Barczyk said and jumped up. He winked at Evan before he turned his back and started packing up the boxing equipment. "Never happened."

"Uhh..." Evan sat up, using his knees to shield his crotch as he tried to regain control of his body. "Yeah. Thanks. Really, I'm sorry—"

"Never happened," Barczyk repeated. It was maybe the strangest part of the afternoon that Evan believed him. Not just that he wouldn't bring it up, but that it would have zero impact on how he interacted with Evan from here on out. "I'm gonna put this bag by my stall and hit the showers. Put the gloves in before you head out. I gotta drop these off at my apartment building so I don't get, like, fined or whatever. I'll meet you at the bar with the guys?"

"Okay," Evan said. He watched Barczyk go, with no sign of discomfort or shame in his light step. The bastard whistled as he hit the gym door, *I'm Walking on Sunshine* ringing out through the empty gym until the door swung shut behind him.

Even sitting on the ground, he felt so off-balance he couldn't stand up yet. He definitely couldn't walk out of here to face Barczyk; he'd have to wait until Barczyk had had enough time to disappear into the showers before he fled.

15

EVAN PAUSED OUTSIDE OF THE LOCKER ROOMS, STRAINING to hear signs of the showers. He couldn't, so instead he held his breath and listened for any noise at all that might signal Barczyk was on the other side of the door. When it was silent, he tiptoed inside, dropped off the gloves, and then he bolted from the training facility. There was absolutely no way he could handle seeing Barczyk right now, especially not if he was wet and any amount of naked.

Evan's condo was on the way to the bar, so he stopped by to shower and change. It was a bad sign that he was still half-hard when he undressed and got in the shower. He shuddered as the hot water hit his cock, reaching full hardness while he desperately tried to ignore it. He'd rinsed out his shampoo before growling, "Fuck it," and taking himself in hand.

He didn't jerk off much. He usually didn't have the energy for it, and he didn't get aroused very often. Sometimes it helped him relax during playoffs or before season openers, those big games where he was all nerves and couldn't sleep. The rest of the time, he kinda just...didn't bother.

The relief he felt once he started stroking was instantaneous. He moaned in surprise at how good it felt. Eyes closed and head tilted up toward the spray, he slowly stroked himself. He was worked up for whatever reason. That was all. That was why he'd reacted like that during his practice with Barczyk. If he handled things—

Except now that he'd thought of Barczyk and their workout on the mats, he couldn't let the image go. His dick jerked in his fist as he remembered the feel of Barczyk straddling his hips. That moment when Barczyk had pressed his hips back against Evan's dick...

Balls tightening, Evan put out his other hand to brace himself against the wall. He jerked himself faster, picturing what would've happened if he hadn't freaked out. What if he'd held Barczyk's waist to keep him firmly in place over his cock? What if he'd bucked up against the swell of Barczyk's ass, again and again? What would Barczyk do? He was such a tease. He wouldn't just sit there and let him. He'd bend down and tease Evan with a kiss, then bite his lip. He'd run his own hardening cock against Evan's abs, those stupid shorts doing nothing to stop pre-come from soaking through.

"Bet I can make you come first," Barczyk would whisper right in Evan's ear before rolling his hips back.

"Fuuuuck," Evan hissed as he came. He hadn't come that hard in... maybe ever. He was dazed by it, with spots in front of his eyes and legs completely jelly. Too weak to stand, he slid down the tiles to the ground and let the water roll off his chest as he caught his breath.

What the actual fuck?

Evan wasn't gay. He'd never been attracted to another guy. He still wasn't convinced he was attracted to Barczyk. Okay, yes, Barczyk was objectively hot, but he was also loud and abrasive and had hurt Evan last season. Hurt people this season, for that matter. No, it must be something about the fake fighting that got Evan all riled up.

He finished his shower as quickly as possible, giving his spent dick only a perfunctory clean because why did it have to make things weird? Hopefully, it'd be satisfied and leave him alone for a while. The last thing he needed this season (or any season) was inconvenient boners around teammates.

———

The guys were already a few beers in when Evan got to the bar, hair still damp but his body more relaxed than it'd been in weeks.

Until he spotted Barczyk.

As soon as Evan saw him, goosebumps rose along his arms and the back of his neck prickled. His entire body became hyper-alert, aware of Barczyk's presence at the end of the bar. Even as Dalton ordered Evan a drink and started yapping away about the woman who owned the bar (or ran it? Maybe designed it? He wasn't paying enough attention to know), he kept an eye on Barczyk.

"She's just so talented," Dalton sighed. "Think I've got a shot?"

"For sure," Evan said. Barczyk said something that made Moreau laugh so hard beer was coming out his nose. "Miss all the shots you don't take."

Barczyk was drinking his own beer, Adam's apple bobbing with each swallow. Evan's fist tightened around his glass.

"Whoa," Dalton said. "I didn't know that applied to non-hockey stuff."

"Yeah. Course." Evan licked his lips. Barczyk was using the condensation from his glass to style his hair into his signature mohawk. His hair looked a grabbable length—

"You're right!" Dalton clapped him on the back. Evan jerked in surprise, the spell broken and his attention back on Dalton. "I'm gonna go ask her out. Thanks, bro."

"You're welcome," he said, trying not to make it sound like a question. He had no idea what the heck he'd said, but he was glad to help. "Good luck."

But then he was alone at the bar. He fisted his joggers in both hands, determined not to look over at Barczyk again and definitely not to get up. Nope. Evan had self-restraint, which was easy anyway because he had nothing to say to Riley Barczyk.

Luckily, he was rescued by Vassiliev and Winchester, who begged him to eat some of the appetizers they ordered.

"It said sampler," Winchester whined. "They didn't say it would be a fucking mountain of fried food."

"It's very good," Vassiliev said. "But it's too much."

Evan dutifully took a few mozzarella sticks and made small talk about the MLB playoffs. He didn't know anything about baseball, but he found he could get away with cheering for Toronto or Pittsburgh. Just mentioning either team satisfied people. Obviously, local support was preferable, but he could claim hometown loyalty (even if Toronto wasn't technically his hometown). It also helped to be able to name specific teams to feign interest; if he admitted he hadn't been to a Blue Jays game since he was three months old, it didn't go over well.

But then someone yelled there were pool tables, and most of the guys flocked over to the back room. As Evan flagged down the bartender to order one last beer, he found Barczyk taking the empty seat next to him and leaning over the bar.

"So I know I'm a great teacher," he said, the slightest of slurs in his voice giving away that he was two beers deeper than Evan.

"But?" Evan rasped, mouth dry.

"But I can't say you've, like, graduated from the Riley Barczyk School of Hockey Fighting." He held up his hands, one still curled around a bottle of light beer. "If you think you've learned enough, I respect it and would agree you'd do a million times better in a fight thanks to me."

This time, Evan knew where he was going. When had he learned to follow Barczyk's line of thought? "But you think I could use some more lessons."

"There's still a thing or two I could show you, yeah."

As always, the smart thing to do would be to say thanks but no thanks. Barczyk had done way more than enough and shown Evan a few things he wished he could unsee (and unfeel and unthink).

But on the other hand, he wasn't throwing the random boner in Evan's face. Barczyk, despite being a total jackass on the ice, was pretty chill off it.

"Uhm." Evan fidgeted on his bar stool. The bartender dropped off his beer, and he used it as a shield. He drank two large gulps while he processed what was going on. When he set it down and wiped his lips with the back of his arm, he saw Barczyk watching the gesture. "Sorry, that was gross—"

"Abs. I spend most of my time with a bunch of grown men who act like teenagers. I'm not going to hold it against you that you don't know how to use a fucking napkin, you heathen."

Evan laughed in spite of himself. "Sorry. It won't happen again."

"You should be, and it better not." Barczyk feigned disgust, but his hazel eyes shone with amusement. "Offer stands for more lessons." He pushed away from the bar and started walking backwards. "If you think you need 'em."

"Okay." It was the safest answer, acknowledging the offer without committing to it. Without exposing how he felt about it or how strung up he'd been only a few hours ago. "Where are you going?" he asked, realizing he was disappointed to see Barczyk go.

He hooked a thumb over his shoulder. "I've gotta show these bozos how to play pool."

"You know how to play pool?"

"Oh please," Barczyk scoffed. "I grew up playing pool in my church's basement during youth group. Assuming this place keeps a nicer table than Father Matthew's did, I'm gonna clean up. If I can run a rack on a crooked table with a bent cue, the sky's the limit on a decent table." He walked backward a few more steps before giving Evan a half-wave, half-salute, then he was gone.

And Evan wasn't just lonely, but alone.

16

His libido was more active than usual. He could count how many times he usually jerked off during the season on one hand; lately that hand was too busy doing other things. It was like he was a teenager again, masturbating every morning to the echoes of dreams he'd rather not try to chase down.

He avoided thinking about anything remotely sexy during the day because he was worried his dick would betray him. The problem was, he wasn't even sure what he thought was sexy anymore. If fighting with Barczyk could set him off, then Evan didn't have a good gauge of what was fueling his sudden surge in sexual desire. Did he have a kink for sparring that he hadn't known about? Was he so touch-starved that he'd mistaken punching and tackling for sexual advances?

There were...other possibilities. Evan wasn't an idiot. There was another common factor, and if he were actually curious, a few experimental fantasies would help him know for sure.

He didn't want to know.

Plausible deniability was his excuse in the rare moments when he got too close to addressing it. As far as Evan *knew*, he wasn't attracted to men, which meant he couldn't be attracted to Barczyk. Done, case closed.

If any chinks appeared in that defense, well...

So despite being hornier than he'd been since puberty, he limited himself to drowsy masturbatory sessions and nothing else. At first he worried that it might leave him feeling on edge all day, but the early release mellowed him out for the rest of the day and got him through his increasingly frequent encounters with Barczyk.

Barczyk, who really treated Evan no differently than he had before, seemed to have adopted Evan as his best friend on the team. He sat next to Evan during travel and team meals. He invited Evan to hang out (though thankfully to very public venues that included other team members, and he was never offended if Evan declined). For better or worse, he also included Evan in his new pre-game routine.

"Abs!"

The whack to his ass took him by surprise. Granted, through his hockey pants, it was about as annoying as if a gnat had landed on him, but it still made him look over his shoulder to see what the heck had hit him. He'd assumed it was an errant puck—it wouldn't be the first time a teammate had hit him by accident during warm-ups—but instead he found Barczyk standing behind him, winding up his stick like a baseball bat.

"What are you"—Barczyk swung and hit Evan on the ass again—"doing?"

"Well, last game I did it, and it was lucky, so I thought I should do it again."

"Lucky? Didn't we lose that game?"

"Yeah, in OT. We should've lost in regulation, but luckily we squeaked by with a point. So if it helped during a game when we sucked, imagine what it could do for us if we play well."

Evan raised an eyebrow. That was absolutely stupid, and while he suspected Barczyk knew it was bullshit, his expression gave nothing away. Plenty of guys had completely insane sounding superstitions that seemed to work for them—Evan's only superstition was a shamrock keychain his grandma had gotten him when he was five; he'd won his first tournament shortly after, so he'd used it since—and he'd learned a long time ago never to question anyone's mojo. And it made sense that

Barczyk, who was more off the rails than most, would have an equally off the rails idea of how to generate luck.

Deciding playing along would be his best bet, he asked, "So if we win, does that mean you're going to do it again next game?"

"Oh, for sure. Except I'll have to up it to three times to keep it going."

"Doesn't seem like much motivation for me to win," Evan said. "The more we win, the more I get smacked."

Barczyk considered him and didn't sound like he was joking when he said, "I'm sure we can figure something out. Like maybe if it works, we can alternate who does the smacking."

Evan pushed Barczyk in the chest. "Stop," he groaned. "We're not hitting each other before games. We're not children."

"Because everyone on this team is so mature," Barczyk countered. He hooked a thumb towards their goalie, Farrell. "It's totally normal to tap the posts 31 times during warmups and after each intermission." Then he nodded to Lawson. "And it's definitely not childish to have to squirt water at everyone who scores as they come onto the bench. And I'm tots not getting tired of Big Katie making us listen to Taylor Swift before overtime. Everyone in hockey is a giant man-child, and we're no exceptions. Just gotta have fun with it while you can."

It was true. Evan was self-aware enough to recognize the bubble of adulthood he lived in where he was half independent adult, half coddled child who had the privilege to play a sport for a living. If he wanted to, he could have the team manage everything for him, from catered meal plans to chauffeurs to his living arrangements. The little ways he took care of himself were small in the scheme of things, remembering all too well how difficult adulting could be from his mom working three jobs. He'd always been embarrassed about how easy he had it now. Leave it to Barczyk to think of it as 'fun.'

"Here." Barczyk spun around and looked over his shoulder. "I'm a good sport. Go ahead, have your turn."

"My turn?" And then when Barczyk leaned forward a little, ass sticking out, Evan understood and felt his cheeks burn. He debated refusing but figured it would only prolong this debacle if he argued. The fastest way out was in, so he lifted his stick, took aim for the area with the most pads, and swung.

Barczyk shot him an unimpressed look. "Jesus, I think that was so lame you gave the other team luck. C'mon, Abs. Like you mean it."

The second time wasn't much harder, but he put more into it. As soon as he made contact, Barczyk let out a dramatic yelp and fell onto his knees, sliding across the ice and acting like he was in agony.

Evan stood there dumbfounded. When he looked around, no one else on the team was paying them any mind...but the fans pressed against the glass were watching with a keen interest Evan didn't think had ever been turned on him before. A few had their phones out and were giggling at Barczyk. When this showed up on social media later, he had no doubt he'd be in the videos. Acting like a child.

"Much better." Barczyk hopped up and skated over. "Let's get that mojo rolling in the game, yeah?"

"You know what would help?" Evan said, desperate to have a normal, hockey-focused interaction. "If we, y'know, practiced some hockey." He grabbed a nearby puck and started drifting backward with it. "Pass with me? Maybe you'll remember how to do it when we play."

Barczyk blinked at him, then barked out a laugh. "I think I can handle that, Abs. I'm good for the occasional apple every now and then."

To be fair, Evan had scored three times so far this season, and he was pretty sure Barczyk had assisted on all three. Since Barczyk had only put up two goals of his own, he had more 'apples' than Evan did. He thought of that as they passed the puck back and forth through traffic. For all his antics and trash talking, Barczyk was talented. He got every pass to Evan, even when people skated through them for their own warm-up routine, all of them beautiful tape-to-tape passes that could go in a hockey textbook.

Instead of being intimidated by the casual display of competence, Evan took it as a challenge. If Barczyk, known more for his ability to trash talk and throw punches, could make crisp passes, then Evan had no excuses.

When it came to game time, Evan felt more centered than he had in a while. All the extra garbage that had been hanging out in his head, he finally locked it away and just played. Be-more-physical what? Learn-to-fight who? Random-boners where?

On their first shift in the third period, Barczyk sent him a beautiful saucer pass for a breakaway. Evan normally freaked out on breakaways. Sure, he was fast, but he'd never had a talent for faking out goalies. Should he deke? Go for the wide open five hole? Drag the goalie to the right side of the net and then try to go backhand into the left? Panic and shoot it wide and look like an idiot?

Before he could choose between any of these options, he got barreled into from behind. Evan didn't know who'd caught up to him, but they were pushing him off course and away from the puck. He nudged the puck into the slot before he lost it altogether. Whoever was on him was dragging him down to the ice, so Evan jerked his arm loose as he tried to turn back around. Someone crashed down at his feet, but Evan ignored the defender.

The puck was sitting in the high slot where Evan had put it. Barczyk was coming in at speed, picked it up, and shot it right above the goalie's blocker.

It was a great shot, way better than whatever Evan might've done if he'd had the chance, and he skated over to congratulate Barczyk on the goal.

"Nice—"

"Fuck yeah, Abs!" Barczyk was jumping up and down, both hands clutching Evan's jersey. "That was a beaut! You did fucking great!"

"Me?" Evan looked around, trying to remember if he'd done anything reasonable in that play. "When I let that guy catch up to me?"

"Wha—? No, when you threw him to the ice like a rag doll and embarrassed the fuck out of him so I could score." Barczyk reached up to sling an arm around Evan's neck and pull him down for a noogie. "Look at you, you fucking goon. Be-u-tee-full."

Evan couldn't help but preen at the praise. His dick enjoyed it too, since it decided this was definitely the moment to remind Evan that, hey, his sudden horniness was almost certainly Barczyk-related. He'd mostly gotten himself pulled together by the time they'd finished skating down the bench and fistbumping everyone.

"Great goal, Barczyk," Coach Jack said. "Nice work on that breakaway, Abernathy. Would've liked to see you get a shot off, but you handled it perfectly. Way to use your body to make the smart play."

"Really?" Evan croaked.

"That's exactly what I wanted from you this season. That physicality. I don't need you smashing people into the boards. You just gotta stand your ground and mean it. Fantastic, kid. Keep it up." He knocked Evan on the back with his rolled-up game notes.

Evan got onto the bench and sat numbly between Barczyk and Vassiliev.

"You put the puck in the perfect spot for Barzy," Vassiliev said with a definite note of approval.

"Thanks."

Barczyk bumped his thigh into Evan's. "Fucking be-u-tee-full," he mumbled, chewing his mouthguard and watching the face-off at center ice.

Evan looked at Barczyk, hazel eyes bright and a brown curl poking out the side of his helmet, and couldn't help but agree.

17

EVAN'S DICK HAD BEHAVED ITSELF SINCE THE TRAINING MAT incident. The Riveters were halfway through a five-game homestand—a decent chunk of time where they got to stay in the greater Pittsburgh area and Evan got used to his own bed again—without any issues during practices or games. It helped that he worked himself hard at the training facility (on the ice and the treadmills; he avoided the mats) that he'd pass out before his head hit the pillow.

He was kind of in the best shape of his life.

But while his head and body were under control while he was awake, he had zero control over his dreams. And like it or not, Riley Barczyk featured prominently in all of them.

"I think," Evan mumbled to himself one morning, "I have a thing for Barczyk."

He was still in bed, panting slightly. Once again, he'd woken up hard and aching, so he'd taken himself in hand and...maybe let his dreams solidify more than usual. As he jerked himself off hard and fast, it was definitely while picturing Barczyk.

Come soaking his hand, he lay there in the uncomfortable admission.

Am I gay? he wondered as he got out of bed to clean up. Didn't seem like he was very straight. But he'd never had any sexual feelings toward a man before. He barely had any sexual feelings ever, which made it harder to sort through whatever was going through his system. Maybe...maybe Barczyk was just an exception. A really random exception, but maybe that meant it would go away as quickly as it'd appeared.

After he'd showered, Evan looked at himself in the mirror. He didn't *look* any different. He didn't *feel* any different. Shouldn't he, like, *know* if he were a different person than he thought he was?

"Because you're not different," he assured his reflection.

His reflection didn't seem to buy it.

Evan tried to shake off the lingering thoughts about Barczyk as he went about his morning routine. He'd accepted his attraction to another man, but what did that mean? It didn't have to mean anything if he didn't act on it. What he'd done this morning when he woke up, that didn't count as acting on it. If he never said anything to Barczyk, never did anything more than be friends and teammates, then this could just be a bizarre blip where Evan had gotten his wires crossed.

There was no reason to make things weird. Barczyk had been more than generous after the...incident...and Evan didn't want to disrupt things. And aside from unwanted fantasies, Evan didn't plan on doing anything about them. It was the idea of Barczyk that turned Evan on (for reasons he couldn't fathom—if he was going to be attracted to men, why the most obnoxious one he'd ever met?), not the prospect of engaging in any actual physical acts with the man himself.

Satisfied he'd figured out his situation, Evan left his condo for practice, optimistic that he could face Barczyk and the rest of the team without embarrassing himself.

———

"Abernathy."

Evan jumped and tried not to look panicked when he saw Coach Mel walking towards him. They had two rinks at the team practice facility, though they usually only used one of them. Today, half the team was scheduled for special teams practice, and the rest (aka Evan, the rookies, and everyone else deemed a liability on the Power Play) were due for work with the skating coaches. Evan was looking forward to a day of edgework, crossovers, sprints, and generally just hating his life.

The last thing he expected was to see any of the main coaching staff approach him, and certainly not Coach Mel.

"Uh," was his super smart response.

"Change of plans. You're with my group today."

Evan stared blankly at her. "What do you mean?"

"Special teams, Abernathy," she said with an astounding amount of patience. Evan appreciated it because his brain was not keeping up. "You're with me today for work on the PK unit. We've liked what we've been seeing from you lately, and we want to try you on the second Penalty Kill line. Don't get too excited," she said when Evan lit up. "This is a trial to see how you do. If you impress us today, we'll keep pulling you into practices and maybe get you some looks during a game."

"I understand. That's still—I *really*—" He took a deep breath and tried again. "Thank you for the opportunity."

"Don't blow it," she warned as she headed out towards the rink.

"I won't!" Evan called after her. This was awesome! He'd wanted more responsibility on the team, more chances to prove himself and maybe work his way into the top six. Granted, the pressure of being on the PK was terrifying, but still!

"You all right there, Abs?" Barczyk asked. He had his newly-sharpened skates in hand, otherwise dressed for practice. He sat down in his stall to put them on. "Never seen someone look so excited for skating practice. Like, *why*? I've been skating longer than I've been doing anything except, like, eating and breathing. I don't need practice."

"Everyone needs practice," Evan said. He'd never been the absolute best at anything, but his ability to practice and work on improving that had gotten him to the NHL over former teammates who had hoped natural talent would carry them all the way. Just because they'd 'arrived' didn't mean the work stopped. "And Coach Mel said I'm working with the PK unit today."

"Hell yeah, Abs!" Barczyk abandoned his half-tied skate to offer his fist. Evan dutifully bumped it, knowing Barczyk wouldn't finish lacing up until he did. "You'd be great at penalty killing. Kinda jealous you don't have to do suicides with us peasants, though."

The last time they'd ended a practice with suicides, Barczyk had dramatically flopped to the ground and wouldn't budge, as if the drill had indeed killed him. It was probably because Coach Jack hadn't been running that practice: even Barczyk had a healthy respect for their head coach, and he saved the theatrics for the skating coaches.

"You ever get PK time?" Evan suddenly felt bad, like he was abandoning Barczyk. *And Vassiliev,* he added belatedly. *You're leaving your linemates, not just one person.*

"No sirree bob." Barczyk moved on to his other skate. "It's too much fun to try to score a shorty. I haven't had a coach risk me on a PK since I was in Squirts and scored a hat trick just from shorthanded goals." He finished tying his skate and looked up at Evan with a proud smile. "In a *playoff* game."

Evan laughed. He had no idea if Barczyk's story was true, but it was easy to picture a 9- or 10-year-old Barczyk ignoring his frustrated coaches and heading down the ice not once, not twice, but three times while shorthanded. Knowing Barczyk, Evan didn't doubt he'd try for a repeat performance.

Barczyk bounced to his feet. "Knock 'em dead. Gotta represent Line Three for me and Vassy. Just don't block too many shots. It's a practice, and Lawsy's got a mean slapper."

When they parted ways, Barczyk going left out of the locker rooms and Evan right, he was surprised to realize he'd *miss* having Barczyk around during practice. What a turn his life had taken in the past month: he'd almost rather give up PK time to skate himself dizzy with Barczyk.

Almost.

———

"And where were you?" Vassiliev asked accusingly a couple of hours later. He was freshly showered and leaning forward against his knees, like he couldn't sit up under his own power if he had to. "How did you get out of skating with us?"

"I was working with special teams," Evan said with just a hint of pride as he took off his helmet. "Coach Mel had me with the PK unit."

"Penalty Kill?" Vassiliev looked impressed. "You will do a good job, I think. Easy to block shots when you are so big."

"Thanks. I think I did pretty well today," Evan said, so excited he couldn't keep it in. "My group only got scored on twice, and we went through a dozen rounds."

"Hells yeah, Abs." Barczyk strutted in from the showers, pulling a too-big shirt on over his glistening skin. Evan caught sight of a gold chain before it disappeared under yellow cotton. "Star in the making, right here," he said and sat on the other side of Vassiliev. Then he winked at Evan.

"I dunno about that—" Evan stuttered.

"You're good," Vassiliev said firmly. "Just young. This is a good chance for you to prove yourself. Take it."

"He will," Barczyk said dismissively, like he didn't doubt it for a second. Evan appreciated the vote of confidence. "I'll try to draw some penalties for you. Give you a chance to show off."

"Don't," Vassiliev said.

Barczyk sighed dramatically. "Fiiine, but I can't promise I won't take any."

"I know you can't," Vassiliev said. "You know, there's no award for most penalties."

"The boos and cheers from the crowd are the only reward I need."

"Pretty shitty reward. I want to play! The more penalties you get, the less our line is out."

As Vassiliev and Barczyk continued to rag on each other, Evan sat back and enjoyed it. He realized he was smiling fondly. He wiped the smile off his face and scowled. He didn't want it to look like he was encouraging Barczyk's recklessness. Or that he liked Barczyk. Or that he was finding Barczyk's enthusiasm infectious.

Vassiliev disappeared a few minutes later, his shoulders hunched and feet dragging as he left the locker room. Evan expected Barczyk to leave with him, but he lingered while Evan finished changing out of his gear.

"I know you're probably not as exhausted as us peons who skated until our feet were bleeding," Barczyk said. Evan made the mistake of looking down and saw Barczyk's bare toes in a pair of flip-flops. He wasn't sure why the image made him gulp. "But if you're looking for more fighting practice, we should figure it out before this homestand ends and we've gotta fly out to Cali."

"Oh. Yeah." He scratched at the back of his neck. "Look, I don't know—"

"I got time next week. We can do it after practice any day." Barczyk pushed up and stretched, the bottom of his shirt pulling up to reveal a few inches of skin. It seemed more scandalous than if he had had no shirt at all. "Just lemme know when you're up for it."

Then he walked away twirling his keys on his finger and whistling *Barbie Girl*. Not once did he look back at Evan, like he didn't care what Evan's answer was.

Or like he knew Evan would give in.

"I won't," he told himself as he grabbed his stuff and headed for the showers. "I don't need Barczyk's help."

Maybe if he said it enough, he'd convince himself.

18

THERE WERE TWO GAMES LEFT BEFORE THEY TRAVELED OUT west, and looking ahead at the Riveters' schedule, they wouldn't be spending much time in Pittsburgh until late December. So if Evan could just avoid Barczyk for the next week, maybe this fighting thing would blow over. As long as it didn't come up in a game (aka he didn't get his ass kicked), he could argue he didn't need any more lessons.

It was a bit of a shame, though. Everything he'd worked on with Barczyk was useful. Evan might never fight in a game again, but if he did, he had some strategies he could use to hold his own. And it was kind of fun. The practice, not real fights. Those were stressful. Tragically, Evan didn't hate spending time with Barczyk. He maybe kind of enjoyed it.

That was the problem. He enjoyed it too much.

They were playing the Nevada Scorpions in a Sunday matinee game. Evan loved home matinees. Late games meant late nights, especially with media coverage or travel to hotels. He'd be in his own bed by 9 p.m., with Netflix on and takeout in hand, fully rested for their morning skate the next day.

"Nevada plays an aggressive game," Coach Jack said in the locker room. "Be ready to get pushed. Don't let them goad you into playing anything other than our game."

"He means you, Barzy," someone called, and everyone laughed.

Coach Jack looked unamused. "We are drawing penalties tonight," he said, enunciating each word, "not taking them." He never looked Barczyk's way, but they all knew the warning was only for one person in the room. "Get this win at home. They're gonna be a lot harder to get once we start traveling. I want higher than a wild-card seed this year, boys. Get it done."

"Yes, sir," they said in unison.

"You going to listen to him?" Vassiliev muttered under his breath once Coach Jack had left.

"I'm never trying to go to the box," Barczyk said indignantly. "The refs got it out for me, I swear."

"Might be your reputation," Evan said. "Preceding you and all that."

"What are you implying, Abs?" he asked with a twinkle in his eyes.

Evan bit his lip so he wouldn't be tempted to smile.

———

During warm-ups, Evan dutifully went to his spot by the player benches. There was no getting out of his new pre-game routine with Barczyk. He'd found it best to get it over with, so he patiently stick-handled while he waited for the inevitable—

WHACK!

Evan sighed and pushed his puck towards center ice. "How many are we at?" he asked. "Five hits? And isn't it my turn to whack you?"

"Is it?" Barczyk skated around and stopped in front of him. "Better make it six. Need a little extra luck if I'm gonna stay outta the box."

"It is your turn," Evan said. He might not be much into this ritual, but it was hard to forget getting his ass whacked the game before. "If there's actually any good luck in this, haven't you ruined it?"

"Nah, it's thought and positive intentions. How 'bout we split it? I do two more, then you can smack me three times. Make 'em count, though. None of those wimpy ones you did last time."

Evan rolled his eyes. He stood there stoically while Barczyk got back in position and hit him twice in quick succession. When Evan swiveled around for his turn, Barczyk was already facing away with his stick slung across the back of his shoulders, bobbing back and forth with the music blaring in the arena.

What a goof, Evan thought as he swung his stick around for the first blow. Barczyk stood there, barely moving until Evan finished his third swing, then he promptly fell to his knees and doubled over like he'd been beaten instead of lightly tapped.

"You done?" Evan said. At least Barczyk couldn't see him laughing.

Barczyk jumped to his feet. "Yep. Let's work that good mojo." He bumped his shoulder against Evan as he skated off, twirling his mouthguard at the corner of his mouth.

The Scorpions came out strong, just like Coach Jack had warned them. Most of their defense was structured around bodying people off of the puck and physically clearing out the slot. Evan was kind of jealous, if only because he was consciously doing as much as he could to be more physical on the ice, and these guys did it as easily as breathing.

As easily as Barczyk did it. Where Evan and Vassiliev would endure the blows and keep playing, Barczyk would shoulder or push back. Once he knew they were gunning for him, Barczyk braced for every hit and laid his own, which only made them come back harder for him. Since a lot of it was behind the play and away from the puck, the refs were letting it go, so it seemed to get worse and worse as the game went on.

One Scorpion knocked Barczyk's stick from his hand, so Barczyk body checked him over the boards onto his own bench.

Another defenseman tied Barczyk up on the boards so he couldn't get to a loose puck, so he grabbed him by the back of his jersey and yanked him back so hard he fell.

When Barczyk was working low in the crease, the goalie knocked him over from behind but managed to lose his stick in the process. Barczyk accidentally-on-purpose stepped on the stick repeatedly with his skate before kicking it into the back of the net. He'd only walked away from that one because Evan and Vassiliev stepped in at the whistle to escort him to the bench.

"You're toeing that line," Evan said at the end of the second period.

They were tied 1-1, and somehow neither team had gotten a penalty. Yet. "Maybe you should, like, chill?"

"Can't now," Barczyk said, gaze fixed on the play. "That'd be putting more of a target on my back."

"He's right," Vassiliev said. "He's annoyed them too much. They won't leave him alone even if he stops."

They were right. Evan watched Barczyk take and dish out more abuse the next shift, and when they went into the locker room, Evan swore he spotted a half a dozen new bruises on Barczyk. It wasn't any better in the third, because Travis Walker made a beeline for Barczyk as soon as their line took the ice. Walker had been with the Riveters for the past four seasons before moving to Nevada during free agency. Evan had been sad to see him go—he was a solid defenseman and would occasionally join him and Dalton for mini-golf—but Evan hadn't thought much about playing against him. It was in fact the first time in Evan's career that he and Walker were on opposite sides of the ice, which was surreal every time he caught sight of Walker.

For better or worse, he'd been ignoring Evan and Vassiliev all game. Walker must've been given Barczyk duty, because he'd been the main instigator and recipient of Barczyk's on-ice attention. It was only a matter of time until their shenanigans were too much for the refs to ignore.

After all the things they let go, it was a weak slashing call that finally got the refs to blow their whistles. Evan was shoved below the goal line and went down. From the ice, he had a great view of Barczyk swatting at Walker from behind. A whistle rang out, and Evan did a double take when he got the puck because there was no way *that* had been the first penalty of the game. The ref pointed at Barczyk and, for the first time, Evan agreed he was getting an unfair call.

"Are you fucking kidding me?" Barczyk screamed as he took his mouthguard out, presumably to make his complaining clearer. "That's fucking embellishment! I barely even touched him!"

"Get in the box, Barczyk," the ref said.

"It's not embellishment! You fucking tripped me, dickhead!" Walker shouted back. He'd been on his knees on the ice, and, despite knowing Walker, Evan was inclined to agree that he was milking it.

"Shows how fucking much you know. They're not even trying to call me for a trip, dumbass," Barczyk shot back. "Right, ref?"

The ref made a face, looking between the two players. "No," he admitted.

"Because he fucking embellished it, and since I barely touched him, he doesn't even know what he's trying to embellish! Never mind how he was roughing up Abs behind the net—"

"I used to be on this fucking team!" Walker yelled, his face red in embarrassed anger. "You've been on the Riveters for two fucking minutes. Who are you kidding, pretending you're sticking up for Abs? I played with him for two and a half years—"

"You're not on the team right now, and you fucking crosschecked him. Don't pretend—"

"Enough!" yelled the ref. "Barczyk, get in the box. Two for slashing. Walker, get out of here before you get two for unsportsmanlike."

"What!?" Walker looked appalled. "I didn't do shi—"

The ref started raising his whistle to his lips, so Walker held up his hands and skated away.

"Smartest thing you've done all night," Barczyk called after him. "Skate away like a little—"

And that's when Walker came back and punched Barczyk square in the face.

———

"Did you see Barzy draw that penalty? Fucking textbook." Dalton fistbumped Barczyk on his way to his stall. They'd won 2-1 against a very disgruntled Nevada bench. Their line had mostly gotten benched after the Walker incident, only going out when Coach Jack was sure he could control the matchups enough to guarantee Walker wouldn't be on the ice with them. In the end, they'd won with a late power play goal from Moreau after a delay of game miscue from the Scorpions' goalie.

Still, the most memorable thing about the game was Barczyk getting Walker to sucker punch him.

Barczyk winked and shot him a finger gun. "All in a night's work." His chest was bare except for his shoulder pads. Despite the bravado, he seemed tired. "Luckily your boy punches like a middle schooler, or I might have more than a black eye."

"He's not our boy," Evan said. He liked Walker well enough, but he hadn't much liked that he'd been competing with Barczyk for cheapest hockey play. He liked it less that Walker had won.

Barczyk turned the full weight of his hazel eyes onto Evan. "Am I your boy?" he asked, unblinking as he watched Evan.

Evan's mouth went dry, which was the only thing that saved him from answering because he didn't trust what he might say right now.

"Of course!" Vassiliev wrapped an arm around him to envelop Barczyk in a side-hug. "Walker is such a shit."

"He's not that bad." Evan swallowed; Barczyk was still watching him. "He wasn't that bad when he played for us," he amended.

"Yeah?" Barczyk teased. "Bet my old teams say that about me too."

Evan couldn't help it; he looked away.

"Walker always was a punk," Vassiliev said, unaware of the tension between his linemates. "But he was cleaner with us. The Scorpions dropped the first seven games of the season. They're playing desperate, and it shows in players like Walker."

Talk shifted as the coaches came in to debrief them after the game, and Evan, for once, relished the breakdown. It gave him somewhere to look other than two stalls to his left.

———

Walker
Yinz wanna go grab drinks later? We're in town until tomorrow afternoon
Miss hanging out with you guys

Ten minutes passed.

Walker
???

Five minutes passed.

Walker

Wtf this isn't about that thing with barczyk
is it?

That guy's a dick I can't believe you're stuck
with him this season

Vassiliev

Well you did crosscheck abs

Kates

It was a little much the way you went down
I don't know if barzy even touched you

Lawson

The punch was also uncalled for

Walker

You fucking kidding me right now?
Abs, tell them this is bullshit
I didn't crosscheck you, that was a clean hit
It's hockey it happens

Vassiliev

No you leave the kid alone
We saw it from the bench it was 100% a
crosscheck.

Walker

It was not!!

Dalton

[a gif of the crosscheck]

Walker

Ok fine sorry abs that was a bit much I
should've laid off you a bit there

Doyle

[a gif of the slashing call against Barczyk,
complete with Walker flopping to the ice
immediately after contact]

Walker has left the chat.

Abernathy

Guys was that necessary?

Doyle

He brought it up

———

Walker

Hey Evan I'm sorry about that hit. The guys
were right that was too much

Abernathy

Don't worry about it. It's hockey.

Walker

I knew you'd understand bro

So is the team really all buddy buddy with
barczyk now??

Abernathy

He's not so bad

Walker

Yeah right

Oh shit you're being serious

For real?? You're okay with that dickhead?? I
remember what he did to you last season

Abernathy

Don't worry about it. It's hockey

Like you said

Walker

Wtf Evan what i did and what he did are NOT
the same

You got right back up iirc

That is NOT what happened when he hit you

Abernathy

Not sure what you want me to say

We're teammates. However much I like or
dislike him I still gotta play with him

Walker

You just like him because he does the dirty
work for you

You never have to get your hands dirty
making the big hits the rest of us do

Abernathy

So you're complaining because he does the
same stuff you do

Walker

That's not what I said

Abernathy

Look I'm not trying to argue

Thanks for the apology. I didn't think anything
of the crosscheck or whatever

No hard feelings promise

Walker

Good

Hit me up when you're in Nevada if you
wanna hang out

19

Evan wasn't in bed by 9 p.m. as planned. Instead, he'd been pacing in his living room as he mulled over Walker, Barczyk, and the game. He felt bad for defending Walker in the locker room when he was essentially doing the same shit Evan didn't like about Barczyk's game. He kept replaying what he'd said in the locker room over and over, wondering if Barczyk saw the double standard. The only difference between the two was that Barczyk had hurt Evan with his antics, but tonight Walker could have just as easily. Watching the re-plays, Evan was grateful he hadn't hit the boards on his way down.

Though he supposed Walker had apologized, something Barczyk never had. That counted for something.

Except he'd also called Evan out for being a wimp. It'd been like a slap to the face. Walker had never said anything about it to Evan during the literal years they'd played together. Had he thought it was a problem the whole time and that the rest of them were picking up his slack? Did others think that but weren't going to say anything?

Fuck.

Abernathy

Hey you have time for another fighting lesson before we travel?

Barczyk

OFC

We could do Tuesday after practice

Just don't punch my face it's sore lol

Don't want to go into Wednesday's game with
a shiner

Abernathy

Tuesday's good. Thanks. I won't punch your
face.

Team gym?

Barczyk

👍

———

Evan squared his feet and swung his right fist. Barczyk deflected it so that Evan's hand only grazed his chest.

"Your punches are looking better," Barczyk said. "You might be ready for the big leagues soon."

"Thanks." Evan tried to sneak another one in while Barczyk was distracted, but he missed and Barczyk jabbed him in the ribs. "Maybe not," he grumbled. When they'd started this whole lessons thing, Evan had seen every near hit as a sign of improvement; now he saw them as misses and hated it.

"You'll never be a prizefighter, but you won't look tragic." That stupid grin with the missing tooth. Evan's heart fluttered; he got distracted and Barczyk punched him in the gut. "Ha!"

Evan's cheeks flushed. They'd been going at it for an hour, and he'd managed not to get hit full on until now. And it wasn't like he had anyone to blame for it but himself and his stupid weakness for Barczyk's stupid face.

"It's all right, Abs," Barczyk said. "There's no shame in losing to the best—*oof!*"

Evan tackled Barczyk to the ground. He enjoyed Barczyk's undignified squawks as Evan punched him with the padded gloves. It was one of those rare moments when he'd turned the tables on Barczyk, and Evan was smiling as he pressed his advantage. He should've never underestimated Barczyk, though: soon it wasn't boxing gloves pushing back against him, but bare fingers tickling his stomach and along his sides.

"Fuck!" Evan jerked away, which only gave more room for Barczyk to attack. Evan squirmed and tried to roll away, but Barczyk followed. "Not"—he heaved a strangled breath between laughs—"fair!"

"Says the guy who tackled me," Barczyk said, mercilessly working his way up to Evan's armpits. Evan desperately worked the boxing gloves off so he could defend himself. He got one off and flung it aside, using his free hand to remove the other glove. Finally, he could retaliate: he grabbed Barczyk's wrists one by one, took a deep breath without giggling, and flung his weight so that he could roll on top of Barczyk and trap him.

And suddenly, Evan's brain caught up with where his body was, and it sucked the air out of him.

It was like the last time but in reverse, with Evan firmly pinning Barczyk down. A low thrum of arousal had been buzzing under his skin since they'd stepped into the gym; he was hard within seconds.

"I—" Evan started, determined to end this and try to salvage his dignity. How could he have gotten himself into this mess *again*? But before he could voice any sort of excuse or apology, two strong legs wrapped around his waist and shifted him so his cock was pressed against Barczyk's rapidly hardening one. Evan shuddered and closed his eyes just so he could take it in.

"You can move," Barczyk said, his voice low and husky and delicious. He rolled his hips to demonstrate the point. They both groaned in unison, and Barczyk whined, "Please move, fuck."

So Evan did. He thrust down against Barczyk, sending a bolt of pleasure through him that he heard Barczyk echo in his ear.

"More," Barczyk said, and Evan was helpless to do anything else. He thrust down again and again, finding a rhythm. His bare feet kept slipping on the mat, but Barczyk's legs tightened around him to keep him in place. "Fuck, Abs. Keep going."

"Do you ever shut up?" Evan bit out as he ground down. He buried his face in the crook of Barczyk's neck, smelling his musky scent and tasting the salty tang of his skin. Shifting his weight so his left hand was free, Evan wound it through Barczyk's hair. He felt a curl wrap around his finger and shuddered.

"No," Barczyk said, though Evan couldn't remember what he was answering. "Shut me up, why don't you?" And then he pulled Evan's head so they were nose to nose. Evan had a split second to realize what was happening before Barczyk mashed their lips together, no hint of finesse in the kiss, just raw need. Startled, it took Evan a moment to kiss back, but when he did, he answered Barczyk's need with his own.

There were too many sensations, so many that Evan could no longer pull apart each individual piece. The rough slide of their dicks together. Barczyk breathed heavily beneath him. His hand still twisted in damp curls. Their lips and tongues pressed together. Barczyk's legs wrapped around him like Evan was the one trapped.

Evan broke the kiss as he reached the edge, a gasp twisting out of him as his vision whited out. His skin tingled in the aftermath, his cock still pulsing even though he was already spent. As out of it as he was, he heard Barczyk groan and arch against him as he came. Evan rolled off of Barczyk before collapsing in a boneless heap next to him.

"Fuck," Barczyk hissed.

Evan grunted in agreement.

"That was fun, Abs." Barczyk's voice wavered, but it was steady when he spoke again. "Could you let go of my hair, though?"

Evan's hand jerked, and he realized he'd been clutching a fistful of Barczyk's curls. He let go and pulled his hand away, surprised and a little pleased at the indent his hand had left in his hair. Then embarrassment flooded him when he realized how out of it he'd been.

"Sorry," he said.

Barczyk shrugged as he sat up. "No biggy." He ran his hands through his hair, sending a few drops of sweat flying. When he was done, there was no sign Evan's hand had been there at all. He leaned over Evan, and Evan's heart raced as he anticipated a kiss. He didn't think he could handle one now that the lust had ebbed and panic was threatening to settle in. But instead, Barczyk only patted Evan's cheek before pushing off the ground, and Evan found he was disappointed.

"Ugh, I ruined these shorts," Barczyk said more to himself than Evan but looked over his shoulder and winked. "Worth it."

Evan lay there, trying so hard to even out his breathing so he wouldn't have to deal with the aftermath of what had happened. "Yeah," he agreed, because he felt like he should say something but wasn't willing to commit to anything more serious than that.

A towel landed on his face. Evan jolted upright, clutching the towel tightly as he watched Barczyk walk out of the gym.

"I'll shower first," he called. "Maybe wait a couple of minutes before you make an appearance." And then Barczyk was gone, and Evan was alone in the gym, once more wondering how the heck things had gotten so out of hand...and if he minded.

Riley

RILEY WAS THE FIRST TO ADMIT IT: HE DID NOT HAVE healthy coping mechanisms. When he was younger, he'd been able to use hockey as an escape, but then he'd gotten too good. Hockey didn't require much of his brainpower anymore. He could be in the middle of a game, and he'd be thinking about what he was doing for dinner or when to return his sisters' calls or how the heck he'd fake it to his grandma that he'd gone to church despite having a game on Sunday afternoon.

Weightlifting and running weren't much better. He was a professional athlete, so those seemed too work-related to be relaxing. Plus, he had to go really hard for it to do anything. Too much opportunity for his mind to wander.

When he had something big, something that was doing a number on him, he needed his brain to shut off. Riley wasn't just good at getting under other people's skins; he was great at doing it to himself too.

You messed around with a teammate.

A teammate you have a crush on.

You thought you were safe because he was straight.

Guess you were wrong, huh? Dumbass. Now you're in trouble.

"Oh my God," he yelled at himself, startling poor Sophia. "Shut up and leave me alone!"

Sophia looked offended, so he stooped to pick her up. She mewed but allowed the indignity once he started petting her.

"Sorry, sweetheart. Not you. I'm the problem here, per usual."

So working out was no bueno, sex would only provide temporary relief until it made things messier, which left...

"Heyyy, bestie," Riley said when Dalton picked up the phone. "You wanna go out for drinks?"

"On Halloween?" Dalton sounded suspicious. "Why?"

"Because we're too old to go trick-or-treating. I dunno, man, why not?" Sensing he needed to pull out the big guns, he said, "I hear there's a place that does spiked milkshakes."

There was a brief pause. "Come pick me up in thirty?"

The burger place was a few minutes away from Riley's apartment building, nestled in the back of a shopping center. He'd found it by accident when he was getting groceries and had been keeping it in his back pocket for a hangout with Abernathy, but he might need to wait on that a bit.

You're not supposed to be thinking about him.

Oh yeah. Whoops.

Dalton was nice. Riley liked him because he was young and energetic and didn't spend his time talking about kids and partners and lawn care like the other guys Riley's age. They could just goof off together, laughing about teammates, talking shit about other teams, and complaining about the coaches.

"They're not so bad though," Dalton said through hiccups. He'd chugged two milkshakes that seemed more booze than milk, and he'd convinced Riley to do a few shots earlier. Dalton was leaning precariously on his bar stool; Riley was prepared to catch him if need be. "They've been great, giving me a chance. Giving Abs one too, even though we're young. I hope they re-sign me at the end of the season like they did with Abs."

"I'm sure they will." Riley wasn't drunk, per se, but he was pleasantly buzzed and looser-lipped than usual, which was saying a lot since he wasn't great about shutting up in general. "Hey, what's Abs' story?"

"Whadduya mean?" Dalton frowned. It made him look young.

Riley shrugged. He wasn't stupid enough to ask what he really wanted to know—was Evan Abernathy less straight than he appeared and would he maybe be interested in a guy like Riley?—because that was a bit much to unload on a third party. Especially since he had dried come in his shorts at home that suggested the answer to both was a resounding yes. So he figured if he was vague, maybe Dalton would offer something.

"He's been freaking out a bit this season, I think," Dalton said after some thought. Riley tensed, worried he was the cause, but then Dalton said, "He's too nice, and he's feeling pressured to play rougher."

Riley nodded. "Yeah, I got that impression. He always been so nice?"

"He's Canadian," Dalton said with a dismissive wave and an over-the-top eye roll. "I could spit on him, and he'd apologize."

"Don't spit on him," Riley said, his fists clenching at his side.

"Duh," Dalton said. "Being mean to Abs would be like being mean to a puppy. A really big puppy. Like a Saint Bernard or something. He's my bro. We were roomies last season. Kinda miss him. He's way easier to room with than"—Dalton cringed—"Winnie. That fucker snores so damned loud and leaves his clothes all over the place—"

"But Abs is doing okay?" Riley interrupted, because he couldn't give a flying fuck about Jacob Winchester right now. Respectfully.

Dalton quirked his head, and Riley held his breath. Fuck, had he pushed too much? Was it suspicious that he kept asking about Ev—Abernathy? But Dalton took a sip of his milkshake and then said, "Yeah, I think so. He's only asked to go mini-golfing once, so he must be okay. I was a little worried when he invited me a few weeks ago. I'm glad you could go with him. My stupid truck." He said that last part with disgust, though Riley had noted he'd gotten the old junker repaired, so he couldn't be that upset with it.

"What's with the mini-golf?"

"That's code for Abs is having a hockey crisis and needs to relax."

"I thought he just liked it." Riley reconsidered their outing to the mini-golf place downtown. Abernathy had seemed into it, but he had the same intensity with hockey, so Riley hadn't thought much of it.

Note to self: take Abernathy mini-golfing. Help him relax the fuck out.

"Oh, he does, but it's his yoga or meditation or whatever. He hasn't asked to go again, so I think he's leveled off. He usually goes through phases throughout the season. Stressed at the beginning, mellows off midway through, goes through it again close to playoffs." He raised his empty milkshake glass to the bartender, a dopey grin on his face, so Riley reached out and put a hand over his mouth.

"He'll have a regular chocolate milkshake. No booze," Riley said. He did a quick self-check and found his buzz was fading too fast. "I'll have a rum and coke, please." Then he took his hand off Dalton's mouth and asked, "What does he do if he's having a non-hockey crisis?"

Dalton worked his jaw and stared blankly at Riley. "Whadduya mean?"

"You said Abs does mini-golf when he's having a hockey crisis. What does he do if something else is stressing him out?"

The blank stare remained. "Abs doesn't stress out about stuff that isn't hockey."

Riley suppressed the urge to shake Dalton. Why was he making this so difficult? "What if he's having girl trouble? Or—" Dalton burst out laughing. "What?"

"Sorry, I shouldn't." He bit his lip in an effort to stop his laughter. Once he had it under control, Dalton said, "Abs doesn't have girl trouble."

"Because he's good at picking up chicks?" Riley asked and hated himself a little for how much he dreaded the answer. Abernathy was nice and polite and handsome and in great shape. Of course, it'd be easy for him to get dates in any city, any time.

Dalton shook his head. "I've never seen Abs with a woman. Or a dude. Or anyone that wasn't a hockey player or working for hockey players, y'know? Like, I was his roommate, and it never happened. I think he's like ace or something."

"Ace?" Riley had felt Abernathy's hard dick pressed against him, had heard him moaning and felt him come. If he were asexual, it was more nuanced than Dalton was suggesting. Though that might explain a few things, like his embarrassment and surprise at what had happened in the gym.

"Why are you making that face?" Dalton asked, squinting as if he were mirroring Riley's expression. "You're not gonna make this a thing, are you?"

Riley relaxed his face. "Nah, I would never. Sorry, I was just surprised, is all."

"Oh. Yeah, I get that." Dalton looked about to say more, but he hiccuped. "I can't believe I missed the mini-golf milkshakes."

"They were pretty good." The bartender dropped off their drinks, and Riley slipped them his credit card. "But hey, this chocolate milkshake looks pretty fucking fantastic. Cheers."

For the rest of their evening together, Riley did his drunken best to forget about Abernathy. If he jerked off thinking about the gym later when he was alone in his apartment, well, no one would ever know but him.

20

EVAN STRETCHED AND GROANED AS SOME OF THE TENSION left his shoulders. His body was tense from all the things he'd kept bottled up, as though it took him physical effort to hold the words back.

"You okay, sweetheart?" his mom asked. The phone rattled with the sound of her chopping vegetables, but it did nothing to mask her concern. "You sound distracted."

Evan tried to pull himself from his thoughts, but it wasn't easy. How exactly did one rescue themselves from a sexual identity crisis where you'd not only kissed a guy for the first time but also gotten off with one? It was all that Evan had thought about for the last sixteen hours. It was what had driven him to call his mom in the first place, hoping that the news of Penalty Kill practice would take his mind off of it.

It hadn't.

All he could think about were the things he was avoiding saying, half-heartedly filling that void with what he could and hoping his mom wouldn't notice his mind was elsewhere. Because instead of being in his condo while he caught his mom up on the early part of the season, he was back at the rink gym.

Thankfully, they didn't have practice today—a break that coincided not only with Halloween but with Evan's need to escape Barczyk. But the clock was ticking on his time to figure his shit out before facing Barczyk again.

Did figuring it out mean I pretend it didn't happen, he wondered, *or acknowledging that it did?*

If we acknowledge it, does that mean it might happen again?

...do I want it to?

The answers lurked just below the surface. He was pretty sure he knew what they were, but he didn't want to think about the implications.

Compartmentalize. Focus on hockey. Don't cause problems for yourself.

He could do this.

"You know how it is," he said vaguely. "New season, same problems." And a few new, very unexpected ones.

"Make sure you eat enough," she said. "I don't care what your dietitians or whatever say. You need a comfort meal every now and then. Cheat days are important! You've gotta take care of yourself, or you won't play at your best."

Taking care of himself used to mean sleeping and eating right, with the occasional mini-golf outing to refocus. It seemed there was another piece.

"I know, I know," he said, then redirected her worry towards her upcoming ski trip. Luckily, there was no way thoughts of Riley Barczyk could derail that conversation.

––––

Two days hadn't helped Evan get his head on straight (har har), but with practice and then a game before traveling out west for a week, he didn't have much choice: he had to show up at the rink and hope for the best.

A lot of the team participated in No-Shave November to raise awareness for men's health, and Evan was no exception. He took his razor out of his travel bag and prepared to look about ten years older within the next few days. He might be one of the youngest on the team, but Evan had no trouble growing a beard.

He'd noticed a lot more stubble going into the end of October. Barczyk, for example, hadn't looked like he'd shaved in a few days (though Evan hadn't noticed until that stubble was rubbing against his bare skin...) and he knew Lawson liked to grow out a proper long beard so he'd gotten a head start. By the time they showed up to practice on November 1st, it was already apparent which of their teammates did have trouble.

"Dalty, your face is a crime against humanity," Turner teased as Dalton came into the locker room. His beard was...well, patchy was a generous description.

Dalton went crimson. "Shut up," he mumbled. "It just takes a couple of weeks to come in."

"Fuck, seeing that almost makes me hope we don't make the play-offs," Moreau chirped. "Hate to see that eyesore all post-season."

"You think he's bad," Antonov said with a conspiratorial grin. "You should see Barzy."

Evan couldn't help it; he perked up. Barczyk looked bad with a beard? That would be kinda great, actually. If he could see an unattractive version of Barczyk, it might solve some of his problems.

The truth was much worse. When Barczyk walked into the locker room moments later, he wasn't sporting a pathetic or shaggy beard. He had a mustache. And not a normal mustache. It was curled up slightly at the ends, like some old-timey cartoon villain. It wasn't much now, but if he kept this up the whole month, it would be ridiculous.

"Oh my God." Lawson cackled. "You look like such a douchebag, Barzy!"

"You look like you're about to rob a train," Doyle agreed.

"You ain't getting laid this month with a mug like that," Kates said, almost like he was trying to warn Barczyk.

"Wrong, wrong," he pointed to Lawson, then Doyle, and then Kates, "and double wrong. I look fantastic, and you know it. Everyone digs a man who can pull off a mustache."

Evan was inclined to disagree—he'd never gotten the appeal and would rather never grow a beard again than have a moustache—but Barczyk did not look as awful as Evan had hoped. It was like his missing tooth or his mohawk or the gold chain: they were just so Barczyk that you knew what you were getting before he said anything. It would've grated on Evan's nerves back in the summer; now he thought it was endearing.

He gulped. He really was in trouble, wasn't he?

"Keep dreaming, Barzy," Lawson drawled. Then he nudged Doyle and stage-whispered, "At least he looks better than Dalty."

The secondhand embarrassment was getting to Evan. Poor Dalton, who didn't have the confidence or swagger Barczyk did to pull off a bad beard (because while Barczyk looked ridiculous, the mustache suited him, and Evan was 95% sure it was because he'd convinced himself he looked good). Not that Evan knew what to say or do to make up for the teasing—

"Don't listen to them, Dalty," Barczyk said. "You look awesome, and you're hot enough you make it work. Not like this dipshit"—he jerked a thumb at Doyle—"who's got a full beard and still can't find a date."

Doyle looked affronted as the whole locker room burst into laughter at his expense. His dating history corroborated Barczyk's jab—he was one of those guys who was married to the game—so he couldn't do more than weakly protest, "What the fuck?"

Dalton looked relieved to have the attention drawn away from his beard. Evan watched Barczyk carefully. At the start of the season, he would've assumed Barczyk had done it because he was such an attention hog. It came second nature to steal the spotlight away from others, whether they appreciated it or not; Dalton being relieved would've been a happy coincidence.

Except...except there had been a glint in Barczyk's eyes. The same one that showed he was about to drop his gloves or get in someone's face, that was how he'd looked defending Dalton. That warning that you were about to mess with the wrong person, and he'd make you pay for it.

Barczyk caught Evan staring, and before Evan could look away, he smiled and twirled the end of his moustache. "Whatcha think, Abs? Hot or not?"

Evan choked on air, his face burning all the way down to his neck.

"Doyle's right," he said, his throat tight, but luckily his voice sounded normal. "You look like Boris from Rocky and Bullwinkle."

"What is a Bullwinkle?" Vassiliev asked at the same time that Lawson and Doyle burst out laughing.

"He does!" Doyle said. "Spot on, Abs."

Instead of being as flustered or off-kilter as Evan felt, Barczyk scoffed. "C'mon, Abs. I'm clearly more of a Natasha."

That only made the locker room louder until some of the coaches poked their heads in. The ruckus died down after that, leaving them all pretending to mind their own business as they got dressed for practice.

A few minutes later, most of the team had filed out of the locker room to warm up. Evan was one of the stragglers—flexing his feet in his skates before lacing up—when a shadow stood in front of him. He knew exactly who it was from the messy tape job around the socks, and it wasn't easy to ignore Barczyk watching him.

"You did me dirty with that one," Barczyk said, voice low; goosebumps prickled along Evan's arms. "I ain't no Pottsylvania baddie."

Evan looked up with an eyebrow raised. "Pottsylvania?"

"Yeah, that's where Boris and Natasha are from, duh. The beautiful land of Pottsylvania."

He stood up so that he could find his equilibrium; it was easier when he was the one looking down at Barczyk. "I never watched the show," he admitted. "But sorry. I didn't—" He wasn't sure what he was apologizing for, since Barczyk wasn't upset. "You knew you'd get shit when you grew that mustache," he said instead. "You can't be upset that people are making fun of you for it."

"You don't like how I look, Abs?" There was heat beneath the teasing, and Evan felt like his skin was going to catch on fire.

"No!" he blurted out. It was his gut reaction, but it sounded too desperate to be the truth. Evan looked around to make sure no one was within earshot before he whispered. "I mean, maybe."

It was barely a confession, given what had happened the other day, but Barczyk lit up. "Mmm, best maybe I've ever heard. Race you to the rink?" And then he was off before Evan could process what had happened.

Were they...flirting...?

Again, his instinct was to deny it. They weren't flirting because they weren't attracted to each other. Obviously.

But they maybe were flirting, because they had gotten each other off only two days ago. They'd *kissed*. Plausible deniability was looking less and less, well, plausible.

He followed Barczyk out to practice, his mind buzzing. He overanalyzed every interaction they had, everything from when they made eye contact to how they worked together during drills. There weren't many opportunities to talk, but even after practice in the locker room, Evan still went through everything Barczyk said or did with a fine-toothed comb.

His conclusion? Nothing. If there was anyone else within fifteen feet of them, Barczyk was the same as ever. He was loud and annoying and said dumb shit, but none of it was remotely sexual. He was no different from when he first joined the team. Evan appreciated that Barczyk could keep his mouth shut about what had happened and not make things weird, but it also unnerved him. How was it so easy for him to pretend it hadn't happened? Was there something wrong with Evan for not being able to get the taste of Barczyk out of his mouth?

Had he hallucinated the whole thing?

He was half-convinced he'd imagined it. It could've been a vivid dream, for the way Barczyk was acting. It wasn't until Barczyk was about to head out to his car for the day that Evan's sanity got a little validation.

"Hey." Barczyk licked his lips once he had Evan's attention. "I know we said we wouldn't have time to do any lessons on the road, but..." He gave Evan a once-over, lingering on his mouth before meeting his gaze again. "I'm sure we could find time."

Yeah, Evan wasn't imagining things. Shit, this was real.

And like every opportunity to shut this down before he got in too deep, Evan ignored the voice of reason in his head and said, "Yeah. Yeah, I think we should."

21

EVAN SHIFTED UNCOMFORTABLY IN HIS SUIT. HE'D BEEN ONE of the first to arrive at the airport for their flight to California, and he'd snagged a seat near the back of the plane. There was definitely a hint that something might happen with Barczyk over the next week, and the prospect was both exciting and terrifying. All night, he'd waited for panic to set in and convince him he should text Barczyk a definitive never mind.

There'd been no panic.

Not to say that Evan was confident this was a good idea. It was a terrible idea for any number of reasons. He'd started making a list of those reasons on a Post-it note, hoping to scare himself into realizing this was kind of a Big Deal. There was a huge difference between spontaneously dry-humping a teammate and another to plan it out ahead of time. But he'd gone through four Post-its' worth before he'd crumpled them all up and tossed them out.

It was a bad idea that could totally blow up in his face...but Evan didn't care. He wanted to feel Barczyk beneath him again and explore his mouth and touch him and—

Aaaand now Evan was getting hard on the team plane. Dammit.

He took off his suit jacket and laid it across his lap until he could get himself under control. When had he become like this? Why did it have to be Barczyk of all people?

Because he's good at getting under people's skin. Are you really surprised he got under yours?

Evan closed his eyes and shuddered.

"Hell yeah, I'm growing this 'stache out."

Evan's eyes snapped open when he heard Barczyk's voice. He was coming onto the plane with Vassiliev behind him. Vassiliev wore his understated light gray suit that he usually wore on the road; Barczyk had a charcoal one that could've been called drab if he weren't wearing a bright yellow dress shirt with it. Even among teammates, he had to stand out.

"You look like a clown," Vassiliev said as he sat down near the front of the plane. "You won't last the whole month."

"Shows what you know." Barczyk took off a messenger bag and tossed it under the seat next to Vassiliev; Evan's heart sank. "I'm fully committed." Then their voices were muffled once Barczyk sat down. They continued bickering, but Evan couldn't hear a word of it. He leaned forward, willing Barczyk to turn around and spot him.

Change seats, he silently pleaded. *Sit with me.*

"This seat taken?"

Evan jumped, startled to see Dalton. He'd been so focused on Barczyk and Vassiliev, he hadn't noticed anyone walk over.

"All yours," he said with a forced smile. Which it shouldn't be! Dalton had been his friend long before Evan had spoken a single word to Barczyk. He liked spending time with Dalton on flights, because Dalton was great at reading Evan's moods and knowing when he wanted to veg out on his phone or when he needed a distraction.

Oh. Evan needed a distraction right now. That tracked.

Dalton plopped next to him and groaned as he settled into his seat. "Thanks, bro. Y'know Jennie? From the bar?"

Evan didn't, but he nodded. "Of course. Jennie from the bar."

"I took your advice that night and asked her out. We've gone out a few times. It's going awesome."

"Congrats," Evan said. He only kind of remembered having a conversation with Dalton about some girl he was into, but he was happy he'd helped. He only wished he'd done it consciously and could take actual credit for it. "That's great. She come to any games yet?"

Dalton beamed. "She was there when I scored against the Cougars. I only score like five goals a season, so I figured it's a good sign I did it when she was there."

"Maybe she's your good luck charm."

"She really is." It was a five-hour flight, and Evan spent most of it listening to Dalton gush about his new girlfriend. He didn't mind, though. Anything was better than agonizing over Barczyk.

———

Their schedule was packed once they touched down in Anaheim. There was a team-building hike, a dinner, and a strict curfew. As wound up as he was, Evan was asleep before he'd decided whether to message Barczyk.

They had practice the next day, along with video review with the coaches for not only the Orange County Mallards but also the Los Angeles Devils and the Bay Area Brawlers, the three teams they'd be facing in quick succession on this trip. There was no curfew that night, but he ended up at a mini-golf place a few blocks from the hotel with Dalton. His phone burned in his pocket, his fingers itching to grab it and text Barczyk, but he resisted the urge.

Not because he wasn't friends with Barczyk. They were, sort of. It would be completely normal for them to hang out. But that moment in Pittsburgh when Barczyk had suggested they have more 'lessons' on the road...it had felt like a promise. Not a promise to act like things were the same; it was a promise to explore the ways they could be different.

So it might drive Evan crazy to keep his distance, but it was for the best. He'd get too riled up otherwise, too distracted. They had a game tomorrow, and he needed to focus.

Besides, he thought as he lined up his shot into the final hole of the course, *anticipation makes it more fun.*

———

The only real, unguarded interaction between Evan and Barczyk was their warm-up butt whacks. The whole thing had always seemed silly to Evan, but now there were undertones. They still did it because enough people had noticed it was Their Thing that it would be suspicious if they stopped, but Evan rushed through it.

"How efficient," Barczyk drawled when it was over. "You've gotta learn to draw out the moment. Make it count."

Evan shot Barczyk a look and skated away. He did *not* want to experience getting hard while wearing full gear. Add that to the list of reasons why this was stupidly reckless.

This probably wasn't what Coach Jack meant when he said he wanted us to help each other...

With that sobering thought, Evan forced himself into game mode.

The Orange County Mallards were on a four-game win streak and came out strong, but once they went down two goals in the first, they seemed defeated. It should've been an easy game after that as both teams went through the motions. And it was easy. Easy enough that Evan, whose record was a nine-goal season, scored early in the third period.

He was pleased by the tally, knowing congratulatory texts would be waiting for him on his phone from his friends and family, and skated past the benches to fistbump the team. Unfortunately, the Mallards took offense to Evan's goal, like he should've stopped trying just because they had.

"Insult to injury," one of their centers said as they lined up for a face-off. "Having some bottom-liner like you score."

Evan gritted his teeth. The Mallards weren't putting up their best effort, but Evan had worked for his goal. It hadn't been easy to get that shot off, and he'd still gotten the puck cleanly over the goalie's blocker. It was a good goal, not some fluky deflection, and he resented the implication that he sucked too much to score when clearly it wasn't the case.

"Play better defense," he grumbled under his breath just before the ref dropped the puck.

Evan spent the rest of his shift eating those words. The center stayed on him like glue, no longer caring where the puck was or where the rest of the play was: where Evan went, he went, and he made sure Evan knew it.

After being pinned to the boards well after the puck had been sent up ice, Evan still couldn't get the guy to let him go until a whistle sounded.

"Would you lay off?" Evan grumbled when he was free. He knew by all the unofficial rules of hockey, he was well within his rights to drop the gloves and fight this guy. But as far as he'd come with his fighting, he wasn't ready to punch someone.

"Aww, big guy wants me to go easy on him?" He laughed and pushed Evan square in the chest, right on his Riveters' logo. "Why don't you go back to the minors, kiddo? You ain't ready to tango with—"

And then the guy was eating glove as Barczyk pushed him backward by his face.

"Personal space, bro," Barczyk said, chewing his mouthguard. "Take a step back, or I'll be happy to make you. Like honestly, give me an excuse, please. I'm bored beating you guys on the scoreboard. Lemme beat one of you guys down for real."

It was weirdly chivalrous the way Barczyk had stepped in, like he saw Evan's indecision.

"Cute that you're babysitting, Barczyk," he said, his tough-guy facade still in place even as he took a step back. "That what the Riveters pay you to do?"

Barczyk shrugged. "They pay me for a lot of things. Getting assists. Looking good. Taking out the trash. Not my fault your team pays you to *be* trash—"

A ref swooped in and blew his whistle until they scattered. Still, Evan skated away with his hands clenched in his gloves, wishing he'd at least elbowed the other center. Something, *anything* to show he didn't need other people to fight his battles for him.

Despite the mounting evidence to the contrary.

"No one's babysitting you, Abs." Barczyk grabbed Evan's jersey and guided him to the bench. "I know you can handle yourself. I just enjoy doing this shit more than you do. I don't mind."

"I know you don't," Evan grumbled as they took their spots next to Vassiliev. "*I'm* starting to mind, though."

Barczyk's answering look was unreadable, and soon they were absorbed back in the game. Evan noticed Barczyk stayed close against him, shoulders and knees pressed together more than the cramped bench warranted. The proximity should've irritated him, but it was comforting. Barczyk wasn't just on the team; he was on Evan's side. And yes, so were the other players. Vassiliev would have his back, Lawson and Doyle and all of them would stand up for him, but Barczyk understood him.

Somehow, by accident, he'd become actual friends with Riley Barczyk.

22

Evan's phone pinged while he was brushing his teeth. He ignored it until he was done, then nearly dropped it into the sink when he saw who'd texted him.

Barczyk
Curfews suck
Does coach do this often?

They'd had another curfew imposed on them, and Evan suspected they'd continue to for the rest of their California road trip.

Abernathy
Sometimes on the road yeah
Especially after we win
There was an incident a few years ago with some of the guys drinking too much
The first time you text me is to complain about curfew?

Evan, like a teenager, stared at his screen and held his breath waiting for a reply. Luckily, it came a few seconds later.

Barczyk
Nah the first time i'm texting you is to tell you
i'm in room 329
Y'know
If you wanted practice

Evan walked numbly out of the bathroom and sat on the edge of his bed. The murky future of whatever Barczyk had been hinting at back in Pittsburgh was finally here. He'd purposely not thought about it too much so he wouldn't freak himself out, and now the full weight of what Barczyk was saying fell on him.

His phone buzzed in his hand a minute later.

Barczyk
Or just hang out, no pressure

"Yeah, right," Evan grumbled. Barczyk likely meant what he said, but Evan felt a metric shit ton of pressure. He needed to clear this up. He needed to go tell Barczyk that he was straight. The last time had been a mistake. Evan was confused and horny and they should stop the lessons because it was messing with Evan's head. Yes. These were the things that needed to happen so Evan could put this behind him before it derailed his entire season.

He would text Barczyk back a simple *no thanks* and not put himself in situations where he might give Barczyk the wrong impression. Any second, he'd type those two words and then put away his phone and go to bed, because they had a curfew and were traveling to San Francisco tomorrow.

But when Evan's hand started moving, that wasn't what he did.

Abernathy
I could use some practice
Be there in ten

———

Evan's heart thundered in his ears. He was doing this. He was going to Barczyk's hotel room to...

To what? It would probably be a repeat of what happened last time, though on a bed instead of a training mat. Fuck, why did he want this so badly? Why was he so fucking turned on when they weren't even in the same room yet?

He shifted uneasily on his feet outside Barczyk's door. Last chance to turn back. If he chickened out, maybe he'd be so embarrassed he'd learn his lesson and get his dick under control. He heard the elevator door open at the far end of the hall and recognized Doyle's laughter. Panicking, Evan knocked urgently on the door. The laughter was getting louder, footsteps bringing his teammates closer and—

The door opened, and Evan almost fell forward. Strong arms pulled him inside, and the door closed behind him. Evan held his breath as the noise in the hallway grew louder before slowly growing quiet. Only after it was silent again did Evan let out a whoosh of air and turn around.

Barczyk stared at him, eyebrows drawn together and arms crossed over his chest. "You okay?"

"It was Doyle and some of the guys," Evan whispered. Then he realized how ridiculous it was to whisper when they were safely in Barczyk's hotel room. "Sorry, that was dumb." He dragged a hand down his face and groaned into his palm.

"You're kind of cute when you're freaking out, anyone ever tell you that?"

"Really?" Evan peeked out from his hand, bewildered.

Barczyk shrugged. "Cute like a puppy is cute. Not, like, bangable cute."

"Oh." *Was that a hint?* "Sorry, I—"

"Geez, Abs." Barczyk put a hand on his chest; Evan shut up. The gesture also made his dick stand at attention. What kind of magic powers did Barczyk have that did this to him? "Relax. And stop apologizing all the time."

Evan started to apologize again but cut himself off in time. Instead, he clamped his mouth so tightly his jaw clicked and swallowed.

Barczyk's hands came to rest on his shoulders; Evan leaned forward into the touch.

"Seriously, bro," Barczyk said. "You good? For real, we can just chill. I'm not looking to give you an aneurysm. As much as I would love to get my hands on you"—Evan whimpered—"there are plenty of other ways to pass the time."

"Uh huh." Evan closed his eyes and shuddered. He knew what he wanted. He didn't understand why he wanted it, but he did. Maybe this was something he needed to work out of his system. Mind made up, he opened his eyes. "I'd uhm...your hands...you could..." He bit the inside of his cheek to get it together. "You should put your hands on me."

"Thank God," Barczyk said before going on his tiptoes to kiss him. As soon as their lips met, Evan forgot everything he'd ever known. There was nothing besides Barczyk's tongue, his mouth, his hands, his body. Evan groaned as he tried to get closer, wrapping his arms around Barczyk and pulling him in tight as he could, as if it were possible for him to get under Barczyk's skin the way he had with Evan. Barczyk fit so perfectly against him, hard chest and solid muscle.

Evan slid a hand up Barczyk's back, marveling at the broad shoulders before tangling his fingers in Barczyk's hair. He couldn't say why he did it, but he closed his fist in the curls and tugged gently. It sent a bolt of pleasure through him, this bit of control he could exert over Barczyk when normally it was Barczyk who was in charge. He did it again, nudging Barczyk so he could deepen the kiss.

The third time, Barczyk broke the kiss and smiled against Evan's lips. "You got a thing for my hair, huh?"

"Yeah," he admitted. It was so satisfying in a primal way that he didn't understand; he just knew he liked it. "Sor—"

Barczyk kissed him once, quickly, then bit his lip. Evan let out a surprised gasp.

"No apologies," Barczyk scolded. They were so close, Evan could feel the words caressing his skin. "You've got nothing to apologize for here. If I don't like something, I'll tell you. You just do the same, 'kay?"

He almost said sorry again, but he stopped himself. "Okay."

The smile Barczyk rewarded him with was so bright Evan had to close his eyes. He leaned down and stole another kiss, running his tongue along the gap where Barczyk's tooth should be. It was strange; all the things about Barczyk that had annoyed him before were what drew him in now. He was drunk on it, the high of getting to take something from someone who was so confident and never gave an inch to anyone.

He backed Barczyk against the door, trapping him with his body as his tongue continued to claim. Their hips pressed together, hard cocks so close but kept apart by nothing more than a few layers of fabric.

"You know," Barczyk said between kisses, "the bed would be more comfortable."

"Mmm," Evan hummed in agreement. He didn't want to move, didn't want to put space between them, because that might let his doubts creep back in. He wanted this too much, and letting a rational thought take hold might ruin the whole thing. He was already haunted by what he wanted from Barczyk; he didn't want to be haunted by what if's too.

"C'mon, big guy." He pushed Evan back, and he whined at the loss of contact. It wasn't far, and then Barczyk's arms were wrapped around his neck. There was a moment of pressure as Barczyk pulled himself up and wrapped his legs around Evan's waist. Evan brought his hands up to steady him and realized he was now cupping Barczyk's ass.

"Fuck, you're heavy," Evan said to distract himself. He squeezed a hand experimentally; he liked the feel of taut muscle.

"Rude," Barczyk said and started sucking on Evan's neck. "I'm sturdy."

"I think you mean dense."

His head snapped back. "Me? I'm not the one choosing to have a conversation instead of getting off. Calling me dense." Barczyk shook his head, and Evan had to admit, he had a point.

He carried Barczyk to the bed. The room was the same as Evan's—like all hotel rooms, honestly; after all these years of travel, they'd long ago blurred together—and he used that familiarity to help steady his nerves. He got to the bed and hesitated, unsure whether he was supposed to put Barczyk down or how to do it. Never one to hesitate, Barczyk rocked backwards and dragged Evan down on top of him as they tumbled to the bed.

"Oof! Geez Louise, Abs. Giving me shit for being heavy like you don't weigh a thousand pounds."

"I do not—"

"Sorry, you're Canadian. Let me convert it for you. A thousand kilograms."

"Pounds and kilograms don't have a one-to-one conversion—"

"Evan Abernathy."

Evan shuddered, his stomach doing a weird somersault at hearing his actual name.

"My dick is really hard. Your dick is really hard. You're on top of me in a huge bed with nowhere to be until tomorrow morning. Focus. You can teach me all about the metric system tomorrow, I promise, as long as you make me come first."

Evan shuddered at the words. Yes, they'd gotten off together once already, but acknowledging it out loud with actual words was a lot different. *Make me come first* did things to him. It made it about *them*, not just Evan, and Evan loved hearing it wasn't a one-sided attraction. Obviously it wasn't, but hearing it made it real.

"I can focus," Evan promised and kicked off his shoes like that proved it. Then he settled between Barczyk's legs. All his attention went to that point of contact as he ground down a few times. His eyes fluttered shut, and he enjoyed the sensation and the simple, heady pleasure it brought him.

Them, he remembered when Barczyk groaned and rolled his hips up. Evan opened his eyes and took in the man beneath him. The light-brown curls collecting around his ears, the lust-blown hazel eyes watching him lazily, the slight bruise under one of them from when he'd been punched by Walker, plush pink lips inviting him in...

He took the invitation, leaning down to kiss Barczyk again. There was a taste to him, some small remnants of whatever he'd had after the game, and Evan chased it. Wanted every little bit of Barczyk he could steal for himself, because maybe if he took enough, he wouldn't need anymore.

"This is fun and all," Barczyk said, breaking away and making Evan grunt in frustration. "But I wanna touch you this time. Could we...?"

Evan blinked as he pieced together what Barczyk meant. No more clothes in the way. That was...that'd be...too intense? No, that wasn't the issue. It'd be too intimate. It was already hard to wrap his brain around what they'd been doing, this intense, gay desire he'd never felt before. But with their clothes still on, he could at least downplay it.

"C'mon." Barczyk rolled them over so they lay side by side, facing each other. He reached a hand between them, his fingers brushing along Evan's dick through his shorts. Evan's toes curled in his socks because, fuck, that was good. "I'll make it good for you, promise."

A shaky laugh escaped. He didn't doubt it, but he was pretty sure there'd be no coming back from Barczyk's hand wrapped around his dick. He both dreaded and craved doing the same for Barczyk. Bit by bit, it seemed like Evan was wandering farther away from who he thought he was.

Or maybe closer to who I actually am, he thought.

Fucking absurd.

Yeah right. I'm not secretly a guy who wants to jerk off Riley Barczyk.

Except Barczyk was tracing the hem of his shorts and watching him patiently. When Evan stole a glimpse down and saw Barczyk's erection straining against his sweatpants, he couldn't deny that he maybe was a guy who wanted to jerk off Riley Barczyk.

"Please," Evan managed and was immediately rewarded with Barczyk taking a firmer hold of him through his shorts. A few light strokes that made Evan almost swallow his tongue, it felt so good. "Oh, fuck."

"Told you." Then his hand was gone, and Evan wanted to die. He'd never been so turned on in his whole life—there was no way he could stop now—but Barczyk started wiggling his sweatpants and boxers down, nodding for Evan to do the same. Pushing down his shorts and briefs wasn't enough distraction from seeing Barczyk's dick, hard and needy, for the first time. He licked his lips and, without any conscious thought, reached out and wrapped his hand around the shaft.

Barczyk bit his lip, failing to stifle the deep groan that escaped, and mirrored Evan. When Evan drew his thumb up the silky skin, reveling in the hardness and the way Barczyk's dick jerked in his hand, Barczyk did the same thing to him. Evan ran his thumb through the pre-come gathering at the tip and gasped as Barczyk did as well. Encouraged, Evan gave a tentative stroke and was rewarded when Barczyk stroked him too.

"As fast and as hard as you want," Barczyk whispered. "You're in charge, big guy. Whatever you want."

The control helped him ease into the moment. He moved his hand, exploring how he could work different sounds out of Barczyk while learning what he wanted. And it was ridiculously arousing to have even this small amount of power over Barczyk, a man who didn't follow the rules or listen to anyone but was letting Evan control him. Barczyk seemed to enjoy giving that control to Evan.

Soon, desire took over. Evan had drawn things out as long as he could, but he was too close to the edge to keep the slow, tentative pace they'd been enjoying. Tightening his grip, he started going faster. Barczyk matched him, and they locked eyes. A silent understanding passed between them: it wasn't follow the leader anymore; it was a race to get the other off first.

Evan was so keyed up and Barczyk clearly had the advantage of experience—the way he could change the pressure of his grip and tease at Evan's slit while never losing his rhythm was a testament to his expertise—but Evan was eager to prove himself.

And not above cheating. He used his free hand to grab Barczyk by the back of his neck and draw his lips close. He nibbled at his lower lip, pulled at his curls, pressed their foreheads together and wouldn't let Barczyk regain any ground he'd taken. He pushed up onto his shoulder so he could look down at Barczyk, giving the illusion that he was trapped. Evan didn't say anything, but the message was clear: I'm in charge, you're here for me, and that's that.

Never in Evan's life had he thought he was so possessive, but he felt it in every stroke, in every kiss he stole. He wasn't used to taking advantage of his size like this, using it to exert his will. Was this what Barczyk felt on the ice when he tricked other people into fighting him? And why was Barczyk giving in so easily to him?

It was hot, whatever the reason, and Evan wasn't sure he'd ever be able to give up the thrill of feeling in charge.

Barczyk came first, warm come coating Evan's hand. It was satisfying, having won, but he didn't have long to enjoy the upper hand: Barczyk let go of Evan's dick and took his wet hand. He wrapped Evan's fingers around his cock and guided him through jerking himself off,

Barczyk's come easing the way. And like that, Evan's handle of the situation dissolved because fuck fuck fuck—

When he came, it was like a tidal wave crashing over him. It stole his breath—thankfully, because he had no idea what kind of noises he would've made otherwise. As he lay there, Barczyk milking him through the aftershocks until he'd started to grow soft and his heart had almost found a normal rhythm, he wondered how Barczyk always managed to turn the tables on him. He collapsed back down on his shoulder, mindful to avoid their come but not willing to go too far yet; he liked Barczyk's heat, felt calmed by his presence even as some small piece of him freaked out about what it meant that he had Barczyk's come on him.

Why *Barczyk*?

He enjoyed a few long minutes of blissful silence when his brain shut off and let him relax. Then he blinked, and his mind was flooded with coherent thought again. He still didn't want to move, to burst the bubble they were cocooned in. If time kept going, they'd have to leave this moment. Then there'd be questions and consequences.

But it couldn't last forever. Barczyk was watching him with hooded eyes like he was about to fall asleep, and Evan wasn't equipped to handle the intimacy of sharing a bed. Sex was enough of a mess; they shouldn't complicate things more than they already had.

"You look so dumb with that mustache," Evan blurted out. It was the first coherent thought he could latch onto. He'd been surprised that it hadn't felt any different kissing Barczyk with the mustache, but that was probably more about Evan having a beard than anything else.

Barczyk blinked awake.

"I look great," Barczyk said, and suddenly they were no longer convenient lovers but teammates. Evan thought that was the end of it, and he was glad that they'd shifted back to their usual selves without any awkwardness in between, but a moment later came a quiet, "You really don't like it?"

Guilt rolled through him. "Not my thing," he said, not wanting to be a dick. He shouldn't have said anything at all. What the fuck did it matter to him if his linemate grew a stupid mustache? "Do you care if I don't like it?"

Barczyk shrugged, though he seemed more shut off than he'd been a few seconds ago. "Not really." It was the first time Evan had ever thought he'd been able to hear a crack in Barczyk's bravado.

"It suits you," Evan said and meant it. He wanted to lean in and kiss Barczyk, but he held back. He didn't know what they did, but kissing after they'd come felt like a bad idea. Like they'd firmly switched back to teammates from whatever they'd been for the last hour, and he didn't want to get his wires crossed trying to go back.

Barczyk considered this. "It suits me, but you don't like it."

Evan went pale. "Shit, no. That's not—"

"Don't worry, I'm just fucking with you." Barczyk pushed off the bed. In the five steps it took him to get to the bathroom, he'd kicked off his joggers and boxers, and tossed aside his shirt. "I'm gonna shower," he said, pausing in the doorway to wink at Evan. "You're always getting me dirty."

Evan stared after him long after Barczyk had disappeared and the water started running. Once Barczyk started singing *Mambo No. 5*, Evan decided that was his cue to leave. He cleaned himself up as best he could, then escaped back to his room for his own shower and a night of wondering if this had been worth it at all.

23

They didn't talk about it.

As the team loaded onto the bus for their trip to San Francisco the next morning, Evan watched Barczyk. There was no sign that anything had happened; he was the same as always, and didn't act any different when he grabbed Evan's arm and made him sit next to him.

"Missed you at breakfast," Barczyk said. "Most important meal of the day."

Evan had skipped breakfast, but not on purpose. When he'd gotten back to his room, he'd spent the next hour thinking about what had happened in Barczyk's room over and over and over until he'd gotten hard again. He'd jerked off, reliving the whole thing, and then passed out. For once in his life, he'd slept so soundly, he'd missed his alarm. It was only Dalton banging on his door to check on him that had woken him up in time to join the team.

"I overslept," he grumbled. "I had to grab some fruit from the lobby on my way out." He held up a banana and an apple as proof, like he needed to show he hadn't been avoiding Barczyk.

"Hmmm," Barczyk hummed. "Slept good, huh? You should do whatever you did last night again. Make sure you're well-rested."

The bus engine whirring to life saved him from having to answer.

Tablets were passed around with their video to review of the Bay Area Brawlers, and Evan found it a minor miracle he could focus on the tiny screen after Barczyk stretched out and laid his leg over Evan's. It was a good sort of problem, though. He preferred this small acknowledgement that things had shifted between them.

Anything was better than Barczyk sitting with someone else, leaving Evan desperate and lonely and distracted.

Yeah, because having company in my desperation is such an improvement.

"Number 35 is an agitator," Barczyk said, half to himself as he replayed a video. "You leave him to me."

Evan's heart fluttered in his chest. Yes. This was definitely better.

———

They were supposed to arrive a full day and a half ahead of their game, but traffic had them getting into their hotel late. Coach Jack seemed harried by the delay, his plans for a team lunch ruined because they'd missed their reservations. He stood in front of the bus, taking off his Riveters cap and running a hand through his hair.

"No curfew tonight, boys," he said in resignation, like it pained him to make this concession. "Be responsible. I don't need a repeat of Portland."

Everyone whooped and cheered. They had the good sense not to make their plans too loudly, instead escaping the bus before Coach Jack could change his mind and disappearing into their rooms to conspire via text. Evan ignored his phone altogether while he settled in. They'd be arguing for the next hour, and he'd rather wait to get the final decision than try to follow along as everyone bickered. There'd be a dozen suggestions, factions forming as the more energetic begged for a trip to clubs while the older crowd looked for fancy steakhouses or cigar clubs. Ultimately, they'd agree on a bar within walking distance of the hotel and break off from there.

Evan wasn't sure how much he was up for tonight. He never had much social battery, and he was wondering how best to weasel out of the more mentally taxing plans when someone knocked on his hotel room door. He froze in the bathroom, his toiletry bag clutched to his chest. Had he told anyone his room number? Who'd seen him go into his room?

Was it Barczyk?

Another knock. Slowly, Evan put down the bag and walked to the door. He looked out the peephole and was relieved to see Dalton on the other side.

"Hey, what's up?" he asked as he opened the door.

"There's a mini-golf place down the street." Dalton's eyes were bright. "They've still got a half hour before they close for the night. You in?"

Evan relaxed muscles he hadn't known he was clenching. "Really? That'd be—" He frowned. "I don't wanna keep you from whatever else is going on."

Dalton snorted. "You haven't been reading the texts? Everyone's busy showering or hanging out at the hotel bar for now. C'mon, we gotta be quick, or they won't let us on the course."

Not about to turn down a chance for mini-golf, Evan grabbed his card key and followed Dalton to the elevator. "Thanks, man. I hadn't even thought of looking up a place. I appreciate it."

"No worries. I'm not looking to drink much tonight. Besides, don't thank me. Thank Barzy."

Evan stopped short and recovered just before the elevator door closed on him. "Barzy?" he asked as neutrally as possible. He didn't think he could handle Barczyk's innuendos in front of Dalton. "He's coming along?"

"Nah." The elevator doors opened, and Dalton started walking out of the hotel and down the street. "He found the place and said I should take you, but he got roped into some pool tournament once they found out there were tables in the hotel game room."

Disappointment curdled in his gut, but Evan ignored it. Mini-golf was supposed to be about restoring his equilibrium, and being around Barczyk did the exact opposite.

They got their putters and started the course. Only ten holes, but it should be enough to do the job. Evan shed his baggage and fell into the game, assessing each hole and making his plan. The course wasn't the best maintained in the world, and it was pretty standard except for one hole that had a weird bump along the main path.

As they started the final stretch, Evan felt his phone buzz in his pocket. Against his better judgment, he took it out.

Barczyk
What's your room number

Evan looked up. Dalton had just missed a jump, and the ball had rolled back to the start. He had some time.

Abernathy
419
Why?

Barczyk
How far along is your mini-golf game?

Abernathy
We've got three holes left. Why?

Barczyk
Go back to your room after you guys are done
Text me when you're back there k?

Abernathy
Why???

Barczyk
It's a surprise

"Five," Dalton grumbled, and Evan fumbled with his phone like he'd been caught watching porn or something.

"Huh?"

"Five strokes. You've got the scorecard, right? Try not to embarrass me with a hole in one or something."

Evan didn't get a hole in one. He couldn't even make par the last few holes, his head on backwards with the prospect of Barczyk in his room tonight. Whatever Barczyk had planned, it wasn't going to be an innocent surprise. He didn't think there'd ever be anything innocent about them hanging out alone again, even if they never did anything.

The feel of Barczyk's dick in his hand was branded in his brain. Sure, put them in a hockey game, and he could probably forget it, but just the two of them alone with a bed...

"You wanna go again?" Dalton offered when he added up the scores. "You didn't do great."

Evan shook his head. He'd made par for the course, but only because he'd done well through the first few holes to balance out the way he bombed the end. More mini-golf would just illustrate how out of it he was. The last thing he needed was Dalton getting suspicious.

"Nah, I'm good. I think I just need to lie down for a bit."

"Yeah, traffic today blew. People always complain about Pittsburgh traffic, but it's nothing compared to other cities."

They walked back to the hotel, Dalton babbling about his girlfriend and the brewery a bunch of them were going to check out tonight and how he thought they'd do against the Brawlers. It was the perfect background noise, familiar and requiring little of him, while Evan's mind wandered.

Not that it ever wandered farther than Room 419.

"I'm gonna get changed," Dalton said when he dropped Evan off at his room. "I can swing by in a bit to grab you before I head out if you want."

"Sure," Evan said without paying attention. He was too busy opening up his text messages.

Abernathy
Back
You plan on going out with the guys later?

A small icon appeared to show Barczyk had read his messages, but there was no indication that he was typing a response, so Evan tossed his phone aside and collapsed face first onto his bed. What was he doing? This was so dumb. If they were caught, there'd be such a mess, the least of which was explaining that he was straight and had this strange Barczyk-exception he couldn't begin to explain.

He might've fallen asleep, because the next thing he knew, there was a knock at the door. Evan jolted off the bed, head groggy, and stumbled towards the door.

"Look, Dalty," he said as he opened the door. "I don't think I should—"

Barczyk pushed into the room. Not only did he close the door, but he put the privacy latch up.

"Barczyk." Maybe he was still asleep. "What're you—?" He was cut off by a kiss that tasted of salt and tequila. Dream or not, Evan didn't much care and had just relaxed into the kiss when Barczyk pulled away. "Wha—?"

And then Barczyk dropped to his knees, and Evan figured out what was next right as Barczyk kissed his crotch. Evan's cock had woken up before he had, because it jerked towards Barczyk's mouth and grew thick in record time.

"Surprise," Barczyk said as he worked his mouth over the bulge in Evan's shorts. Fuck, that was a good look for Barczyk.

"Surprise," he echoed, a hand coming up to rest on the back of Barczyk's head. "Good surprise."

Barczyk laughed and looked up at him. "Ain't it, though?" He kept his gaze locked with Evan's as he ran his hands up and down Evan's thighs. His face was right next to Evan's dick, close enough that Evan just needed to shift a few inches to rub himself against Barczyk's cheek. The fucking tease didn't move though.

"Yes," Evan admitted and swallowed, his mouth dry. Then, "Your mustache is gone." It wasn't completely true. The outline of his mustache was darker than the rest of his stubble, but the ends had been trimmed. In a day or two, it'd be impossible to tell he'd had a mustache at all.

"Yeah. Heard it didn't look great."

Before Evan could unwrap that mess, there was a loud knock at his door. He jumped and felt his cheeks going red even though whoever was out there couldn't know what was going on only a few feet away.

"Yeah?" Evan croaked.

"Hey, Abs." It was Dalton. Evan gulped and looked down at Barczyk pleadingly. What would they do? "We're about to head out to that brewery. You coming?"

"Uhm—"

Barczyk hooked his fingers into the hem of Evan's shorts and started working them down his legs; the head of his cock was free within seconds, dangerously close to Barczyk's lips.

"Tell them you have a headache," Barczyk whispered, his breath ghosting over the sensitive skin. A bead of pre-come formed, and Evan thought about how easy it would be to force Barczyk's head over and urge him to lick it up; he didn't.

"I have a headache," Evan repeated mechanically, but it must've been too quiet because Dalton knocked again.

"What was that, Abs?"

Evan clenched his hands into fists—one still gripping Barczyk's hair, the other hanging uselessly at his side—and leaned his head back against the wall. He was rapidly losing control here. "I have a headache," he said too loudly. "Count me out."

Go away, Evan begged. *I don't have the willpower to walk away from this...*

There was a long, drawn-out silence before Dalton said, "Okay, bro. Sorry you're not feeling good. Want me to get you some Advil or something?"

That was when Barczyk took him into his mouth.

"I already took some," he gritted out. His eyes were clamped shut because he would lose it if he looked down. He could barely hold it together as he felt Barczyk's mouth suck around the tip of his dick, his tongue tracing around the head as his fingers teased at Evan's balls. This was the best torture in the world, and Evan wasn't equipped to handle it.

" 'kay. Feel better!" And then, mercifully, came the sound of footsteps walking away.

Barczyk hummed around his dick, and Evan whined pitifully before he realized Barczyk had been talking.

"What was that?" Evan dared to look down. It was a mistake, first because he got a great view of his dick straining against the inside of Barczyk's cheek, and second because he got to watch as Barczyk popped off of his dick, his lips rosy and wet.

"I said, you sure you don't wanna go drink with them? I'm cool if you want a rain check."

At least part of Evan's brain was working, because he said, "And pass up a chance to finally shut you up? Hell no."

Barczyk laughed like it was the best joke he'd ever heard. "Shut me up then," he teased. He didn't resist when Evan guided him back to his dick.

Like pretty much everything else, Barczyk was good at giving head. He once again read Evan like an open book and got him off hard and quick. Without batting an eye, he swallowed Evan's come and guided Evan gently to the ground when his legs nearly gave out.

"Fun, right?" Barczyk said, pleased with himself. Evan had found Barczyk attractive in a number of ways—his competence and confidence high among the reasons, but there was also a raw male energy that did weird things to Evan—but this was the first time he'd thought Barczyk was cute. "What?" he asked, as though he could see the shift in Evan's face.

Cute sounded a little too far from sexual attraction for Evan's liking. Experimenting was one thing, but cute seemed too...too...*romantic.*

So instead of unpacking that, Evan leaned forward to kiss Barczyk. He shuddered when he tasted his own release on Barczyk's tongue, but it helped remind Evan this was about sex. This was a weird, convenient thing where they got each other off. He had no idea why either of them liked it, but it was acceptable. He could accept it, anyway.

"Can I return the favor?" Evan asked. He'd be terrible at it. He'd never had a dick in his mouth, been so rarely on the receiving end, but it would make it impossible for him to have compromising thoughts like *Riley Barczyk looks cute.*

"You don't have to," Barczyk said seriously. "I was just—"

"I know I don't have to. I want to."

And that was how he ended up on his knees in front of Riley Barczyk. Evan pulled down Barczyk's loose joggers and his plaid boxers. He stroked Barczyk to full hardness. Later, he'd have a dozen excuses to explain why he did this, but right now, he couldn't deny that he wanted Barczyk's cock.

"Oh, fuck, Abs. That's real good. Yeah, just like that. I didn't...never would've...you could've had me...that's—"

That was when Barczyk was relatively coherent. His babbling didn't make a whole lot of sense after the first couple of minutes. He knew it was Evan's first time giving head but, as always, was so stupidly encouraging and gentle. How could Barczyk be gentle? Why was he so nice and patient?

"Gonna...gonna come..." He tapped urgently on Evan's shoulder in warning. "Abs, you don't have to—" Evan didn't budge, just kept bobbing his head back and forth with the same sloppy rhythm he'd been using, kept working his hand on the bottom of his shaft. "Evan," he whined and then started to come.

Evan almost choked, though he wasn't sure if that was the come hitting the back of his throat or the helpless way Barczyk had said his name. It was stupid, but half the time Evan thought his teammates didn't know his first name. He never heard it during the season, and it threw him to hear it at all, never mind like this. He swallowed as much as he could and rested his head against Barczyk's hip. Maybe he should pretend he hadn't heard that. Add it to the list of things he needed to lock away and ignore.

"We should..." Barczyk took a deep shuddering breath and patted the top of Evan's head. "We should get cleaned up. If we hurry, we can catch up with the guys at that bar or whatever."

"I have a headache," Evan said shakily. He couldn't get up yet, couldn't look at Barczyk. Definitely couldn't go into the bathroom to clean up and face his reflection. "Remember?"

"Oh." He could feel Barczyk shrug. "You made a miraculous recovery. Yay."

Evan huffed. "I think I'll pass." He pulled back enough to glance up at Barczyk. "Rain check?"

Barczyk laughed.

24

"You guys have been playing so well this season," his mom said. "You've grown since that playoff loss last season. Coach Jack and the GM have done well picking up new pieces and fitting them into the system."

Evan nodded, remembered she couldn't see him, and grunted in agreement as he rummaged through his fridge. They'd just returned from the California road trip, and he had very little edible food available other than crackers, protein bars, and slightly stale bread.

"Three for three in California," she went on. "You guys rarely do that well. How many points did you pick up, sweetie?"

Evan gave up on finding food and opened up Uber Eats. "You know I got four," he said with a fond eye roll. He'd forget in a couple of weeks, but she'd remember for the next few seasons.

"That one assist to Barczyk in San Francisco was particularly good." A pause. "He's been having a good month. That hat trick against the Brawlers was, what, his first in a few years?"

Evan shuddered, remembering how Barczyk had celebrated after that game. Evan had only given three blowjobs in his life, and all had been in the last week. "Yeah, something like that," he said dismissively.

Then, because it would be suspicious if he didn't say more, he added, "He fits in pretty well with me and Vassy."

"I agree. Vassiliev and you have a similar style. Last year, your right winger was too similar to you two. Barczyk brings that little extra oomph to the line." Another pause, longer this time. "Things are going okay with Barczyk being there, right? He's not giving you any trouble, is he?"

Oh, there's plenty of trouble, just very little of it's on the ice.

"No. He's pretty easygoing when there's no puck involved. Nice. Not pushy."

Really hot...

He pushed the thought away. His sexual identity crisis was something he was keeping to himself, if only because there was no way to bring it up without exposing the root of it. His mom was understanding and wouldn't judge him for any of it, but Evan didn't want to talk about it. He had too much rattling around in his head without adding his mom's questions or concerns into the mix. Once he understood things better, he could bring it up.

"Oh, good," his mom said in relief. "I know how much you worried about having to share the team with him. He seems to be up to his usual antics on the ice, but I'm glad it doesn't carry over into the locker room."

"He's been pretty tame lately, I thought." He didn't know why he wanted to defend Barczyk, who had drawn two unnecessary penalties when they were in L.A., but he did.

"Maybe. Though I appreciated his penalty got you some PK time. You looked good, sweetheart. Think they'll keep giving you chances?"

"I hope so. I'd like more responsibility, and I think this is a good way for me to prove that I'm more than a third-line center."

"You're a great center. The problem is that Turner and Moreau are also great centers, and they're more established on the team and in the league. You'll get your chance, sweetie."

Evan was about to talk about how much he could learn from them when his mom's tone shifted.

"What's with the butt-tap thing you do with Barczyk? I watched that L.A. game with your Aunt Linda, and we couldn't figure it out. The commentators said you've been doing it since Vermont."

"Oh." His cheeks were bright red, and he was glad his mom hated video calls so he could downplay things. "Barzy does it for good luck. Seems to work, so I play along."

"Barzy," his mom scoffed. "I've always thought hockey nicknames were ridiculous. How hard is it to call the man Riley and be done with it?"

Evan might have a stroke if he had to call Barczyk 'Riley.' He felt like some Victorian gentleman who shied away from using people's Christian names, because it truly caused him an unreasonable amount of anxiety.

"How's Aunt Linda doing?" he asked, hoping this would be his Get Out of Jail Free card. "How was the ski trip?"

"It was great! The cabin was perfect. Close to the slopes without any of the crowds. I'm not as spry as I used to be, but I could still beat Linda, and that was enough."

"Isn't Aunt Linda like eight years older than you?"

"Nine," she said. "And that doesn't matter. She skis more than I do, and I was still faster. I know you don't have any siblings, so you don't understand, but it's important. Oh, did you get to hang out with your cousin in L.A.?"

"Billy's more than a decade older than me," Evan said. "We haven't hung out since I was old enough not to need a babysitter anymore."

His cousin Billy was Aunt Linda's oldest son and played for the L.A. Devils. He'd always been nice to Evan despite the age difference, but they didn't seek opportunities to hang out when they played against each other. They said hi on the ice before the game—mostly to satisfy their mothers—and that was it.

Besides, he'd been busy.

"But it would be nice if you boys could hang out," his mom said.

Billy was married with two kids and projected to retire within a few years. Aside from their mothers being sisters and both men playing hockey, they had very little in common. Not that Billy wasn't a nice enough guy, it just always felt forced when they had hung out those first few seasons together because of their moms' nagging. Both had been relieved when Evan had suggested they stop.

"You travel so much," his mom said. "It's such a great opportunity to see family."

He didn't bother with his usual reminders—they didn't get a lot of time in other cities, he was working, sometimes their schedules didn't overlap. Instead he mumbled, "I know, I know," to appease her.

———

Evan was jittery. The nature of professional sports meant there were constantly people around, especially when they were on the road. His small little bubble of alone time had also vanished in San Francisco when he'd spent that first evening with Barczyk. Since then, Evan hadn't been alone to do anything except shower and sleep, and his empty apartment felt too big and lonely. He was a bit of an introvert, so it'd never bothered him to live alone (it'd been such a relief to lose the roommate part of away games this season), so it wasn't some sudden need to socialize that was driving him crazy.

He wanted to see Barczyk.

He wrote and re-wrote a text message about a dozen times before settling on a hopefully neutral one that didn't sound like he was looking for a booty call.

Abernathy

You busy? I was thinking I could use another fighting lesson

Barczyk didn't reply, and Evan hated himself for this show of weakness. Barczyk had other things going on besides Evan. It wasn't like he was at home, as lonely and bored as Evan, waiting and hoping Evan would reach out. He was probably out with the guys—it wasn't as if Evan was his only friend on the team or even his only linemate.

So Evan went through the boring chores that had built up over his West Coast trip. He ordered groceries. He did laundry. He paid his bills. He did dishes. He—

He definitely didn't sprint to his phone when he heard it vibrate with an incoming text.

Barczyk
Thought you might've outgrown that kind of practice

Abernathy
You said I wouldn't be able to graduate from the barczyk school of beating people up until American Thanksgiving

Barczyk
I have never in my life put the words American and Thanksgiving together
But yeah I guess I did promise that

Abernathy
So are you free tonight?

Barczyk
I might be. But believe it or not they never trusted me with a key to the rink so if you wanna practice you'll have to do it at my apartment building

Evan remembered a distant, naive version of himself who'd thought he could stay out of trouble with Barczyk if he kept things professional. He'd lost any semblance of a professional relationship weeks ago. Semi-public sex and hotel room hook-ups weren't any better than going to his apartment (though that might be a tad more intimate), so he figured keeping distance was a lost cause.

Abernathy
That's fine text me the address? I can be there in an hour

Barczyk
👍

25

EVAN DIDN'T GO TO BARCZYK'S APARTMENT BUILDING WITH any expectations, but as soon as he got there, he realized he'd subconsciously created some, and they didn't match up with the actual experience. When Barczyk opened the doors of the complex for him, Evan was surprised they didn't head for the elevator. When they ended up in a stairwell and went down instead of up, Evan understood he'd assumed they'd go to Barczyk's actual apartment.

When they got to the gym area, he shifted on his feet. There were other people there. Half a dozen or so people, all working out. Two teenage kids perked up when they saw Barczyk and waved enthusiastically, but after Barczyk acknowledged them, they respectfully went back to the squat rack and ignored him.

That was nice, except it didn't magically make them invisible, and Evan would really prefer not to be seen. He hadn't been able to control his dick when they'd practiced that first time, and that was well before things had...progressed. What was he supposed to do if they weren't alone? He wasn't sure he could control his reaction to Barczyk without gear. Look at Barczyk, for fuck's sake! He had a stupid muscle shirt with the sleeves cut so ridiculously low that you could practically see his whole chest! And he had a bright green headband on that kept his curls at bay.

Barczyk dug out the boxing gloves they'd been using from a plastic crate of equipment, caught Evan's expression, and raised an eyebrow.

"Problem?" he asked.

Evan cleared his throat and tried (unsuccessfully) not to fidget. "I didn't know we'd have an audience," he grumbled as he pulled at the hem of his tee. A real t-shirt, thank-you-very-much. Loose and properly covering his torso. Like a gentleman.

Barczyk walked over and handed Evan a pair of gloves. "They ain't watching us, Abs," he said, voice low.

Evan subtly scanned the room and saw that Barczyk was right. No one was paying them any attention as they went through their own workouts.

"Right now," Evan said.

"You plan on putting on a show?" Barczyk teased. His voice at that wavelength did things to Evan, and his dick stirred in interest.

"I'd really rather not," he said pointedly.

Barczyk's gaze flicked down Evan's body. He didn't smile, but his lips twitched. "Mr. Abernathy, did you text me for a booty call disguised as a fighting lesson?"

"No!" Evan whipped his head around to make sure no one had overheard; everyone kept working out as if nothing had happened, and Evan breathed a sigh of relief. "I swear, I didn't—"

"Abs, relax," Barczyk said. He stepped back and started putting on his gloves; Evan did the same. "We're professionals. We can handle working out together."

It was exactly what he needed to hear. Of course they could. They *were* professionals. They were coworkers, technically. They were practicing for their job. There was nothing inappropriate about this unless they made it inappropriate.

Again.

Okay, so they didn't have a great track record, but they went through practices with the team all the time. This was basically the same.

"You're right," Evan said, "So—"

"Besides," Barczyk interrupted. "We can always go a few rounds upstairs in my apartment after."

And that was when he came at Evan with a right hook that hit Evan square in the jaw. Which was also exactly what Evan needed: he was so annoyed that he switched into fight mode. Not that his fight mode was, like, the Hulk or anything. It was more that he had no brainpower left for anything besides dodging, blocking, and punching. The only thing he avoided was tackling or getting tackled, because the less skin contact the better. Getting Barczyk in a headlock was less compromising than pinning him.

The give and flow of the practice was familiar, but Barczyk's unpredictability kept him on his toes. Whenever Evan got too comfortable, thinking he'd figured Barczyk out, he'd end up getting sloppy and whacked for it.

When they were done, Evan was sweaty and sore and relaxed.

"Honestly," Barczyk panted as he tried to regain his breath. "There's not much more I can teach you. I think once you're in a real fight, you'll be fine."

"Really?" Evan beamed at the praise, then frowned. "So have I officially graduated from the Barczyk School of Hockey Goons?"

"Your diploma's in the mail." Barczyk sauntered over to a table and grabbed a couple of towels. He tossed one at Evan before vigorously rubbing his hair.

Evan toweled off his face, wondering how best to say what he wanted to. "Does that mean...that...we're done...uhm..." He winced at how terrible he was at this.

Barczyk peeked out from his towel. "We done with fighting practice? We can still do it for funsies, especially if you think you're getting rusty, but I don't think you need it anymore."

"Oh." He slumped in disappointment. He had never wanted these lessons in the first place. Why was he upset they were over? "I appreciate you taking the time to—"

"There are a few"—Barczyk licked his lips—"*other* skills that you could use some work on. I'd be willing to help you practice those some more. If you wanted."

Evan noticed the gym had cleared out while they were practicing.

They were alone, nothing but the whir of the fans and the sudden weight of possibility settling between them. He gulped.

"I did kinda notice that I uh...that you're better than me at...some of the stuff from the hotels," he said.

Barczyk dropped his towel on the floor and walked over to Evan so they were chest to chest. Ish. With their height difference, there wasn't a lot of overlap.

"I am pretty good at that stuff," Barczyk agreed, voice husky. He was so handsome. Evan didn't know how he hadn't seen it before because, fuck, fuck he was so screwed here. He could drown in those hazel eyes and wouldn't notice.

"Mhmm," Evan hummed.

Barczyk put a hand on Evan's hip, slipping under his tee to rest on bare skin and drawing him closer. "If you wanna kiss me, Abs," he said, "just kiss me. We don't have to fight first. You say the word, and I'm in."

That was all the invitation he needed. Evan leaned down and kissed Barczyk, reveling in the salty taste. It was a gentle, quick kiss. Evan didn't want to stop, but Barczyk drew back, their noses still pressed together.

"You wanna practice in my apartment?" he offered. "I've got a few things I could teach you."

"Yeah," Evan said. "I'd like that."

———

They only stayed in Pittsburgh long enough to play Buffalo again (this time with a loss, though both Evan and Vassiliev scored) and the Chicago Storm (a low-scoring 1-0 win where Barczyk drew three penalties). In the five days they were in town, Evan had spent three of them at Barczyk's apartment. Not that he'd seen more than the bedroom as they'd stumbled down the hallway, kissing and undressing before unceremoniously pushing each other onto the bed and getting off as quickly as possible.

He never stayed long after. Barczyk would kiss him and then pop off the bed and into the shower. It wasn't so much a dismissal as an invitation to escape that Evan always took. They had a good thing going, but he was pretty sure it was limited to friendly blowjobs. He didn't want to rock the boat by suggesting he wanted more than that. Because he didn't, and he got the impression that Barczyk didn't either. This was a casual, mutually beneficial hookup. And it was working out well for them on the ice: their line had found the chemistry that'd been lacking earlier in the season, and they were on fire.

Though Evan did wonder what would happen if he stayed. If he were still there when Barczyk got out of the shower. Would they make out lazily on the couch before a second round? Or would they order takeout and watch TV? Would Evan spend the night for once? If he did, would they sleep in each other's arms?

The one time he'd felt brave enough to try, he'd lingered on the edge of Barczyk's bed and listened to him sing an off-key rendition of *Shake it Off*. All Evan had to do was stay put. Barczyk would be surprised, but the worst that would happen is they'd hang out. He was sure Barczyk wouldn't be a dick about it—he saved that for opponents on the ice.

But then Barczyk's cat had sauntered into the room. She'd looked at Evan with a feline air of superiority, like how dare he still be here when her owner was done with him. She'd sat there in the doorway, looking at him and judging him.

So yes. Evan had been chased away by a cat. Not his finest moment.

"There any good mini-golf courses in Baltimore?" Barczyk asked as he plopped down next to Evan on the plane. "Dalton says the one in San Fran sucked ass."

"I did not," Dalton protested. He was sitting across the aisle with Winchester, an UNO deck on the tray table. "I said that I thought it must not be a good course 'cause it gave Abs a headache instead of taking it away. Bro totally tanked the last few holes, and he never does that. I mean, he did when he hurt his shoulder last season, but normally he's golden."

Evan tensed at the mention of his shoulder. His Barczyk-injured shoulder. He worried that Dalton would remember it was Barczyk who'd nearly sent Evan on Injury Reserve, and...what? Would Evan have to say there were no hard feelings? Or would Barczyk apologize months and months too late? Evan wasn't sure what he wanted, but he didn't want to say any of it publicly. He didn't want Barczyk forced into an apology he didn't feel.

Worse, he didn't want to hear Barczyk say he wasn't sorry at all.

So Evan quickly said, "It's November, guys. I doubt there'll be much mini-golf until we hit Nevada and Texas."

Everyone accepted his redirection back to mini-golf, and Evan let out a shaky breath.

"It shouldn't be so bad in Maryland," Barczyk countered. "They're in the south, right?"

"They're only one state farther south than us." Winchester shuffled the UNO cards. "They're not fucking Florida. You two playing or just yapping? Dalty cannot handle the distraction when we play. As if this isn't a kids' game."

"Deal me in," Barczyk said. "Abs?"

He shook his head. "I'm gonna nap."

"Bor-ing." Barczyk winked before turning his back to him, full attention on the UNO game. Though Evan appreciated that he leaned back against Evan just a smidge, a comforting gesture that helped Evan relax enough to drift off.

26

Baltimore was a tough one. They lost 4-1, which was doubly depressing since it'd been the Blue Crabs who had knocked them out of the playoffs in May. Evan didn't think the Crabs were all that much better than them, but seeing them again and hearing the crowd had brought back bad memories. The Crabs had gotten in their heads before the Riveters ever took the ice, and it showed up again and again on the scoreboard.

"You didn't even fight someone," Vassiliev grumbled in the locker room after the game. "We got our butts kicked and nothing to show for it."

"I tried!" Barczyk protested. "I couldn't get anyone to bite. Not even Nilsson! He's been harder to piss off ever since he made up with his brother or got a boyfriend or left Portland or whatever the fuck it was that made him level-headed."

He looked disgusted, though Evan suspected he was more frustrated that he couldn't get under Lars Nilsson's skin anymore as opposed to anything Nilsson had actually done.

"That team's been locked in the past couple of years," Evan offered. "They get some of the fewest penalties of any team."

"Locked in," Barczyk mocked. "They've got no fighters is what it is, so they've gotta avoid playing rough altogether. Look at their captain. Jake Campbell's a pipsqueak—"

"Isn't he taller than you?" Vassiliev asked. "Like everybody?"

"—and barely throws the body. No wonder they got clobbered in the Conference Finals. If you can't play tough hockey, you ain't bringing home the Cup."

Evan said nothing. He'd come to appreciate the physicality Barczyk brought to the game, but he still didn't think instigating fights had a place in hockey. Pushing and shoving in front of the net or along the boards, fine. Tricking someone into throwing a punch, kind of dumb.

"You know who *will* fight you?" Vassiliev said later after they'd had their turn with the media. "We go to Philly next, yes? They will not make things easy for you."

The hair on the back of Evan's neck bristled. You didn't just leave the Philadelphia Gliders and expect there to be no hard feelings among the fans. Philly fans were passionate, to put it politely, and took every player's departure as a personal offense. The more beloved the player had been, the longer Philadelphia held their grudge and the more vocal they were for blood.

If it were someone like Evan, someone mild-mannered and flying under the radar, it would only be a few boos here and there when he got the puck, and their interest would wane at the end of the season.

Riley Barczyk had been one of the most popular players in Gliders' recent history. They'd eaten up his antics and relished every hit, every punch, every takedown. It didn't help that there was nothing quiet or subtle about Barczyk's playing: the fans would know he was there, the Gliders would know, and both would do their best to show Barczyk that they didn't appreciate him being on the wrong side of the ice.

Probably for the rest of Barczyk's career.

"They didn't make it easy when I played for them, either," Barczyk quipped. "Ten years no playoffs, but the fans got the balls to tell us how to play. I ain't playing for charity. I'd like another Cup, thank you very much."

"And you think you could do that in Pittsburgh?" Evan asked.

175

He'd wanted so desperately to make the NHL, then to get his footing with his team, and then to get a solid contract. It wasn't that Evan didn't want to win the Stanley Cup, it was more that it was so far down on the list that he hadn't let himself think about it the past few years. Sure, he'd indulged last season when they were in the playoffs, but he'd come so far and fought so hard. He told himself he was satisfied with what he had.

He had to be. Chasing the Cup was The Dream, but it was so damn hard. Players way better than him worked their entire careers for it and never won. Evan could play his heart out, but if his team wasn't up to it, it'd always be out of reach.

Barczyk shrugged. "I don't see why not," he said. "We get our foot in the door come April, we'll see what happens."

Vassiliev stood up and flicked Barczyk's ear on his way out of the locker room. "Try not to get murdered in Philly," he said. "Can't win the Cup if you're dead."

———

In Evan's hotel room, when his chest was covered in come and Barczyk was cleaning himself up with a washcloth, Evan asked, "You're not worried about Philly at all?"

Barczyk froze for a split second, then chuckled. He tossed aside his washcloth and got another. Evan heard the faucet run before Barczyk hopped into the bed next to him and cleaned up his chest.

"No, I'm not worried about Philly," he said while he worked. "They'll go at me hard, but it's not my first rodeo. I knew this was coming the moment I left, and I knew it'd be worse once I picked Pittsburgh."

"You could get hurt," Evan insisted. He wasn't sure where the worry came from, but he wanted Barczyk to take this seriously.

"Abs, it's hockey. I could get hurt literally at any time. I once had a goalie take himself out for three weeks because he stepped on a puck while coming onto the ice. I had a teammate in Squirts give himself a concussion because he smacked himself on the benches after retying his skates. I even had a coach sneeze so hard once that he gave himself a hernia."

"Which is why most people don't go looking for more danger. What happens if—?" Barczyk pinched his nipple, and Evan wiggled out of his grasp. "Hey, quit it."

"You up for a friendly wager?" Barczyk asked.

"What is it?" Evan was instantly suspicious. He wasn't sure he trusted what Barczyk's idea of a 'friendly wager' might be, but he was too curious not to at least ask.

"Let's see who gets more hits in Philly."

Evan didn't like that he was still lying down and had to look up at Barczyk, so he sat up. They were eye level, though it didn't help him read what was going on in Barczyk's head any better.

"But they'll be after you," Evan said. "All night."

"Oh, 100%." That toothless grin. "Scared of a challenge?"

What was he doing here? Was he trying to distract Evan, or was he trying to convince Evan that this was the right way to play?

...or was he worried about what Philly might do to him, so he was trying to get Evan's help deflecting their attention?

A month ago, Evan would've scoffed at that. Riley Barczyk wasn't scared of anything. Not old teams, not bigger players, not the hits or the fights, not his reputation. He didn't need help and certainly wouldn't ask for it.

It felt like he was asking for it now.

"What's the wager?" he asked, trying to sound aggravated about it.

"Well, if you get more hits than me," Barczyk said, pausing slightly before his big reveal, "I'll let you fuck me."

Evan's brain short-circuited. He sat there, unable to process what he'd heard for so long that Barczyk felt the need to keep talking, which only made it worse.

"Hey, it's okay," Barczyk said. "If you lose, you don't owe me anything. You're new to laying the body. I'm not like trying to trick you into anything here. I know it's a long shot and all that. And even if you win and change your mind, that's cool."

It was Barczyk's babbling that did it. Evan shook loose the cobwebs in his head so his brain could boot back online. Before he could think it over, he interrupted: "Okay." He held out his hand. "If I get more hits than you in Philly, I get to fuck you."

Barczyk grabbed his hand and shook it a little too hard and a little too long. "Deal."

Riley

RILEY HATED UNO, BUT HE LIKED HAVING SOMETHING TO do with his hands. With Abs napping beside him, he needed a distraction, especially when Abs looked so fucking handsome in his blue suit. Like, not fair. Not fair at all.

Evan Abernathy was, in general, not fair. He was attractive and nice and put up with Riley, which was a trifecta Riley hadn't encountered much in his twenty-eight years. And he played hockey, which was a huge bonus. All of these things would be great in a guy who was into Riley despite Riley being so...so *Riley*.

The problem was that he still wasn't sure Abs was into him like that.

Oh, Abs was into the sex stuff. He maybe hadn't figured out if he's bi or gay or pan or whatever, but men didn't suck dick that enthusiastically without being a little queer. Riley hadn't forgotten what Dalty had said about Abs being ace. Even if that weren't the case, it sounded like Abs was going from 0 to 100 and hadn't given himself the time to adjust.

Riley didn't want to fall for a straight-ish guy. He also *really* didn't want to be used in Abs' gay experimenting.

Not that he was opposed to experimenting. That was how he'd

ended up where he was, after all, but he tried to be upfront with his hook-ups. And back when he was young and dumb (er...young*er* and dumb*er*), those hook-ups had never lasted long enough for feelings to get involved.

Feelings were starting to get involved here.

It was on him for getting himself into this mess. It was a bad idea to fool around with teammates, and a worse idea to fall for someone who wasn't emotionally available for a relationship with another man.

Was *Riley* emotionally available for a relationship? Hmm, he might need to figure out an answer to that one before he got carried away. Pretty shitty of him to judge Abs when he didn't have his own shit figured out.

Dalty won another round of UNO. Riley tossed over his stack of cards in disgust. He had to draw twenty friggin' cards because he didn't have a blue! He didn't even get a wild or a +2 or anything from that stack. What a stupid game.

"You playing again?" Dalty asked as he shuffled the deck.

"Sure," Riley grumbled. What the fuck else was there to do?

They arrived in Philadelphia just before noon, and everyone was given an hour to settle in before they had to head out for practice. An hour wasn't much time, but maybe he could figure out which was Abs' room and they could—

"Barczyk. A moment, please."

Riley froze. Uh oh. He turned on his heel and walked back to Coach Jack with his hands buried in the pockets of his suit jacket, wondering if he should apologize in advance or play dumb.

Play dumb? Bro, you have no idea what you did. You are *dumb.*

"Yes, sir?" Riley asked. He might be a jackass on the ice, but his very Catholic mother had instilled in him a healthy respect for authority. Especially when said authority controlled your career.

"How are you doing, Barczyk?" Coach Jack asked, his expression maddenly unreadable. "You settling in with the team all right?"

Riley shrugged. "I'm doing fine. Can't complain. The boys took me in, no problem." Most usually did. He could only remember one time a guy never warmed up to him—they'd fought before, and Riley had broken his nose or something, he couldn't remember—so he'd just kept his distance. They were adults and professionals. If people on the Riveters didn't like him, they kept it to themselves, and he did the same.

Coach Jack nodded. His blue eyes were laser-sharp as he assessed Riley. "You ready to face the Gliders tomorrow night?"

"Why wouldn't I be?" he huffed. "I ain't injured."

"It can be hard to face former teams. Lots of emotions. Lots of pressure." He trailed off, giving Riley a chance to weigh in.

"We already played the Nor'easters," he hedged. "You didn't seem concerned then."

"Because I wasn't, and I'm not now. But you and I both know there's a world of difference between Vermont and Philadelphia."

Riley opened his mouth to say something asinine, remembered who he was talking to, and thought better of it. When did anyone give him credit for all the times he *didn't* open his big fat mouth?

"Yes, sir," he said instead.

"I'm tired of the media asking me about this game," Coach Jack continued. "I hate this kind of storyline. Makes the game all about one player when we're trying to build a team that can go all the way. Granted, the fans eat this up."

"They sure do." He'd gotten used to the theatrical side of professional sports when he joined the league, and he'd taken advantage of the spectacle that went along with it. It was how people knew his name, after all: Riley Barczyk, league pest. He was proud of that notoriety.

Abs doesn't approve.

The thought came out of nowhere, and he reeled a little. Why did it matter if Evan Abernathy did or didn't approve of how Riley played hockey? He didn't play for anyone but himself. Besides, if he played by everyone else's rules, he wouldn't even have been drafted.

"If I were a Gliders fan"—Riley struggled to tune back in as Coach Jack kept talking—"I'd be happy if my team won and showed the league they don't need you. But if I were a Riley Barczyk fan, which I am, I'd want to see his triumphant return to a city that was dumb enough not to lock him down for another season. So, which storyline are they going to be running?"

On the one hand, he appreciated Coach Jack taking time to talk to him one-on-one, period. That wasn't a courtesy every coach gave, especially not for an experienced bottom-six player who was doing his job. On the other hand, he fucking hated this babying bullshit.

"No storyline needed," Riley said. "They're just another team. Same as the last game. Same as the one after. They're not in my head."

"Let's hope you're in theirs," Coach Jack said. "Feel free to play rough. I hate losing the Battle of Pennsylvania. Nothing makes Pittsburgh more ornery than losing to fucking Philadelphia."

"Yes, sir." Then Riley made his escape before Coach Jack could extend their heart-to-heart.

He bypassed the elevator, taking the steps two at a time up to the fourth floor to forget the conversation. He meant it. He didn't give a shit that he was playing the Gliders. They'd come at him hard to make a point, and he assumed he'd match their intensity without even thinking about it.

That didn't mean that this game was meaningless, though. He had a lot riding on it.

If you get more hits than me, I'll let you fuck me.

His foot caught on a step, and he almost stumbled into a wall. Instead, he only jammed his toe, and he cursed under his breath all the way to his room.

———

Riley had, in his opinion, done a very admirable job of ignoring the crowd. Not completely, obviously, because where was the fun in that? The fans still trying to get his autograph, he gave it to them. The ones with more creative signs during warm-ups (whether positive or negative), he posed for them. For the little girl wearing a Barczyk jersey, he gave her a stick. And the group of teenagers who gave him the finger, he pretended he was going to toss them a puck over the glass, then dropped it back on the ice and skated off.

"And now to honor Riley Barczyk and his three seasons on the Gliders, please turn your attention to the Jumbotron!" the announcer boomed over the crowd. Riley leaned over the bench to stare up as the screen showed nothing but him. His favorite kind of entertainment.

He'd expected a tribute video before the game. This one was nicer than the previous ones the Kings and Nor'easters had done for him. Way better than the one from the Rough Riders. That one had looked like an intern had made it an hour before the game and had included a clip that hadn't been him at all. Dicks.

The Gliders, for all their faults, did him right. There were interviews from the coaches and other players, and the highlights were legit. Great goals, pristine passes, and of course the hits. Chef's kiss to them on the selection there. They even got his fight two seasons ago with Dustin Crowne when he'd knocked out the poor bastard.

" 's a good punch," he said and turned to joke with Abs about it. "Maybe one of these days you'll—" He stopped short at how pale Abs looked. "Hey, you okay?"

"They going to show *every* hit you ever made?" Abs' voice was shaky, but not like he was angry or annoyed. More like he was worried.

"Nah," he said and nudged Abs' shoulder. "We'd be here all night. We got a hockey game to play." He'd hoped that would be enough to get a smile or maybe an eye roll, but Abs' eyes stayed fixed on the screen like he could turn it off by sheer force of will.

And then it clicked.

Shit.

Riley had to wait for the applause as the video ended. He waved at the crowd, boo-cheering him, and winked for the cameras. It was a nice moment, but he was happy to see it done: he was officially no longer a Philadelphia Glider, and so didn't have to feel bad for what came next.

As things settled down for the start of the game, he leaned in close to Abs who jumped at the sudden proximity.

"Look, Abs," he said, as low as he could over the noise of the arena. "I'm sorry if I stressed you out with our deal. I don't give a shit if you don't get a single hit."

"Are you trying to back out?" Evan asked. He didn't look sick anymore. Rosy-cheeked and with lips pressed into a thin line, Abs looked about ready to shove Riley over the boards onto the ice.

Riley raised an eyebrow and took a moment to admire what an angry Evan Abernathy looked like.

The verdict: kinda hot.

He made a mental note to rile Abs up more often. This wasn't the time or the place, though. Not about this.

"I'm not," he said gently, though he thought most of it was lost in the roar of the crowd as the game started. "It's just a lot of pressure, and I didn't want to...." There was a lot he could say here, but the honest answer was he didn't want to ruin things. He couldn't say that, because that would mean there was a thing and it could be ruined.

Luckily, Abs didn't push. "It's fine." He swallowed, his Adam's apple fucking delicious as it bobbed. "I'm looking forward to it."

The universe decided that was the time for them to prove it: Moreau dumped the puck and rushed over for a line change.

Riley had been one of the resident Tough Guys™ on the Gliders. With him gone, that only left Brock Warner, a large defenseman who never went out of his way to deliver hits but could send guys flying if he wanted to, and James Marsh, their fourth line center who'd learned from Riley that throwing his body could earn him minutes. He had none of Riley's finesse with the puck or with drawing penalties, so Riley figured Marsh would be his biggest problem tonight.

As expected, the Gliders didn't play nice. They were definitely targeting him. Not always physically, but with tight coverage and challenging him way more than they did Abs or Vassy. Their mission was clearly to keep Riley off the score sheet; giving him a few bruises was just a bonus. He'd been a target before and didn't mind it. Facing an old team gave him the advantage of knowing how all of them played...and knowing exactly how to piss them off.

At the next face-off when the ref's back was to him, he knocked Fernsteiger's stick out of his hand. There was no payoff on that one for a couple of shifts, but it drew a slashing call when Fernsteiger tried to do the same stunt to Riley but wasn't smart about his timing and did it right in front of the ref.

When Pope iced the puck, Riley knew he wouldn't be able to get to it fast enough, but he still skated in hard specifically so he could snow the goalie. He knew Mackintosh was pretty chill for a goalie and wouldn't mind too much, but he also knew Warner was on the ice. He oversold the crosscheck a touch, going limp right as Warner hit him so he'd flop spectacularly.

"Not smart. You made him mad," Mackintosh said just before Warner landed on top of him.

"Barzy, you little shit!" Warner yelled and pushed Riley's face against the ice. He hadn't liked Riley's bullshit much when they were team-mates, no surprise he liked it less now. "Give me an excuse to pummel you! I dare you!"

Before Riley could answer him, the weight pressing onto his back lifted. When Riley pushed himself off the ice, he turned and saw Abs dragging Warner away. Warner, for his part, seemed surprised that someone could drag him anywhere. Using Warner's confusion to his advantage, Riley pushed to his feet and went to intervene on Abs' behalf. Warner wasn't much of a fighter, but he was still way more skilled than most guys. He'd give Riley a run for his money—no way Riley could let Abs get his ass handed to him.

"Hey, no harm done." Riley grabbed a fistful of Abs' jersey and yanked. Abs didn't move at first—if anything, he tightened his grip on Warner—but another hard tug, and he let Riley pull him away. "See, we're all friends."

Warner glared at them both. "Friends," he scoffed. "Barzy, we weren't friends when you lived here."

"Aww, Warner, you're breaking my heart." Riley skated backwards with Abs in tow. They had a lot of ice to cover for that icing call. "I've missed you so much. I thought we could have a movie night and paint each other's nails."

Warner only rolled his eyes and went to his bench, muttering what sounded a lot like, "Fuck off."

A whistle blew. "Riveters! Let's go!" the far ref called. "Stop dicking around! It was an icing, not a timeout!"

Riley shot a thumbs-up to the ref that hopefully wasn't too patron-izing. "Don't get in a fight," he told Abs. "We're counting hits, not punches."

"What's the difference?" Abs mumbled. Riley couldn't tell if it was a joke. He chose to think it was.

"We'll check the stats after the game," Riley said. "I've only got two so far, I think. Officially."

"No bonus points for snowing the goalie?" That one was *definitely* a joke.

"Nah. It'll get me some comments on the fan blogs, though." He grinned, happy to have things the way they belonged.

Him and Abs, playing hockey. Who gave a shit about the other team?

27

EVAN HADN'T SEEN MUCH OF BARCZYK SINCE THEY'D LANDED in Philly. From the second they got off the plane to the moment they could safely escape into the hotel, the media had hounded Barczyk. Their closed practice had been the only respite, keeping out the reporters who'd crowded around the arena entrance and begged for locker room access. During a friggin' practice! It would've driven Evan crazy, especially when fans spotted them and added to the chaos, but attention had never seemed to bother Barczyk.

He thrived on it.

Evan hadn't bothered trying to see Barczyk after practice—Barczyk had stayed after the rest of the team had cleared out of the locker room, slowly working through everyone with media clearance as they waited for their sound bites—and took his dinner to his room for some peace. He took some melatonin in the hope of knocking himself out. The more time he had to think, the more he'd freak himself out.

Because if he started thinking, sooner than later he'd have to think about the deal he'd made.

Tomorrow night, he might be having sex with Riley Barczyk.

Which was absurd! He'd gone into the season hating Barczyk! Also, straight! None of this made any sense!

It was also ridiculous to think this meant any more or less than what they'd already been doing. They'd been having sex for weeks. The only difference between that stuff and this was whatever baggage he wanted to put on it.

Unfortunately, his brain wanted to put a lot of baggage. Like he could still say he wasn't gay, but that was the point where he'd have to acknowledge he maybe was a tiny bit.

But this whole situation was easy to avoid! He could lay a few hits to appease Barczyk without giving it his all, then he would lose their deal and nothing would happen. There was no reason this had to be a thing at all.

Of course, every time Evan considered it, he found himself grinding his teeth. Baggage or not, he really wanted to win. He'd never allowed himself to imagine fucking Barczyk; as soon as Barczyk had offered, it was all Evan could think about. Evan was helpless, too weak to refuse what Barczyk was so willing to offer, which meant he'd be as physical as possible against Philly.

More physical than he'd ever been. Barczyk got hits as easily as he took shots. It was like breathing or skating for him, barely a consideration. In some strange alternate reality where Barczyk didn't want to play physical tomorrow night, it wouldn't matter: the Gliders wouldn't let him walk out of this one without a few bumps and bruises to show for it.

Whatever. It at least gave him an excuse if someone asked Evan why he'd suddenly tried to bully his way through a game. He could say he was looking out for his linemate, which was true. That he might get rewarded for it later was nobody's business.

"Stop thinking," he grumbled to himself. He rolled over, took another melatonin, and this time blissfully drifted off into oblivion.

———

Game day was more of the same: it was Riley Barczyk versus all of Philadelphia, per every sports news outlet. Admittedly, it felt like that. A lot of obscene gestures and rude comments were directed their way as they went from the hotel to the arena, all of them met with Barczyk's wide grin. He looked a little tired, though; Evan wondered if Barczyk had slept well, and if he hadn't, what had kept him up.

Not that Evan got a chance to ask. Evan might as well not have been there for how little Barczyk said to him in the locker room. There were a lot of cameras, so he got it. There was rarely such a thing as a private conversation in the locker room, and this was almost as bad as playoffs. Vassiliev and Evan both had to scooch down the bench to make room and stay out of the limelight.

On the ice, it should've been business as usual, but still no. Evan watched Barczyk from a distance as he worked the crowd during warm-ups. Just like when he'd first arrived in Pittsburgh, the fans sure loved to hate him.

"This will all go to his head," Vassiliev said. He sounded amused. "I don't know how we'll survive if his ego gets any bigger."

Evan laughed because he was supposed to, but he didn't have the heart to say anything. Instead he waited by the bench in their usual spot, stickhandling and trying not to notice how quickly the time was disappearing. With only two minutes left and most of the team already back in the locker room, Evan decided to join them. He spared one last glance at Barczyk, rocking back against the boards so that they shook as fans banged on the other side, before disappearing down the tunnel.

Instead of being ready to play, Evan felt more off-kilter than before. He hated to admit it, but he was a little hurt that Barczyk was too busy for him. They hadn't done their butt-tap ritual. It was stupid to miss something so childish. He'd never wanted to do it in the first place. It was just to humor Barczyk.

Excuses were easy to find. None of them made him feel any better.

———

"Smart hockey, people!" Coach Jack reminded them again and again, whenever they got on or off the ice. He was hammering it into their heads because the Gliders had come out hard. They had a chip on their shoulder about Barczyk, no doubt about it, and kept taking potshots at them. Even the veteran players needed the reminder, because they looked about ready to pick a fight.

"Smart. Hockey!"

Normally, Evan would be all on board for that. Smart, non-physical hockey was what he'd always aspired towards. But tonight, there was more on the line than accolades and standings points. For the first time in his entire hockey career, from when he first laced up as a kid until now, Evan wasn't trying to play disciplined. He was there to hit anyone who got too close to Barczyk, and hopefully reap the rewards for it.

It wasn't just about the bet with Barczyk. Sure, Evan wanted to fuck Barczyk, but he saw the way the Gliders were targeting him. After Brock Warner all but tackled him to the ice, a protective instinct had ignited in Evan. These jerks had encouraged Barczyk to play the roughest style of hockey possible, their fans had cheered when Evan had hurt his shoulder, and now that he wore a different jersey, they were pissed at him.

Barczyk, though? He was always defying Evan's expectations. A rough player going against his former team—especially a team like the Gliders—seemed like the perfect opportunity for him to run wild. He didn't. Barczyk played the same as always, physical and aggressive, but no worse than usual. If anything, he was more reserved. Not because he wasn't trying to get under people's skin, because he definitely was, but he was more strategic about it. Like instead of throwing stuff at a wall to see what stuck, he was a laser-guided missile going for a precision strike.

So far, the refs had let it all go. Everyone, Evan included, got rougher and rougher. There wasn't a thirty-second stretch of game without someone getting hit. What had started as everyone-targeting-Barczyk had spilled over so that every line was doing their best to retaliate for something dumb someone had done earlier. By the end of the second, Evan didn't think anyone knew what offenses anyone was upset about anymore. They were fired up, and no amount of pleas from the coaches could do much about it.

"This is kinda fun," Barczyk said as they got ready to start the third period. "It's like a playoff game, except with no stakes."

"So I'm getting my ass kicked for nothing?" Vassiliev scoffed. There were murmurs of agreement down the bench.

"You know it's bad when even Abs is roughing guys up," Woodward said. "You see the way he threw Warner around like a rag doll? Somebody find a photo of that later and send it to me. I'm gonna make it my lock screen."

Evan raised his shoulders as if he could disappear into his jersey. "It wasn't that big of a deal."

"It was fucking fantastic," Barczyk said. He was chewing his mouth-guard, holding it right next to his missing tooth. "I'm gonna give him so much shit for that after the game."

"Let's focus on getting out of Philadelphia in one piece," Coach Jack said. "We're up a goal. I want smart fucking hockey. I'm gonna brand it on all of your foreheads. This is not a playoff game, and I want the intensity saved for later in the season. We are a playoff-bound team, and the Gliders aren't. We are not letting them dictate the play here. Clean checks, then you skate away."

"I'll play as clean as they do," Woodward said once Coach Jack's attention was elsewhere. Evan was inclined to agree.

"Five minutes to go," Barczyk whispered to him as they skated out for a face-off deep in the Gliders' zone. "Think we're about tied in hits."

Evan shivered. He had no idea if it was true. He'd only been able to keep track of his own hits for the first two shifts, then he'd been too distracted trying to play this weird version of hockey that felt more like football. All he knew for sure is that both of them had been active.

Evan won the face-off, and he had to wrench his head back into the game.

They spent most of the shift in the offensive zone, though they had garbage chances. When the Gliders regained the puck, Evan prepared to go for a line change because he was gassed.

Except the Gliders defenseman with the puck, instead of making the smart play and passing the puck up or clearing the zone, took aim and shot it point blank at Barczyk. He hit low on Barczyk's chest, right below the shoulder pads. It was too well-aimed to have been an accident, and even from fifty feet away, Evan could see Barczyk wince in pain and then snarl.

He could see it happening, the way Barczyk was about to lose it on his former teammate.

Usually, he'd stay out of it. Finish his line change and let things sort themselves out.

Evan turned on his heel and raced back. He hadn't planned on doing anything other than keeping Barczyk out of trouble, but the defenseman lifted his stick like he was about to swing it at Barczyk, and Evan's aim shifted. He no longer cared about stopping Barczyk from doing something stupid; he was too busy being the stupid one.

Bam!

Because the guy had no idea Evan was coming, he never braced for the hit. He stumbled as he tried to catch his balance, feet swinging wildly as he hit the ground and got his left leg tangled under him, and couldn't get his arms out to move to protect himself. His chest hit the ice first, then his head. It was an awkward fall, and Evan instantly regretted causing it.

"Sorry," he choked out. "Shit, I didn't mean—"

He was drowned out by a series of whistles. "Twenty-one, in the box! Two minutes for charging."

"I—" His jaw snapped shut. He couldn't argue the call. He'd done it, no question. In the moment, he hadn't thought twice about it. But part of him wanted to protest. *Look at how they've been acting all game! It's not my fault! I'm not a goon!*

Barczyk skated over and tapped the defenseman (who seemed fine, thank fuck, just shaken up) with the blade of his stick. "FAFA, amirite?"

"Get to your bench, Barczyk." The ref sighed in exasperation. "I've got enough to deal with. I don't need you causing more ruckus."

"I would never." He sent Evan a loaded look but did as he was told, leaving Evan to face the consequences of his actions.

"I appreciate it when you guys don't argue," the ref said as he led Evan to the penalty box. "Makes my job easier."

"Probably be easier if we didn't commit any penalties." Evan waited patiently for the attendant in the box to open the door for him.

The ref laughed. "That'd be nice, but I won't hold my breath. The day hockey players stop doing dumb shit on the ice, I'll hang up my skates and retire. You guys'll keep me plenty busy until then."

Evan settled into the box and looked up at the Jumbotron. They showed his very blatant charge from several angles, each one earning hysterical boos from the crowd. When Evan looked at the Gliders' bench, he was relieved to see the player joking around with his buddies.

He looked happy to have been the one to draw the first penalty and waved off a trainer who leaned over to talk to him.

No harm done, Evan supposed. But he wasn't proud of himself. He hadn't meant to hurt anyone, but Evan had meant to knock him over. Maybe that was how Barczyk did it. He'd found a way to harness that part of himself where he could focus on the check and separate it from the possible consequences. It had been freeing (and a little gratifying) in those seconds between deciding to teach that guy a lesson and realizing what he'd done.

"Don't sweat it, kid."

Evan turned to look at the penalty box attendant. The guy was in his late sixties and probably called every player a kid, so Evan let it go. "Sweat what?"

"You look upset about the penalty. Don't sweat it. You've been having a good game, and this team, they do a good job of getting under people's skin." He paused, giving Evan a chance to take in the screams of the arena and the sound of someone hitting the boards not far from them. "You accept you did a little too much, you sit your two minutes, and then you forget about it. You've gotta learn to let it go, son."

"Sure," he said. Then, "Thanks." He turned back to watch the game, because what else was there to do?

I accept that I did too much, he thought. *I went too far, and it's fine. I'm going to let it go and not let it change how I play this game.*

He repeated it like a mantra as the penalty timer ticked down. When the attendant opened the door for him, Evan jumped onto the ice, and the impossible seemed to happen.

He let it go and played some really good hockey.

28

"ABERNATHY!"

Evan froze as he took off his elbow pads. The locker room was filled with reporters, again crowded around Barczyk as they asked about the aftermath of his first game against the Gliders. As the lone goal scorer, Doyle had his own troupe of reporters around him, as did Farrell for the shutout. Evan very rarely had the press interested in him, and it always seemed out of politeness. A few extra quotes they could add to their collection and use if necessary.

But when he looked up, there was a trio of reporters in front of him with their cell phones out. They waited for his acknowledgement, so he swallowed the lump in his throat and said, "Hi."

Needing no more invitation, they went at it.

"This was an exceptionally physical game for the team," a woman with dark brown hair said. "You're not known for your hits, but you were among the most aggressive players out there for the Riveters. Could you tell us a little about that?"

"Uhh..." His brain, helpful as ever, refused to come up with any actual words for what felt like a full minute. "I was?"

The woman nodded, more patient than he deserved. "The Riveters recorded over forty hits tonight, which is closer to what we see in a playoff game. You were responsible for seven of those, including the one against Aimo Kinnunen in the third. You average less than a hit per game over your career. What was it about tonight's game that inspired you to change your performance?"

"Seven hits?" And then, because he wasn't as smart as he should be, he asked, "How many did Barczyk get?"

"Five," the woman said, her lips quirking in a smile. "Should I take it that's the answer to my question?"

The other reporters laughed, and Evan tried to smile but wasn't in control of his face at the moment. He'd beaten Barczyk. Holy shit.

"Wow, that's a first," he said, which earned another laugh. He joined in, letting their amusement catch hold so he wouldn't have room to think about later. "Yeah, Barzy's a good role model for how to play a physical game. It's not how I prefer to play, but there are some teams and some situations where it's needed. Tonight felt like one of those games."

"Did you feel the Gliders were being unnecessarily rough in how they played?"

Evan hesitated. He'd had enough media training to know what would sound good to fans and what might piss people off. As a kid, he'd hated when players had given generic, bland answers, but those were the safest.

"Philly's a physical team," he hedged. "They came out hard, so we matched that intensity."

"Did you think they were targeting Barczyk and your line?"

Evan felt like he was backed more and more into a corner. He did think that, and the reporters knew it. They just needed him to say it so they could get their sound clip and sensationalize a game that was over. The Riveters still had to play the Gliders two more times this season; the last thing he needed was a target on his back.

Though after that hit to Kinnunen, maybe he already had one.

"Teams know what kind of player Barzy is," he said, choosing to ignore the Gliders altogether. "Anyone who's smart tries to keep him contained, because he can cause a real mess for the other team if they're not careful."

Sensing they wouldn't get anything juicy out of him, they offered a few more questions about the game and the upcoming schedule. He answered politely, even if he didn't expect to see a word of it used in their coverage of tonight. Which was fine—Evan didn't make it into sports blogs often, and he kind of preferred it that way. He also didn't want to give the wrong impression. He was not an instigator who was going to deliver big hits all of a sudden.

Evan had showered and changed long before the media was done with Barczyk, so he let himself get shuttled back to the hotel. They had an afternoon flight to Pittsburgh, then an evening off. They'd have a whole two home games before they were off again. Four and a half days at his own condo. He used to look forward to those stretches at home, no matter how short, but all he wanted was to make tonight last as long as possible.

A bunch of the guys dragged him to the hotel bar to buy him a drink.

"You outhit Barzy in Philly," was all Lawson said as he ordered a round of shots and put the tab on Barczyk's room.

Evan wasn't in a rush—no matter how much he wanted to be—so he stayed with his teammates for an hour. Long enough for them to be shooed away by the coaching staff.

"No repeats of Portland," Coach Mel warned as Evan and a few others disappeared in the elevator. "Finish your drinks upstairs in your rooms."

There was a lot of grumbling, but they did as they were told. When the elevator let them out on the floor where most of them were staying, they grouped up and disappeared into either Woodward's, Doyle's, or Calhoun's room. They were too loud to notice Evan hang back, and he was glad he didn't have to make any excuses as he fished into his pocket for his room key—

And found not one, but two keycards.

He took them out and stared at them in confusion. Two identical cards, except one had a piece of paper with the hotel's stationary attached.

Room 445
Come get your prize ;)

A strangled noise escaped Evan's throat before he could stop it, and he closed his fist around the keycards. He looked up and down the hallway to see if anyone had heard him. Everyone was long gone, hidden away in rooms to continue celebrating in peace. No one was there to witness his heart trying to beat out of his chest.

With trembling legs, he walked in the opposite direction of his room. He found Room 445 next to the stairwell and stared at it. There was no way Barczyk had beaten him here. Should Evan wait until later? Give him a chance to settle in before he showed up, begging for his reward? Maybe he—

A door opened down the hall. "All right, all right!" Kates shouted. "I'll get some dang ice!"

Panicked, Evan did the only thing he could think to do: he put the keycard to the door and rushed inside before anyone could spot him.

The room was pitch black. It took him a few tries to find the light switch, and then he was blinded. He stumbled into the room as his eyes adjusted. When he got his bearings, he stopped short.

He was in Riley Barczyk's hotel room.

It was a stupid revelation to have, because he'd been in plenty of hotel rooms with Barczyk. He'd just never been in one of them without Barczyk. He wasn't sure why that mattered, but it did. It was the difference between being a guest versus being an intruder. It didn't matter that Barczyk had invited him: he wasn't there, so Evan shouldn't be.

He lingered in the middle of the room. But the only thing more awkward than staying would be leaving only to return later, so he sat at the edge of the bed. There were no real signs that Barczyk had stayed here last night. Housekeeping had made everything pristine once more, with only a few items cluttered by a duffle bag and next to the sink. Maybe it would've been easier if there was something personal in the space. A book or a pair of sunglasses or chapstick or something. Nope, it was a sterile hotel room that could've belonged to any of his teammates.

Was that the problem? Did he want to see evidence of Barczyk? Would a half-chewed mouthguard or boxing gloves help?

No, he thought as he grabbed the TV remote and put on the first movie he could find. A distraction would help.

He watched *Star Wars: The Empire Strikes Back* with painfully long commercial breaks until finally, *finally* the sound of the door unlocking interrupted. Evan turned off the TV and jumped to his feet, all nerves and a sudden jolt of desire that had him half-hard before Barczyk had slipped into the room. Barczyk froze when he saw Evan, then broke into a grin.

"Fucking goon," Barczyk said. He was still in his suit from the game, navy with a golden tie. Evan was too, though he hadn't noticed until just then. He should've changed, because his rapidly growing erection was straining against the suit pants and left him exposed to Barczyk's gaze. Barczyk had definitely noticed, because he licked his lips as he dragged his eyes down Evan's body.

"I didn't think it was possible to beat you." Evan's voice was so husky he didn't recognize it. Fists clenched at his sides, it took a painful amount of concentration to stand still. He wanted so badly to act, to devour Barczyk and take and take and take, but he didn't know how to start.

"I'm only human." Barczyk chuckled as he pulled off his suit jacket, revealing how fucking perfectly tailored his shirt was. It hugged every inch of muscle, from his chest to his biceps. Evan's mouth watered, and he swallowed thickly when Barczyk ran a hand down his own hard cock. "I've got my weaknesses."

And then they were all over each other. They collided halfway between the door and the bed, arms tangling together and lips meeting. Barczyk's hair was still a little damp from his shower, and Evan moaned as he buried his fingers in those familiar curls. He used his grip to tilt Barczyk's head back to deepen the kiss. Barczyk undid the buttons of Evan's shirt and wiggled it off him, then did the same for himself while Evan explored Barczyk's mouth.

Soon their bare skin pressed together. Barczyk grabbed Evan's ass to pull him closer. Their dicks were still trapped by layers of fabric, and their height difference made it such a tease whenever Barczyk rubbed against him.

"Bed?" Barczyk offered, like he could read Evan's growing frustration.

Not trusting himself to speak, Evan nodded. He let Barczyk push him onto the mattress and obeyed when he nodded for Evan to lie back against the headboard.

"I, uh..." Evan was distracted as Barczyk crawled onto the bed after him and undid his belt, ignoring the bulge of his dick. "I thought..."

You said I could fuck you were not words he was equipped to say out loud, so he let Barczyk work off his pants.

"Don't worry." Barczyk leaned down to kiss Evan's dick through his briefs, then ran his nose up the shaft. "I know what I promised." He pulled at the hem of Evan's underwear and sucked the head of his dick into his mouth.

"Oh, fuck." Evan fisted the sheets. "You and your fucking mouth."

Barczyk laughed, the vibrations going right to Evan's balls. He sucked Evan off for a few minutes, playing a dangerous game because Evan wasn't capable of lasting long when Barczyk put that talented tongue to work. Why hadn't he liked Barczyk, exactly? Fuck if he knew.

Too soon, Barczyk pulled off of him with a wet plop and finished undressing them both. Evan stayed still while he watched Barczyk dig through his bag for a bottle of lube and condoms.

"Condoms?" Evan asked, confused. "We get screened all the time—"

"It's cleaner." Barczyk tossed him one. "I just prefer it."

Evan put the condom on. He wasn't about to argue about safe sex. He'd just finished rolling it on when Barczyk straddled him. He stayed up on his knees, barely any contact between them, so Evan hooked his hands around his legs and rubbed the warm skin with his thumbs. A few months ago, he never would have thought of himself as so tactile.

There were a lot of things he was learning about himself.

"You ever done this before?" Barczyk asked as he popped open the lube container.

"This?" He shook his head.

Instead of teasing him about his inexperience, Barczyk nodded. "You ever try it on your own?"

Evan laughed nervously. "I hadn't even thought about it until you suggested it," he admitted. "But it's all I've been thinking about since."

Again, Barczyk didn't roll his eyes or mock Evan. He accepted his answer without comment and focused on squeezing a healthy amount of lube onto his fingers. "I'll make it fun, don't worry." He winked and moved his hand behind him.

Evan reached out and grabbed his wrist. "Can I...?"

Barczyk raised an eyebrow. "Open me up? Abs, not that I don't trust you, but you're new at this. I'm not interested in getting hurt 'cause we didn't do this right."

"Oh." He let go of Barczyk's wrist. "Of course. That's—"

"I'll show you how, though." He took Evan's hand in his and guided it to his ass. "Slow and steady, Abs. Slow and steady..." Evan put his hand over Barczyk's, feeling what Barczyk did as he explained it with raspy breaths. One finger tracing his rim before pushing inside, then two working him open. Barczyk took one of Evan's fingers with his and together they stretched him open. "Fuck yeah, like that. You learn quick, Abs..."

Barczyk took over when they got to three fingers, his dick dripping a steady stream of pre-come that had Evan's mouth watering.

"Almost done." Barczyk's cheeks were red, and there was a sheen of sweat on his forehead. "Lube."

Evan grabbed the bottle and slicked up his dick, the contact making him moan. He'd been so lost watching Barczyk, he'd forgotten his own arousal. This was the hottest thing he'd ever seen—how was he supposed to last long enough to see Barczyk come? He coated his cock with a generous amount of lube. He looked up and caught Barczyk watching him with lust-blown eyes.

"Ready?" Barczyk asked.

That was a loaded question. Evan was absolutely ready to feel Barczyk's tight heat wrapped around him. He'd never have thought he'd want this, but right now he needed it more than air. But was he ready for the consequences? Almost certainly not. For Barczyk, this was probably nothing, but for Evan, this was more than casual sex. This was a big step, and Evan was terrified of where it was leading him.

He wasn't ready to find out...but he also wasn't willing to turn back.

"I'm ready," Evan said.

Barczyk took over, nudging Evan to relax against the headboard. He lined Evan's dick against his hole, Evan holding his breath as he felt the first hint of pressure. And then he was pushing past the rim, Barczyk slowly sinking down. Inch by inch, Barczyk guided Evan's dick inside him while Evan did his best not to move, not to push, not to beg for more. It was driving him insane how good it felt, that promise of how much better it would be with Barczyk riding him. He was hypnotized by the sight of his cock disappearing, of Barczyk's eyes fluttering shut and the strain of his leg muscles, the way their breathing seemed to sync perfectly.

"Fuck," Evan muttered. "Fuck."

"Uh huh," Barczyk agreed as his ass pressed flush against Evan. He groaned and looked unsteady; Evan's hands settled on his waist, holding him in place. He resisted the urge to thrust up into Barczyk and instead just enjoyed this surreal, impossible moment.

He was balls deep in Riley Barczyk. What even was his life?

"Dunno why I'm always surprised," Barczyk said breathlessly, "when a big guy has a big dick."

That did it: Evan laughed, rescued from spiraling into a crisis. "I'm not that big."

"Easy for you to say." He shifted his hips, the sudden movement making Evan's fingers dig into his hips. "You're not being split open by your massive dick."

"That's—" His breath hitched as Barczyk clenched around him and he momentarily forgot English.

"Uh huh," Barczyk said proudly, like rendering Evan speechless was what he'd been going for this whole time. "Gimme a minute and I'll make it way better for you."

Evan wasn't sure that was possible, but he was in no position to argue. He was completely at Barczyk's mercy and wasn't as upset by it as he thought he'd be. Still, he didn't want Barczyk to win so easily, so he managed, "If you say so."

The wait was agonizing bliss: it gave him time to map out Barczyk's hip bones with his thumb, to enjoy the weight of him, and to soak up his warm body wrapped around his cock. It was more than he thought sex could be, and still his body craved more. This was too gentle, too subdued. He wanted to move, to claim or be claimed or get lost somewhere in between.

When Barczyk cleared his throat, Evan licked his lips in anticipation.

This was it, the more he so desperately needed, that he'd been willing to challenge everything he knew about himself for.

But what Barczyk said wasn't at all what he'd expected.

"Hey," he said. "I got a weird request."

Evan would do literally anything Barczyk asked him right now. "Uh huh?"

"Could you..." He bit his lip. His voice sounded strange, so unlike his usual self that Evan found a tighter grip on his sanity so he could pinpoint what was off.

"Could I...?" Evan asked and worried it might be something he wouldn't be able to give.

"Could you, uh, maybe call me Riley? Just for tonight?"

Oh shit. Barczyk was shy about asking for this. He looked so nervous and vulnerable, and somehow Evan had done that.

It's not just fooling around for him either, part of him warned. *You're both stepping off the deep end here. This is a bad idea. This is a terrible, crazy, stupid—*

Evan reached up and pulled him down, rubbing their noses together. "Okay," he said. "Riley." And then, for the first time, he kissed *Riley.*

It was different from kissing Barczyk, bizarre as that sounded. Barczyk was his annoying teammate, who was kind of a jackass. He was loud and obnoxious and didn't give a shit what people thought about him. He gave good hand jobs and better blowjobs and laughed about how messy it was afterward.

Riley was all those things too, obviously, but he was sweeter about it. He moaned into every kiss and shuddered when Evan touched him. He looked Evan in the eye as he rode him, slow at first like he knew Evan would lose it otherwise.

"Fuuuuck," Bar—*Riley* groaned loudly. Evan panicked briefly—someone might hear them, and there'd be no hiding what was making Riley sound like that—but then Barczyk moved faster, and Evan didn't have room to care about anyone or anything else. "I was so worried you wouldn't win that bet."

"Make...an easier...bet...next time..." Evan panted.

"Next time?" Riley laughed. "No way. You're not getting off that easy. What, you think because I like your dick you don't have to earn fucking me?"

"Jesus," Evan hissed. "You can't talk like that."

"Why not?"

You're going to make me come too soon didn't seem like the right thing to say, so Evan kept his mouth shut. Though given what Riley said next, maybe Evan shouldn't have.

"It was so fucking hot watching you smash into Kinnunen for me. I was going to do something really fucking stupid to him, but damn, that was so much better. Fuck me, I'm gonna watch that hit on repeat when I get home and jerk off to it."

"No, you're not." His cheeks burned, and his chest tightened with a confusing mix of pride and embarrassment.

"Swear to God. Hottest thing I've ever seen. Except maybe you on your knees sucking me off. No highlights of that, though."

"You're the worst." It only sounded a little fond.

"The worst? Don't make me stop. I swear, Evan"—Evan tried not to think about how his toes curled when he heard Riley say his name— "don't test me. I'll stop right now and make you tell me how amazing I am before—"

"Riley," he begged. "You know you're amazing." He teetered precariously on the edge. How was he expected to have a conversation under these conditions? "Please, I can't..."

"I do know I'm amazing." He grabbed Evan's hand and wrapped it around his dick, urging Evan to jerk him off while he kept up his grueling pace. "But I'd like to hear you say it."

Evan looked up into Riley's hazel eyes, and out tumbled a truth Evan hadn't fully appreciated until then: "You're amazing, Riley Barczyk."

29

Beep beep beep!

Evan woke up groggy and disoriented. That wasn't unusual, given how much he traveled and found himself in different but almost identical places. The hotel rooms blurred together, and it made it jarring when his alarm jerked him awake.

This morning was worse than usual, and his brain wasn't helpful in piecing together why. He reached out blindly, trying to find his phone and turn it the fuck off, but he found he couldn't move. His body tensed under the warm, heavy weight pinning him to the bed. And then the weight moved, elbowing him in the ribs before climbing over him to turn off the alarm.

"Snooze," Barczyk grumbled before collapsing right on top of Evan. He was draped across Evan's chest, their bare skin clammy in the places where the sheets offered no protection, and Evan remembered in perfect clarity where he was and how he'd ended up there.

He was in Barczyk's hotel room. They'd had sex. And then, in a fit of madness that he blamed on exhaustion, Evan had stayed the night. They never stayed the night.

Shit. Shit shit shit shit SHIT—

Evan took a deep breath, held it in, and then let it out until there was no air left in his lungs. Right. Not the time to freak out.

Very carefully, he wiggled out from underneath Barczyk. (*Riley*, some stupidly fond voice corrected, but he ignored it.) Barczyk didn't seem to notice. He stayed where he was, sprawled across the bed at a ridiculous angle with a tangle of sheets and pillows around him. That mess hadn't been from having sex, Evan was sure of that. Barczyk must be a restless sleeper, because there was no way that was Evan's doing. Maybe it'd make it easier to pretend he hadn't spent the night in bed with Barczyk, since Barczyk was unlikely to notice amongst the mess that someone else had been there.

As quickly as he could, Evan gathered his clothes and cursed himself for not having changed out of his suit beforehand. How the fuck was he supposed to sneak back to his room in his fucking game day suit? If anyone, *anyone* saw him, they'd know he hadn't slept in his room. Granted, they wouldn't guess he'd been balls deep in Barczyk, but he didn't want that kind of attention.

He was tempted to grab some of Barczyk's clothes, but that made him feel shitty. He already felt like an ass for running away; he didn't need to add stealing into the mix. So he put on his undershirt and briefs, bundled up his suit in a towel to hopefully limit the chances of someone spotting it, and slipped out of the room just as Barczyk's alarm went off again.

The hallway was empty—it seemed pretty early, thankfully—and he got to his room without any trouble.

Except the trouble had followed him, because as soon as he locked the door behind him, his head exploded in a mess of *what the fuck did I do last night am I gay do I have feelings for Barczyk what the actual fuck?*

A hot shower could soothe him out of this sort of anxiety spiral. How could the world be bad when you had a nice, relaxing shower to help you forget your troubles? Except every inch of skin he touched, he remembered that Barczyk had touched those same places. And then he had to deal with his dick being extremely interested in those memories, the same dick that had come inside Barczyk a few hours ago. Arguably the only reason he was in this mess was because his dick had no chill around Barczyk for some God-forsaken reason, and it had the audacity to get hard during his nice shower?

If he'd had the willpower to ignore it, Evan might've felt better. He didn't, and after jerking off to images of Barczyk riding him like a fucking pro, Evan was more miserable than he'd started the day.

How had he let things get so out of control? He did not like Riley Barczyk! He didn't like his stupid curly mohawk or his ridiculous missing tooth or the sound of his annoying voice or how he had to go on tiptoes to kiss Evan or how his hazel eyes looked more green after he came or how he could be teasing and patient at the same time or—

Evan pinched himself, because the list forming in his head didn't seem to have an end. Whether it was things he liked or disliked about Barczyk, it wasn't a good sign that he could rattle them off so quickly. Or that none of them were hockey-related.

"I'm so fucking fucked," he grumbled. He pulled on some clothes and headed downstairs for breakfast, determined to get some time away from Barczyk. Maybe food and caffeine would help him sort this out.

It did, but only a little. Piling a plate high with eggs and bacon, he grabbed a cup of coffee (and filled it with cream because as desperate as he was to get his mind off Barczyk, he didn't actually want to taste coffee), and found a seat at a crowded table between Dalton and Winchester.

"Fucking beast over here," Dalton said as he mussed Evan's hair. "That hit last night?" He did a chef's kiss, saw some ketchup on his fingers and licked it off, and then went back for more hash browns. "Fantastic, bro."

"I see Barzy's rubbing off on you," Winchester said.

Evan choked on his coffee. "What?"

"Barzy. Seems like he's rubbing off on you," Winchester repeated. "Like you learned how to deal a hit through osmosis or some shit."

"Oh. Right. Yeah, I guess." Evan kept his head down and poked at his food, no longer hungry. He needed to get himself together. If he didn't want people finding out that he and Barczyk were fooling around, he needed to not lose his shit every time Barczyk's name was mentioned. They were linemates, for fuck's sake! It was unavoidable.

Barczyk was unavoidable. Why had Evan let himself think this was okay? His questionable sexuality aside, the last thing Evan needed was the scandal of sleeping with another player, period. And how was he ever going to get space to figure things out when they saw each other basically every day?

"You all right?" Dalton asked as the table cleared out. "You barely ate."

"I've just got a lot on my mind." He forced a giant bite of eggs into his mouth, hoping Dalton would take a hint and not talk to him. Evan wasn't in the mood.

Dalton did not take the hint.

"What's up? Normally you only freak out about hockey stuff, and the season's been going pretty well for you. Your line's doing great."

Evan chewed and grunted.

"And I know the coaches are happy with your play lately. You've stepped it up this season with the physicality. I know S'more's got a couple seasons left on his contract, but JT's out after this season. If he signs somewhere else, they'll probably be ready to move you up to second-line center. The way you've been playing..."

Dalton continued to babble, and Evan let him. Hockey had always been the center of Evan's world. Maybe it could ground him now before he drifted too far off course.

———

Evan didn't see Barczyk until the plane ride back to Pittsburgh. He held his breath as Barczyk got on the plane. They made eye contact, and Barczyk headed toward him—

"Barzy! You in for some Mario Kart?"

Barczyk kept his eyes locked on Evan a few heartbeats longer before turning away and smiling. "Sure, bro. But I only play as Princess Peach."

With a Barczyk-free hour and a half ahead of him, Evan should've relaxed. Instead, his throat tightened uncomfortably, and his chest ached.

———

Abernathy
Minigolf ASAP.

Dalton
It's fucking November bro it's freezing out

Abernathy
The place in the strip is indoors
And they have milkshakes

Dalton
K but you're buying

Abernathy
Deal

"This is like a record, right?" Dalton asked as Evan scored another hole in one. It was his third in a row. "You're locked in."

He was. He needed to be. He took way too long at each hole, breathing in mini-golf and breathing out everything else while he lined up his shots. It'd been working so far: he'd only thought of Barczyk fifty times instead of a thousand.

Fifty-one, he corrected.

"So what's the issue, bro?" Dalton asked. "Mini-golf is for when you're stressed. What are you stressed about? You're having a good season."

Evan bent over to collect his golf ball and buy time to think it through. He liked Dalton. They were nearly the same age and had gone through the same development on the Riveters, and Dalton had been a great roommate and friend. Maybe he could confide in him a little, just enough to take some of the pressure off.

"I'm uh..." He stood back up and fidgeted with the ball. How much exactly should he say? "I've been hooking up with someone lately," he settled on, because it was true but didn't reveal much. No genders, no names, no locations.

"Oh, wow." Dalton seemed genuinely surprised. "That's a first. Congrats?" A pause. "Or maybe not, if it's leading to mini-golf levels of stress?"

They moved on to the next hole. "It is kind of stressing me out," he admitted. "I'm not good with this kind of...stuff."

Dalton nodded. "So end it?"

Evan stopped short. End it? Yeah, that was probably the most logical thing to do, but his knee-jerk reaction was *absolutely the fuck not.*

"Sorry," Dalton said. "Hit a nerve?" He dropped his golf ball and kicked it into place, not even looking at the course before hitting it down the purple turf. Evan made a face at the terrible form and the surprisingly terrible bounce that landed him at least three strokes away from the hole.

"Fuck, Dalty. Don't worry about hitting nerves. Worry about hitting the ball. How many times we gone putting, and you still suck?"

Dalton stared at him, blinking like Evan had just spoken French to him.

"What?"

"That is the meanest chirp you've ever said to me. Like, you're spot on, but wow. Usually it's all 'good try' or 'maybe next time do this' or 'not so hard' or some shit like that." He pointed at Evan. "You weren't nice about it, though. Like, wow, my feelings got a little hurt there."

"Sorry. I didn't mean—"

"Aaaand he's back." Dalton cut him off with a wave of his hand. "It's fine. I do suck at this, but I'm more here for the company than the, uh, sport. But if you wanna coach me through how to fix this fuck-up, I'm all ears."

They finished the last five holes like that, Evan finishing in one or two shots and then helping Dalton make his just over par. They returned their putters, then found a table in the back of the bar area and ordered some milkshakes.

"You sure know the way to a guy's heart," Dalton said after his first sip. The wording made Evan uncomfortable in ways he refused to think about.

"How are things going with your girlfriend?" Evan asked. "It was your one-month anniversary the other day, right?"

Dalton beamed. "Yeah, while we were in Maryland. I'm taking her out tomorrow after the game to this nice place downtown. She's the best."

"I'm glad," Evan said and meant it. It was good to see someone so helplessly in love and know it was working out. "Must not be easy for her, dating a hockey player."

"She's super busy with her work, so it's not too bad. Sometimes I'm in town and she's the one traveling. Dose of my own medicine, right?" Dalton's expression shifted, and he grew more serious as he asked, "Is that the problem with your hookup situation? That you travel too much?"

Evan wasn't sure what his face did, but it felt kind of like a grimace. "Not exactly."

Dalton raised his eyebrows, urging him to go on.

"It's just...I'm not much of a hook-up kind of guy. It's really casual, which I like, but when I'm with him, I can't always think clearly and—" He snapped his mouth shut. What had he just said?

There was a moment when it seemed Dalton didn't notice, but then his eyes went wide. He opened his mouth, closed it, opened it again, and then said, "So you've been hooking up with a guy? Is that why you're stressing?"

That was just the tip of the iceberg, but that was the safest answer. It was also very true that Barczyk's being male-shaped was one hurdle his mind was having trouble leaping over.

"Yes?" He realized it sounded like a question, so he added, "Yeah, kind of."

"I can see why that would...complicate things," Dalton said, brow pinched together. "Tell me to fuck off if this is none of my business, but is this an experience issue or are you worried you'd get in trouble with the team if they found out?"

The blood drained from his face. Oh God, if the Riveters found out he was having sex with Barczyk... "Both," he said. "Definitely both."

"Okay. Well, if your guy doesn't care about the inexperience, I don't think you should."

Evan pushed aside his milkshake. He'd lost his appetite. "It's not that I'm worried about the inexperience. I just...never thought of myself as gay. And I'm definitely not straight, even if this is just a random blip or exception or whatever. So every time I'm with him, it's like I'm a different person than I was before, and I don't know what to do with that."

"Do you not want to be attracted to men?" Dalton asked.

Evan thought about that. Was his problem that he had some sort of internalized homophobia that he was working through? Maybe. He couldn't remember ever being attracted to a guy before, not consciously, so it was more the abrupt shift in his internal compass that was freaking him out. Had it always been like this? How had he not noticed? Would he still be interested in men after this thing with Barczyk ran its course?

Would it run its course?

It wasn't just this sudden interest in men that was throwing him. It'd be a hell of a lot easier to figure this shit out if it weren't Barczyk. If he could've had this internal crisis about literally anyone else, it might've been easier to wrap his head around it. He didn't want to sort through questioning his sexuality while also navigating it with someone he'd thought he'd hated.

"No," Evan said. "I don't think it's that."

"Well, that's a relief. I don't think that's something you can change." Dalton took Evan's abandoned milkshake and started pouring it into his own. "So it's just kind of a weird adjustment for you, and you're stressing out about people finding out while you figure it out?"

Huh. That was a piece of it. Like, he could talk about this to Dalton because Dalton hadn't known Evan his whole life. Lately, Evan felt like he had no idea who he was anymore, and he didn't want his family back home hearing about this before he'd gotten an actual answer himself. Never mind that this could tank his career. There were some players in the league out, thanks in part to Lars Nilsson's very public self-outing a few years ago, but Evan wasn't blind or deaf. Not every team was as supportive as the Crabs, and Evan didn't want people around the league talking about him for this. He wasn't established enough to risk his career over something he was just finding out about himself.

But the biggest piece, the part that made Evan's stomach do flip-flops and his heart skip a beat, was that it was all because of Riley Barczyk. If Evan had already known he was gay, if he were already out among friends, if he already had the team's support, the fact that he craved Barczyk in a way he'd never craved anyone or anything before, that would've always scared him shitless.

"I'm worried what figuring it out might mean," he said. There were a lot of possibilities, twists and turns, and no obvious end point. Evan didn't know which one he was aiming for, never mind how to get there. "Do I figure it out on my own, or do I figure it out while I keep hooking up with this guy?"

Dalton's face scrunched up like he'd bitten into a lemon. "Uh, that might depend on the guy. But you can kinda do both, right? I assume he's local, and we're not in town that often. Think it through on the road and enjoy your nights together here. Win-win."

"Win-win," he repeated, defeated. If only being out of Pittsburgh meant any escape from Barczyk. It was ten times worse when they were in the same hotel and he knew Barczyk was only a few doors away. There five whole days in town, filled with practices and games, gave him no break. He'd just have to put some distance between them while he could. Clear his head and see if Barczyk was really as intoxicating or if Evan was getting caught up in the moment.

"Thanks," Evan said to Dalton as they headed to the parking lot. "This helped."

"No problemo. You helped me work up the nerve to ask out Jennie, so I owed you one." He pulled Evan into a hug and patted his back. "Good luck, bro. Hope it works out."

"Me too."

30

EVAN MANAGED TO AVOID BARCZYK FOR A WHOLE DAY.
There was an optional skate the next day, and while Barczyk took the
ice, Evan didn't. He went home and caught up on the chores that always
piled up while he was out of town, and when a message went out on the
team chat about meeting up, he said he was busy so Barczyk wouldn't
message him privately.

But he couldn't reasonably ignore Barczyk when they suited up for
their game against the visiting Ohio Otters. In the locker room, Evan
kept his eyes fixed on his gear as he got ready. He had no plan, but they
needed not to be suspicious. It hadn't been long enough for Evan to
forget that night in Philly, and he was sure it'd be obvious on his face if
he so much as looked at Barczyk. If he had to talk to him, they were
doomed.

On the ice during warm-ups, it felt safer. The growing crowd made
his problems seem insignificant. He was just one person of the thousands who were here, the thousands more still arriving. Evan Abernathy
sleeping with his teammate and having feelings about it seemed so dumb
in a place this big.

Better yet, it gave him the cover he needed to interact with Barczyk
and have no one think anything of it.

"Did we ever figure out a lucky number?" Evan skated to a stop beside Barczyk, his stick up and ready to smack him.

"My lucky number's seventy-three," Barczyk said, working his mouthguard from the left side of his mouth to the right. "So maybe not that."

"Twenty-one isn't sounding great either." He whacked Barczyk once, twice, and watched him drift a few inches forward each time. "We play it by ear?"

"Works for me."

They switched spots, and Evan leaned over, bracing himself. Barczyk stood behind him and whispered, "Don't worry, Evan, I'll go easy on you." And then backed away and hit Evan harder than he'd expected. Or it could've been what Barczyk said, because Evan went down hard, knees hitting the ice with a loud thud.

"Abs!" Barczyk cackled. "What the fuck? People are gonna think I'm beating you to death over here."

He hopped back onto his feet. "Well, *Riley*," he hissed and enjoyed the way Barczyk gulped. "I was a little blindsided by—"

"Oh shit, I forgot." Barczyk's attention had shifted behind Evan, and he pushed past him at a near sprint. "BRB!" he called over his shoulder and raced to center ice.

Evan stood there dumbfounded. He watched as Barczyk practically jumped into another player's arms at center ice. A player on the Otters, which was weird since Barczyk had never played for them. When the hug broke apart, Evan recognized Ryan Russell, alternate captain and very publicly out NHL player, pat Barczyk affectionately on the head.

They talked for a solid minute—Evan checked the timer on the scoreboard as it marked that warm-ups were drawing to an end—with both smiling and laughing. Evan didn't like or understand why he was clenching his jaw or that he was breathing so shallowly or the way he wanted to skate over there and insert himself in their conversation, but he relaxed as soon as the two took off their gloves to shake hands and went back to their respective teams.

It made him feel a little better when Barczyk came right back to him.

"So what's the game plan? We being responsible today or are we—?"

"You know Russell?" Evan blurted out, watching the other center.

Russell was at his bench talking with a teammate, looking relaxed and cheerful in a way Evan hadn't felt in months. The bastard wasn't just talented; he was handsome and friendly too. Good thing he was already dating someone or else—

Or else what!? Why did it matter?

"RJ?" Barczyk shrugged, smiling way too fondly for Evan's liking. "Yeah, we played together in Juniors, and we were in Vermont together."

"Oh." Evan had known that. Or he should've. "Are you guys still close?"

"Nah, not really. We just chat before games. Tradition or whatever. Nice guy. Way nicer than me. I bet I'll smash him tonight, and he'll still apologize to me for getting in my way or some shit." He laughed. "Kinda like you, actually."

A teammate Barczyk had spent years with. A teammate just like Evan. How much like Evan?

Evan wanted to scream. Barczyk, oblivious to Evan being about two seconds away from an aneurysm, bumped his shoulder against Evan's as he skated off, like some giant cat showing affection. The horn sounded for the end of warm-ups, and Evan took one last look at Russell as he disappeared from the ice. Evan made a mental note not to let Ryan Russell score or win a single face-off against him tonight.

Spoiler: Ryan Russell did win face-offs against Evan. A lot of them.

Russell was on the first line for the Otters, so he shouldn't have matched up against Evan very often, but Russell's line was absolutely destroying the Riveters' first and second lines, so Coach Jack used his home ice advantage to put Evan, Vassiliev, and Barczyk against them. Russell was killing Evan at the dot, but otherwise they kept down the scoring chances. A small win.

"Hey, Abs." Barczyk grabbed Evan's jersey and kept him from going to the face-off circle for yet another impending loss to Russell. "Just tie him up. I'll come in and grab the puck."

"You don't think I can win a stupid face-off?" Evan snapped, surprised at his own annoyance.

Barczyk didn't even flinch. "Against RJ? Probably not."

"Why, because he's better than me?"

Again, Barczyk wasn't fazed by Evan's pissy attitude. "At face-offs?

Yeah. But he's top five in the league, so, like, he's better than most people."

Evan, for the first time in a long time, wanted to punch Barczyk.

"But," Barczyk continued, "he's smaller than you. So tie him up. He won't be expecting it."

With no better ideas, Evan did what Barczyk suggested; instead of trying to win the puck back to the defense, Evan stepped forward and bodied Russell away from the puck.

"Yoink!" Barczyk yelled as he swooped in from behind, scooped out the puck, and rushed down the ice. Evan's momentary thrill of victory died when Russell pulled away and chased Barczyk down the ice. Evan scrambled after, and it wouldn't have been so bad, except even after the goalie covered the puck, Russell and Barczyk kept pushing and shoving. Not unusual, since Barczyk usually got a few extra shoves after the whistle, but this was too...playful.

"Back it up, Riles," Russell said, his glove in Barczyk's face. "I'm not playing this game today."

"I ain't doing shit," Barczyk said. He took off his own glove and threw it at Russell's gut. "Fuck off, RJ."

"You fuck off."

"No, you fuck off—"

"How about both of you fuck off and line it up or go back to your benches," the ref snapped, though he didn't seem bothered by Barczyk and Russell's fighting. Like he didn't think that any trouble was going to come of it, which was the opposite of how refs normally treated Barczyk.

They lined up for another face-off. Russell won.

"Riles?" Evan asked when they were back on the bench a minute later. He hated how pathetic he felt bringing it up.

Barczyk shrugged. "Everyone called me that in Juniors." He chugged some water from his water bottle, then sprayed some at Evan. "What'd they call you?"

"Abs," he said. He'd played for Team Canada when he was 17, the winter before he was drafted. He knew some players jived with their teams and loved the experience of playing for their country. Evan had found the whole thing overwhelming as it led into the tournament, and then underwhelming during and after. It hadn't made a big impression on him, at least not the way it seemed to with Barczyk and Russell, sort-of-friends years later.

"Oh," Barczyk said, and that was the end of it.

The Riveters lost 3-1. It was one of Evan's worst games in a while. No shot attempts, no hits, two whole face-off wins (neither against Russell), and a minus one rating. The only consolation was that Russell hadn't scored, and Evan felt like a dick for caring. Ryan Russell hadn't done anything to him, ever. His only crime was having known Barczyk before Evan had.

"You seem stressed," Vassiliev said after the game. "You didn't play so well, but we won. Don't sweat it."

"I'm not stressed," he said, voice tight and an octave higher than usual.

Vassiliev held up his hands in surrender, but his face said like *hell you're not.*

Evan had played hard that game but still had too much energy, so he bypassed the showers and went to the small gym at the arena to run until he couldn't feel his feet anymore. That was normal, right?

31

Barczyk
Come over?

Abernathy
I'm not good company right now

Barczyk
You need to unwind
I saw you in a post-game interview after the otters
You looked like you either needed to go five rounds in a ring or get laid
Lucky for you I'm happy to help with both

Abernathy
I'm fine

PROUD OF HIMSELF FOR RESISTING TEMPTATION FOR ONCE this goddamned season, Evan was about to head to bed to toss and turn for a few hours, when instead of getting another text message, his phone rang.

He stared at Barczyk's name on the screen, willing himself to let it go to voicemail. He cracked after five seconds.

"I said I'm—"

"Evan."

That shut him up.

"Come fuck me," Barczyk said. "I'm hard, I'm open, and I'm waiting for someone to tire me out."

Evan swallowed so loudly he was sure Barczyk could hear it.

"I didn't do anything to earn it," he said. Not because it wasn't tempting, but that was what they did, right? All these scenarios to make it okay. Evan needed to practice fighting, or he was learning how to give blowjobs, or he'd won a bet. That was their relationship.

Wasn't it?

"Earn it?" Barczyk's breathy chuckle had Evan reaching for his dick. That sound should be illegal. "I'm sure I can think of a thing or two."

Evan wavered. He couldn't remember why he'd been against this, why he'd been trying to put space between them when Barczyk was whispering in his ear that he wanted Evan.

"You got other plans, that's fine," Barczyk said. "But if you're just sitting at your place doing nothing, I promise I can show you a good time."

"I—"

"I'm willing to beg. On my knees, on my back, however you want me, I'll beg. *Evan*, please."

"I'll be there in twenty minutes."

"The door's unlocked."

———

"Why do you taste like peanut butter?" Evan said between kisses.

"I got hungry. Sue me." He held Evan at arm's length for a moment. "Riley, remember?"

Evan nodded, blushing because not only had he needed the reminder, but Barczyk knew it. "Get on the bed, Riley."

Riley hadn't been kidding about being open and ready. When he climbed onto his bed, ass up, his hole glistened with lube. On his hands and knees, Riley looked beautiful, and Evan forgot his own bullshit long enough to marvel at him. Russell and the Otters could have their stupid win; Evan was the one who got to have *this*.

And yeah, he didn't win a bet this time, but he'd earn it later. He'd keep Riley out of a fight, or he'd score a game winner, or he'd kill a penalty. He'd prove he was worth Riley or the Riveters or anyone having faith in him.

His knees were about to buckle, so he climbed onto the bed behind Riley. Evan held his hips, like the gentle touch would help him calm himself down. He took his time with the condom and lube, then with lining himself up. His body screamed for him to do it already, to push inside and take what they both wanted. Enjoy the time together and figure his shit out later and all that.

"C'mon, Ev. I'm dying here. How long are you gonna—*fuuuck*," he hissed as Evan pressed the tip of his cock against his hole and put just the barest pressure.

"You said you'd beg," Evan said. Big words, considering he didn't have much restraint left, but hearing Riley's voice was one of the weird kinks he'd picked up lately.

"Please, for the love of God, get your dick in me. Fill me up. It's a waste of your dick and my ass not to have the two together, so please, please, *please* fix that."

Riley could probably talk forever and not get tired, but Evan couldn't hold out any longer. It was a different experience from last time when Riley had controlled the pace. Evan tried to mirror the slow, gradual push. He watched as he buried his length inch by glorious inch, sometimes stopping or pulling out a little. Riley's legs trembled, so Evan tried to bear his weight until he'd finally bottomed out. He stayed like that, flush against Riley's ass and holding him close.

A perfect moment.

The rest of the night was like an out-of-body experience. He fucked into Riley as hard as he dared, and all he could think of was their sparring matches. This was way better, and he didn't have to hide his arousal, wasn't embarrassed when Riley took himself in hand and jerked off to the rhythm Evan set. He felt Riley clench around him as he came, saw the come stain the sheets, and couldn't tell if the moans were his or Riley's.

His own orgasm barely registered, because as much as it was a release, it only brought with it a few moments of peace before all his doubts and confusion returned. What was he doing here? Why did he keep digging himself deeper into this mess when he didn't know what the fuck he was doing? He stared up at Riley's ceiling like it held the answers he needed. Harsh truths or easy outs, he just needed a direction.

"Hey." Riley kissed him, and it kept some of the panic at bay. "Go clean up. I'll meet you in the kitchen."

It helped having someone tell him what to do.

He waited until Riley had disappeared before he hid in the bathroom. A shower sounded great, but he was scared of what thoughts would slip in. He grabbed a washcloth and did his best not to look in the mirror. Back in his sweats and the old Team Canada shirt he'd worn over, he lingered in the bedroom.

There was definitely more personality here than in his hotel room. There were movie posters on the wall and a shelf that was nothing but framed photos. There weren't any of the awards, trophies, and memorabilia hockey players usually collected (Evan was no exception—his 'office' was just piles of pucks he'd been given throughout his career in the NHL, plus a bunch of medals and trophies he'd gotten as a kid that his mom insisted he box up and take with him), and Evan kind of liked that. Riley Barczyk as a person, not a hockey player.

But Evan couldn't hide in here forever, and unless he was going to climb out the window, he had to face Riley eventually.

Riley. Barczyk. Barzy. Were these different people? Barzy, his teammate who helped him work on his game. Riley, the guy he was fucking.

Barczyk, the asshole who hurt him last season.

It seemed easier to believe they were different than one and the same. It also made one less thing for Evan to unpack in his head. *Maybe I'm gay* was enough of a challenge without adding, *I really like sex with Barczyk.*

Riley was kind of great, though. A sentiment that landed heavily as he stepped into the living area and found Barczyk at his kitchen island, plating a tower of sandwiches. It looked like a whole loaf of bread had been sacrificed for this meal, and there were two protein shakes waiting on the smooth marble next to the plate.

"I'm starving," Riley said, sucking jam off his finger. He was in a pair of boxer briefs and nothing else, just his bare skin and that gold chain and a mess of curls. It looked like he hadn't cut his hair since he arrived in Pittsburgh, less mohawk now and more mess. Evan wanted to see it get longer and longer. "Hope you like PB&J. I didn't get groceries since we're heading to Canada in a couple of days." He pointed to Evan's shirt. "You visiting fam while we're up north?"

Evan looked down at his shirt and rubbed a hand over the maple leaf self-consciously. "Yeah, probably."

Riley raised an eyebrow at him. "Probably? Bro, we leave in two days. You might need to figure that out. Aren't you from Toronto?"

"Toronto?" Fuck, was it already that trip?

"Sit," Riley said, so Evan did. He pushed over the plate and said, "Eat." He waited until Evan had taken a sandwich before he grabbed one himself. "Toronto, Ottawa, Quebec, then we dip back here for a game and head out west again. You sure you're okay?"

He didn't want to answer, so Evan took the biggest bite he could manage and let the peanut butter save him for a minute. He chewed thoroughly because he needed every second to think. What was he supposed to say? *Most of my brainpower has gone into not freaking out about how much I like your dick, and the rest of it's reserved for hockey?*

Riley would like hearing that.

Evan swallowed and grabbed a protein shake for good measure, chugging half of it.

"I've got a lot on my mind," he said. It sounded lame even to him.

There was a moment when he worried Riley (Riley! When had his brain accepted that switch?) might ask the obvious question, but he squinted at Evan like he could read it on his face.

"Well," Riley said as he dug into his own sandwich and talked around it. "If you wanna fuck, lemme know. It's my favorite distraction."

"Don't talk with your mouth full," Evan said. "It's disgusting."

"Oh please, you love my mouth when it's full."

"Not when it's full of food, dumbass." It sounded too harsh, so he muttered, "Sorry. You're not a dumbass. But it's still gross."

"I mean"—Riley swallowed and took another bite—"I can be, for sure. A dumbass. Just gotta embrace it, y'know?"

Evan tried very hard not to smile. It wasn't working. "Stop."

"Stop what?" Riley asked, sandwich still in his mouth.

"You're the worst."

"Nope." He went back in for another bite, and Evan reached over the island to stop him; Riley let him. "I'm the best, Abs. I'll convince you one of these days."

Evan wasn't sure which possibility he dreaded more: that Riley would try and fail, or that he'd already succeeded.

32

EVAN HAD FUCKED UP BY LETTING THE EASTERN CANADA trip slip under his radar. He sent his mom and his cousin his schedule for Toronto as soon as he got home that night, then he sent out a few messages to friends in Ottawa. He'd lived in Ottawa for a few years as a teenager, and he was still close with his billet family; he tried to visit when he was in town. Maybe being back home in Canada would help him feel normal again.

You're not just magically gayer in America, he told himself.

I'm magically gayer when I'm around Riley, he argued back. *So who the fuck knows?*

The trip gave him something to focus on, at least. And plenty of excuses to avoid Riley if needed. Evan *should* avoid him, though he wanted to less and less. Their warm-up routine was comforting. Riley's encouragement on the bench and at practice was reassuring. His loud mouth during games was entertaining. His presence on plane rides was soothing. He'd gone from Evan's biggest stressor this season to the thing that helped Evan hold it together.

And the thing most likely to shatter him apart.

"That's not fair," Evan mumbled to himself as he packed his duffle for the trip. "If you said you were done with him, he'd let you walk away. You're doing this to yourself."

It didn't make it any easier.

———

His cousin's schedule didn't align with his, which wasn't uncommon. With each team having their own practices, outings, and training, it didn't always work out that Evan got to see the people he wanted to when he traveled. But his mom would bend over backwards to see him whenever she could, so he was unsurprised to find her waiting outside the locker rooms after their practice in Toronto.

"Mom!" He leaned down to pull her into a hug and already felt lighter. Home was where the heart was and all that. Evan didn't think it was possible for him to feel stressed when Carol Abernathy was around.

"Hi, sweetie," she cooed, not letting go until Evan had to stand up straight so his back wouldn't cramp up. "Ready to head out?"

A few of his teammates waved as they passed, on their way out to museums, restaurants, or the hotel. Their game wasn't until the next evening, and most planned to enjoy their afternoon in Toronto now that their team responsibilities were done for the day. That meant Evan had a half day with his mom, and since she was in charge, he assumed that meant a trip to the aquarium (her favorite) and a meal.

"Sure, I—"

"Is this Mama Abernathy?"

Evan's stomach did an uncomfortable flip. Oh no.

"Riley Barczyk," his mom said, her tone unreadable. "The man himself. Nice to meet you in person." She held out a hand. "Evan's told me a lot about you."

Riley shook her hand. "Only the bad stuff, I hope."

His mom rolled her eyes, but Evan could tell she was amused. "Something like that. Though I have a league full of commentators who already do that."

"They don't like me much in Canada, eh?" He winked, and the impossible happened: his mom laughed.

"On the contrary. We love to hate you. They ever let you boys into the Olympics, you'll be the bane of our existence, I'm sure." She gave Riley a once-over, her gaze critical as she assessed him. "You've been doing well for the Riveters, so I'll give you a pass. For now."

"Yes, ma'am." Riley clapped Evan on the shoulder. "See you at the hotel. Have fun, Abs' mom! Keep him out of trouble."

Then Riley was gone, and somehow Evan had survived the encounter.

"He's charming. I'll give him that," his mom said as they walked to her car. "Wish he hadn't hurt my baby so I could like him. Though you seem to have warmed up to him."

Evan escaped into the car so she wouldn't notice him blush. By the time she'd situated herself in the driver's seat, his cheeks weren't burning hot anymore.

"He's not as bad as I thought," Evan said carefully.

"Good," she said, backing out of the space and setting her GPS. "Let's grab some food. I've got us tickets to the aquarium this evening."

They didn't talk about hockey for the rest of the day. It was like a factory reset, where Evan felt like himself for the first time in ages. He could enjoy a beer and burger with his mom, while she caught him up on all the family drama (the drama being no worse than someone forgetting someone else's birthday, or the aunts squabbling over the next family vacation location, or the moms placing bets on whose son would go farthest in the playoffs this year). And while his mom squealed over shark eggs and manta rays, he knew that whenever he figured out his Riley-situation, his mom wouldn't judge him.

That was a small relief.

———

His mom was rinkside for warm-ups, as usual when they played the Terrors. Her seats would be higher up—anything lower than the 200s, and she said she couldn't see enough of the game—but she knew he liked to see her while he was there. When he'd been really little, he'd liked to find his mom in the bleachers. It'd been easy enough in rinks that couldn't hold more than a few hundred, but it'd gotten harder over the years.

In Toronto's arena, it was impossible. It could hold over 18,000 spectators, and unlike many arenas around the league, they'd had a sellout crowd every game for decades.

It took Evan a few minutes to spot her against the boards, and he skated over to her. She wore her signed ABERNATHY jersey (embarrassing) but thankfully didn't have a sign. This time. She waved excitedly to him and nudged everyone around her. He couldn't hear through the plexiglass, but he could read her lips as she pointed at him: "Look! Look! That's my son!"

He stayed a little longer, tossing a couple of pucks over the glass for the kids near his mom, then he skated off. There was something he needed to do.

Riley was waiting for him at their usual spot, the top of the left circle. Instead of doing something productive like stickhandling or shooting, he was bopping along to the music. Katie Perry, maybe? Fuck if Evan knew.

"You're late," Riley said.

"Sorry—"

"Holy fuck, Abs. I'm just giving you shit. Do not apologize for saying hi to your mom. We play in Boston, I'm gonna have a little cheering squad."

"You're from Boston?" Evan joked. "I'd never have guessed."

Riley took off his glove to give him the finger. "Hey, fuck off. I've done a lot of work to lose this accent. You should watch old interviews. I sound fuckin' hilarious. You can take the boy out of Massachusetts, but..." He shrugged.

"You're not actually from Boston, right?"

"Nah. Salem." He motioned for Evan to turn around. "Come on, big guy. Hometown ice isn't saving that ass."

Evan spun around, mostly so Riley wouldn't see how his words affected him. "I'm not *from* Toronto."

"Close enough, Mr. Canada." Riley whacked him three times in quick succession, then once more for good measure. "You better score. I just paddled you in front of your family. I don't want it to be for nothing."

"Wha..." He trailed off, looking first down the ice—his cousin was paying them no mind—and then back over to his mom. She *was* watching, though he was too far to see her expression. "Well, fuck me," he grumbled. She knew about their weird routine, but it was different having her a hundred feet away versus seeing clips online.

"Only if you ask nice," Riley said. "My turn."

Ignoring the innuendo, Evan did exactly what Riley had done—four butt taps, and Riley was his usual theatrical self as he hit the ice at the end and yelped—and skated away.

Admittedly, a lot of Evan's current issues were his own internal bullshit; some of it was definitely Riley, always throwing him off balance in little ways. As off-kilter as it left him, Evan liked that about Riley. Riley didn't tiptoe around things. He pushed Evan's comfort zone, but without throwing him off the deep end.

He was in the deep end anyway, but that was his fault.

Riley

THE RIVETERS PLAYED A SUNDAY MATINEE AGAINST THE Ontario Ice Owls, and Riley planned to make use of the free evening. He'd looked up nice places in Ottawa to take Evan for dinner. That was important, he thought. Evan didn't take care of himself enough, and he'd been acting weird the last week or so.

Since Evan wasn't up for talking about it, Riley could treat him to a relaxing evening of fine dining and good sex. Least he could do, right?

They were in the locker room post-game—a 4-2 loss to the stupid Ice Owls, fucking embarrassing, but hey, Evan had scored so silver lining and all that—and Riley was trying to figure out how to bring it up. He had a whole plan, complete with a wager about who could suck the other off first, and just needed an opportunity to talk to Evan alone. Maybe on the team bus back to the hotel—

Lawson stood up in the center of the locker room, finally emptied of media and coaches. Cupping his hands around his mouth, he announced, "Team party tonight. I got us a room at a bar near the hotel. Dinner and drinks in ninety, got it? Get showered ASAP. We lost, so no way I can argue us out of a curfew. We've gotta get our fun finished up by 9 p.m. sharp."

Goddamnit.

Whatever. They could show up and slip out. Riley could salvage this. Dinner could wait for another night, but who wasn't relaxed after blowjobs and beer?

"Can't," Evan said. He tossed aside his gloves and ran a hand over his chin, a month's worth of beard tempting Riley to do something stupid. "Got plans."

"Plans?" Riley asked, and it came out angrier than he intended.

"You going to see your girlfriend?" Lawson asked loudly. Half the guys laughed, and a few made kissy faces. Riley felt like he couldn't breathe. What the fuck?

"Don't stay out too late," Woodsy said, waggling his eyebrows.

Evan just rolled his eyes. "I'll be back before curfew, don't worry," he grumbled. The teasing continued a little longer, though Riley didn't hear any of it.

Dalty, stupid Dalty, said Evan didn't date. Now, all of a sudden, he had a girlfriend the whole fucking team knew about? And was going to see her instead of hanging out with the team?

Was *that* why he'd been acting weird lately?

If he considered things objectively, Riley doubted Evan had an actual girlfriend for no other reason that Evan wasn't the type to hook up with Riley if he were already in a relationship. But there was something to this story he was missing, and it might explain the weird vibe Evan had been giving off.

Riley was having trouble being objective, though. All he could feel was jealousy and annoyance and hurt. He hadn't gotten Evan to himself at all on this stupid trip to Canada. First his mom (yes, Riley knew he couldn't complain about that one), and now some random chick. Even at the hotels, he hadn't been able to get Evan for more than five minutes without the team interfering. Stupid celebrating their 5-0 blowout of the Terrors.

Stop freaking out and fucking ask, dumbass.

Oh. Right.

He didn't get a chance until they were on the bus. Riley had to cut ahead of five guys to make sure he got a spot next to Evan, and he couldn't even be ashamed of how unchill he was being. This was A Big

Deal, and there were basically no answers that wouldn't hurt him somehow, but he still had to give Evan a chance to explain.

There were a lot of subtle, totally normal ways to lead into asking what he wanted to know. Riley had never been good at subtle, so of course when he plopped down next to Evan, the first words out of his mouth were, "So you've got a girlfriend?"

Jesus fucking Christ. He felt like he was back in middle school and had the same inability to function like a normal human being around someone he liked.

"Huh?" Evan looked up from his phone, his frown lightening when he saw Riley.

A chance for Riley to prove he wasn't a complete spaz, and instead his stupid brain doubled down. "Lawson said you have a girlfriend. You're gonna hang out with her today or something."

"Oh, that." There were no signs of embarrassment or guilt, which was a plus. "She's not my girlfriend."

"But there is a girl?" For fuck's—could he just take his foot and insert it permanently into his mouth?

Evan blushed. What did that *mean*? Fucking hell.

"Kind of? There's literally a girl—Amy—but I'm not dating her. I've *never* dated her. I lived with her family when I played in the Canadian Junior Hockey League. I was so homesick when I moved to Ottawa, which I know is stupid since it isn't even that far from Peterborough. I could've been a lot farther from home, but still. Her family was great. We still talk, and I try to visit when I'm in town. Her parents are out of town, so it'll just be the two of us tonight."

"She's part of your billet family," Riley said slowly, like he might've misunderstood. A wave of relief washed through him when Evan nodded. "Cool that you still keep in touch."

"I'm glad she was available at such short notice." Evan said it like he was confiding something in Riley. "I completely spaced out on the schedule and didn't text her until, like, four days ago."

So she rearranged all her plans just for you? Fucking fantastic.

"Uh huh." He grabbed the first available topic change he could think of. "Nice goal today. Season highlight for sure."

Riley was proud that Evan blushed again, this time deeper than when they'd been talking about stupid Amy From the Billet Family (who was probably a lovely person, but Riley didn't give a shit; he didn't like sharing).

"It was all right."

"Nope, it was *not* all right. It was fucking fantastic. Backhand bar down? Those ain't easy." He liked this part of being on a team. Hyping up his teammates, making sure they stopped to enjoy the little moments that made up a big season. Some guys put their nose to the grindstone, so to speak, and were too focused on the prize to enjoy the journey there. Yeah, Riley remembered when he won the Cup with vivid detail, but his fondest memories from his career were the mundane moments where he was hanging out with his bros.

You maybe lifted the Cup a couple of times, but you lived with your team every day for months, maybe years.

Evan, more than most, seemed like he needed those confidence-boosters. Not because he had his eyes set on the Cup, but more because he seemed...adrift. Letting hockey push him forward instead of getting steady on his own feet.

Riley could be his anchor.

"Yeah," Evan said. He had that small smile that barely looked like a smile, but on him it was the equivalent of a grin. Riley hadn't noticed that smile until they'd started their fighting practice. How pleased he'd get whenever he managed to punch Riley. His victory smile, private and contained unless you knew exactly what it looked like. "I guess it wasn't bad."

"It was great," Riley agreed sincerely. "I'm jealous. Half of my goals this season have been garbage goals."

"You're really good with trash," Evan joked. He had told exactly zero jokes when the season had started, so Riley delighted in them every time, even as they became more frequent.

"Dick," he said far too fondly. Riley had stopped being able to ignore how much he liked Evan, but he hoped Evan wouldn't spot it yet. He was hoping Evan might catch feelings for him too before then, though he wasn't sure how likely that would be.

For the rest of the bus ride, Riley was determined not to let on how disappointed he was that Evan wouldn't be his tonight. He could be nice and not ruin Evan's night with his friend because of his foul mood.

And then when he went out with the team, Riley could get hammered enough that he wouldn't care that he'd end the night alone.

33

EVAN CHECKED HIS PHONE TO MAKE SURE HE WAS AT THE
right place and headed into the restaurant. Amy had texted him the
address and time, most recently updating him she was seated at a table in
the back and had ordered appetizers.

Rubbing his palms on his pants, he scanned the tables along the
back wall until he saw her strawberry-blond ponytail. Amy Peters caught
sight of him and waved him over enthusiastically, getting up to hug him
when he was close enough, and Evan tried not to let his nerves show. He
remembered all the talk about him seeing his 'girlfriend,' and the anxiety
living in his head rent-free right now was like the queasiness of going on
a date, but it had nothing to do with feelings for Amy.

The guys always gave him shit for Amy ever since they'd met her two
years ago and determined they were a 'cute couple' and that she was
'super smart' since she knew about hockey, and it had always bothered
him. Not because Amy wasn't awesome, but because they made it
sound like the only way a girl would go near Evan (or vice versa) was if
they were dating. Like female relationships had to be sexual and
couldn't just...be. She was like a little sister, he supposed, though he
wasn't sure what having a sister was like. A good friend for sure, and
that was what he needed.

It was also why he was scared shitless of this dinner.

"You scored!" Amy said when she let him out of her bear hug. "Mom and Dad'll be so mad they missed it!"

They sat down and caught up. Evan relaxed into her stories as Amy told him everything that had been going on with the Peters family since he'd last checked in. Amy was a vet tech, and after a string of stories about weird pet incidents, Evan had regained some of his equilibrium.

"So what's going on with you?" she asked. "Like, besides the hockey stuff."

They didn't talk much about hockey anymore, not since he'd gone pro. Like his mom, Amy watched as many of his games as she could and texted him encouragement throughout the season. She'd made it clear when they were teenagers that they were friends outside of his being a hockey player; she wanted to hear how he was doing with all the non-hockey stuff that didn't make it into the news reports and media coverage.

"Uhm..." The answer was almost always 'not much.' His life had been 99% hockey since he could remember. All the exciting things were hockey-related, whether good or bad. Evan had always struggled to pick out pieces of his life to offer her, often having to settle with times he got to play with a teammate's dog or a particularly cool mini-golf course he'd found somewhere.

Today he had a very non-hockey thing he wanted to get off his chest.

"I uhm...I kinda started...seeing someone...." He made a face, both at how awkward he sounded and because he wasn't sure if he could call what he and Riley were doing qualified as 'seeing someone.'

But before he could backtrack or add qualifications to that, Amy clapped her hands together. "Oh my God! Evan, that's so exciting! I'm so happy for you! What's his name?"

"Well, he's—" He stopped short. He expected to have to do this whole thing about how it wasn't a woman, but then what Amy said hit him. She hadn't even gone gender-neutral. She'd straight up asked what *his* name was. "How'd you know?"

Amy blushed, her shoulders rising to her ears. "Oops, sorry. I shouldn't have assumed. That just slipped out." A pause, then a quiet, "But I was right, wasn't I?"

"Yeah..." Evan scratched at the stupid beard he'd finally get to cut this weekend now that it was December. No-Shave November and Play-offs were the bane of his existence. "I just...I dunno, I was expecting to have to explain that I might be gay—" Amy made a sound; Evan narrowed his eyes. "What? I can't be gay?"

"Sorry. No, you can definitely be gay. Like, *obviously* you're gay? I'm just surprised you didn't realize I already knew—"

"You already knew? Fuck, Amy, *I* didn't know until Ri—" He cut himself off. Names were a bad idea. His sexuality was his business to share, but having sex with a teammate wasn't. He trusted Amy, but he shouldn't make that call without discussing it with Riley first. He certainly wouldn't appreciate it if their roles were reversed. "I didn't know I was attracted to men until a couple of months ago."

Amy blinked at him. Then she topped off both of their glasses of wine as she muttered, "Shit, you're serious. Jesus, Evan."

"I can't believe you knew I was gay and never told me," he said and laughed, because this was ridiculous. He'd thought he'd have to convince Amy he wasn't straight, but she'd known the whole time!

"I can't believe you were gay and didn't know!" Amy said, laughing too. "That's too cute. And makes me feel a bit better that you never told me. When we were kids, I thought you didn't trust me or something."

"You're literally the first person I've told," he said. "I trust you."

Her eyes went wide. "That's so friggin' sweet. I'm seriously honored." She held up her wine glass. He raised his too, then they both took a long drink before she asked, "Do you feel better now that someone officially knows?"

Evan traced the brim of his wine glass. "Kind of? I mean, yes, but I'm also confused about how you knew before I did. When did you figure it out?"

"Uh, like, within a week of you moving in? Evan, sweetie..." She reached across the table and squeezed his hand. "My friends hit on you the entire time you lived with us, and not once did you notice. My very hot, very obvious friends. And you were polite and stuff, and yeah, you were oblivious, but it was also clear you weren't interested at *all*." She took her hand back and made a face as she went back to poking at her salad with her fork. "But you were super interested in the neighbor across the street."

"Neighbor?" What neighbor? He couldn't remember anyone who — "Oh my God. The basketball player!?"

Amy tapped her nose. "You gave him the biggest puppy-dog eyes. It was so cute. He wasn't gay, but he was so sweet not to burst your bubble."

"I wasn't interested in him," he said automatically, but when he considered his new, fully understood appreciation of the male form, he did have a lot of mental images of Bobby Knightley without a shirt. "Wow, I had a crush on him. Why didn't you tell me!?"

"I honestly didn't think it was possible to have a crush on someone and not know it," she said.

"Fair," Evan grumbled and buried his face in his hands. This was not how he'd anticipated this conversation going. "This is so embarrassing."

"Awww, don't be embarrassed. No judgment. You never seemed super sexually driven anyway, and this is the type of thing hockey players don't talk about. It's a Big Deal, so I totally understand that you maybe didn't want to analyze it too much if you didn't have to. Granted, I always thought you didn't want people to know because you were worried about how it'd affect your career. And it's not easy to be a queer player in professional hockey, so I didn't say anything. I mean, look what happened to Lars Nilsson because of it, and no offense, but he's a much better player than you. It didn't occur to me that you hadn't said anything because you didn't know."

Evan sighed. "Do you think I should keep it quiet?"

"Honey, you started this conversation with 'I might be gay' and not 'I'm gay.' You should figure that stuff out before you hold a press conference."

"Yeah, fair."

"So Carol doesn't know?" she asked a few minutes later. There was no hint of an accusation, but Evan felt bad anyway.

"I'm...not ready to tell her. My mom's the best, but I just..."

If Evan got right down to it, it wasn't really about his mom. His mom would be supportive (whether she already suspected like Amy had, he had no clue), but she'd ask questions. Completely valid questions like what made him figure it out. Which would lead to more questions, and all of those questions pointed to Riley Barczyk.

And Evan was barely ready to confront his sexuality head-on. He absolutely wasn't ready to tell his mom that he was sleeping with Barczyk.

"I'm not sure what she'd think of the guy I'm hooking up with," he muttered into his glass of wine. The glass was annoyingly empty, so he poured himself another. "And I don't understand that whole situation, anyway."

Amy stared at him as she processed this and said, "You know damn well that sounds intriguing and mysterious. Are you worried she won't approve of the guy? Because that's kind of a red flag. Or is it because this is just sex and that's embarrassing? Because I get that."

"She—" He stopped short. What was it his mom had said about Riley? He was a charmer? Riley being a bruiser on the ice wouldn't bother her—his mom could be old school and appreciated a good enforcer, especially one who could also score. If Evan had gotten over Riley hitting him last season (had he?), she could move past it. So while she would probably never expect the words 'Mom, I think I'm gay' to be connected to Riley, that wasn't *really* Evan's concern.

He had no idea what he was even doing with Riley. Aside from lots of sex, there was no real acknowledgment of what they were.

"It's complicated," he said. "It's *mostly* sex, and it's kind of casual."

"Gotcha. Do you wanna talk about it? You mentioned a relationship, but I didn't know if that was just a segue into the whole gay-thing, or if that's what you actually wanted to talk about."

"I do kind of want to talk about him," Evan said, because he did. The relief of Amy knowing he was gay had taken an enormous weight off his mind. Sharing Riley might help ease that burden more...except the idea of saying it out loud made him nauseous. He wasn't sure if it was confusion or fear or a selfish desire to keep Riley to himself. "But like I said, it's complicated. I don't know how much I could really say."

"Would it help if I asked questions? That way you could choose what you did or didn't share."

Worth a shoot. "Sure."

Slowly, Amy got a very broad picture of things. They were having sex regularly whenever Evan's schedule allowed. It'd been going on sporadically for a few months. Evan didn't know where it was going, denied feelings being involved, but said he wanted it to continue for now. No, they hadn't talked about it. Yes, Evan was more physically attracted to his current hookup than he could ever remember being before.

Amy took it all in, but then grew quiet after dessert was dropped off. She stabbed her chocolate cake while she chewed over whatever she was going to ask next.

"I'm not going to look at you as I ask this, because you have a terrible poker face and I don't want you to accidentally confirm or deny something you don't mean to, but..." Amy took a deep breath, her gaze fixed pointedly at her plate. "Are you hooking up with another player?"

Evan stared at her dumbly. "Huh?"

"I changed my mind. Don't answer that," she said, holding up a hand. "It's better if I don't know. Dating a professional athlete is always complicated, so I can see that being a huge stumbling block for any relationship. Dating a queer professional athlete is harder. *Two* queer NHL players sounds like a nightmare."

Evan swallowed. "It's happened," he said defensively.

"Oh, I'm sure it's happening right now." She still wouldn't meet his eyes. "And there's exactly one public example of it, and they're engaged." She looked up. "I guess what I'm saying is...be careful. Whether you're with another player or not, that's not the point. A lot could go wrong very quickly. Unless you're ready for a lot of press and attention, just make sure the two of you are on the same page. It's a lot for someone who's comfortable with their sexuality, and you're new to the whole gay thing, apparently."

"Yeah, you're right," he grumbled, because she was. If he couldn't wrap his head around being gay, how could he ever hope to do it with a national audience? And Evan couldn't even say for certain they were in the same book, let alone on the same page. "We're being careful," he promised.

"Good." She offered him a bite of cake and then wiped her hands. "This is a big deal. We're gonna celebrate at the bar."

"Celebrate what?"

"Figuring out who we are is an accomplishment, no matter how old we are when we do it. You don't have to be anywhere tomorrow morning, do you?"

"Flight to Quebec isn't until noon, but I have a curfew. Gotta be back at the hotel by nine."

"Grown ass men with a curfew," she said with an eye roll. "What a life."

"It's gonna be rough when I gotta grow up, eh?" He was only half-joking. He did worry about what would happen when he retired and had to do things without the structure of an NHL season or the day-to-day routine of practice, games, and meetings. A life when he no longer spent half his time traveling...weird.

"Probably," she said. She held up her wine glass. "To figuring out this adult bullshit one step at a time."

He clinked his glass to hers. "Maybe I'll get there one day." They each finished off their glasses.

"Don't worry, Evan," she said. "We all get there. Eventually."

34

EVAN STUMBLED INTO THE HOTEL AT 8:55 P.M. WITH THE stink of stale beer and perfume following him from his Uber. His stomach sloshed uncomfortably from wine and beer, and he desperately wanted to get to his room so he could down an entire bottle of aspirin and five glasses of water. Or, at the very least, so he could be close to a bathroom if he ended up throwing up.

Each step felt like lead. He barely recognized a bunch of his teammates in the hotel bar across the lobby, singing off-key to a song he didn't know. When he squinted over, he thought he saw Riley in the middle of them like a band conductor. Evan smiled and took a few steps to the bar, but the room swayed and his stomach gurgled in warning.

Instead, he made a beeline to the elevator on unsteady feet. The dull mechanical hum of the elevator almost put him to sleep, but the ping and lurch when he arrived on his floor woke him up long enough to stagger to his room. After two tries to make his key work, he was inside. He kicked off one shoe, made it as far as the bed, and collapsed face first.

He'd planned on finding Riley to hang out, but his brain was sluggish and his body wasn't cooperating much, either. Maybe if he took a little nap, he'd sober up enough to invite Riley over.

Mmm, Riley...

He woke with a jolt, unsure of where he was or the time. He had to piss, though, so he wandered to the bathroom, ended up in a closet instead, and had to turn around to try again. He drank a glass of faintly metallic tap water, then another, and the last responsible decision he made before passing out was setting an alarm on his phone.

There were some notifications begging for his attention, but his blurred vision couldn't make them out. He ignored them all, wiggled halfway under the covers, and decided that whatever it was, it could wait until morning.

———

Evan wasn't much of a drinker. He didn't remember how much he'd had with Amy at the restaurant bar after dinner, but it was well past his comfort level. It'd been too much fun, relaxing and forgetting all his worries while playing stupid games like Rock Paper Scissors and a very drunken version of I Spy.

A lot of it came back to him when he woke up with a headache. Some of it went away when he figured out how to turn off his alarm, but not enough. It was rough, making himself presentable enough to wander down for breakfast, and his stomach rebelled at the thought of eating.

"You look like ass, bro," Dalton said as he sat down next to him with a plate piled with three waffles covered in eggs and syrup. Evan closed his eyes and breathed through his mouth so his stomach could settle. "Late night with your girl?"

"Amy's just a friend," he grumbled. He'd been over this with Dalton last season, but he didn't have the energy to put up much of a fight.

"I know. I'm just giving you shit. Looks like you overdid it, though."

"I did." Evan listened to the sound of Dalton chewing until he could hazard a bite of his plain toast. "Remind me to never drink again."

"Abs, if we win the Cup, I'll be pouring you that first beer myself. You want a mimosa or something? Hair of the Dog or whatever?"

"Ugh." His stomach threatened to violently expel his toast. "Absolutely not."

Dalton shrugged. He'd almost finished his breakfast platter. "Suit yourself."

Evan had managed a whole quarter of toast when Riley showed up wearing sunglasses and a wrinkled shirt, clean-shaven for the first time in months. He sat down with nothing but a huge mug of coffee and proceeded to dump five packets of sugar into it without saying a word to Dalton or Evan.

"You gonna drink your breakfast?" Dalton asked. "They've got actual food."

Riley gave him the finger and added more sugar.

Evan frowned. Everyone was prone to being surly in the morning, especially hockey players who'd spent the night drinking, but Riley wasn't usually grumpy after. He might be tired and yawn more than usual, but there wasn't much that could keep him quiet. Riley sitting there, dark shades obscuring his eyes, and silently giving attitude was weird.

"You all right?" Evan asked, and Dalton laughed.

"What?" Riley said, glaring at Dalton.

"Abs looks like he had to crawl out of bed this morning, and he's asking you if *you're* all right." Dalton ran a finger through the syrup on his plate and sucked it off. "Funny, because you probably outdrank Abs by like ten beers, and he's the one who looks green." He stood up and took his plate. "You just look like a douche," Dalton said and walked off.

"Ten beers?" When Riley didn't argue, Evan asked, "Why'd you drink so much?"

He shrugged. "Bored, I guess. You?"

"I didn't have ten beers—" Riley tilted his head enough to glare at Evan over his sunglasses, this tiny peek at hazel enough to stop him short. "I was being dumb, I guess." He gulped. "Maybe next time we can be smart and entertain each other."

Riley's lips quirked in an almost smile, but then he rubbed his eyes under the sunglasses and any trace of amusement was gone. "We'll see." He reached over and took a slice of toast from Evan's plate and took a huge bite of it. With his mouth full, he asked, "You don't have any family or friends waiting to steal you in Quebec, do you?"

Evan watched Riley's mouth longer than he should've. He shook his head and said, "Je ne français."

Riley snorted, sending crumbs flying. This time his smile didn't disappear. "Even I know that was crap. I thought you were Canadian."

"I am," Evan said. "Not *French*-Canadian. That's completely different."

"Uh huh. Sounds like an excuse to me." Riley wiped the back of his mouth, sipped his coffee, and asked, "You have fun with your friend?"

"Yeah. She's one of the few people who don't make me talk about hockey. Get to be Evan and not Abs for a bit."

Riley was quiet. Evan wished he would take off the stupid sunglasses. He didn't like that his misery was obvious, but he couldn't tell what was going through Riley's head. Not that he could do that anyway, but he liked having a fighting chance.

Abruptly, Riley pushed away from the table. "For the record," he said, "you can be Evan any time you want with me."

And then he walked away, leaving his coffee and Evan behind like he didn't care about either.

35

EVAN STILL FELT LIKE SHIT WHEN THEY ARRIVED IN QUEBEC. He did what he had to with the team until they let everyone go to their rooms, where he promptly took a shower and then slept for twelve hours. He woke up the next day feeling a bit more human, but he'd skipped breakfast in favor of more sleep; his stomach rumbled as he brushed his teeth. They had meetings to go over footage in an hour, but they were using the hotel's conference rooms. Maybe if he was quick, he could grab something just to tide him over until lunch.

When he opened his hotel room door, Evan nearly tripped over something tucked into the doorjamb. He bent down to find an ordinary paper bag, but it became magical when he opened it and found fresh beignets. There was no note or anything, and no clues as he looked up and down the hallway, but there was really only one suspect. Only one person on the whole Riveters who wouldn't just notice Evan had missed breakfast, but do something about it.

Abernathy
Thanks for the beignets you're the best

He saw that Riley had opened and read the message. He never got a response.

They lost to the Fleur-de-Lis. Badly. It was a 5-1 game where they had to pull their goalie and put in the backup, both of whom looked annoyed. Evan couldn't blame them; it wasn't their fault the Riveters were hemor-rhaging shots on goal and tanking the goalies' stats.

It'd been a normal, completely winnable game to start but had taken a turn in the first period, and the Riveters had never quite recovered.

Evan had seen it coming, too.

He knew Riley was off his game when he gave Evan a single slap with his stick, not breaking his stride as he skated by. That was their whole warm-up routine, reduced to two seconds. To be clear, Evan wasn't blaming the loss on a superstition gone wrong. It was more a sign of Riley's mojo being off, and that didn't bode well for their line.

If only the damage had been contained to their line, but alas, it wasn't.

Riley took a season high and league-leading six penalties for a total of 25 penalty minutes, including a game misconduct at the end of the third. The first two calls had been, in Evan's opinion, a little soft. Not super surprising, given that was more or less standard in Quebec. The fans were loud, and their outrage tended to sway the refs. Unofficially, of course, since the refs denied calling the game differently in any arena or at any time of year.

But after Riley took the first few penalties, it only fired him up more. His play became more aggressive and dumber. He didn't seem to care about the puck, or hockey, or winning. He was angry and was looking to take it out on anyone within reach wearing navy and silver. After the third bad penalty, Coach Jack clearly thought he was a liability and started limiting his minutes...which meant Dalton often filled in on the third line and the fourth line more or less got scrubbed.

"What the fuck is up with Barzy?" Dalton asked the first time he was sent out instead of Riley. "He's way too fired up for a fucking Wednesday night."

"Woke up on the wrong side of the bed, maybe," Vassiliev grum-bled. "Fuck if we know."

Evan worried he might know, and that Vassiliev was closer to the mark than he might think.

The fight that led to the misconduct...that hadn't been fun to watch. Riley had seemed to calm down a bit during the second intermission, so Coach Jack trusted him with more minutes. They needed him on the ice to help wear down the Fleur-de-Lis and get back some semblance of control.

"Just win me this period," Coach Jack said before the start of the third. "That's all I'm asking."

It was apparently too much to hope for.

Despite controlling his temper, Riley was on the wrong end of a boarding that knocked him onto the Quebec bench. It was called immediately, much to Evan's relief...until he realized Riley hadn't noticed the ref's arm go up to make the call. Or he didn't care, which might be more to the point, because he pushed himself off the bench, locked eyes on the nearest Quebec player, and charged at him. He dropped his gloves and tackled the player, some defenseman closer to Evan's size than Riley's, and started throwing punches.

The defenseman—not expecting to be attacked for a teammate's bad decision—didn't even get his gloves off before Riley had knocked him to the ice. A ref and linesman were there in seconds to pull Riley off, but such an unsatisfying end only made Riley more fired up than he'd been after the check.

"If you dumb fucks could fucking ref a goddamned game fairly—"

"Barczyk!" The ref had to put Riley in a headlock to drag him away. "Calm the fuck down!"

"—let them take cheap shots at me all fucking night! I stand up for myself and you assholes—"

It didn't get any better from there. The five-minute major for fighting was expected. The game misconduct wasn't, but it wasn't exactly unearned.

"You're kicking him out of the game for running his mouth?" Coach Jack snapped at the refs. "If you start enforcing that, you'll need a bigger penalty box."

"He's out of fucking control, Brooks," the ref said. "We don't have to take this kind of abuse from a hothead."

"Game misconducts are for intent to injure," Coach Jack said. "Your hurt feelings don't count."

The ref went red in the face and skated away. Riley was already gone anyway. He'd stormed down the tunnel—seven minutes left in the game —to wait out his time in the locker room. Evan couldn't blame him.

"No press!" Coach Jack said to Riley once the game was over. They all hung their heads. A few guys had complained about the game on the bench. Some thought Riley had lost them the game back in the first; others were happy *someone* had shown life. But no one was happy about taking a beating from the Fleur-de-lis.

"Lawson, Woodward, Calhoun, and Moreau," Coach Jack continued, pointing to them each in turn. "That's it. You four can talk to the press and answer for we stunk out there tonight. All of you can expect a long, uncomfortable flight back to Pittsburgh tomorrow."

Evan tried his best to get Riley's attention in the locker room. He waited and silently pleaded for Riley to look at him, just so he could see Riley's smile and his stupid missing tooth and know Riley was over whatever had led to that mess on the ice.

Not once did Riley look Evan's way. Or at anyone. He'd taken off his gear while they'd finished the game, and he sat there at his stall staring into space. Riley was one of the last ones into the showers. When he showed up on the bus back to the hotel—the last one on board—he hadn't re-tied his tie or tucked in his dress shirt.

He also ignored the empty seat Evan had saved for him, opting instead for one near the front next to one of the coaching staff.

That also made him one of the first off the bus, and he'd disappeared into the hotel before Evan had any hope of catching up to him.

Abernathy
You ok?
Wanna hang out?
We could watch a movie or get a drink
Not ten though I promise

There'd been no response by the time Evan had gone back to his own room. He changed quickly, determined not to be wearing his fucking game suit when he tracked Riley down. There'd been no sign of Riley in the lobby, bar, or hallway. Fuck. Where should he try next?

A door opened down the hall, and Evan whirled around.

"Hey, Nover!" he called as he ran over.

"Abs," Antonov said. "What's—?"

"You know where Barzy's room is?"

Antonov narrowed his eyes. "Why?"

"I just..." What was a plausible reason? Oh right, the real one. "He had a rough game, and I just wanted to see how he's doing."

"I don't know if that's a good idea," Antonov said. "If Barzy isn't downstairs looking for a drinking buddy, he needs to cool down on his own."

"If he tells me to fuck off, I'll fuck off," he promised. "Do you know what room he's in?"

He hesitated long enough that Evan thought he wouldn't tell him. Maybe he didn't know, and Evan was wasting his time. But Antonov sighed and pointed to the stairwell. "He's up a floor. 756, I think. Two down from the ice machine, right side."

"Thanks!" He was already in the stairwell.

You're just going to check on your linemate, he told himself, taking the steps three at a time. *That's allowed.*

Evan knocked on Riley's room and waited. This was the first time he'd gone without being invited, and for the first time with Riley, Evan worried about rejection. Which shouldn't be a big deal, right? It'd sting, but they were just messing around. There wasn't much to reject, right? It'd be awkward for a bit, but they'd get over it. Whenever things had run their course, they'd go back to being teammates. That was always how it'd end. Riley had shown he could keep his personal life separate from hockey, and Evan could do the same. They could be professional.

There was a sound on the other side of the door, and Evan held his breath. His hands were buried deep in his pockets, and his heart was pounding like crazy. It would suck if Riley looked through the peephole, decided not to bother, and Evan had to walk away. Fuck, that would—

The door clicked open, and Evan was pulled roughly inside by his shirt. He stumbled forward and almost tripped, lips meeting him in a rough kiss as the door was slammed shut behind him. Evan groaned into the kiss, hungry for the taste of Riley after so long without.

So long? It's only been four days.

That should've set off alarm bells, but it didn't; Evan was too busy kissing Riley. With one arm wrapped around his waist to pull him tighter, the other working into Riley's hair, Evan moaned as he slipped his index finger into a curl. He stepped forward into Riley, hoping to find the bed so he could press their bodies together and feel more of him. Instead, they bumped into a wall, but it let him trap Riley and sink deeper into the kiss. Their cocks, straining against their clothes, ground together, and this time it was Riley who moaned loudly; Evan greedily swallowed the sound.

Riley broke the kiss. "Get on your knees," he rasped. Evan didn't move right away, too stunned by Riley's lust-blown eyes. It'd been too long since he'd been this close, gotten a chance to pick out the brown and the green specks. "Now," Riley repeated, with a nudge on Evan's shoulder.

Evan didn't think about it; he dropped to his knees and started mouthing at Riley's dick through his sweatpants. Riley made an almost pained noise and cupped his hand under Evan's jaw.

"You still haven't shaved." He ran his thumb along Evan's beard and used his other hand to wiggle his sweatpants and boxers down just enough to free his dick. He guided the tip to Evan's lips, leaving a smear of pre-come. Evan's tongue licked it off without him thinking about it, and he savored the taste of that familiar musky flavor. "Suck me off, Evan."

He didn't need to be told twice.

Despite weeks and weeks of practice, Evan was pretty sure he wasn't an expert at giving head. It could be overwhelming when he tried to keep a steady rhythm but got lost in the smell and the taste and the feel of Riley. He closed his eyes so he could focus on the weight of Riley's dick in his mouth. When he breathed in, he inhaled soap and a hint of citrus. He probably smelled exactly the same, but on Riley it made his mouth water.

"Faster," Riley said, breaking Evan's train of thought. He let Riley guide his head back and forth, Riley fucking into his mouth with shallow thrusts. And then, once he thought he'd gotten the rhythm Riley wanted, he took over. His hands came up to hold Riley in place, his hips flush against the wall so he couldn't thrust into Evan's mouth anymore. Evan moved as fast as he could, his tongue teasing around the shaft, and hummed low in his throat.

"More," Riley begged. "Fuck, Evan, more..."

So he gave Riley more. He gave Riley everything.

His jaw muscles burned, and his knees hurt where they dug into the rough hotel carpet. He felt like he could barely breathe, but when Riley's legs started trembling, it was worth it. He eased Riley's left leg over his shoulder to bear some of his weight.

"You're the fucking worst," Riley babbled. "You drive me fucking crazy, holy fuck. How am I supposed to...why do you have to...Evan, Evan, Evan..." There wasn't anything intelligible after that, just variations of his name in that broken voice, half prayer and half curse. As if Evan had any of the power here.

Evan got little more than a whimper in warning before Riley came down his throat. He waited until the pulses stopped before he slowed down, swallowing every drop and keeping Riley's cock in his mouth until it softened. When he pulled off, Riley grunted. Evan looked up and marveled at how fucked out he looked, head thrown back against the wall, his hair a mess as if he'd been pulling it, and a drop of sweat trailing down his neck.

You look beautiful, he almost said but caught himself. That wasn't a word in their shared vocabulary for these hookups. Hot. Fuckable. Sexy. Those were allowed. Safe.

Beautiful...where the fuck had that come from?

Evan guided Riley's leg back to the ground and got up with shaky legs. He had no plan except easing the weight off of him, but as soon as he was standing, chest pressed against Riley's, Riley's eyes flew open.

"You wanna fuck me?" he asked. His voice sounded raw, like he'd the one who'd had a dick down his throat.

That did sound amazing, but Evan didn't think he'd last very long. And as much as he'd love the feel of Riley's tight heat wrapped around him, he didn't want to move. They were touching, head to toe, and he couldn't bear to give that up. So instead, he found Riley's hand and brought it around his dick, straining uncomfortably in his joggers.

"Your hand," he said. *I want to watch you when I come,* he thought but was too scared to say it. When Riley looked down to get Evan out of his joggers and wrap his hand around his aching dick, Evan nudged his face back up. Their eyes locked, and he hoped he wouldn't have to explain.

Don't look away. Please...

He leaned down to rest his forehead against Riley's, so all they could see was each other. They shared the same air, breathing in and out together even when Evan's hitched as he got closer and closer to the edge. His whole world was Riley Barczyk.

As predicted, Evan didn't last long. Only a minute or two of Riley's hand working him and he came, spurts of come soaking into both of their shirts. It was more relief than pleasure, and he let it wash over him.

"Don't faint on me," Riley said. "You'll crush me."

He moaned and shifted so he could rest more against the wall instead of Riley, but he couldn't quite force himself to stand up yet. He had an arm around Riley's waist, so he pulled him closer. He'd just wanted to check on Riley. He hadn't planned on having sex. Was this all their relationship was?

Did he want it to be something else?

"Can I, uhm..." Evan dreaded each word as he pushed them out. "Could I stay here? Tonight?"

Riley stiffened, then relaxed. "Kind of presumptuous."

"Sor—"

Riley pinched him. "Shut the fuck up, Evan. Yes, you can fucking stay the night. Take off your nasty shirt first."

They were in bed a few minutes later, the lights off and curtains sealed tightly. Riley fit perfectly in Evan's arms, the two of them tucked in the comforter to keep out the winter chill. It was nice and comfortable and definitely not how they did things.

Evan liked it a lot.

36

DESPITE A COSY MORNING OF MAKING OUT IN RILEY'S ROOM and exchanging handjobs in the shower, Riley was just as surly the next day. He avoided everyone, eating breakfast in his hotel room and sitting by himself on the plane with his headphones unable to contain the loud music playing while he stared out into the clouds. Evan worried. Riley was a go-with-the-flow guy, and yet here he was, stuck in the mud.

Evan wanted to believe Riley's current foul mood had nothing to do with him. Things had been nice last night and this morning, right? If Riley were upset at Evan, he would've said something. Or, more likely, he could've told Evan to fuck off and not yanked him into his room for sex. Or he could've told Evan to leave instead of letting him stay. There was just enough evidence for Evan to pretend he wasn't connected, so he took hold of it fiercely.

Once or twice, he reached out while they were back in Pittsburgh, but Riley seemed uninterested with hanging out with Evan or anyone from the team.

"He's worried about his misconduct," Lawson confided with a group of them at the end of practice. As soon as the coaches ended practice, Riley had sprinted off the ice and disappeared.

"What do you mean?" Dalton asked. "The game's over. We lost. Damage done."

"The league is required to review all game misconducts for further disciplinary measures," Lawson said. "With Barzy's track record, they might come down hard on him to make a point."

"All he did was yell at the ref!" Dalton was indignant. "And fight a guy! There's someone who does that in every game, every night!"

"Sure," Lawson said with a shrug. "But only one of them is named Riley Barczyk."

Dalton shared a worried look with Evan. "Think he likes mini-golf?" Dalton asked with a weak smile.

"Not enough for it to help," Evan said. The only thing he could offer Riley was orgasms, and that hadn't helped either.

It might've been making it worse.

———

They didn't talk much over their stay in Pittsburgh—two home games plus practices—because Riley seemed to need the space. Evan had to admit, he needed it too. After talking to Amy, he'd acknowledged that he was gay in a way that made it settle inside him like a fact instead of a hypothetical. This thing with Riley wasn't some random glitch in his system; it was just the first attraction strong enough for him to recognize it for what it was.

So what exactly did that mean? Was he using Riley as a very willing but oblivious experiment? Did he have feelings for Riley that were more than sexual? Did he want to pursue those feelings?

Evan couldn't settle on answers. He'd think he understood things when he was alone at his condo or hanging out with Dalty or the guys...and then he'd lock eyes with Riley at practice or on the bench, and his stomach would flipflop and his heart would yearn for something he didn't want to think about too hard.

The only exception to giving Riley space came in the form of their pre-game ritual. Obviously, they had to talk and work well together during games or they were fucked. For a second, it looked like Riley was coming over for their butt taps, but he skated right by Evan. The next time he came by for a lap, Evan stepped into his path so quickly his choices were collide or stop.

Thankfully, he picked stop.

"You owe me like ten whacks," Evan said.

Riley stared at him blankly. "Abs"—Evan was starting to hate his own last name—"that was just for shits and giggles. It doesn't help us play any better."

"Sure," he said, because Evan knew it didn't manifest any actual luck. Sometimes it wasn't about the superstition but the routine, the way it could ground you before a game. It wasn't to give you something to blame or credit; it was about getting yourself to switch gears into game mode. Evan thought they both could use that. "But we lost 5-1 and you took a bajillion penalties last time when we didn't do it properly."

Riley's jaw dropped. "A *bajillion* is stretching it," he said.

"Half a jillion? Sorry, I can't count that high. Must've lost track." He savored Riley's indignant scowl and the dimple that meant he was trying very hard not to smile. "My point is, we gotta clear out the bad mojo and bring back the good mojo. So..." He lifted his stick like a baseball bat. "Turn the fuck around, Barzy."

"You used to be such a nice guy," Riley grumbled but he turned around.

"I know," Evan agreed. "Someone must be a bad influence." Then he swung.

———

By the end of their homestand, Riley was back to his old self: loud, obnoxious, and full of energy.

Evan had really missed that. Funny how things changed.

"Albuquerque and Nevada in December," Riley said the day before they headed out. "Best time of year for that trip."

"What, you not enjoying Pittsburgh winters?" Woodward teased.

Riley rolled his eyes. "I played in Vermont for two seasons, Woodsy. I grew up in fucking Massachusetts. I can handle the cold. I just like not freezing my ass off when I walk to my car."

It was good to have him back.

"Hey, Abs."

Evan froze at the sound of Riley's voice directed at him. He'd been on his way out of the training facility, but he'd gladly wait in the frigid parking lot if it meant Riley was talking to him outside of hockey.

"What's up?" he asked in a terrible impression of a normal human being.

"Should be pretty nice out west," Riley said, with far more calm than Evan had managed. His words steamed in the air. "You should bring some clothes besides suits and workout clothes. Something nice. In case you wanted to go somewhere besides the hotel and the rink." He knocked Evan with his shoulder as he walked by, heading for his car at the opposite end of the lot.

Evan stared after him long after he'd disappeared around a corner, wondering what that was about...and what qualified as 'something nice.'

———

Instead of agonizing over what Riley's seat choice might be on the plane to New Mexico, Evan was proactive. He got on board and found a spot among the other younger players like Dalton, Winchester, and Pope. It did get him stuck playing Connect Four, but hey, he needed something to take his mind off of the cute right wing a few rows behind him laughing loudly with their goalie Farrell.

Back in August, that laugh had grated on his nerves every time he heard it. Now he wanted to pocket the sound and save it for later.

When they arrived at the hotel, the team braced for their usual warning about a curfew. Coach Jack looked about to say it, but Lawson stepped forward and said, "Hey, Coach. Think we could have a late curfew tonight? Let the boys unwind and enjoy the warm weather."

Like a good captain, he wouldn't let anyone else get chewed out if Coach Jack got pissy about the request.

Coach Jack narrowed his eyes. "Warm weather? It's 50 degrees."

"And back home it's 30. It's practically shorts weather."

"Hockey players," he grumbled before mulling it over. Coach Jack crossed his arms over his chest and made eye contact with each of them in turn. "If I'm happy with practice, you can have a free evening. As long as you don't play like shit tomorrow night, I can let you boys have your fun. Don't cause trouble, and you won't find yourselves in any."

This was met with quiet enthusiasm as they rushed off to their hotel rooms before Coach could change his mind.

"So what was the Portland incident that caused this curfew thing?" Riley asked once a bunch of them were safely in an elevator.

"You never been on teams with a curfew before?" Vassiliev asked.

"Oh, I have. Nothing as strict as when I was in Juniors, but I've had coaches lay down the law. Sometimes it's a Barczyk-only curfew, but I earned that restriction. So what'd youse do to earn yours?"

The four of them shared a look, because none of them wanted to admit it. The silence drew out long enough that they reached the third floor and two guys escaped. When the doors slid shut again with just him, Riley, and Vassiliev left, Evan sighed and figured he should get it over with.

"There was an incident with indecent exposure," he said. "There was a very drunken strip poker game going on in a hotel lobby."

"It wasn't the main lobby," Vassiliev said. "It was relatively secluded. And it was very late at night."

"Vassy, were you one of the indecent ones?" Barczyk teased. He looked delighted by the prospect.

Vassiliev looked offended. "I am good at poker," he said. "I still had my shirt, socks, and boxers. I was very presentable."

Riley burst out laughing as the elevator dropped him and Evan off on the fourth floor. Vassiliev waved good-bye as he disappeared behind the metal doors, and it was, as usual, Evan and Riley alone.

"I'm guessing you weren't at the poker game," Riley said, wiping tears from the corner of his eyes. "Fuck, that must've been fun until it wasn't."

"I was asleep in my room several floors away. Dalty and I stayed away from that kind of stuff. We weren't old enough to drink when that went down, so we would've gotten it a lot worse than the other guys did."

"How much trouble they get into?"

"A lot," Evan said. Coach Jack had decided that if they had energy to be up at 3 a.m. playing poker and drinking, then his practices weren't hard enough. So aside from their individual punishments, the entire team suffered from excruciating drills for the next month. Coach Jack didn't let up until the end of February, only because he wanted them to save their energy for playoffs. They'd learned their lesson, though.

Hopefully.

"So assuming we don't fuck up at practice," Riley said as he stopped outside a door, "you wanna grab dinner? I know a place."

"Sure," Evan said. He was tired of hotel restaurant food. "What kind of place?"

"A food place," Riley said. He laughed when Evan rolled his eyes. "A nice one. Great Yelp reviews and everything."

"A nice one," Evan repeated, a record scratch in the back of his head. "Where we should wear nice clothes."

"Yeah, that's how it works."

"Just the two of us?" Evan asked uneasily. Riley huffed, a hint of whatever had happened on the ice in Quebec peeking through, so Evan quickly said, "Sounds good. A nice food place for dinner. Perfect."

Mollified, Riley went into his room. Evan turned away before he could be disappointed not to be welcomed in. And then he walked mechanically down the hall with his hands shoved in his pocket. He was so busy stressing out over it, that he reached a dead end and had to double back to find his room...two whole doors down from Barczyk's.

"I'm an idiot," he grumbled. His hotel room didn't disagree.

37

PRACTICE WAS DEEMED ACCEPTABLE BY THE COACHES, AND
the team cheered at having curfew moved to midnight. If they played
like shit tomorrow, it'd come back to bite them in the ass, as Lawson
sternly reminded them.

"Best fucking behavior," Lawson warned with one breath, then
with the next asked, "Who wants to go do shots at that bar we hit up last
year?"

Evan jerked off in the shower before his dinner date with Barczyk to
ease the tension. He laid out his travel clothes, glad that Riley had given
him the warning before leaving (and doubly glad he had heeded it).
When they traveled, he typically packed a suit or two for game days,
workout clothes, and maybe a henley or pair of jeans in the winter.
That's all that hockey players wore most of the time: league-mandated
fancy suits, and team-branded sports apparel.

He'd have been embarrassed as hell wearing a suit to dinner with
Riley (nothing said date more than a fucking suit), and he was glad he'd
brought a pair of khakis and a sweater. Of course, he'd neglected a jacket
besides the nice peacoat he wore when they traveled, and he didn't have
the confidence to pull that off without the accompanying formal attire.
Was his Riveters hoodie okay, or should he be a weirdo and use his suit

jacket? Could he borrow something? Who dressed nicely on the Riveters and might've brought a blazer? How would he explain what he needed it for? Shit shit shit—

A knock on his door ended his internal spiral. He took one last look in the mirror, straightened out a wrinkle in the pants (crap! He should've ironed them), before opening the door.

"Hey, our Uber is almost here. Ready?"

Riley was wearing faded jeans that were tight around his thighs but loose everywhere else, a belt with a ridiculously big buckle, and a black polo with the collar popped and his gold chain peeking out from the low V where all three buttons were left undone. Evan's eyes locked in on that bare skin, the slight hint of chest hair, before dragging his attention back to Riley's face. His very amused face.

"Ready. Just gotta grab my—" Evan hesitated, looked to Riley for a clue and saw he had no coat or hoodie or anything with him, and flipped a coin in his head. "Hoodie," he settled on, but Barczyk had slung an arm around Evan's shoulders.

"It's pretty warm out," Riley said. "We'll be in the car and the restaurant. I don't think you need anything." Without waiting for Evan to agree, he pulled him out of the hotel room and down the hallway, Evan's door clicking shut behind them and echoing in the empty hall.

Whenever Evan worried things between him and Riley would get awkward (and there'd been a lot of opportunities for it), Riley rescued him. He chatted up the Uber driver on the way, getting into an argument about the Rockies and the Red Sox that required nothing of Evan except his presence. When they were led to a small table toward back of a fancy but tiny restaurant, Riley gushed about the place to the hostess and got them through the server's spiel about the overly complicated menu, and then they were alone, and there was no one to rescue Evan from having to acknowledge he was maybe on a date with the guy he was having sex with.

...which honestly didn't seem like a problem at all when he worded it like that.

"You want a beer?" Riley offered. "You look like you could use a beer."

Evan nodded. "Just one."

"That's usually how they come. One at a time." Riley went through the menu and ordered them a couple of beers and a plate of nachos, then appraised Evan with a thoroughness that made him squirm in his seat. "You like spicy food?"

The question came out of left field, having nothing to do with any of the thoughts buzzing through Evan's head. He had to remind himself they were about to get dinner, so the question made perfect sense.

"Not really," he said. "Didn't have a lot of it growing up and never got a taste for it."

"Guessing there aren't many Mexican places in Peterborough."

Evan shook his head grimly. "We don't even have a Chipotle." Riley's chuckle shouldn't have done things to him, but it did.

"They got some decent places in Pittsburgh, though. Chipotles galore. Some decent Tex-Mex places. You never branched out?"

"You make it sound like I've never eaten a taco before."

"Have you?" Riley cackled when Evan tried to kick him under the table but missed. "I'm just trying to figure out what we should order at this Mexican restaurant in New fucking Mexico, or if you're gonna be stuck with house salsa and plain chips."

This time his foot connected, and he enjoyed Riley hissing in pain as the server dropped off their beers and nachos. Riley ordered for them, dishes Evan had never heard of like mole poblano and posole.

"I'm putting a lot of faith in you," Evan said.

Riley clinked his beer bottle against Evan's and took a long sip, his Adam's apple bobbing with each swallow. Jackass.

"Have I ever steered you wrong before?" He winked and then said, "You were drafted by Pittsburgh, right?"

This was another non sequitur, and it hit him as hard as the question about spicy food. What was Riley doing?

"Yeah," he said, suspicion leaking into his voice.

"You like the city? Seems like a good fit for you."

"I like it," he said, biting the inside of his cheek. On the one hand, this was a topic where he could actually contribute; on the other, the abrupt shift in conversation left him uneasy. "I never thought I'd end up there, but I'm really glad they drafted me."

Riley nodded, digging into the plate of nachos. "Glad they're treating you right. I know a lot of buddies who got drafted and never quite got their feet under them, and sometimes it was because the teams weren't supportive."

"You were drafted by the Kings, right? Were they good?" Evan cautiously picked up a chip, one devoid of jalapeños and sauce, just in case. He nibbled a corner, deemed it safe, and ate the rest in one mouthful. It was good.

"They were decent," Riley said. "Gave me plenty of minutes, considering I was a small rookie with anger issues."

"Anger issues?" Evan had never considered Riley to be particularly angry. Aggressive, sure, but it didn't seem malicious. He was relatively level-headed, as far as hockey players went. More than most, even. He lost his cool and yelled at the refs, which Evan wasn't a huge fan of, but Riley didn't smash his stick or throw tantrums.

Except he had in Quebec. Was that what he'd been like all the time as a rookie?

"Oh, for sure," Riley said, chips in each hand as he poked around the plate to find the best ones. "I was a fucking ball of rage that first season. Had something to prove and hated anyone telling me to calm the fuck down. Granted, I needed to, but I wasn't ready to hear it. Won a Cup that year, which maybe helped me mellow out a bit. Like, hey, look at me, I did it. Only played three minutes in that final game because I was too much of a liability. That, more than anything, calmed me down a bit. I can play the way I play, so long as I'm in control of it. If my emotions take over, I'm not helping anyone, least of all myself."

"Guess that makes sense," Evan said. All he could picture was Riley's snarl after he was pushed onto the Fleur-de-Lis bench and went looking for blood. It was easy to picture a younger version of Riley, less in control of his emotions, going 110% every game. Evan might not always care for that style of play, but he respected how much guts it took to do that game in, game out. And it wasn't like Evan was the only one who criticized Riley for it: every hockey news circuit complained about him. Riley just didn't care.

Evan couldn't relate at all, but he thought he could see the satisfaction of winning the Cup outweighing what others thought. Riley had already achieved The Big Thing, so he could let the criticism slide off of him.

"First season, eh?" Evan asked.

Riley's eyes lit up. "Did I just get a wild 'eh'? And yeah, very first season in the league. Part of me was relieved, and part of me was like, what the fuck? Where do I go from here? Turned out the answer was pretty straightforward." He leaned across the table, so Evan did too. "I do whatever the fuck I want, and as long as I score goals and draw penalties, teams'll take me anyway. Gotta say, hockey's a lot more fun when you're playing for yourself."

Evan let that settle in. "When is that?" he asked. "When do I get to play for myself? Do I have to win the Cup before people stop getting on my case for not being physical enough?"

"I mean, you don't have to do that shit." When Evan gave him a dubious look, Riley held out his hands in a wide shrug. "You don't. People see how big you are and that you don't hit, then they see tiny guys like me who do, and they want the best of both worlds. Doesn't mean you have to do anything. Hell, you play some fine fucking hockey as is. Get some confidence, and no one'll be able to tell you shit."

Evan didn't believe a word of it. He couldn't, not when all he'd heard this season from coaches was how he needed to improve his game. It wasn't as though Riley hadn't been agreeing with them.

"Then why were you giving me fighting lessons?" Evan said, more bite than he'd intended slipping in. He blushed, not just because of his tone, but because they'd done a very good job of pretending the lessons and the orgasms associated with it had never happened.

But as usual, Riley was unfazed. "A little 'cause I was jealous. If I were as tall as you, I would fucking wreck people. Or maybe I wouldn't, because I wouldn't need to. I dunno. And maybe I saw a teammate who could use my help, so I offered it. I didn't make you take the lessons, and I think we can both agree it's helped, if only to get your head screwed on right about the whole thing. But you ain't playing much different than you were at the start of the season. You're just a little more open to using your size, and that's made all the difference."

They were interrupted as the server dropped off their meals. Evan had no idea what he was looking at, but the server said it was the mole poblano. Hungry enough to be curious, he took a bite and hoped for the best. Spicier than he was used to, but not painfully so; he dug in.

"Good, right?" Riley said. "You plan on doing the long haul in Pittsburgh?"

"I hope so," Evan said. He wanted to say that was the dream, playing out his career for one team, but given who he was talking to, it seemed rude. "I like playing for the Riveters. I like Coach Jack. I like my teammates. I like how close it is to home."

"It's nice that they almost always make the playoffs," Riley agreed. "More chances to win the Cup." He sipped his beer and put it down carefully, with more care than he did anything. It made Evan nervous for a reason he couldn't name. "Teammates and coaches change all the time. Teams change, y'know? A good vibe can die out when people retire or management changes or just because that's life. You'd still want to stay in Pittsburgh?"

"I mean...maybe not," Evan said. The Riveters had been home for the past three years. People had come and gone, but the team had felt more or less the same over that time. The changes were so gradual, it was only looking back that Evan could notice things that were different from when he'd started. But at its core, it had been a good organization to be a part of; that didn't seem likely to change in one or five or ten years. "I just know I'm happy where I am. If that changes..." He shrugged. "I guess I'll reassess then. But I've got a few more years on my contract and a limited trade clause—"

"A limited trade clause? Fuck, Abs, they must want you long haul. I've *never* gotten a limited trade clause."

"Have you ever asked for one?"

Riley's mouth snapped shut. "No," he gritted out.

"I thought you liked the flexibility of moving around." Evan could never deal with that level of uncertainty, but spontaneity was Riley's thing. Where Evan saw security, Riley might feel trapped.

Evan's stomach lurched. Stupid spicy food.

"I do," Riley said. "It's easier not being tied down when things go south."

Evan sat there, bunching up his napkin on his lap. He wasn't hungry anymore. In the back of his mind, he'd been trying to find the right time to ask if this was a date; now he wasn't sure he wanted to know. Either way might be disappointing.

Though as usual, Riley sensed Evan's distress and bailed him out. They dropped the hockey talk and went into mini-golf, then a detour into pool, and ended the evening with judging what other sports the other would be good at if they'd never played hockey.

"Volleyball," Riley said. "Tall people play that, right?"

"You'd be great at pickleball," Evan countered. "Or maybe rugby."

Riley snapped his fingers and pointed at Evan. "Cheerleading. You'd be a great cheerleader. The one who throws and catches people."

When they got back to the hotel after being crammed together in a too-small Uber, they went their separate ways. It didn't feel as much like a date when he ended up alone without so much as a kiss goodnight, but it also felt like the best first date he'd ever had.

38

"I GET TO HIT YOU THIS TIME, RIGHT?" RILEY ASKED. "YOU got me both games in Pittsburgh."

He swung his stick towards Evan's torso; Evan caught it before it hit him. "Not the front," he scolded. The only thing worse than having a pre-game superstition was doing it wrong.

"Is it reverse good luck if we do it backwards?" Riley grumbled but moved so he was behind Evan.

"Reverse good luck? You mean bad luck?"

Riley drew the blade of his stick down Evan's body, starting at his head and following his spine down, then across his ass before a light tap. Why the hell was this so sensual? Illegal. Mostly because it was really uncomfortable to be half-hard while wearing a cup.

"No," Riley said. "Reverse good luck. Big difference." Riley deemed seven swings enough to avoid 'reverse bad luck' and skated away with a look over his shoulder that made Evan want to follow him.

He didn't, though.

Instead, he did some stickhandling while studying the Albuquerque Turkeys. The Turkeys had been a great team...over a decade ago. They'd had some ups and downs recently, including two big ones in the same season: a few years ago they'd made it to the Stanley Cup Finals after

266

years of not even making the playoffs, only to lose to the Ohio Otters. Evan couldn't imagine that kind of emotional atomic bomb going off in his life. He was disappointed whenever the Riveters lost in the playoffs, but it was somehow easier when it was a first or second round exit. A Conference Finals loss would be heartbreaking.

A Game Seven Cup Final? Fucking devastating.

The Turkeys had rebounded somewhat since then. Last year they'd made a respectable playoff push, losing in the second round; this year they were on track to make the playoffs again. They were scrappy, especially since they were in the midst of a losing streak at home. On the road they did fine, but in Albuquerque they'd lost five of their last six. That always made Evan wary; teams didn't like to lose in front of their own fans.

Of course, teams never liked to lose. No one got this far in their career without having a competitive streak a mile wide. Evan had always used his to push himself forward. Strive to do better and contribute where he could. The Turkeys seemed to have more of a collective mind set; they used it to fuel their *team* moving forward. There'd be no easy shifts, no weak spots to exploit, just a determined team that was going to play hard from whistle to whistle.

When Evan glanced over at the Riveters, he worried Coach Jack had been wrong to give them so much freedom last night. They were ready to play, sure, but they weren't ready to fight for a win. He saw it in the lazy, disorganized way they warmed up. There was always a point in the season where the switch flipped, and you went from playing game by game, getting your feet under you, to digging in to earn as much ground as you could before playoffs. The Turkeys had made the change already; the Riveters hadn't.

———

Most of them hadn't locked, Evan was forced to amend during the game. There were a few among them who had. Doyle was having a great game. Their backup goalie Reese was bailing them out of some sloppy defensive zone plays. Moreau had won most of his face-offs.

And then there was Riley, hitting everything that moved.

It wasn't as out of control as it'd been in Quebec. This was more his usual style, throwing his body and running his mouth in equal measure. Tonight he seemed to remember they were trying to win a hockey game, and he was making great plays too. Evan and Vassiliev weren't having spectacular games (okay, Evan was sub par but Vassiliev was doing fine), but Riley seemed determined and able to carry their line. He got three scoring chances just in the first period, and that was with only about three minutes of ice time.

"Much better," Coach Jack praised him several times throughout the night. "That's what I want to see, Barczyk! Play hard, but control it!"

"You're having a good night," Vassiliev said in the locker room. "You want to share some of that luck with the rest of us?"

"I already did," he said, looking Evan right in the eye before turning to Vassiliev. "Not my fault you can't hit an empty net."

"I hit the post!" Vassiliev said. "I'll get the next one!"

The game was going so well that Evan was still having fun despite his own mediocre performance. He had Riley joking on the bench again, and the tension from Quebec was gone. *This* was what Evan wanted: he wanted to get along with his linemates and enjoy hockey and win games. They were up 3-2, so if they buckled down during the third period, they'd be good.

And that was when Riley took out Luc-Henre Baptiste, star center of the Turkeys.

In Riley's defense—and crazy that Evan was the one making that defense in his head—it looked like an accident. Just an unfortunate play where they collided awkwardly along the boards. It looked eerily like when Riley had done that to Evan last season, or at least how Evan imagined it had gone (he'd never worked up the nerve to watch the replays). They hit the boards. They both went down. Riley got up and kept playing. Baptiste didn't.

Once they realized he was hurt, the refs blew the whistle and trainers went onto the ice to check on Baptiste. They all stood there watching, but Evan turned to watch Riley instead. It was like they'd been transported back in time to that night in Philly almost a year ago, the one where Evan had been on the ice worrying about his shoulder and his career and his future, and Riley had been...doing what?

Standing there expressionless, apparently. Riley leaned on his stick, his eyes fixed on Baptiste but otherwise showing no emotion. He didn't look happy about the injury, but he didn't look upset about it, either. No worries for Baptiste and no remorse for having caused it.

This was the Riley Barczyk that Evan hated. He'd never gone anywhere. He'd just been hiding behind toothless smiles and grabbable curls and offers to help Evan. Help Evan what? Become a player like this? Just admiring his handiwork after potentially ending someone's season?

Evan turned away and went to the bench. He wasn't sure he could stand to look at any of it anymore.

When Baptiste finally got up and was guided off the ice, the arena broke into cheers. Evan joined the other players as they tapped their sticks against the ice or boards. That show of respect for an injured player, teammate or rival, had always gotten to Evan.

But he also knew it wouldn't be of much comfort to Baptiste that Riley or anyone else was doing it. He didn't remember what it'd sounded like for him in Philly. He'd been too worried and wanted to get to the medical staff as quickly as possible. Baptiste was probably thinking the same, praying over and over *please don't be too bad, please let me be okay.*

The refs huddled together by the penalty box and determined Riley deserved no penalty for the play, much to the aggravation of the Turkeys and their fans. The Turkeys weren't a physical team, but Coach Jack deemed it wise to pull back on Riley's minutes.

"Fucking garbage," Riley grumbled as Evan and Vassiliev both went out on the ice without him. "What do they think I'm gonna do, hurt the same guy again?"

Hurting people is the problem, yes, Evan thought.

"Maybe they're worried about retaliation," Dalton said as he followed, once again Riley's replacement on wing. Riley looked about to snarl something less than friendly, so Evan stepped between them to guide Dalton to the face-off.

The rest of the game passed in a blur. When they got back to the locker room, there was the usual post-game rundown by the coaches as they stripped off their gear.

And through it all, Riley said nothing. No one said anything about Baptise, and it pissed Evan off. He was so angry he nearly threw his elbow pad across the room when he took it off.

This was why he hadn't liked Riley in the first place. Sure, he'd gotten to know him better, and he wasn't an irredeemable jerk, but he wasn't some angel. He was callous and took no responsibility for his reckless behavior. Baptiste, Evan, the dozens of others he'd injured—they weren't a blip on his radar. Riley Barczyk only cared about Riley Barczyk, and if you were on his team, he might pretend to care.

As pissy as he was, Evan knew he was being unfair. He might be trying to spin this as Riley being a jerk, but it was more about Evan's hurt feelings. Riley wasn't a complete asshole. He just played an aggressive style of hockey and was unapologetic about it. If Evan didn't like that about Riley, that was Evan's problem.

A really big problem, because this was more than the injuries and their careers. Evan realized he didn't care about the hit in Philly anymore. Yeah, it had sucked, and yeah, he thought it was kind of shitty that Riley didn't remember or care, but it was hockey. What had he been expecting? A handwritten apology? It wasn't Riley's responsibility to care about someone's hurt feelings on the ice. Reckless as he was, Riley didn't *want* to injure anyone. It was an unfortunate side effect of the game, and instead of letting it paralyze him like it did Evan, he embraced that physicality.

No, Evan could let go of the resentment about his shoulder...what he was having trouble with was how much he liked Riley, and what that said about him. Not that he was sexually attracted to him, because that obviously said Evan was some sort of queer, but that he liked Riley romantically. This wasn't about the sex anymore—that would've made it so much easier—and Evan worried if this reflected something about himself. Because it was one thing to accept Riley for his faults, but Evan didn't know if he could handle those things in himself.

Was he the type of person who might someday send someone into concussion protocol and not bat an eye? Would he someday be desensitized to Riley doing it?

Why could he now accept these things about Riley but not himself?

And that was it, wasn't it? As angry as he was about the hit to Baptiste and all that other muck about Riley's playing, Evan was upset at Riley for being so unapologetically Riley. Then here was Evan, apologizing for anything and everything that he did that might make other people uncomfortable. Evan, who couldn't very well apologize to himself for the discomfort of the past few months.

There was an increasing amount Evan was discovering about himself through Riley, too much to process, and it was easy to think of Riley as the problem. He was the one making Evan confront these uncomfortable truths about himself—his sexuality and kinks, his capacity to be more aggressive, the kind of person he was attracted to—and now that Evan knew this was what was happening, it had him on edge.

And it wasn't fair to blame Riley for any of it when all he'd done was exist and encourage Evan, but Evan bristled when Riley did his locker room interview after the game. He knew what was coming, and he didn't want to hear it. He was at max capacity of garbage floating around his brain; the last thing he needed was more. If only he could shut off his ears.

"Could you tell us a little more about the hit to Baptiste?" one reporter asked. Evan braced like he was about to get punched.

Riley ran a hand through his sweat-damp curls. He'd taken off the top half of his gear, nothing on his chest but his gold chain, and left on everything below his waist. Pretty standard for hockey players, but a power move during interviews to show the reporters how invasive it was to come into the locker room. Evan had never had the guts to talk to reporters without at least a shirt on.

"It's too bad he got hurt on that," Riley said. "I know I play rough, but I'm never trying to send a guy to the hospital or anything."

"You have a long history of rough play, as you say," another reporter said. "Do you ever apologize to opponents afterward?"

Evan looked up so fast his neck hurt. It was like someone had pulled the question out of his head. For a second, he worried *he'd* been the one to ask it.

Riley shrugged, flashing a hint of a smile. "Not really? I walk a thin line, sure, but I play hockey. They play hockey. They step onto the ice knowing what's coming. I don't apologize when I steal the puck from people or block a shot or do anything that's part of hockey. I'm not gonna pretend I'm sorry for playing the body. It's hockey. They literally pay me to do it."

But what about hurting them? Evan thought, though this time the reporters didn't pick up on his question. They moved on to other topics, more generic ones that required no thought and never got real answers, while Evan sat there, miserable.

39

Evan's night passed in a blur. He must've showered and changed, because the next thing he noticed, he was getting off the bus at the hotel. He might've even continued the night in that daze, except Riley was walking over to him with a look that usually meant one of them was going to end up with a dick in their mouth soon.

And it would be *so* easy to melt into oblivion with Riley's help. Forget the storm raging in his head and enjoy a night with his willing teammate...but he'd been doing that for too long. He needed to take a breath and figure out how to stop his head from exploding.

"Rain check?" Evan asked as soon as Riley was close enough. There was a flash of confusion, maybe even hurt, so Evan said the first thing that came to mind. "I promised Dalty we'd hang out."

Riley's brow pinched, right between his eyes, and Evan was struck by the impulse to reach out and smooth the crease away.

"Oh." Riley stuffed his hands in his suit pockets. It was unfair Evan had to keep his distance when Riley always looked so good in his game suits. "You guys were roommates, right?"

"Yeah, the last two seasons. It's weird not seeing him as much this year."

Riley bit his lip like he wanted to say something, but he shrugged. "Have fun. Maybe I'll cash that rain check tomorrow in Nevada."

Evan's dick perked up at that, a very insistent *yes, please!* that he tried to reel in. Maybe tomorrow he'd be in a better headspace to fall into Riley's bed (he really hoped so...), but not tonight. He let Riley walk away and then scanned the crowd as quickly as possible. Avoiding was one thing and lying was another; he needed to find Dalton.

He spotted Dalton at the far end of the lobby and rushed over. "Dalty! Hey, hold up!"

Dalton was about to get on the elevator but stepped away and waved off the guys inside. "What's up, bro?"

"You busy?" he asked, huffing a little from how fast he'd run to get over here.

Dalton stared at him. "It's almost midnight, bro. No, I'm not busy."

"Good. You wanna hang out?"

"Hang out? Abs, there's no mini-golf open right now."

"Ha fucking ha," Evan grumbled. "Do you wanna hang out or not? I'll buy some beer from the hotel shop if you want me to."

Dalton looked him over, apparently decided it was worth losing some sleep, and nodded. "Sure. You grab some beers and meet me in my room when you're ready. I wanna change out of this fucking suit first."

Evan grabbed the first two beers he could reach in the mini-fridge, stopped by his room to change into sweats and a Riveters tee, then knocked a little too urgently on Dalton's door. He was in fact still knocking when Dalton opened the door and smacked Evan's hand away.

"The fuck? Don't worry. I didn't fall asleep." Dalton took one of the beers, opened the door wider, and nodded for Evan to follow. "Take a seat, I guess. Sorry, it's kind of a mess. I wasn't planning on having company."

"No roommate?" Evan asked, startled. Still on his entry contract, Dalton would normally have someone like Winchester or Pope room with him on the road. It was a rare treat during the early years to get a room to yourself.

"Nope," Dalton said with a grin.

Evan closed the door and sat in the stiff plush chair next to the window, cradling his own unopened beer in his hands. The cold bottle and the condensation were more comforting than the alcohol would be, so he held it tightly. "Sorry. Thanks for humoring me. I know it's late, and it must be nice to have space to yourself."

Dalton sighed and rubbed a hand down his face. "Ugh, I'm being a dick. Don't be sorry. I'm not mad. You don't usually need to, like, talk, so this must be serious." He opened his bottle. When it began to fizz, he brought it to his mouth to suck up the overflow. "So what's up?" he asked as he wiped the edges of his lips with his shirt.

"I—" Evan wasn't sure where to start. "I'm stressed out and don't know what to do."

"Is this about your guy friend?" Dalton asked.

Evan winced. He'd already gotten some support on that front from Dalton before, and Amy's advice had helped. If he was still having trouble sorting things out, he needed to attack the problem from another angle.

"It's about Barczyk," Evan said.

Dalton froze, his face going pale, before he let out a laugh and held his chest. "Jesus, Abs. Sorry, for a second I thought you were saying Barzy *was* your guy friend. Fuck, mini-heart attack."

Evan gave a fake laugh and rolled his eyes. "Yeah, ridiculous, right?" Did he like that it sounded ridiculous that he was having sex with Riley? Not really. Did he like the small amount of privacy it allowed? Kind of.

"But it's about Barzy...?" Dalton prompted. "Did he say something? I know he's got a big mouth. He might've just been dumb and not realized it. Not that I want to excuse anything if he was being a dick." Dalton cut himself out, took a deep breath, and said, "I should just let you tell me what he did before I get carried away."

Without saying it, Evan knew what Dalton was worried about: that Riley had said something homophobic or otherwise insensitive. More importantly, he understood Dalton was ready to help kick Riley's ass if necessary, which Evan appreciated. He'd get his ass kicked by Riley, but still. Not wanting anyone to get hurt on his behalf, Evan needed to clear the air.

"He hasn't said anything. It's nothing about this season," Evan said. "It's about last season."

"Last—?" And then understanding flickered in his eyes. "The thing with your shoulder? What about it?"

"This is going to sound dumb, but uh..."

Evan put his beer on the floor, because there was no way alcohol was going to help. He sucked in a deep breath, held it, and then...unloaded, for a lack of a better word.

"He's never apologized for it, and I get it. He doesn't apologize for any of what he does. And this is probably me being overly sensitive that he doesn't care, but he *doesn't care*. He doesn't care that he could've really hurt me. He doesn't care that he sent Baptiste to concussion protocol. He doesn't care about any of it, and I feel kind of like an asshole for being on the ice with him when he does that shit.

"And then all season, I'm getting the coaches telling me I gotta play more physical. Be more physical, kid. Use your body. So I do all that, and they're happy. Great job, kid! Way to knock 'em down! And then what? Do I end up like Barzy, where I don't even remember every person I've sent to the medical staff?

"And if I don't say anything to Barzy about how I feel about all this, am I complicit? Does it even fucking matter if I approve or disapprove, because he's a grown-ass man and not my responsibility? Like, what do I do to get past this?"

The more he spoke, the faster and faster he went until he probably wasn't making any sense by the end. When he finished, Evan took a few deep but shaky breaths and felt like his heart was about to beat out of his chest. Fuck, it felt good to let that out.

Dalton didn't look like it'd felt good to hear it. He looked like he'd just watched a train wreck and was now expected to help pull bodies from the wreckage. After thirty seconds of silence, he put his beer on the nightstand next to the bed and crossed his arms over his chest.

"That was a lot."

Evan buried his face in his hands. "Fuck. Yeah, it was."

"You feel better?"

Evan peeked between his fingers. "A little?"

"Good. So here's the thing. You're not Barzy's babysitter. None of us are. Yeah, as his linemate, you might have to step in and help now and then, but nothing he does is your fault. Don't take on the burden of his behavior, past, present, or future. You guys play very different styles of hockey, and you both do it well. Stop overthinking things."

"I wish," Evan grumbled.

Dalton gave him a sympathetic look. "Sorry, bro. I don't have any better advice on this one. Unless you want to talk to Barzy about it." He paused, waiting for Evan's firm shake of his head, before he continued. "Would you even feel better if he apologized? Or if you were on a different line?"

"Not really," he admitted. In August, he would've loved that. But since then, Evan had to acknowledge the burden of getting over it was on him. Feathers were going to get ruffled and egos were going to get bruised during games, and the chip on his shoulder might've been put there by Riley, but only Evan could take it off.

Honestly, it wasn't any specific thing that he was upset about. It was the whole situation, the small but steady accumulation of worries and bullshit and stress. Riley could've handled everything perfectly from the start, and it wouldn't have made Evan feel any better about it.

"Then there's nothing to do," Dalton continued. "Except, like...play hockey? And I get where Coach Jack and them are coming from. Sometimes I see you looking like you're scared of your shadow, but lately you've looked a lot more confident. It started with being more physical, sure, but you haven't hit anyone in a few games, right? You still look better than you did in pre-season." He put up his hands. "I'm not trying to say you looked bad, by the way. It's not a hockey thing so much as an attitude thing. You *look* like you're an NHL player and not a rookie."

"Thanks?" Evan said, unsure if it was a compliment.

"You're welcome?" Dalton said with the same uncertainty. "For real, bro. You've been doing great. You're earning that contract they gave you."

"Yeah?"

"Totally." He bit his lip. "Do you think it's got anything to do with your guy friend?"

Evan blushed and turned away so maybe Dalton wouldn't notice.

"I know that's not what you're here to talk about," Dalton said. "But I hope things are going well with your guy."

They were, and they weren't, but Evan didn't want to go into that in case he said something incriminating. "You know how it is," he said vaguely. "What about you and Jennie?"

Dalton lit up. "She's the *best*."

Evan did open and almost finished his beer as he repaid the favor and listened to Dalton. Not that Dalton had any problems except travel. He gushed and gushed about his girlfriend. Evan kind of envied him for how simple things were for him. Maybe one day Evan would figure his shit out, and he'd be able to brag about his boyfriend without worrying about all the other baggage that went along with said boyfriend.

Maybe.

40

EVAN STUMBLED OUT OF DALTON'S ROOM AROUND 2 A.M., planning to be responsible and go to his own room.

His feet took him to the wrong door. His hand knocked, and his heart let him fall into open arms. Then the rest of his body betrayed him piece by piece, and Evan couldn't blame anyone but himself.

He never made it back to his own room that night.

Riley

EVAN WAS ACTING WEIRD.

Which was maybe presumptuous on Riley's part. He'd known Evan for all of five months. Some of these guys had known Evan for years, and no one seemed to think he was acting off. Though Riley liked to think he had more *intimate* knowledge of what made Evan tick, and to his eye, Evan wasn't acting very Evan lately.

Or...was he? He'd been quieter than usual on the bench and during practices, and the more Riley thought about it, the more it reminded him of the Evan he'd first met in Pittsburgh. Shy, never speaking up, restrained. And then after their game against the Turkeys, he'd been nearly catatonic in the locker room. He'd been so out of it, he hadn't noticed a few reporters trying to get his attention. Riley had flagged them down when it was obvious Evan wasn't up for interviews.

It'd really worried Riley when Evan had blown him off at the hotel.

Now, Riley knew he could be A Lot. Whatever was bothering Evan, it made sense he'd want to minimize distractions so he could screw his head back on properly. And Riley was a big boy. He could handle a night on his own, thank you very much.

It'd just hurt a little, seeing Evan jog off to spend time with Dalty.

He hadn't much minded being woken up at 2 a.m. with a slightly drunk Evan. That had taken away a lot of the sting, both of the rejection earlier and having to crawl out of bed at two in the fucking morning. He'd thought maybe Evan was feeling better. He just needed some time with his best bro. Perfectly reasonable.

Except the fucker wasn't in Riley's room in the morning. At first, Riley thought he'd dreamed Evan's appearance—a good dream, honestly—but no, there was definitely an Evan-sized imprint in the bed. He thought they were past Evan disappearing in the middle of the night. He thought they had something a teensy bit more solid than late-night hook-ups.

And so, with 36 hours until game time, Riley started a downward spiral.

———

It was his fault. Not Evan's. It was Riley's fault he'd been neglecting his therapy appointments for the last few months. Granted, he was avoiding them because he didn't want to talk *about* Evan, but again, he could only blame himself for it. Riley's issues were all anger-related anyway, so a relationship with anyone shouldn't matter. Hell, sex usually mellowed him out. Hard to be angry when you're getting off regularly, y'know?

Except the next evening as he got ready to play the Scorpions, he realized he was a little angry at Evan.

Frustrated, he corrected. *I'm frustrated with him.*

As he jumped onto the ice and did a lap around their zone more quickly than was advisable, he thought about why. Things were going well, weren't they? The sex was good. They had fun. They'd gotten better chemistry on the ice. It was greedy of him to want more from Evan. Greedy and unnecessary. This was better than he'd hoped his move to Pittsburgh would be.

And yet...

He did three laps before it was too dangerous and he had to stop. Too many people, too little space, too many pucks flying. Fuck, he was keyed up. Not a good sign. Maybe he'd do some breathing exercises before the actual game, because he felt about ready to explode. If he didn't get a handle on this, he was going to be a disaster.

Hope the penalty box is comfy...

"Barzy."

Riley snapped back to attention and had to look straight up to meet Evan's eye. "Sup?" he asked.

"What's the point of a mouthguard if it's never in your mouth?"

It was a great opportunity for a dirty joke, but Riley couldn't think of one.

He rolled his eyes—the only sass he could muster—and sucked it back into his mouth. So preferred to chew it than wear it. Sue him. "What's up, Sasquatch?" he asked around the stupid piece of plastic.

"I'm feeling like we need some whacks to get us going," Evan said with that adorably small smile that was mostly in his amber eyes. Riley would do a lot for that smile, including continuing this fake warm-up superstition. Whose bright idea was this, anyway?

"We ever pull the statistics on this?" Riley was nearly incomprehensible with the stupid mouthguard in properly, so he pushed it off with his tongue and settled it at the corner of his mouth. "How many wins to losses?"

Now it was Evan's turn to look fondly exasperated. Evan Abernathy, fond of him? That'd be nice.

"Not enough data. Gotta go for a full season before we know for sure." He started to turn around, but Riley tapped him with his stick.

"You go," Riley said. It wasn't a good idea for him to whack Evan right now. If he went too hard, he didn't want to wonder if it'd been on purpose. So he turned around and let Evan hit him a few times with his stick. The routine did help him calm down. Maybe that was why people had their superstitions.

It was going pretty well. There was more hockey than anger going through his head, which was always a good sign. That meant that when he ran his mouth, he was in control of what came out.

And then Travis motherfucking Walker decided to be an asshole.

Maybe Walker was bored. Or trying to make a name for himself on a new team. Hey, maybe the guy didn't like having all his teeth and thought Riley could help him out. There was no way of knowing what went through Walker's mind when he first crosschecked Riley, or even when he slashed him, but it didn't matter. Riley knew what kind of trajectory Walker was on, knew he had a short rein on his own temper, and so he'd looked the other way when Walker was being a classless dick.

Up until he blatantly tripped Evan.

All the fuck no's on that one.

Riley got up to full speed before he charged into Walker, sending the larger player sprawling onto the ice. There were whistles and shouting, though Riley ignored it in favor of watching to see if Walker was going to come up fighting.

He did spring to his feet, red-faced and pissed, but he saw who it was who'd hit him and wisely chose not to drop his gloves.

"What the fuck, you piece of shit!?" he screamed at Barczyk.

"You've been acting like pond scum all period," Riley drawled. They hated when he didn't yell back. The calmer he was, the more worked up other people got. They didn't need to know he was fucking seething under the surface. "It was only a matter of time until it came back to bite you on the ass."

"Fucking rich, coming from a guy like you!" Walker seemed a lot braver now that the refs were here, yelling at them about penalties.

"You see me going after anyone that doesn't deserve it? You want to stay on your feet, then make sure you let my boys stay on theirs."

They were ushered to the penalty boxes—Walker with 2 minutes for tripping, Riley with 2 for charging—and Riley felt he'd made his point. He was willing to leave things at that (like, *mostly*; he was still going to fuck with Walker at face-offs, but he wasn't going to go out of his way to hit the guy or anything), but the fucker just didn't know when to accept the L.

"You talking about Abs?" Walkers yelled from the other penalty box. "You of all people do *not* get to give me shit about Abs."

Riley had a lot to say about that, but he was acutely aware of how public this conversation was with the fans banging against the glass right behind him. So instead of engaging, he held up his hand in Daniel's direction and mimed him running his mouth.

Undeterred—there was no fixing stupid, after all—he kept talking.

"Don't pretend like you're some knight in shining armor," Walker snapped. "You aren't rescuing him from me. Just because they all seem to have forgotten what you did to Abs last season, doesn't mean I have."

The fuck?

Riley spared him a glance. "Did last season? You're reaching, bro. Learn to play some hockey, fuckhead."

It looked like Walker said more, but the arena erupted in cheers. Riley looked up to see a replay of the Scorpions scoring. Ugh. Riley hated when the other team scored during his penalties. Worse, it was four-on-four, so Riley still had to sit out the rest of his two minutes.

But the thing about being stuck in the box was he had a lot of time to think. So he thought about Walker sitting a few feet away, so confident that he was the good guy and Riley the bad guy. What was it he'd said?

What you did to Abs last season.

He'd never fought Evan before, that was for damn sure. Riley couldn't remember ever doing anything to Evan in particular...but he didn't exactly remember every hit he'd ever dealt. Was it possible there was some truth to what Walker had said?

And if so, why hadn't Evan ever brought it up before if it was such a big deal?

41

AFTER GETTING TRIPPED BY WALKER, EVAN WAS UPSET. THE trip was bad enough—he'd seen the footage on the Jumbotron and was pretty sure it'd been intentional—but Evan couldn't shake the feeling that Walker had targeted him because they'd played together. Like he knew Evan wouldn't retaliate, so it was a freebie.

Though Walker should've learned from the game in Pittsburgh: just because Evan wouldn't fight him, didn't mean he could get away with being rough.

Riley had swooped in and put Walker in his place, which only added to Evan's annoyance about the whole thing. Riley thought Evan couldn't take care of himself. Riley was still going around hurting people. If Walker had gotten hurt, was any of it Evan's fault?

The answer to that last one was of fucking course not, but guilt decided it needed to make an appearance along with the mess of everything else he'd been feeling lately.

There was also the tightening in his gut, like Walker had awakened Riley's bad side. Some nights Riley was a ticking time bomb, waiting for the wrong trigger to set him off, and his shouting match with Walker had all the makings of setting him off.

Except...it didn't. Riley came out of the box, scowling and surly, but he played a somewhat lackluster (though physical) second and third periods. He didn't instigate anything, ignored the Scorpions trying to rile him up (notably, Walker wasn't among them), but also didn't drive play the way he usually did.

He was just...there. He barely spoke on the bench, with a faraway look on his face, like his mind was elsewhere. Riley was normally the loudest person on the team, yelling support and chirping the other team as they skated by. On the days when he was pissy and fighting everyone that moved, then he was muttering expletives at everyone within earshot.

Obviously, Evan was concerned. And it wasn't just him who'd noticed.

"You were very quiet tonight," Vassiliev said as they boarded the bus back to the hotel. "You didn't let Walksie get under your skin, did you?"

A vein pulsed in Riley's temple. "What?"

"Walksie. Walker. He's young. He can be a loudmouth and rub people the wrong way." Vassiliev paused. "Like you, a little, but less focused."

"Less focused?" Riley asked, and Evan was relieved to hear he didn't *sound* terrible. Not as energetic as usual, but not upset.

"He's more like atomic bomb." Vassiliev made a noise like an explosion. "You're a precision strike."

"Or he's like a sledgehammer," Kates added as they all settled into their seats. "And you're a scalpel."

"Oh, lemme try!" Winchester said. "He's like a pack of hyenas, and you're like a honey badger."

"The fuck does that mean?" Kates looked appalled by the comparison. "You're terrible at analogies."

"I thought these were metaphors," Winchester said.

"Simile?" Dalton offered.

And as a third of the team argued literary devices like weirdos, Evan waited for Riley to get drawn into their bullshit. But he didn't. Instead, he stared sullenly out the window as they drove through the bright lights of Las Vegas to their hotel, a couple of miles from the arena, tucked away from the main strip.

When they filed into the hotel lobby, another late night before another early morning, Evan had to push through the crowd to get close enough to Riley.

"Barzy!" he called, shouldering past Moreau and Antonov. He had to reach out and grab Riley's shoulder before he dipped into the elevator. Which was dumb, because he had no plan here. What was he supposed to say that he could say with most of the team in earshot?

But when Riley turned to look at him, Evan didn't really care about the audience.

"You all right?" Evan blurted out.

"Why wouldn't I be?" he asked. His smile was the lopsided, carefree one he flashed in interviews, but his eyes scanned the lobby.

I don't know, Evan thought desperately. *That's why I asked.*

We can't both be freaking out...

But Evan just shrugged and stuffed his hands in his suit pockets. "Dunno," he said and swallowed. "Just checking."

Riley rubbed a hand over the stubble on his face. "Just tired. That mid-season travel slump, y'know?"

He did look tired. Was that why he was so muted? Evan hoped it was that simple, but he doubted it. "Sure. Sorry, I'll uh...I'll let you sleep."

They parted, and Evan hoped for a text inviting him over to Riley's room, but it never came. He was too much of a coward to invite Riley over; he wasn't sure he could handle Riley saying no.

———

They flew home to Pittsburgh for a blessed two and a half weeks in town. Evan wanted to kiss the ground in relief when they landed, because he wanted the comfort of his own condo and bed. He didn't kiss the ground, mostly because it was below freezing, and he wasn't going to spend an extra second outside if he could help it.

Unfortunately, returning to Pittsburgh made it harder to come up with excuses to see Riley.

Riley, who'd avoided Evan on the flight. Riley, who had dark circles under his eyes. Riley, who looked about one minor inconvenience away from shouting expletives in the airport.

Evan thought maybe they needed some space, but Evan had just gotten into his Uber when his phone pinged.

Barczyk
You wanna do some fighting practice?

Not really. Not because he didn't need the practice, but he had a bad feeling about squaring off against Riley right now. He wasn't sure if it was Riley or himself he didn't trust; something was wrong, and it was like a powder keg ready to blow. But he could hardly say that, and he wasn't in a position to be picky about when and how they hung out.

Abernathy
Sure I'm getting a little rusty. When?

Barczyk
My apartment this evening? 5 ish?

Abernathy
I'll be there. Dinner after?

Barczyk
Maybe.

———

Evan walked into Riley's apartment complex with the same mix of dread and anticipation he had the first time. It was funny how the source of his dread had shifted. He wasn't worried about sex with Riley...he was worried about Riley.

He was worried about *them*, and what that meant.

The gym was empty except for Riley, who was swinging at a punching bag. Instead of his spandex shorts and muscle shirt, Riley wore joggers and a loose Riveters tee that was far too faded for his five months on the team. Barefoot and with a headband to keep his growing curls at bay, he looked good, fluid and lithe as he moved. He always looked good, though. Evan stood in the doorway to admire him for a few more seconds before he walked over.

"Got the place to ourselves," Evan said in a hopefully cheery voice.

Riley took a few more swings before he stopped. "Reserved it," he said with a shrug. His eyes roamed over Evan as Evan took off his hoodie and boots. "Grab some boxing gloves. Let's jump right in."

The routine of swinging and blocking was more familiar than he'd realized. Evan had to talk himself through the first round or two, but his body remembered what to do. It was grounding in the same way mini-golf was, that slight mental exertion to take his attention off all the other stuff flitting through his mind.

"Not bad," Riley said after fifteen minutes of exchanging light jabs.

"Learned from the best," Evan said with a smile. Riley didn't smile back, and Evan felt his own fade away.

"I'm gonna get a drink. We'll go again in a minute." Riley walked off to the water cooler at the far end of the gym. Evan was thirsty, but he didn't feel like he was invited. What was going on?

"Hey," Evan said as they squared up again. "You sure you're okay?"

Riley shrugged. "Good enough."

"Do you—?" But then Riley was swinging at him, harder and faster than before, and Evan's attention went from Riley's strange mood to defending his face. This time, he felt like that punching bag hanging in the corner more than a practice partner. But he powered through, doing his best to fight back. He needed to weather the storm, because it seemed more and more like this practice was for Riley's sake rather than Evan's. Too much frenetic energy, and with no game or practice for the next two days, this was the closest outlet he'd get. Evan could do this for Riley.

He was panting by the time Riley backed away again, a dangerous glint in his hazel eyes.

"Thanks," Evan said and, groaning, took a seat on the mat. "I need a break."

Riley sat down a few feet away. He crossed his legs and circled his arms around them. "Watch the shoulder when you swing," Riley said, his tone off. "Wouldn't want it to get hurt."

Evan froze. "My shoulder?"

"Yeah. Heard you injured it last season."

There it was. The perfect opening to bring it up and clear the air...but he didn't. There was something weird about this whole evening, and his skin prickled with goosebumps. It was like he stood on the precipice of a cliff and where to step to come down safely.

"My shoulder's fine," he said, and he could tell from the look on Riley's face that he'd just misstepped and fallen over the edge.

"Then why do I have guys like Travis fucking Walker telling me I'm a jackass for having injured you last season? Why can I Google 'Barczyk Abernathy hit' and get tons of GIFs of me nailing you along the boards and blog posts going off about how dangerous that play was and poor Abernathy could've been seriously hurt? Huh? How come all that exists out there, and you're telling me 'it's fine'?"

There was a flicker of shame that ran through him; Evan turned away from Riley and stared at the small cracks on the mat. Funny how you couldn't see them until you got close.

"Yeah, you hit me last season," Evan said. "You hit people all the time, though."

"And most of the time, those people aren't shy about telling me off for it. I join a new team, and if someone's got a bone to pick with me, they pick it. We laugh about it, we share a beer, and it's like it never happened. If you were upset about it, why'd you never say anything?"

"I got over it," he said. He chanced a glance up at Riley, but his expression was inscrutable.

Riley licked his lips. "When?"

"Huh?" His heart lurched.

"When did you get over it?"

Although he should answer, he didn't want to admit how recently it'd been; he stayed quiet.

"You weren't over it when I came here," Riley continued on, ignoring Evan's silence. "How long were you pissed at me and wouldn't even tell me? Because God forbid Evan Abernathy have to be the bad guy even for a second. What else haven't you told me?"

This was an answer Evan felt better about giving, so he said, "You're the first guy I've ever been with."

That seemed to derail some of Riley's anger. "Ever?"

"Yeah."

"Like—?"

"First *ever*," Evan said. "First anything. Period. End of sentence."

Don't make me spell it out...

Riley blinked at him. "Oh."

"Oh?" His mouth had gone dry, but he forced out, "Was that...not okay?"

"Huh? No, it's just..." Riley sighed and looked up at the ceiling. "I mean, I had an idea you didn't have a lot of experience 'cause of what Dalty said but—"

"What do you mean?" Evan interrupted. That couldn't be right. "You talked to Dalty about me?"

"Evan, I talk to everyone about you," Riley said. It was the hardest blow he'd landed all evening.

"Riley, I'm—"

"So what's all this been? Am I the demon from your past I've been teaching you to beat? Why didn't you say anything?" His voice was raised, but he wasn't yelling; Evan wilted under Riley's gaze.

"You didn't remember," he said, pleading for Riley to understand.

As he saw Riley's body language shift, it wasn't because of some mutual understanding. Evan watched Riley close off, the veneer of calm dissolving as he took a deep breath through his nose and his brow furrowed into a deep scowl.

"Probably," Riley said carefully, "because there wasn't much to remember."

Evan stiffened. "My shoulder—"

"You miss a game?" Riley asked coldly. Evan didn't say anything, just stared incredulously at Riley. "Practice?"

"I missed a practice," Evan said. "Just because it wasn't bad, that doesn't mean it was okay. It could've—"

"Evan." Riley said it so forcefully, Evan's jaw snapped shut. "Hockey is a very physical, dangerous sport. You cannot step on the ice if you're not willing to face the possibility of getting hurt while you're on it." Evan tried to look away, so Riley smacked his hand against the mat. "I'm serious. Stop ignoring this. I'm sorry I hurt you, and I'm glad it wasn't worse, but you can't play like this where you're scared. And you can't put that burden on everyone else, that they need to play differently because that's not what you want."

"I don't—"

"You do," Riley said firmly. "You blamed me for this shoulder thing for maybe a whole fucking year because that was easier than accepting that hockey's dangerous and sometimes shit happens. You're annoyed that the coaches tell you to play more physical. You want to be the injured party here because poor Evan, nice Canadian boy, doesn't want to play the same sport as the rest of us."

He pushed off the mat and pointed a finger at Evan. "Play how you wanna play, but don't get bitchy at the rest of us for doing it differently."

That was Evan's chance to say something, to defend himself or fight back or, hell, maybe agree and apologize. But he sat there, trapped under the weight of this argument. All those uncertainties about where he stood with Riley, all his guilt and anxiety, they pressed on his chest. This was why he hadn't wanted to talk about the hit with Riley. It served no purpose, just got Riley defensive and made Evan miserable.

"I'm not fighting any more battles for you," Riley said. He looked disappointed at Evan's silent acceptance. He turned around and walked away, and suddenly Evan could move.

"Riley, wait—" He jumped to his feet. He could still catch Riley. He could fix this.

"Go home, Evan," he called over his shoulder. "I've got nothing left to say to you right now."

He realized once he was alone that Riley had apologized. Months and months of wanting nothing but some acknowledgement and sympathy, and he'd finally gotten it.

It didn't make him feel any better.

42

EVAN DROVE HOME, REPLAYING THE ARGUMENT OVER AND over. Was *he* the bad guy in all this? Riley seemed to think so, and he had valid points. Evan had felt uncomfortable with Riley on the team, and he should've cleared the air early in the season.

...but that would've only made Riley feel better. He could've wiped his hands of the whole thing earlier. He'd have said his minimal sorry, Evan would have been forced to accept it, and Evan would have continued to be frustrated and upset. It was only after months of spending time together that Evan could even trust Riley's apology—that he hadn't meant to hurt Evan or anyone, that was just an unfortunate byproduct of how he played. In August, he would've thought Riley was full of shit.

And Riley didn't care about what others thought of him. If he rubbed someone the wrong way, he shrugged it off or joked about it. Not saying anything about the shoulder incident wasn't the problem. If it'd been Dalton or Lawson or Vassiliev or literally anyone else on the team, Riley would've said sorry and moved on, regardless of how that teammate felt about his apology afterward.

The problem was that it was *Evan* who'd held it in.

Evan, who'd been holding onto resentment but been perfectly willing to accept Riley's help. Willing to do a lot more than accept help.

In the Abernathy-Barczyk duo, he didn't think any of them had done anything wrong...but Evan had been pretty shitty to Riley. He understood why Riley was upset and felt taken advantage of.

"I *am* the bad guy," he mumbled as he parked his car and laid his head against the steering wheel. "Fuuuuck."

He went inside his lonely apartment and plopped down on the couch to stare at the blank TV. All he wanted was to talk to Riley and fix things, but, as usual, Evan didn't know how to do that. He wanted things to go back to the way they were a few weeks ago, when they were having fun. How had he fucked this up so badly?

That was an answerable question, so he grabbed a pad of paper and a pen from his coffee table, tore off the top pages with his packing and grocery lists, and started jotting down notes.

> *How did I fuck this up?*
> - *confused about sexuality* → *probably gay*
> - *upset about hit* → *needed to let that go, should've talked to Riley*
> - *frustrated* → *I'm not a fucking kid, I shouldn't have to change how I play*
> - *avoidance* → *kept all this bottled in too long.*

He went back to the first one and circled it several times, then drew an arrow to a blank space and started over.

> *definitely gay.*
> *experimenting with teammate = bad idea*

Well, that was a start. Seeing it all on the page helped him see all the pieces that had collided to get him into this mess. But he already knew there was a problem. That wasn't going to help him solve anything.

How do I fix things?
- apologize to Riley.

It was a shitty way for Riley to find out, hearing it from someone else. It didn't matter that Evan had moved past it. For Riley, this was a brand new issue. But after that very obvious answer, he was stumped. Clearing the air about the hit was only one side of the issue: that fixed things with Barczyk, his teammate and league pest. He was more concerned with how to fix things with Riley, his...his what? 'Guy friend'? Teammate with benefits? Hookup buddy? All of those sounded dumb and didn't quite hit on what it was they were doing.

- need to figure out what I want from Riley (sex? relation-ship? go back to just teammates?)

His heart skipped a beat at the word relationship. What would that even look like?

"Horse before the cart," he mumbled to himself. He had three possibilities written, and he wasn't sure which one was the best choice. It was smartest to smooth things over and go back to being teammates with no sex involved. Friends, or friendly at least, with no more late nights together. Professional. No more Riley, just Barzy.

A wave of sadness hit him at the thought, so unexpected it made him want to cry. Evan didn't know if he was capable of being a good boyfriend to Riley, if only because that side of himself was so new and raw. How could he build any sort of relationship when he hadn't known he was attracted to men this time last year?

But he didn't want to let Riley go.

I like Riley Barczyk.

His hand trembled as he wrote, but slowly he gained confidence. The scariest part was admitting it, after all; everything else wasn't so bad.

Plan:
- *give Riley space*
- *reach out to talk*
- *apologize*
- *try to get back together*
- *prove I'm worth a second chance*

Carefully, he tore off the page along the perforated edge, then he hung it up on his fridge with the lone magnet. He had a plan, right there in black and white. He had no idea if it was a *good* plan, but it was something.

———

Every day when Evan left his condo, he'd walk by the fridge and tap the paper as he passed. That little reminder of what he needed to do, like when he'd been a kid working on perfecting his edge work or his toe drags.

It didn't make it any easier to have Riley ignore him during practice. He was good at subtly finding ways not to end up in the same group as Evan, or to put space between them during drills. When they had training in the team gym, he gave Evan a wide berth and never went near the area where they'd practiced fighting. During team meals, Riley surrounded himself so thoroughly that the closest Evan could've hoped to get was five seats away.

"I'm guessing," Dalton said as he sat down next to Evan at one of those lunches, "that you tried to clear the air with Barzy, and he wasn't thrilled."

Evan tensed, a denial on his lips, but then he deflated. He didn't see the point. "Yeah, kind of."

Dalton scooped a big spoonful of pudding out of the plastic container, and Evan held his breath. He worried Dalton would accuse him of being a baby about the whole thing, or say that Riley was being childish to care. But all he said was, "Bummer."

It was kind of nice, having one person be level-headed.

"Think it'll be a problem at tonight's game?" Dalton asked. "He's pretending you're invisible. Not a big deal in practice, but kind of a problem if your linemate's ignoring you on the ice."

"It'll be fine," Evan said. He was confident it would be, if only because Riley cared too much about winning and playing well to let something this petty get in the way.

Dalton shrugged. "Hope so. You two have been killing it together. Hate to see that get messed up over some drama."

Dalton was the only one who seemed to notice anything was off. Even Vassiliev, stuck between them in the locker room, didn't pick up on the tension that was so thick it felt like it was choking Evan. Or maybe he was too polite to comment.

During warm-ups, Evan was unsurprised that Riley ignored them. Their pre-game routine was over, and that more than anything told Evan how annoyed Riley still was. It'd been four days since their argument, and Evan had hoped he'd have softened by now. Riley never took things personally, not what players or the media or the fans said. If he got upset during a game, it never lasted longer than the game itself, like the final buzzer flipped a switch and he could move on.

For such a divisive player, he didn't hold grudges. He remembered all the heavy hitters and the people likely to come after him, the weaknesses to exploit and how much each ref was likely to let him get away with, but it wasn't like he was some villainous mastermind the way Evan had imagined. Riley was just good at reading the ice, and he did it objectively.

His ignoring Evan wasn't objective. It wasn't malicious either, but there was actual emotion behind it.

Which had to be a good sign. That meant he cared. If he'd really gotten over Evan, things would be like at the beginning of the season when Riley would actually talk to him or look in his direction. Evan still had a chance.

Right?

Their first shift was...fine. Not amazing, but not a total shitshow. It felt like he and Riley were rusty, and it was only Vassiliev holding their line together. They could turn it around.

On the bench during a game, there was nowhere else Riley could be except next to him, and Evan was determined to take advantage.

"Hey." Evan nudged Riley with his knee. Riley's head snapped around so hard, Evan's neck hurt in sympathy. "Next face-off, I'm going to win it to you, 'kay?"

Riley stared at him as if he'd spoken in Swedish. "You talking to me?"

"No, I'm talking to fucking Farrsy in net," Evan snapped, some of his frustration leaking through. He took a deep breath, reeled it in, and said, "Yes, I'm talking to you. Next offensive zone face-off, be a little toward the top of the circle, and I'll win it to you."

Riley just stared at him, chewing his mouthguard. As much as Evan wanted to turn away, he didn't; he stared right back. Riley looked away first.

They didn't get a chance for Evan to make good on his promise until their last shift of the first period. They finally got their offensive zone draw to the right of the goalie, perfect for Riley as the right wing to take a shot right after the face-off. Assuming Evan could win it. He checked over his shoulder to make sure his teammates were in position, then squared up at the dot. As he looked the other center in the eye, he saw something. It was another third-liner, just like him, but younger. He looked so determined, so into it, like everything hinged on this one stupid face-off.

Evan had lived that way for years until he got his contract. So intent on making every play count.

...so easy to throw off.

"Don't fuck up," Evan said as the ref dropped the puck. The other center blinked, and Evan won the face-off.

Right to Riley, waiting exactly where Evan had told him to. Evan pushed the other center to clear more of the path to the net. Riley shot, the puck whizzing past Evan before it hit the goalie. The goalie, not expecting a shot so soon, fumbled it and dropped it right into the net.

Evan threw his arms up, pushing away from the poor rookie to throw himself at Riley, who looked stunned that he'd actually scored. He didn't have time to brace himself as he was crushed between both Evan and Vassiliev, then Riley whooped loudly.

"Fuck yeah!" he screamed and head-butted Evan, a feat only possible because Evan was hugging him so hard he'd pulled Riley into the air. "Let's get another one!"

"You greedy bastard," Vassiliev said, tapping both of them on the heads. "But I agree. Two more at least!"

And suddenly, it was back. That spark that had driven them on the ice for months was rekindled. All Evan had wanted was a tiny bit of what they'd had before, a reminder to Riley of how good things could be if they were on the same page. What he got was an inferno. They went on a rampage in the second period, driving play and spending their entire shifts in the offensive zone. They did so well that Coach Jack gave them extra minutes. Every time they were on the ice, it felt like they were about to score.

At the start of the third, they did.

It was the dumbest way they could've scored. After all they'd done this game, it was another stupid bounce that went in. Riley was in front of the crease, being a menace as usual, while Vassiliev and Evan passed back and forth, trying to open something up. Frustrated and tired, Evan took a shot. A weak shot, one he barely got any of his stick on. He'd be embarrassed by that shot most days, except when it got to the crease, it deflected off of Riley's skate into the back of the net.

It was such an ugly, stupid goal.

The goal horn went off, and the arena erupted. Evan threw open his arms and cheered, expecting nothing more than to enjoy the view of Riley celebrating. Instead he got an armful of Riley, who squeezed him so tight Evan couldn't breathe. When he let go enough for Evan to draw in some air, he lost it immediately: Riley pulled him down and kissed him hard on the cheek.

"Let's fucking go!" Riley screamed and head-butted him again, as though their heads knocking together could somehow undo having *kissed* him. In the middle of a fucking game! All Evan wanted to do was reach out and kiss him back. He couldn't, but his heart thundered with the possibility that maybe he'd be able to again soon.

He was hyper-aware of Riley the rest of the night, something he didn't know was possible. He thought he was *always* that aware of where Riley was, what he was doing or saying. Riley had wormed his way into Evan's brain months ago, but it turned out there were spaces he hadn't quite gotten to yet.

Although the Riveters tried their best, they couldn't get Riley the hat trick on the night. When the other team pulled their goalie in the last few minutes of the third period, Coach Jack sent Riley out and everyone, even Farrell, gave him the puck every chance they got. If it'd been Evan out there, desperate for his first career hat trick, he'd be flinging the puck down the ice every chance he got. Riley, either not selfish enough or more level-headed than he was given credit for, made the smart play every time: whether it was a pass or a clear, he only tried for the empty net twice, one time hitting the post and the other time icing it.

No one was surprised when he got the first star of the night, and Evan watched in the locker room with everyone else as he was interviewed on the ice.

"What a great performance tonight!" the reporter gushed. "Those were two great goals tonight."

"Thanks," Riley said. He was breathing a little heavily, and his face was red, but he glowed with happiness. It looked like the Riley he'd seen in a dozen hotel beds.

"Were you worried when they reviewed your second goal to see if it was a kick?"

"I mean, I didn't kick it, so no. I've got plenty to say to the refs most games, but they're usually right when they have time to review footage."

"Usually?"

Riley shrugged. "No one's perfect. Not even me." He winked, and the reporter laughed. "But in all seriousness, I owe both those goals to Abs. He made the play both times, and I just got to cash in. Probably why I never got that third one, since he wasn't on the ice with me anymore."

"Is that why you, uh, showed your appreciation to him after that second goal?"

"You mean when I laid a big wet one on him? Yeah, I've gotta be careful. No one's gonna pass to me anymore if I keep doing that, right?"

The locker room lost it at that, and Evan couldn't hear the rest of the interview as his teammates threw tape balls at him and made kissy faces. When it died down, Vassiliev put a hand on Evan's shoulder and said very solemnly, "I won't kiss you unless it's the Cup-winning goal."

"Thanks, Vassy," he said, matching his tone. "I appreciate that."

Vassiliev gave his shoulder one more squeeze before he let go. "Be careful," he teased. "If Barzy will kiss you for that, imagine what he would do to you in a game that matters."

43

EVAN THOUGHT THAT GAME WAS THE BREAKTHROUGH THAT would get Riley talking to him. If Riley would kiss him in front of tens of thousands of people—even if only on the cheek—then he must be willing to talk to Evan again.

Not so much, apparently.

Instead of being a big momentum shift towards fixing things, it was a tiny nudge. Riley continued not to initiate any conversations with Evan during team time...but he didn't resist when Evan talked to him. He stopped finding excuses to get out of Evan's group during drills, and he would allow himself to be within ten feet of him at the gym. So, progress, right?

And at games, though, it was almost like a time machine. There were still no pre-game butt whacks, but once the puck dropped and the crowd was roaring, once their adrenaline was going and there was no time to think, then it was like things were before.

When Evan scored against the Prowlers, Riley's eyes lit up, and he tackled Evan the same way he always had. When Evan got some Penalty Kill time two games in a row, it was Riley he heard on the bench more than everyone else, shouting encouragement. And if someone gave Evan trouble, either physically or running his mouth, there was Riley to put him in his place.

I'm not fighting anymore battles for you, Evan heard clearly every time Riley pushed or chirped someone on his behalf. Evan felt like a burden at those times, because Riley still had to look out for him when he'd made it clear he didn't want to. So he tried to play that physical game the coaches wanted from him, if only to spare Riley having to babysit him.

But going from the arena where he felt at any moment Riley might pull him in for another kiss on the cheek, to the locker room where Riley seemed to forget Evan was there, gave him emotional whiplash. Instead of soothing him with the possibility of how things could be again, it taunted him that it might be over.

He told himself to keep giving Riley his space, but every time he heard Riley's laugh, it killed him to see he was still being kept at arm's length. His laugh, his smile, they weren't for Evan. There was no secret keeping them tied together, one that promised if they could just get through this practice or that game or these team activities, they'd get those stolen moments together where Riley was all his.

And then, as they finished up their December homestand and were days away from traveling again, Evan began to worry: how long was too long to give Riley the space he wanted? Was Evan risking any hope of fixing things by waiting? Fuck. He needed to get Riley alone just so he could say sorry. That was the first step, apologizing for holding onto that stupid shoulder thing and not talking it out sooner.

It was impossible. Riley would let Evan talk, but only in the very public places where it couldn't get too serious. There was no privacy at the training facility and definitely none on the bench. There was nowhere Riley allowed him to be that was an acceptable place to say any of the things that needed to be said.

One night in his condo, Evan grabbed his notepad again in frustration. He vented for a full page about how much he'd fucked up and how lonely he was. It stopped making sense at the end, so he tore the page off and crumpled it into a ball.

"Not productive," he grumbled as he tossed it across the room.

For the millionth time, he took out his phone and stared at his recent text messages to Riley.

Abernathy

Hey can we talk?

Do you wanna go grab a beer or a milkshake?

Nice goals tonight

You going to Lawson's holiday party next weekend?

You okay after that fight? Looked like you took a bad one at the end

Going to the bar with Dalty, Winnie, and Daniels...

None of these messages had been met with any response. He couldn't even tell if Riley had read all of them. As much as Evan wanted to talk to Riley, texting was like shouting into the void. Bearing his heart on a string of text messages...no thanks. He turned off his phone and put it aside to avoid the temptation of scrolling back through their older messages.

He sat there on his couch, head in his hands as he leaned forward to stare into space. He fucking hated this.

The notepad caught his eye again, the jagged edge where he'd ripped a page bugging him. He picked up the pad and tore off the leftover pieces from earlier. Then, without thinking about it, he picked up his pen and started writing.

> Riley,
> I'm sorry. You're right, I should've said something. I was holding onto that hit way too long and holding it against you when I shouldn't have. It was messed up that I never said anything while we were... Well, I should've either buried it months ago or told you. I'm sorry.
> - E.A.
> P.S. I miss you.

Very carefully, he folded the top of the page before gently tearing it out. He made it look as innocent as possible as he folded it into a square, writing RILEY on the outside. Evan left it by his wallet and keys so he wouldn't forget it. The next day at practice, he found a chance to tuck it into Riley's jacket pocket. There were a few other people in the locker room when he did it—on a gym day, there wasn't much hope of avoiding that—but no one was near their stalls and, more importantly, Riley was busy on the squat rack. He put the note next to Riley's keys, so he'd have to find it, then sneaked back to the treadmills.

It might not be much better than texting into the void, but Evan was tired of doing nothing. This was better than a text message, anyway. More personal.

Evan went through his run, his skin buzzing in anticipation. How long until he could expect Riley to read it? Would he message Evan? His imagination went wild, and he was in a good mood as he finished up his workout and showered. When he went back to the locker room to grab his stuff, he noticed Riley's stall was empty. Evan's heart thudded double time. Riley had his note! Any moment now, he might hear from Riley and—

He stopped on his walk out to his car. He felt something in his pocket next to his wallet, and when he pulled it out, his heart just about died in his chest.

In his pocket were the torn-up pieces of his letter.

Riley

RILEY WAS DETERMINED TO MOVE ON FROM EVAN Abernathy.

Clearly he'd felt more for Evan than Evan had felt for him. Riley thought there'd been something more than sex and goals building between them, but finding out Evan hadn't much liked him when he joined the team *and* that he'd never been with another man, Riley felt used. Not that Riley wouldn't have been up for helping a friend experiment, but he'd like to have *known* if that's all it was.

And what was this shoulder thing? It pissed Riley off. It was about respect, and it seemed like it'd been lacking.

So he was going to keep his head down, ignore Evan, and get over this ill-fated crush.

It was really easy to stick to that plan when he wasn't near Evan. Or thinking about Evan. So, basically, never.

"I should move on," Riley grumbled. "But I don't know if I want to. I dunno what to do, Sophia."

He was on his bed, listening to a podcast about...robots? (fuck, he hadn't been paying attention for a while now and had no clue what they were talking about—wasn't this a podcast about movies?) and petting

306

Sophia. She blinked at him impassively, which he took as a command for more pets and an invitation to keep talking.

"We had a real good thing, I thought," he said and scratched under her chin. She looked like a damn queen receiving her due worship from the peasants. "I liked him a lot."

She opened ocean-blue eyes and stared at him. *Liked?* she seemed to ask.

"Fine," he grumbled. "I *like* him a lot. But he doesn't talk to me. He didn't tell me he'd never been with men before. He didn't tell me he'd previously hated my guts. What the fuck kind of relationship is that?"

No response from Sophia, except to close her eyes once more.

"Yeah, yeah," he said. "You'll get your pets."

The Evan Question had been nagging at him since he'd confronted Evan. Riley couldn't regret anything he'd said, wouldn't take any of it back, but he felt trapped. He wanted to be with Evan again so badly, but it was obvious they saw each other differently. It felt like Evan didn't respect him as a partner, and it seemed like Riley had over-valued where their relationship was going.

Ugh. That last part was on Riley. He should've brought up that, hey, he kinda had feelings for Evan, and did Evan feel the same way? But he hadn't, because he'd been scared of it being one-sided. Not that Evan would be a dick about it. He might've misjudged some things about Evan, but the guy was polite to a fault.

Sometimes, that softened his resolve to take a step back. Riley could picture it so easily: Evan, still anxious about the hit last season, seeing Riley join the team. His hurt and frustration that it'd never registered to Riley. He could see it in the way he'd been almost cold to Riley at the start of the season; it wasn't just that Evan didn't want to play a physical game, he thought Riley was heartless for not remembering.

...was he?

No. Riley played a rough game, sure, but he'd never tried to hurt anyone. He'd busted some noses and bruised some egos, but he'd never sent a guy on Injury Reserve. Never broken anything or anyone beyond repair, nothing a few days rest wouldn't heal. Evan included.

And Evan had warmed up to him. However he'd built Riley up in his head, Riley had gotten him to see through all that and give him a chance.

So did he owe Evan a second chance in return?

Yes was his gut answer, but his pride was too wounded to deal with that right now. Evan had hit on Riley's insecurities enough that Riley knew he needed space to lick his wounds and recover, or else they'd be as much of a mess as before. He hadn't been sure Evan had wanted to reconnect, except for that stupid letter...

Riley had almost gone to Evan right then and there and said it was fine, they could start over. As much as he wanted Evan back in his arms, it wasn't smart to jump back into bed so soon. He'd already let himself get caught up in his attraction and desire. Next time—if there was going to be a next time—needed to be done right. Part of doing that right was waiting to make sure Evan wouldn't change his mind and thinking through how much of himself Riley was willing to put out there. Because right now, he could survive losing Evan Abernathy; if they started where they'd left off, in another month he didn't think that'd be true anymore.

So he'd torn up the note to avoid temptation and stuffed it in Evan's jacket pocket, mostly so Evan wouldn't be waiting for a call that wasn't coming. But he wasn't strong enough to get rid of it completely...he'd torn off the part where Evan had put his initials and said *I miss you*. He'd rolled that up and slipped it into his wallet. Just a little sliver to remind him Evan cared, if only a little.

———

As captain and responsible adult with a wife and kids and house (yikes, that was a *lot* of responsibilities; Riley could barely handle himself and a cat), Lawson was in charge of throwing team parties. Their schedule hadn't allowed for any so far this season, but their current homestand in Pittsburgh was long enough and close enough to Christmas that they were having a holiday party on the only Friday night they didn't have a game.

They also only had an optional skate the next afternoon, meaning they'd all be able to sleep off their booze and not look like ass on the ice.

Riley loved this sort of party, especially mid-season. Aside from all the team bonding, it was nice to let loose. Riley desperately needed to let loose in a way that wouldn't result in fights or penalties or black eyes. He'd been on his best behavior on the ice (for him, anyway), like he had something to prove to Evan. The strain was getting to him.

You think you don't have to play the way I do? Well, I can play your way too. Just watch.

So he'd dressed up in his nice khakis that made his ass look good, his fancy loafers, and a light-green button-down with short sleeves. It was the shirt that his sisters assured him brought out his eyes, showed off his arms, and that he could unbutton to be 'as slutty as he wanted.' And then, because he'd already dressed as fuckable as he could, he decided to go the extra mile and do the little things that only Evan would appreci-ate: he styled his hair to show off the curls, left the day-old stubble, and used a bit of mascara to bring out his eyes.

Yes. Riley knew he had nice eyes and wasn't afraid to weaponize them.

As he checked himself out in the mirror, he had to admit he'd done a damn fine job.

Of what? he asked himself as he put on his jacket and headed down to his car. *Are you even trying to sleep with him right now? Because you probably could without the extra effort.*

Showing him what he's missing, duh. He looked at himself in the rearview mirror and winked. *And that I don't need him.*

Riley had purposely gotten to Lawson's place on the early side of things. He wasn't emotionally equipped for taunting his kind-of-ex while sober, and he didn't trust himself to pre-game alone. Getting drunk at your team's holiday party was acceptable; showing up already smashed less so.

"Barzy! Welcome." Lawson grabbed his hand and pulled him in for a hug, their arms squished uncomfortably between their chests. The bro-est of hugs that was more chest bump than embrace, as if there was some need to assert dominance or the gesture would appear too soft. Riley refrained from rolling his eyes. "You're just in time. Woodsy is making martinis. Help yourself to whatever's in the fridge."

Riley tucked his jacket into the massive hallway closet and followed the chatter to the kitchen.

"Evening, boys," Riley said as he stepped inside. "Somebody hand me a drink, stat."

"Look who's all dressed up," Woodsy said. "You know this isn't a club, right? No one to pick up at the team holiday party, Barzy."

That's what you think.

"Some of us just like to look nice." He found a cooler next to the kitchen island and dug around for the beer with the highest ABV he could find. "You should try it sometime."

One beer, two martinis, and a round of shots of something that tasted like ass later, Evan showed up. He'd clearly not taken the same approach as Riley, because he was wearing possibly the ugliest Christmas sweater in existence, complete with pompoms and tinsel and a strange design that Riley was a bit too drunk to understand. But Goddammit, Riley still wanted to climb him like a tree.

Which is why Riley very pointedly turned away from Evan and rounded up people for a game of pool before his dick got any stupid ideas.

Lawson, like many people with too much money and a large basement to fill, had a pool table at one end by a wet bar. The wet bar was actually nice—perfect for keeping Riley liquored up while he played—but the table was crap. Ugly brown felt, inadequate clearance on all four sides, no ball return, and cue sticks that were begging to be shaped and properly chalked.

All of which he apparently said out loud while racking with a shitty plastic rack, because Big Katie said, "You got a lot of opinions about tables. I'm just happy when I don't have to share a cue."

"Did you, like, major in billiards?" S'more asked, proving once again that Riley shouldn't feel bad for him for the stupid nickname.

"If you make over 7 mil a year, shouldn't you be able to maintain a pool table?" Riley snapped. He closed his eyes to regroup, then let S'more break as an apology.

They played more rounds than Riley cared to keep track of. The only sign he was doing well was that he got to keep playing. Half the team seemed to cycle through, either to watch or lose to Riley. But he was sobering up too much, so mid-game he passed his cue off to Dalty and disappeared back upstairs to find food and booze. Lots of booze.

"Hey! Mr. Pool Shark."

Riley whirled around (too quickly—oof, his stomach) to see Nover pointing above Riley's head. Riley looked up and spotted the mistletoe hanging in the doorway.

"Wha? You want a kiss or something?" He pulled the massive winger in and kissed him on the cheek, just like he had to Evan a few games ago. It wasn't half as good, but he wasn't surprised. "Merry Xmas!"

Nover laughed and handed him a glass of water. "You should slow down."

"It's a party," Riley said. He took the glass and might've dumped it down the sink, except Nover blocked his way to the kitchen and watched him until he drank half of it. "Happy, Mr. Buzzkill?"

"I will be happy if no one throws up," Nover said and patted Riley's shoulder. "Not my house, but still my team. Take it easy."

"Take it easy," Riley mumbled as Nover walked off. He still had the glass, which gave him the perfect excuse to head to the kitchen for another drink. Though before he took two steps, he looked up and saw Evan. Their eyes locked, and for a second, Riley forgot why he was upset. Did it matter, when Evan was *right there*, and did he really care if they lasted a lifetime or one more night, so long as Riley got that last hour or two with him?

He took a step forward, then another.

"Riley," Evan started, and Riley stopped and shook his head.

Fuck, he shouldn't do this when he was drunk. It was questionable whether he should do it at all, but being drunk set a bad precedent.

So instead of falling into a trap that would hurt both of them, he turned on his heel and went (hopefully) in the direction of the kitchen.

The rest of the party was a blur, which was exactly what he wanted. There were shots, followed by karaoke Christmas carols, followed by beer pong, then more shots until Riley ended up dancing out on the back deck with a few of the others who'd gotten too hot inside. It was shitty music, something one of the Europeans had put on, but it was music. He had a beer in one hand and a cigar in the other. A mostly unsmoked cigar, because Riley couldn't stand smoking, but he appreciated the aesthetic. Despite his thin shirt and the chilly air, he was sweaty and wanted nothing more than a pile of snow he could jump into. Sadly, it hadn't snowed once since he'd come to Pittsburgh. Stupid global warming.

"All right." The music cut off abruptly, and the five of them on the deck groaned in disappointment. "Sorry to be a buzzkill," Lawson said, "but it's almost two, and I gotta shut us down before the neighbors complain."

"Boo!" Riley said, both hands cupped around his mouth (not easy, given the cigar and beer bottle). "Booooo!"

"They don't call me The Law for nothing," Lawson said, unfazed. "Let's get you guys inside and sobered up." And he made sure to throw an arm around Riley and drag him in.

Riley made it to the kitchen island and sat on the stool—it way too high and way too wobbly for such a nice kitchen—and laid his hands on the cool marble counter.

"Ugggh," he moaned before burying his head in his arms. "I drank too much."

"You sure did, bud," Lawson said. "Why don't I set you up in a guest room?"

The last thing he wanted was to have to deal with Lawson in the morning before he cleaned himself up for that stupid skate and was about to say as much. He could get himself an Uber, thank you very much. He wasn't a baby.

"I could drive him," Evan offered, voice soft, like maybe he thought Riley was already asleep. "His place is on my way back."

"No," Riley said petulantly. He had no defenses left. If he were alone with Evan, he'd do something stupid like have car sex or ask Evan to marry him. "Guest room."

"Probably a good idea. More likely to throw up if he's in a car, I think," Lawson said. "C'mon, Abs. Help me get him to your old room."

Riley let himself be manhandled down an endless path of long hallways and twists and turns that would make it impossible for him to find his way out again. A light switch clicked on, and the world didn't get much brighter, which is when he realized he'd shut his eyes along the way. He opened one just a crack to reveal a room so bland and clean it could be a hotel room. It had a bed and a nearby bathroom, though, so it was heaven as far as he was concerned.

The person guided him right up to the edge, and then Riley threw himself onto the fluffy down blanket, sighing in contentment. Yes, this was where he would sleep off his too-much booze and his heartache and maybe never leave again because it was so comfy. He felt someone taking his loafers off one at a time, then felt someone nudging him under the blankets. A hand carded through his hair, latching onto a few curls, and he melted into the touch. He craved that touch, wanted to wrap himself in it the way it'd wrapped him in the blankets.

"You need anything?" a voice asked. A beautiful voice. His favorite voice. But it was a memory or a dream.

"No," he grumped. "I need everything."

The voice didn't respond for a while, but the hand kept moving through his hair. "Water? Aspirin?"

"Time machine," Riley said. "Go back and fix my fuck-ups."

The hand stopped. "How far back would you need to go?"

Hmm, that was a tough one. A week ago and fix his fight with Evan? No, that would just prolong the inevitable. The beginning of the season so he could apologize to Evan like he'd wanted Riley to? Ugh, but it wasn't his fault! He'd just been playing hockey! He could go back and never offer to help Evan learn to fight, stop himself from ever getting into this sticky situation.

...except Evan would always be handsome and nice and adorably shy. Riley had been screwed from the moment he'd signed his contract with the Riveters, and he hadn't wanted to go anywhere else able to afford him.

"January 26th," he finally said, his voice slurring at the edges as he started to drift off.

"Why January 26th?" The voice wobbled.

"I wouldn't check Evan." He yawned and wrapped his arms around the pillow, pulling it in tight. He buried his face in the soft fabric and inhaled deeply. It reminded him of Evan, like some faint bit of his scent was deep inside. "Then he wouldn't be mad at me, and then I wouldn't be mad at him for being mad at me."

The silence stretched on, and Riley thought he'd fallen asleep. He jolted when the bed dipped beside him, like someone getting on next to him, but stilled when he felt a kiss placed on his cheek.

"Go to sleep, Riley. Try not to think about January 26th anymore. Start thinking about December 19th."

"When's that?" he asked.

"Tomorrow, Riley. It's tomorrow."

And then the weight next to him was gone, and the room was flooded with darkness. Even though he was alone, he didn't feel like it.

44

After the party, Evan had hope.

The torn-up note had felt like Riley tearing apart Evan's heart and shoving it back in his face. Then Riley had shown up at Lawson's house like sex incarnate. It'd made Evan want to claw his eyes out. Riley had looked *so good*, and he was doing it *on purpose* to torment Evan, to show him what he'd had and lost.

Evan had only helped Riley to the guest room—*his* old room, once upon a time—because he wanted to make sure Riley was okay. It was probably his fault Riley had been drinking so much, and Lawson had been busy wrangling everyone else to kick them out. It was the least Evan could do, right?

Drunk Riley was so pitifully cute. Which was not the type of thought Evan was used to having about anyone, and certainly not one he'd ever thought he'd have about Riley Barczyk. But Drunk Riley was also Honest Riley, apparently.

I wouldn't check Evan. Then he wouldn't be mad at me, and I wouldn't be mad at him for being mad at me.

Hearing that had given Evan an absurd amount of hope, because everything seemed fixable. Evan wasn't mad anymore, and it sounded like Riley was close to giving up his own anger.

And then Evan went to the training facility the next day, and that hope fizzled a little.

Riley showed up late, wearing sunglasses and nursing an iced coffee (in fucking December?), and sat in the back as the coaches talked about the season so far, their upcoming schedule, blah blah blah. Evan couldn't help it; he zoned out. His entire focus was on Riley, two rows behind him and five seats to his left. He could hear Riley sipping his stupid coffee, and he swore he could smell Riley's cologne. Fuck, why'd he sit here? It'd be too obvious if he turned around—

He lasted a very commendable ten minutes before he gave in and stole a glance at Riley. With his black-tinted Aviators, it was impossible to tell where Riley was looking or if he was even awake, but it felt like they locked eyes. Evan snapped back around, cheeks on fire, and tried his very best to listen to what Coach Jack was saying.

Ugh. It was like being in high school all over again.

Most of the team opted out of skating that day, and a few of the veteran players cited needing a maintenance day to duck out as soon as the meeting was done. Evan was not in that kind of position, too young and healthy to get out of doing something. He just planned to try to do whatever Riley did.

"Barzy!" he called as he ducked through the crowd to get to him before he left the meeting room. Riley either didn't hear or ignored him, and it wasn't until they were in the hallway that Evan caught up to him, grabbing the sleeve of his hoodie to hold him in place. Riley turned and looked at where Evan was holding him, then up at Evan. Aviators or not, he did a good job conveying bitchiness.

"Abs," he said, oddly formal and distant.

And Evan realized with a sickening drop of his stomach that Riley didn't remember Evan tucking him in last night. He tried not to let his disappointment show. Whether Riley remembered shouldn't matter, anyway. It was the *feelings* that counted, and Riley wasn't as aloof as he wanted Evan to think.

"You feeling okay?" Evan asked.

"Great," Riley said. "Like a freight train ran over me."

Evan laughed awkwardly. "You seemed kind of out of it last—"

"You getting on the ice today?" Riley looked at his watch. Evan wanted to scream.

"Wasn't planning on it," he said slowly, "but if you wanted to work on something—"

"I'm cycling." It wasn't an invitation, and Evan took the hint.

"Oh. Cool. I guess I'll...do...something." His shoulders fell as he heard himself. But Riley tilted his head down so the sunglasses slid a smidge to reveal hazel eyes. Amused hazel eyes. Success! Kind of!

"You do that, Abs," he said and walked off.

The days dragged on as they finished up their homestand and flew out to Detroit for a game against the Motor City Racers. It was the only thing standing between them and a short holiday break. Evan wasn't sure if he craved or dreaded that break. This felt like the tipping point, the last chance to do something before Riley disappeared for five days and maybe got the good sense to realize a relationship with Evan was a terrible idea. But how could Evan convince him otherwise if Riley wouldn't have a real conversation with him?

Evan spent maybe an hour pacing back and forth in his hotel room, running through every version of Riley-forgives-him and Riley-never-wants-to-see-him-again when there was a knock on his door. He froze mid-step and stared at the door.

It's Riley here to put me out of my misery and say we're done.

It's Riley here to forgive me.

There was a secret third option, apparently, because the knock sounded again followed by a curt, "Abs, it's me. Open up."

Dalton.

Surprise washed away any chance he got to analyze whether this was better or worse than Riley showing up, and he walked over to answer the door.

"Hey, Dalty," he said. "What's up?"

The wind was nearly knocked out of him as Dalton pushed a heavy box into his arms.

"Merry Christmas!" Dalton said, nudging Evan back into his room and closing the door behind him. "Open it!"

"Thanks," he said. Shit, he hadn't gotten Dalton anything. They'd never gotten each other anything, in fact, even when they were roommates.

"Don't worry, I won't be mad if you didn't get me anything," Dalton said, as if he could sense Evan's hesitance. "Yet. I accept Amazon gift cards and bottles of wine."

"You don't drink wine."

"No, but Jennie does."

"Fair enough." Evan hesitantly tore a corner of the wrapping. Once he got a peek of golf balls and putters, he tore the rest off in record time. It was an indoor mini-golf kit, complete with a putter, a putting green, golf balls, and little obstacles you could set up. "This is literally the best gift anyone's ever gotten me," he said in awe, staring at the box and worried he was about to cry.

"Right?" Dalton beamed at him. "Now you can mini-golf whenever! C'mon, let's set it up. I'm dying to try it out."

They pushed as much of the furniture aside as they could and set up a mini-mini-golf course. Dalton grabbed a couple of drinks from the mini-fridge ("Part of your gift to me, Abs. Duh."), and they played. They took turns with the putter and setting up different holes, and it was only after he'd finished his first beer that Evan realized something inside him had unclenched. He was relaxed for the first time in weeks.

And he hadn't thought about Riley once in almost an hour. A record!

"How are things going with your guy friend?" Dalton asked, the damn mind reader. And he asked it just as Evan had lined up a shot; he missed so badly the golf ball veered off the green and rolled under the bed. Dalton whistled. "That bad, huh?"

Evan knelt down and used the putter to corral the ball into reach, giving him time to figure out what the hell he would say. Would Dalton figure out his Barczyk-troubles and guy-troubles were the same, Riley-shaped problem?

"We're taking a break," Evan said as he got back to his feet and set the ball back at the beginning.

"Shit. Sorry, bro. That sucks." He watched Evan valiantly try to regain his inner calm. At least he waited until Evan had taken a slightly better shot before asking, "Think you'll get back together?"

"I hope so, but I think I messed it up."

Dalton frowned at him. "You're giving up? You seemed really into this guy."

"No, I just—"

"Have you tried, like, sending flowers?"

Evan gave up on mini-golf. He leaned the putter against the bed and sat down heavily. "To a guy?" he asked.

Dalton leaned against the wall across from Evan, arms crossed over his chest. "Guys can like flowers. Besides, it's not about the flowers. It's the gesture. Showing you care and that you're thinking of him, even though you're apart. You could also send a card, chocolates"—he started counting off ideas on his fingers—"a watch, a care package with his fav snacks, a houseplant—"

"A *houseplant*?" Evan asked incredulously. "How is that different from flowers?"

"Flowers die. Houseplants need to be nurtured. Like a relationship. It shows you're invested in a future, but it's not as intense as, like, getting a pet or moving in together."

Evan stared at him. "Who the fuck are you, and what have you done with Eddy Dalton? I lived with you for a year and a half, and you didn't know shit about relationships. You get *one* girlfriend, and suddenly you're an expert?"

"Am I giving you bad advice?"

"No, that's why I'm having trouble here." Evan rubbed his temple. "I need to think of a gesture."

"Gestures don't have to be things, BTWs. But if you're on a break, that's probably your best bet. Especially with us being on the road so much and the holidays coming up." Then with a smug grin he said, "My advice should count as a second gift."

"Don't push your luck."

They played a little longer, but once they ran out of overly-priced beer, Dalton helped him pack everything back into the box and left him to his now too-empty and quiet hotel room. Since paper and pen were working for him, Evan took the pad of paper from the desk and the cheap pen and started writing a list of ideas. He wrote everything he knew about Riley's likes, from his style of clothing to the beer he drank to the movie posters he'd seen scattered on Riley's bedroom wall. He Googled gift ideas, starting with romantic ones and then more broadly when those didn't suit Riley.

He liked the idea of a care package, since he wanted to take care of Riley like he almost had at Lawson's place but hadn't been allowed to. He ordered a bunch of things to his place so he could assemble the package and drop it off once they were back in Pittsburgh, then he found a place that made custom ties and bought a duo of matching Riveters ties: one yellow with green wrenches, the other green with yellow wrenches. Something that would be waiting at Riley's door when he got home.

It wasn't much, but like Dalton had said, it was about the gesture itself. Reaching out and showing that he cared. More than that, that he *knew* Riley. Evan *saw* him, not just the exterior of Barczyk the pest or Barzy the teammate. He saw Riley underneath all that, and he cared about that person.

Satisfied that this might be the little nudge Riley needed to, y'know, have a meaningful conversation with Evan in the near future, Evan tucked himself into bed and stared at the ceiling until he fell asleep.

45

THE MOTOR CITY RACERS WERE THE ONLY THING THAT stood between them and a flight back to Pittsburgh for the holidays. The Riveters were restless in the locker room, too focused on their plans with family to have their heads in the game. Never a good sign, in Evan's experience, but he couldn't exactly claim to be doing any better; he caught himself staring at Riley more often than he could reasonably claim was platonic.

On the ice before the game, Evan skated to his and Riley's usual spot above the left circle. Not that Riley had engaged in their pre-game ritual lately, but Evan stood vigil on the off chance he'd change his mind. He stickhandled absentmindedly until there were only a few minutes left on the clock. He sighed and passed away his puck...and inspiration struck.

He leaned forward a little, resting his hands on his thighs like he would when Riley was about to swing his stick at him. Then he mimed being hit, staggering forward in the dramatic way Riley sometimes had before hitting the ice. He twirled in a half-circle on his knees, too nostalgic to care about how ridiculous he must look doing the routine alone.

When he got up, he spotted Riley at the bench, watching him. He stood with one foot on the ice, the other on the bench, as if about to go back into the locker room but had stopped. Had he seen?

Evan skated over faster than he'd ever skated during a warm-up—he didn't want to risk Riley disappearing down the tunnel—and stopped so hard he sprayed snow across the ice. His mom had sometimes compared him to an overgrown puppy; this was one of the rare times he kind of agreed with her.

"Hi," he said cheerfully. "Ready to play?"

Riley appraised him, a slow crawl up his body from skates to helmet before he asked, "You doing solo whacks now?"

"Well, my good-luck partner left," he said. "Guess all the good mojo's mine tonight."

Riley smiled, a split second of amusement before he smoothed it out. "We'll see, Abs. We'll see."

The Racers seemed to be experiencing the same lethargy as the Riveters. It was a dull game to watch, and that included when Evan was actively playing. No one seemed to be trying, and both teams mustered up a combined and pitiful total of seven shots on goal in the first period. It had the feel of an exhibition match or a pre-season game, and it wasn't easy to break out of that mentality.

Coach Jack stood in the middle of the locker room, hands in his pockets as he chewed gum and considered what to say. Evan expected to get chewed out for their lackluster performance, but he calmly said, "You think I want to be in Detroit today? My kids are at home, setting up the Christmas tree and baking cookies, and I'm stuck here watching this piss-poor attempt at a hockey game. You wanna go home with a win, or do you want to end the year with a loss? Figure it out, exploit the Racers' laziness, and put some pucks in the net."

"The goalie has faced no shots," Vassiliev said conspiratorially. Only mostly true: the Riveters had put up three so far. "He's not warmed up anymore. We fire everything and something goes in, yes?"

"Were you *not* shooting the puck?" Riley asked in mock offense. "Some of us have been trying to score the whole time."

"You don't even look awake out there," Vassiliev snapped back. "Not a single hit! Did you forget how to play hockey?"

"You want me to shoot, or you want me to hit?"

"You always do both!"

"And you haven't been doing either!"

Well, Evan thought, *at least they're fired up.*

Just wish it weren't at each other.

In the second period, they got hemmed into the defensive zone for a good forty seconds. Evan's legs were burning, and all he wanted was to get off the ice. When one of their defensemen managed to lob it through the air over everyone's heads and out to center, that was what Evan planned to do...until he saw Riley sprinting out for the loose puck.

Sensing a chance, Evan and Vassiliev went with him. Riley knocked the puck away from one defender and went down ice one-on-one with the other.

"Hey!" Evan called, banging his stick on the ice to get Riley's attention. "Drop!"

Without looking, Riley left the puck for Evan and drew the defenseman away. Evan came in, ready to take a shot when the other defenseman came out of nowhere and did a diving slide in front of Evan as the goalie squared up. Evan grabbed the puck, wondering if he should still shoot—there was no chance it was going in—and in that split second, he saw a white jersey out of the corner of his eye. Taking a chance, he passed the puck over to what he hoped was a Riveter.

There was barely time to see it was Vassiliev before he shot into the wide open net.

Tic-Tac-Toe. Riley to Evan to Vassiliev. Perfect line chemistry at work.

"Oh thank fuck," Evan said. If they'd messed this up, he had zero energy to regain possession of the puck or help on defense. He and Riley hit Vassiliev at the same time, followed by the defensemen.

"No kisses," Vassiliev said with a laugh. He knocked Evan and then Riley on the heads. "But good work."

"I know, I know," Evan said. "Saving it for the Cup."

They skated down the bench for fistbumps and finally, *finally* got to sit down.

"We were dead if you didn't score that," Riley said. "I was about to lie down there on the ice and take a nap."

"You were the idiot who chased the puck when we should have

changed," Vassiliev said. "If you were tired, you should have gone to the bench."

"You don't sound very grateful for that goal I got you."

"I said good work! You want a thank-you card?"

"Yeah, actually. I'll give you my address."

Evan hid his amusement behind his water bottle.

Their goal woke up both teams a bit, and it started to resemble an NHL game again. Both goalies were putting on a masterclass of glove saves and toe kicks that would look great on their highlight reels. Evan prayed the other team's goalie would slip up, because a one-goal lead was an uncomfortable way to play. It made him tense, like any mistake could be disastrous and cost them the game. In a lot of ways it was harder than when they were down, because the coaches shortened the bench when they needed to score and put the third and fourth lines out less, meaning it was less likely Evan would be the reason they lost.

With a lead, everyone got shifts. Equal opportunity to fuck things up.

They lined up for a neutral zone face-off. Evan was running through options—win it back and hope the defense got it but risk giving the other team the zone, or win it forward out of danger but limit the chances that they'd get possession, or tie it up and let someone else make the decision—when he felt a weight on his shoulder.

"Evan."

His name went through him like a lightning bolt.

"Relax," Riley said. "You're gonna break your stick if you grip it any harder. It's fine. We're winning." He patted Evan's chest, right on the Riveters' logo. "Chill. You've got this."

As far as pep talks went, it wasn't much, but it did the trick. Evan shook his head to clear the last of his doubts and squared up. He won the face-off to Pope, and the game was on.

It was two shifts later that they were able to break through again. It was a partial line change, with Evan and Riley out with Woodward. Vassiliev was a great winger, and Evan enjoyed playing with him, but Woodward's ability to stay calm under pressure was next level. He dangled repeatedly through the Racers' defense, buying time for Riley and Evan to get open. Riley, being Riley, started a shoving match with a defenseman just outside of the crease. A *loud* shoving match, with Riley yelling all sorts of obscenities that would be a lot more enjoyable to listen to if Evan weren't trying so damn hard to make space.

Eventually, Woodward's slow crawl through the zone seemed to piss off the defender covering Evan, and he went to double-team Woodward to get the puck back. Woodward must have eyes in the back of his head, because as soon as Evan had breathing room, he sent Evan a beautiful pass through everyone. Wide open, Evan took a one-timer and hoped it was on net.

It was on net. The puck slid beneath the goalie's arm on the blocker side and hit the inner post before lodging itself in the back of the net.

"Wow," Evan mumbled.

"Abs!" Woodward grabbed him in a hug, tried to pick him up, and gave up when he remembered Evan was bigger than him. "Beautiful shot. Way to go, kid."

Riley was next, colliding into his back. "I told you!" he said over and over again. "I told you! I fucking told you!"

Evan turned, mouth going dry when he saw how excited Riley looked. He wanted to lean down and kiss his cheek, but he'd already been warned about kisses after Vassiliev's goal. Besides, Riley hadn't been the one to pass to him; he'd have to kiss Woodward's cheek too, and he didn't think he could pull that off the same way Riley could.

Instead, he settled for fistbumping Riley and saying, "Your turn. Third line's all scoring tonight."

Vassiliev echoed the sentiment several times on the bench and then during the second intermission, outlining all the ways they were going to get Riley a goal. Some of them were as simple as 'pass Riley the puck' and others were more outlandish, like getting him the puck behind the net so he could get a Michigan goal, or Riley scoring while lying on the ice. But the details didn't matter much: their only game plan for the third period was to get Riley Barczyk on the board and solidify their line's success to end the calendar year.

They had some chances in their first few shifts, though the goalie stopped most, and the Detroit defense iced the puck on their other good opportunity. There was something electric in the air. Evan could feel something big coming. All they had to do was capitalize on it.

One of their shifts seemed like it would be a dud. There was a lot of back and forth between zones, with no team establishing any real control. In a few more seconds, Evan would head back to the bench to regroup for another push later. He just needed to wait for a whistle or for the puck to go deep in the Racers' zone so he could safely go for a line change. Riley, to a fault the one to drive play, was fighting along the boards for the puck while the rest of them watched, no one ready to commit until they knew who would win the battle.

Riley started to pivot away with the puck. The Racers' player, a winger Evan kind of recognized, turned and tried to stick lift Riley. He missed, his own stick going straight up into Riley's face. It happened all the time, and the way Riley jerked his head didn't mean much. It was instinct to dodge errant sticks and pucks.

It meant something when Riley immediately collapsed onto the ice, dropping his stick and cradling his face in both hands.

It wasn't until Evan saw the splash of red on the ice that he understood Riley had been hit.

Oh fuck.

Evan wasn't quite sure what happened after that. One second he was standing there, sick to his stomach. The next, he was skating forward. And then, before he knew what he was doing, he'd dropped his gloves and had his left hand wrapped in someone's jersey and was swinging his right fist full force at someone's face. Once, twice, three times in quick succession. Again and again, he swung without any idea if he was making contact with anything breakable or if he was just beating his hand bloody against the guy's helmet. He didn't actually care, since he figured his message was pretty clear either way.

You hurt Riley Barczyk? You're gonna get fucked up.

Oh, he thought blandly as hands came around him and started yanking him hard. *This is what it feels like. Wanting to punch someone.*

It felt like being really fucking angry.

He let go, and the guy fell backward. Evan, restrained by two refs, was dragged away. It wasn't until he was shoved into the penalty box that he noticed the medical staff walking out to Riley, still doubled over on the ice. He leaned forward, face pressed against the glass so he could watch as they helped Riley to his feet. He barely heard the arena half-heartedly applaud as Riley was guided to the bench and down the tunnel, his hands now clutching a towel pressed to his face.

"Sit your ass down, Abernathy," a linesman called as he skated by. "You're in there for a while."

He sat down.

After talking to both teams, a ref came to explain the situation to the crowd: "Number 28, Detroit, double minor for high-sticking." The arena swelled with angry boos. "Number 21, Pittsburgh, five minutes for dropping the gloves. Power Play Pittsburgh."

This earned even louder and more incredulous boos as the fans screamed over the seemingly unjust call. Evan was glad he wasn't a ref and hadn't had to figure that one out.

There was angry pounding on the glass behind him as the fans told him in no uncertain terms how much they hated him. Watching as Number 28 on Detroit had been helped off the ice to go to his own locker room, Evan couldn't argue: he'd earned the fans' ire.

He also couldn't make him feel as bad about hurting that guy as he should. Not yet, anyway.

The next five minutes sucked. It wasn't so much the penalty, but the isolation. He was trapped in no man's land, unable to hear how Riley was doing. When Number 28 appeared back on his team's bench with a puffy nose and swollen eye, whatever possible sympathy Evan might've felt dried up. Riley was still back with the medical staff. That was the easiest way to know a hockey player was seriously hurt: they weren't ready for their next shift.

When he was released back to his team, there was only a minute, and a half left in the game and still no Riley.

"Attaboy, Abernathy." Coach Jack smacked him hard on the back. "Those were some great punches. Way to stand up for your teammate."

"How's Barzy?" he asked. He hoped no one noticed how strained he sounded.

Coach Jack made a face. "Getting stitched up. Lucky he had his mouthguard in for once, or he'd be missing another tooth right now."

"Why isn't he back on the bench?" he asked, but the game was starting again and Coach Jack's attention was gone. He turned to

Vassiliev. "Why isn't he back on the bench?" he repeated, because if someone would know, it should be Vassiliev.

Vassiliev shrugged. "The game's almost over. I think they didn't see the point."

Riley would want to come back out, though. Any of them would. Was it worse than they were saying? But why would they lie?

At the end of the game, Evan was ready to storm into the locker room to find Riley, but he was intercepted and directed off for media coverage before he'd left the tunnel.

"Why? Why me? Can't I change first?" He bristled as he was guided to a crowd of bright lights and reporters. Normally it was players like Lawson or Turner or Woodward who got pulled aside like this, reappearing in the locker room after everyone else had gotten a head start getting undressed and cleaned up. But mics and cell phones were shoved into his face before he got an answer.

"Great game!" one of the bolder reporters called out. Evan couldn't see who it was past the lights. "First Star of the game. Your first career Gordie Howe hat trick. Your second career fight ended with a pretty definitive knockout. How's it feel?"

Evan blanked. He'd dreamed of moments like this since he was a little kid practicing hockey with plastic sticks in his living room. Recognition of all his hard work throughout his career, of his skill and commitment. He remembered the beginning of the season and how desperately he'd wanted that watch during their home opener. Here he was, the one hand-selected for the post-game interviews and everyone who'd ever known him watching at home, proud of him.

Yet all Evan wanted to do was go to the locker room.

"It's pretty incredible," he said, because what the fuck else was he supposed to say? He channeled that other Evan who'd yearned for this and tried not to sound like a robot. "Feels great," he added with what hopefully passed for a real smile. Maybe tomorrow it *would* feel great.

They asked other questions about him and his line and the team. Blah blah blah. Like he, a third-liner who'd spent the dwindling minutes of the third period in the penalty box, had anything insightful to say about the Riveters making the playoffs. The only real answers he had related to him and Riley and their growing chemistry over the season, but he had to lie through his teeth for those questions.

Well, it's definitely not because we spent months fucking each other. It must be some other reason.

Finally, they let him go, and he couldn't hide how eager he was to escape. He practically ran into the locker room and—

Riley wasn't there.

46

It was after midnight, and the hotel hallways had long cleared out. There was no celebrating their win, and no need for a curfew: everyone was in bed, eager to sleep through the tail end of this road trip and go home. Everyone, of course, but Evan.

He double-checked that the coast was clear before he sneaked out of his room and down a floor. It hadn't been easy finding out where Riley's room was, but after some needling, he'd gotten it out of Lawson. When he arrived, he knocked a few times but got no answer. Not that he'd been expecting one. They'd said Riley needed to go to an actual hospital to get patched up because they were concerned about his face or something. No one knew more than that, or seemed to care.

How could you not care for details when a teammate went to the hospital?

He supposed, if he wanted to be generous and objective, they cared but weren't concerned. They trusted Riley would be fine, and they'd worry if they were told to worry.

Evan was going to worry until he had Riley standing in front of him, and he could see the damage for himself. So he stood there, holding his breath as he prayed Riley would answer the door, groggy and annoyed at having been woken up and with nothing more than a busted lip. Maybe he'd tell Evan to fuck off, and Evan would be glad to hear it given the circumstances. As the seconds dragged on, it seemed less and less likely.

Riley must still be at the hospital. Never a good sign.

The normal thing to do would be to go back to his room, text Riley, and try again in the morning. Evan had long ago abandoned being normal when it came to Riley, so he sat in front of Riley's room and got as comfortable as he could. He leaned back against the door and waited.

And waited.

And waited.

And at some point, he fell asleep.

———

"The team cheap out on rooms or something?"

Evan jumped, banged his head against something, and squinted into the fluorescent lights to find the source of the voice.

Riley stood above him, dressed in what looked like a fresh Riveters shirt and his suit pants. His shoulders sagged, and he smelled like a mix of sweat and antiseptic. But he looked like he was all in one piece, walking under his own power, and that was enough to ease the vise around Evan's heart. He leapt to his feet, and the new vantage point let him see the long gauze bandage next to Riley's right eye.

"You're okay," Evan said, so relieved he didn't hide it. "Right?"

"I'm fine," Riley said. It sounded like he wanted to put more bite into it than he did, but he was too tired to muster it. "I don't need you checking up on me just because you feel sorry for—"

"That's not why I'm here," Evan said.

Riley glared at him. Not as effective with the bandage.

"I was worried," Evan continued, when it became clear Riley had nothing to say. "They said you were fine, but I wanted to check for myself." As Riley again did nothing but stare at him, Evan wilted. "And I guess I have. Checked. So...I guess...I can go back to my room..."

Riley stepped around Evan, took out a keycard, and opened his hotel door. Evan held his breath, terrified this was a dismissal, but Riley looked over his shoulder. "You coming in or what?" he grumbled. Evan didn't need to be told twice.

Riley flicked on the lights as he moved deeper into the room, and unsure about the protocol here, Evan lingered by the door.

"Need anything?" Evan was suddenly eager to do something, to be useful. It might give him the excuse to stay if Riley otherwise decided this was too uncomfortable.

Riley, back to him, grunted, "Glass of water? I gotta take some pain meds."

Evan did as he was told, filling up a glass to the brim in the little kitchenette. It was good to use his hands, a physical task to distract him, and he wished there was more to it than just...pouring water. It was over too quickly. But it wasn't about him right now, so he dutifully walked over to hand Riley the drink—

And just about dropped it when he saw Riley's face.

Riley had taken off the bandage and was inspecting the long gash along the right side of his face. The puckered skin held tight by a dozen stitches went from his cheekbone up along his temple, dangerously close to his eye. It glistened with whatever antibacterial goo they'd smeared it with, making it look angrier than it might otherwise.

Evan stood there, absolutely frozen as he took in not only the injury, but how really fucking close Riley had been to getting hit in the eye. Didn't they wear the stupid visors to *prevent* that kind of thing?

But Riley, satisfied, turned away from the mirror and caught Evan staring at him.

"Gonna have a gnarly scar," he said, his voice not quite as full as usual.

"What—?"

"It was so close to my eye, they wanted to get a plastic surgeon, so they took me to the hospital." Riley cracked his neck, and his eyes fluttered shut in relief. When he opened them and saw Evan hadn't moved a muscle, he rolled his eyes and turned away. "You think this is bad, you should see the other guy. Heard he got his ass whooped. You got that water?"

Evan jerked back to life, water sloshing over the side as he rushed forward with the glass. Riley ignored him as he pulled a white paper bag out of his pocket and started rummaging around to get the right bottle of meds. He popped a few in his mouth and mumbled, "Thanks" around the pills. He swallowed and then cast Evan a sidelong glance. "What're you doing here?"

He reeled as if he'd been slapped. "I wanted to check on you," he said, defensive. Like he couldn't believe Riley didn't believe him. "I couldn't sleep—"

"You were sleeping when I found you," Riley said. He crossed his arms over his chest. "Try again."

Evan gulped. He'd wanted his chance to talk, right?

"Because I miss you, and I was worried, and I needed to see that you were okay," he blurted out in a rush, the words tripping over themselves to get out. "Because the coaches' standards for you being okay and my standards are clearly not the same."

"You know," Riley said, drawing out the words so they hit Evan one at a time, "I wasn't too happy to have to leave a game and go to the fucking hospital, but I'm not mad at the guy who did it. Like, yeah, control your fucking stick, but whatever, it was an accident." He ended on a very pointed note, just in case Evan hadn't put the pieces together.

He had. Many times over since Riley had been taken off the ice.

"I don't give a fuck about my shoulder." Then he winced and back-tracked. "Okay, I obviously care about my shoulder, but I'm not upset. I get it. I can't hold on to that stuff if I plan on playing long term. There's no room for that kind of shit. It was my first injury scare, and it left more of an impression that it should've. I was hurt, and I didn't want to acknowledge it wasn't because you were *trying* to hurt me. I could've just as easily tripped over my own feet and gotten hurt. It was just conve-nient that it was you with your reputation. I'm sorry."

Riley closed his eyes and let out a couple of breaths through his nose before he opened them again. "It's fine. I...understand. It's hard to sepa-rate intention from the results. I'm...sorry I didn't let you apologize earlier." He licked his lips. "Can we be done with last season?"

"Yes," Evan said, not giving Riley a chance to change his mind. He offered his hand. "Fresh start."

"Fresh start..." Riley looked at Evan's hand but didn't move to take it. "For...everything?"

No! he wanted to say, to scream, but maybe it was for the best. Get rid of the baggage and start over. He took Riley's hand but didn't shake. "Fresh hockey start?"

Riley's eyes bored into his. He looked so tired and fragile. "What else is there?"

In for a penny...

"Riley." He pulled his hand away. "I don't give a shit about you hitting me. I don't care about hockey right now. I'm here because I care about *you*. You think I'd be in anyone else's room right now if they'd been hurt? I'd be asleep in my bed, knowing I'd find out the damage tomorrow with everyone else. If you want to start over, fine. We'll start over. But don't think that means I can forget how much I've missed you."

All he'd said was that he'd missed Riley, a sentiment he'd shared in his note and that he felt was written in every look he sent Riley's way, but the confession felt like a bomb had detonated between them.

And Riley, always with something to say, was quiet as he opened up a drawer in his nightstand. Evan watched with faint concern that the pain medication was making him loopy as Riley found his wallet and dug around for a small, crumpled piece of paper. He handed it to Evan.

"Open it," he said, so Evan did. He carefully unfolded the tiny, rumpled thing and was surprised to see his own handwriting staring back at him.

E.A.
P.S. I miss you.

"I thought..." Evan coughed to clear his throat. "I thought you tore it up."

"I did," Riley said. "But I read it first." He took the paper from Evan and put it back in his wallet. "I watched the game highlights on the news while they patched me up. About the only thing they had on TV. You got a mean right hook."

"I had a good teacher." Evan swallowed. "What are the chances of us...I don't know. Trying again?"

"Trying what again?"

"Riley..."

"Evan. I'm fucking exhausted. They numbed my face, and I still felt every fucking time they pulled that needle through my skin. I thought things were one way between us, and I was wrong. I'm too tired right now to pretend I know what you're saying. I already assumed things for you before. I can't do that again. So please say what you fucking mean so I can't misinterpret it in the morning and get hurt in a month when it turns out I was wrong."

"I—" Evan hesitated. Not because he doubted his feelings or Riley's or anything about *them*. It was a lot to put out on the table all at once. "I didn't know I was gay until that first time in the gym with you, and I haven't been able to get you out of my head since."

Riley's eyebrows shot up, though it seemed to hurt him, and he flinched. "You didn't know you were gay until you were...twenty-two?"

"No idea," he confessed. "Like, none."

"You're sure?" Riley asked. "Because I got that you weren't experienced, but I thought it was because you had, like, a low sex drive. Not because you hadn't touched dicks before."

"I'd touched a dick before."

"Yes. Singular. Your own. That's not very many dicks, Ev." He waved a hand. "We're getting off topic here. So, what? You were freaking out because you were having an existential crisis about wanting the dick of someone you secretly hated?"

"I wasn't freaking out." Riley gave him a sharp look, so he backtracked. "It wasn't that bad."

"If it were a normal amount of freaking out," Riley said, "you would've talked to me about it."

His shoulders slumped. "I'm sorry."

"Fucking Canadians and their apologies. Evan. I know you're sorry. I'm sorry. Everyone's sorry. It's meaningless if we don't learn something from it. So what's the lesson we're trying to learn here? Things are broken right now, but what part are we trying to fix?"

Riley radiated desperation and exhaustion, and all Evan wanted to do was tuck him into bed like at the Christmas party and get him through the night. Evan didn't know how to get from here, this minefield of a conversation that felt like he could destroy everything with a wrong step, to that point where he could wrap Riley in his arms and take care of him. But Riley's defenses were down, so he tried to lower his.

"I want to be together," Evan said. "I want to get to be with you every night after practice and games. I want to sit next to you when we travel and talk to you about whatever the fuck you want to talk about. I want to take care of you right now when you're hurt and deserve to be taken care of. I want things to be like they were, but better because I'm done with my bullshit. Please. Can we fix this?"

"Why?" The question was so quiet, it barely disturbed the air between them. He had to read it on Riley's lips because he wasn't sure he'd heard it correctly. "Why would you want that with me?"

Evan stepped forward, one foot then another until he'd closed the gap between them. As gently as he could, he put his hands on Riley's cheeks, mindful of the stitches. He traced a line parallel to the mark, watching to see if it hurt.

"I think," he whispered, "that I'm falling for my teammate...and I don't know what I'd do if I couldn't be with him anymore. I've never felt like this for anyone, ever. That's got to mean something, right? How could I not want to try to make it work with you?"

Riley whined. "Evan," he warned, and he didn't have to say anything for Evan to understand.

Don't say shit like that if you don't mean it.

"It's true. It's so fucking true, and if there's the slightest chance you'd want me back—"

Before he could finish, Riley's arms were around his neck and pulling him down to mash their lips together. Evan groaned into the kiss, so relieved and happy to be allowed to have this again with Riley.

"No one like you has ever given me the time of day," Riley muttered between kisses, then buried his face in Evan's chest. Evan could feel him breathing in his scent. "Nice guys don't like guys like me, for all the reasons you didn't like me. I should've known it was too good to be true before."

Evan wrapped his arms around Riley and held him as tightly as he dared. "You are a tiny ball of anger," he teased, twining his fingers through Riley's hair. Fuck, he missed his hair.

"Fuck off," he said into Evan's shirt.

"Some might say it's your best quality."

Riley pinched him.

He kissed the top of Riley's head and stepped back. "You need sleep."

"No, I—" He yawned, flinching as his mouth stretched wide but still unable to contain it. "Ugh, I need sleep." He eyed Evan warily. "You gonna...hang out? Stay?"

"Can I sleep? Believe it or not, your doorway wasn't very comfortable."

Riley's whole body released whatever last bits of tension it'd been holding onto. "Fuck, yes. Sleep. I've slept like shit without you."

So he helped Riley undress and got him settled in the puffy hotel comforter, then he climbed in after him. He'd expected to wrap himself around Riley, encasing him in that protective layer he thought Riley would crave after getting hurt, but instead Riley pulled him in and laid his head on Evan's chest. Ear pressed to Evan's heart, he took one deep breath after another until slowly his grip relaxed. Trapped—though was he really trapped if there was nowhere else he'd rather be?—Evan rubbed circles on Riley's back until his snores joined Riley's.

47

Evan technically didn't sleep well. He was woken up every time Riley moved, which got more frequent as his pain meds wore off, so Evan watched the sun rise bit by bit, more of the hotel room coming into view as Riley rolled back and forth, dislodging blankets and pillows. And sometimes kicking or punching Evan as he did.

Even so, Evan wanted the night to last forever.

It couldn't, and soon Evan's bladder demanded he get up. Soon the team would wake up, and everyone would start venturing downstairs for breakfast and crowd the lobby as they impatiently waited for their flight. Evan would have to face reality sooner than later. Might as well get a jump on it.

In the two minutes it took for him to use the bathroom and clean himself up a bit, Riley had managed to turn so that his feet were buried under the pillows and a bunch of sheets were wrapped around his head at the foot of the bed. What a weirdo.

"Mornin'." Evan sat down next to him. Riley stirred, wrinkling his nose and mumbling something, but didn't open his eyes. Indulging because he could, Evan ran a hand through Riley's hair and checked the cut along his face. No blood, but he counted ten, no, eleven stitches. An accident, of course. A play gone wrong that thankfully hadn't ended up worse.

He'd have to get used to that. Watching one of his favorite people throw himself into harm's way on purpose, again and again.

"Why are you staring at me?" Riley mumbled, eyes still closed. "Am I that cute?"

"You'd be cuter if you had all of your face."

"Nah, scars are sexy." Riley yawned and stretched so wide, Evan almost got knocked off the bed. He hadn't done that kind of full-body stretch in years, though maybe it was more necessary if you were the kind of restless sleeper Riley was. "I'm starving. Breakfast?" He pouted with those full lips and hazel eyes, and Evan knew exactly what he was being conned into.

"Fine, I'll get you something. I've gotta go change anyway."

"Thanks, babe." Then he rolled over to go back to sleep.

The endearment sent a shiver down Evan's spine.

Evan found his socks and shoes, mentally going over how much he could feasibly carry up for Riley to enjoy breakfast in bed without it seeming too suspicious. When he opened the hotel door, he came face to face with Dalton leaving the room across the hall.

Dalton stared at him in surprise. Evan froze, wondering if he could convince Dalton that this was in fact Evan's room and whatever he was remembering about his neighbor was wrong.

"Isn't that—?" Dalton asked.

"Get me coffee," Riley called from inside the room, loudly enough that Dalton could hear. He looked over Evan's shoulder into the room, back to Evan, then he slowly backed into his own room and closed the door.

Okay then. That would require a conversation later. But if it had to be anyone, at least it was Dalton.

———

There was no escaping the team forever. They had to rush through breakfast in Riley's hotel room and then pack. Riley grabbed Evan before he could leave, looking scared but casual about it. Like that was how he wanted to feel.

Very Riley, really.

"Sit with me on the bus," Riley begged. Well, ordered, but nicely. "And on the plane." And then, as if he actually thought Evan might refuse, he pulled Evan down by the neck and kissed him within an inch of his life.

" 'kay," Evan breathed. "And back home...?"

It was easy enough to be attached at the hip when they traveled, but they'd never been good at navigating things in Pittsburgh.

"Sure, I'll go back home with you."

It wasn't until they were in the airport about to board that Evan realized he might've accidentally invited Riley to his place. And Riley had accepted the invitation.

The team showered Riley with concern and attention, and Evan tried to stay out of the way while they did. Maybe he shouldn't have wandered so far, though, because while they boarded the plane and Riley told the story of his hospital visit for the tenth time, Dalton pulled Evan aside.

"I feel like you purposely misrepresented your guy-friend situation."

"I have no idea what you're talking about, and I did no such thing. I just...didn't correct your assumptions."

Dalton rolled his eyes. "C'mon, bro. After that mini-golf gift?"

"Abs!" Riley called from the back of the plane and gestured to the empty seat next to him.

"Sorry, my linemate is calling me."

"Does he call you that in bed?" Dalton mumbled as Evan started walking away. "I don't think beating the shit out of someone is a healthy gesture."

Evan turned around and shrugged as he walked backwards. "It worked, didn't it?"

"I didn't say it wasn't effective. You're not getting out of this. You owe me a milkshake, a beer, and an explanation. Abs!"

But Evan had escaped. For now.

Riley passed out before they took off, his head on Evan's shoulder. Evan wanted to hold him, especially when they hit turbulence and he flinched in pain, but he restrained himself. It was barely an hour flight. He could wait.

"You guys made up."

Evan nearly jumped off his seat. He looked across the aisle and spotted Vassiliev a few rows up, watching them.

"Huh?" he asked. He'd been pretty successful playing dumb so far, so he figured that was his best bet. Sometimes it wasn't even an act.

"You and Barzy. You've been...off. No hitting before the game. I knew in the game it was better, and now I see it's back to normal." He grinned. "Good. We'll need more goals if we want to make the playoffs."

Right.

If anyone else shared the sentiment, they kept it to themselves.

———

Arriving in Pittsburgh with everyone eager to fuck off for five days meant they were the last ones off the plane.

"I can carry my own shit," Riley warned. "I don't carry stuff with my face."

Evan held up his hands in surrender.

Throughout the whole Uber ride, crammed into the back of a too-small sedan, Evan was conscious of the fact that Riley had never been to his condo. He'd rarely seen Riley's apartment building, and hiding behind practice and convenience hadn't given him an excuse to have Riley over. Really, he'd avoided it because that had felt too intimate. Having sex with a guy in his own bed had been the last bridge to cross, that one last chance at plausible deniability.

...was he about to have sex with Riley in his bed? Fuuuuck that would be awesome.

Evan's hand fumbled with the stupid condo lock not once, but twice. Then Riley was walking past him inside, and wow, he looked good there.

"There's no Canadian flag," Riley said as he looked around. "Thought Canadians were, like, legally required to have at least five maple leaves per square foot. Sorry, per square metre."

Yes, he pronounced meter wrong. Ass.

"Says the American. Aren't you guys born star-spangled?"

"Touche." Riley plopped down on the couch and let his head fall back against the leather. "Not to be super fucking boring, but I'm hungry and tired. Could you fix one while I work on the other?"

There wasn't a lot that Evan would consider edible in his apartment —he'd planned to go grocery shopping when he got back in town, but he wasn't going to abandon Riley to do it—so he did what he could. Grilled cheese sandwiches and protein bars. Yummy.

He finished plating and was about to decide whether to let Riley sleep or wake him up, but when he looked up, he saw Riley watching him from the couch.

"Not to be that guy," Riley said, voice rough and eyes hooded as he palmed his cock through his pants, "but could you fuck me before we eat?"

Evan swallowed the lump in his throat. "Yeah," he said. "I think we could fit that in."

It started with slow kisses on the couch, with Evan straddling Riley and being mindful of his stitches.

"Just fucking touch my face," Riley said and then bit down on Evan's lower lip.

"Ow! What the fuck?"

Riley wiggled his hands under Evan's shirt and ran his hands up his chest. "You can touch my face. It's not that bad."

"Have you *seen* your face?"

"Yeah, and it's fucking handsome." He huffed when Evan didn't laugh. "I'm not saying we should get out the boxing gloves, but it's fine. Just please stop hesitating like you're worried you're gonna hurt me. Fucking *touch me*. It's been weeks, Ev."

Evan groaned. He closed his eyes and rested his forehead against Riley's. "You're gonna kill me."

"There are worse ways to die." He tilted his head to kiss Evan's chin, then nudged his hips. "I know you're like a virgin or whatever, but you've got lube, right?"

Evan's snapped back open. "I was wrong. I'm gonna kill *you*."

"Ohh, Mr. Nice Guy gets in one fight, and suddenly he's all tough."

This time, he pushed Evan hard enough to force him up. "Answer the question."

"Yes, I have lube," Evan said. God, why was it so embarrassing to admit this to the man he had sex with? "And condoms."

"Fuck yeah. Now show me your bed and show me how much you missed me."

Evan wasn't about to argue with that.

———

The grilled cheese sandwiches had long gone cold by the time they made their way back to the kitchen. Evan stood in the doorway of his room, enjoying the view of Riley Barczyk in *his* apartment, wearing *his* clothes, eating the food *Evan* had made for him. He could get very used to this.

Riley stuffed half a sandwich in his mouth and went to rummage around in the fridge, but no sooner had he opened the door than he slammed it shut and stared intently at the door. It took longer than it should've for Evan to realize what he was looking at.

"Shit, that's—"

"Yuhhgwaatuhpin?"

He'd been expecting Riley to be upset about the list, but he'd never heard *that* string of curse words before.

"...what?"

Riley swallowed, coughed, then repeated: "You got a pen?"

"Oh." That...wasn't what he'd expected at all. "Yeah, in the top drawer there."

Seconds later, Riley had a pen in hand and was writing something on the paper. He clicked the pen shut when he was done and tossed it back in the drawer, looking very pleased with himself. Evan held his breath as he tiptoed over, scared of what he'd find. When he read it, his heart did a somersault.

Plan:
- Give Riley space ✓
- Reach out to talk ✓

- *Apologize* ✔
- *Try to get back together* ✔
- *Prove I'm worth a second chance* ✔

- *Date Riley and win a Stanley Cup together*

Game on.

Epilogue

PLAUSIBLE DENIABILITY.

A strange balancing act, especially when Evan was dating a man who didn't understand the two words separately, never mind together.

Evan had left his condo before Riley had. Driven his own car and parked in his usual spot in the player parking section of the arena. He'd expected to get up to the team area of the arena before Riley had made his appearance. Plausible deniability, right?

He heard the screech of tires making the last bend in the parking garage and sighed when Riley backed in right next to him, so close that their cars almost touched. Then he popped out of his car and pulled Evan down for a wet kiss on the cheek. Which, fine, no one except other Riveters might see them. And the kiss on the cheek was Riley's Thing right now. He scored a goal? He'd kiss your cheek. You scored? Another kiss! Goalie got a shutout? Yep, a kiss. It was kind of a brilliant cover, though Evan would never tell him that.

But the real problem today of all days was when he noticed Riley's game suit. The pale goldenrod pants and jacket, the light cream shirt, and, of fucking course, the yellow tie with green wrenches that Evan had gotten him for Christmas.

"Nice tie," Evan said, grinding his teeth. It was one of Riley's favorites, in fact, so he should've guessed this would happen. Riley hadn't even been dressed when Evan had left the condo, so it'd slipped his mind.

Riley looked down at the tie, then grinned widely. "Thanks. My boyfriend got it for me."

"I know," Evan said. He waited for Riley to see the problem, but when he didn't, Evan held up his own tie. The matching green tie with yellow wrenches. "This isn't what I meant when I said we needed to fly under the radar."

"Twinsies!" Riley said, then punched Evan's shoulder. "C'mon, Ev. No one'll even notice."

Everyone noticed.

Especially when they walked in together, past the stream of photographers and reporters and bloggers and fans, all with a keen eye for the minutiae of players' lives, all of them looking for an inside scoop. Riley, always cheerful in the spotlight, smiled and waved all the way to the locker room. Evan wished he kept spare ties in the car.

The locker room offered no escape. He stowed away the tie as quickly as he could, but as he undressed, a second, more troublesome problem emerged.

"That a hickey, Abs?"

It took a monumental effort not to turn and glare at Riley. Evan could hear his snickers as he turned to face Turner. He mentally went through *I don't know what you're talking about* and *mind your own business* before settling on, "Fuck off."

Turner cackled, everyone nearby joining him. Riley included, the traitor. It was only Dalton's pointed look that actually embarrassed him, and he kept his head down as he changed as quickly as possible. First time in a long time, he couldn't wait to get his neck guard on.

———

The team always went all out for St. Patrick's Day. It was huge in Pittsburgh, and the team's green and yellow tied in perfectly with the city's mania. All their yellow was swapped with a glittery gold—helmets included—and a glittery shamrock was put behind their Riveters logo. It was a sparkly monstrosity, honestly, but the fans loved it.

(The fans in Pittsburgh, anyway. His mom hated it because the gold made it harder to watch on TV since it reflected every bit of light in the arena. Luckily this year she wouldn't have to worry about the TV glare.)

Evan didn't mind them *too* much. They weren't his favorite, but he'd seen worse jerseys around the league. The gold was a little gaudy, but the bright helmets made it easier to find his teammates. He had more issue with them wearing the outfits almost a full week before St. Patrick's day, but it was the closest weekend game to the holiday, and Pittsburgh didn't seem to be as strict about dates for holidays as other places he'd lived. He'd learned that the hard way his first year in the city and been startled to have July 4th fireworks going off on June 28th.

Another problem with the gold: it made them look like a college team, and he pulled at his jersey self-consciously. The jersey that would be auctioned off after the game, his sweat and all. Weird.

"We look fucking golden tonight, boys," Riley called as he stood up in the center of the locker room. He did a little twirl to show off, and half the guys started clapping and cheering for him. Evan rolled his eyes; they really shouldn't encourage him. "Can't lose when you got like six four-leaf clovers on ice at a time, amirite?"

And as goofy as the jerseys looked, Evan couldn't deny that the gold suited Riley. He looked good. Really good. Kissably good.

Evan cut off that thought and packed it away. He needed to compartmentalize the parts of him that played hockey with Riley and the parts of him that did other things with him. Right now, the focus was on hockey.

Later, though...

For the millionth time since they'd gotten to the arena, Evan checked his wrist. He didn't usually wear his watch when he played, but today he had reason to. His mom was coming to town, ostensibly to celebrate Evan's birthday, but he maybe had an ulterior motive in asking her to visit.

"Stop checking your watch," the Ulterior Motive said. They were lined up in the tunnel outside the rink, waiting to get onto the ice for warm-ups, and Riley was bumping him with the butt of his stick. "She's here, I promise."

He'd gotten a text message to that effect earlier. Evan was supposed to pick her up at the airport in the morning, but her flight from Toronto had been delayed because of a late snowstorm. She'd promised him she was more than capable of arranging transportation to the arena, but he worried. He didn't want her to miss the game, though he did like that it had bought him a few hours before he had to explain the real reason why he'd asked her to visit.

"But what if—"

Riley bonked him on the head. It required him to reach up to do it, and then to jump when Evan tried to jerk his head away, but he managed it. "Nope. It went fine. You're gonna see her in the crowd, and you're gonna score some goals for your mom, and then you're gonna celebrate your bday at that fancy place down the street."

"Shhh," he hissed. "Don't jinx it."

Riley didn't say anything else, but his look was a clear, *I do what I want.*

As soon as they got on the ice and did a few laps, Riley and Evan stopped at the top of the left circle. This was Their Spot during warm-ups, their routine now a permanent fixture of their games. There was no rhyme or reason to the number of whacks or who would be the whacker versus the whackee, but it was so much a part of Riveters games that a crowd of fans was pressed against the glass near them. As Evan smacked Riley's ass, they called out the number.

"One! Two! Three! Four!"

Then they awed loudly when that was it. Sometimes they went as high as a dozen, always stopping before they reached thirteen because, as Riley put it, "What's the point of doing a good luck ritual if we're gonna ruin it with an unlucky number?"

"Four!" Riley yelled at the crowd and pointed to the shamrock on his shoulder. "We have to do four today!" And the fans all laughed and cheered, most of them in their own clover-laden apparel.

"You're such an exhibitionist," Evan said. How was this his life?

"Don't act like you don't love that about me," Riley said without missing a beat.

He did. In fact, he loved a lot of things about Riley Barczyk. This just wasn't the right time to admit it.

"Hey!" Riley called and pointed wildly to a spot in the corner. There she was, Carol Abernathy, waving to him from the second row. "See, it is good luck. Told you she'd make it."

More excited (or nervous?) than Evan was, Riley got to her first. "Hi Miss Evan's Mom!" he cupped his hands over his mouth as he yelled at her through the glass. "Welcome to Pittsburgh!"

They read her lips more than heard her say, "Hi Riley! Hi Evan!" And though Evan wanted to stay there and ask his mom about her flight, doing it with plexiglass in the way and before a game was not the best time. He let her shoo him away. They'd have plenty of time after the game. Three whole days of catching up, and there certainly was a lot to catch up on.

They passed pucks for a bit before Riley skated off to center ice and left Evan on his own. They were playing the Turkeys, and Riley had announced over breakfast today that he should apologize to Baptiste for the concussion earlier in the season. And to preemptively apologize for maybe hitting him again today, because one concussion wasn't a free pass for potential future checks.

"It's hockey," Evan had agreed, though he was pleased Riley's hockey now included at least acknowledging the other people.

Not that it stopped him from being a pest.

"What the fuck!?" Riley screamed during the first period. "That's some bullshit right there!"

"Barczyk," the ref warned. And that was it, a single stern note that had no impact on Riley.

"What? Just because he's Dylan fucking Everett, he can interfere with me? Fucking blatant, too. C'mon!"

"He's talented but a troublemaker," Vassiliev grumbled as he and Evan watched. "He's gonna get a penalty if he keeps this up."

"He's got a talent for getting into trouble," Evan agreed. He couldn't pull his eyes away from Riley as he continued to mouth off. Evan was barely paying attention, too busy staring at Riley's lips and remembering other talents Riley had and how good his kisses tasted.

Despite Riley's pre-game predictions, their line didn't score. Neither did any of the other lines, and they lost 2-0. But their line also managed not to get any penalties, *and* Evan got a shift on the Penalty Kill late in the second, so that was a small consolation.

"Didn't even score for your mom," Riley scolded him. "Terrible son. What kind of Canadian are you, anyway?"

"I'm in the NHL," he pointed out. "I'm not *that* much of an embarrassment."

They changed and showered in record time. Because their line hadn't done a whole lot, neither of them was selected for media coverage, and they were able to slip out to find Evan's mom before most of the team was out of the locker room. When he saw her, Evan felt his stomach clench with unexpected nerves.

"Mom!" he called. No, he realized. Not nerves. Excitement.

"Evan, sweetie!" she cooed as she hugged him. She saw Riley standing off to the side, waiting awkwardly. "Riley," she said uncertainly. "Good to see you again. When Evan got me those seats next to the penalty box, I thought maybe he wanted me to babysit you."

Riley's eyes crinkled as he smiled. "No, ma'am. I was on my best behavior today. Only ten f-bombs, honest."

She tried not to smile. "I think I heard one or two of them." She turned back to Evan. "So what's this big surprise you invited me to town for? I admit I'm very curious."

Evan took a deep breath, then said: "Mom, I want you to meet Riley Barczyk. My boyfriend."

About the Author

A.L. Heard is a romance author who writes love stories set in every world, whether in NHL locker rooms, Victorian ballrooms, or magical kingdoms. Her debut hockey romance novel, *Hockey Bois*, was released in 2021 and her first historical fantasy novel, *Tessa of Hundrfeld* arrives in 2025. A longtime fanfiction writer turned indie author, she currently lives in Pittsburgh. Between writing projects, she teaches languages, she's a teacher, hockey-player, hockey mom, and spends her weekends exploring local breweries.

Social Media:

- Bluesky: https://bsky.app/profile/ashheardwrites.bsky. social
- Instagram: https://www.instagram.com/ashheardwrites
- Goodreads: https://www.goodreads.com/author/show/ 20974405.A_L_Heard
- Ko-fi: https://ko-fi.com/jhoom

Other Titles by A.L. Heard

- Hockey Bois: A Beer League Romance
- Drop the Gloves
- Vampires Don't Play Hockey
- Tessa of Hundrfeld: Book 1 of The Shadow Queen
- The Lady or the Duke? A Victorian Era Decide Your Fate Story

www.ingramcontent.com/pod-product-compliance
Lightning Source LLC
Chambersburg PA
CBHW050920030726
47503CB00007BB/2389